TOR BOOKS BY BRANDON SANDERSON

The Stormlight Archive
The Way of Kings

The Mistborn Series
Mistborn
The Well of Ascension
The Hero of Ages
The Alloy of Law

Warbreaker
Elantris

THE RITHMATIST

THE RITHMATIST

BRANDON SANDERSON

ILLUSTRATIONS BY
BEN MCSWEENEY

TOR®

A TOM DOHERTY ASSOCIATES BOOK
NEW YORK

THE RITHMATIST

Map and interior illustrations by Ben McSweeney

A Tor Teen Book
Published by Tom Doherty Associates, LLC
175 Fifth Avenue
New York, NY 10010

www.tor-forge.com

Tor® is a registered trademark of Tom Doherty Associates, LLC.

Library of Congress Cataloging-in-Publication Data

Sanderson, Brandon.
    The Rithmatist / Brandon Sanderson.—First edition.
        p.   cm.
    "A Tom Doherty Associates Book."
    ISBN 978-0-7653-2032-2 (hardcover)
    ISBN 978-1-4299-5316-0 (e-book)
    [1. Fantasy.]   I. Title.
    PZ7.S19797Ri 2013
    [Fic]—dc23   2012043417

Tor books may be purchased for educational, business, or promotional use. For information on bulk purchases, please contact Macmillan Corporate and Premium Sales Department at 1-800-221-7945 extension 5442 or write specialmarkets@macmillan.com.

First Edition: May 2013

Printed in the United States of America

0 9 8 7 6 5 4 3 2 1

For Joel Sanderson,
whose enthusiasm never stops

THE RITHMATIST

BASIC EASTON DEFENSE

The Easton Defense is versatile against multiple opponents, but is difficult to produce both because of its use of the nine-point circle and the difficulty in building a nonagon missing three sides.

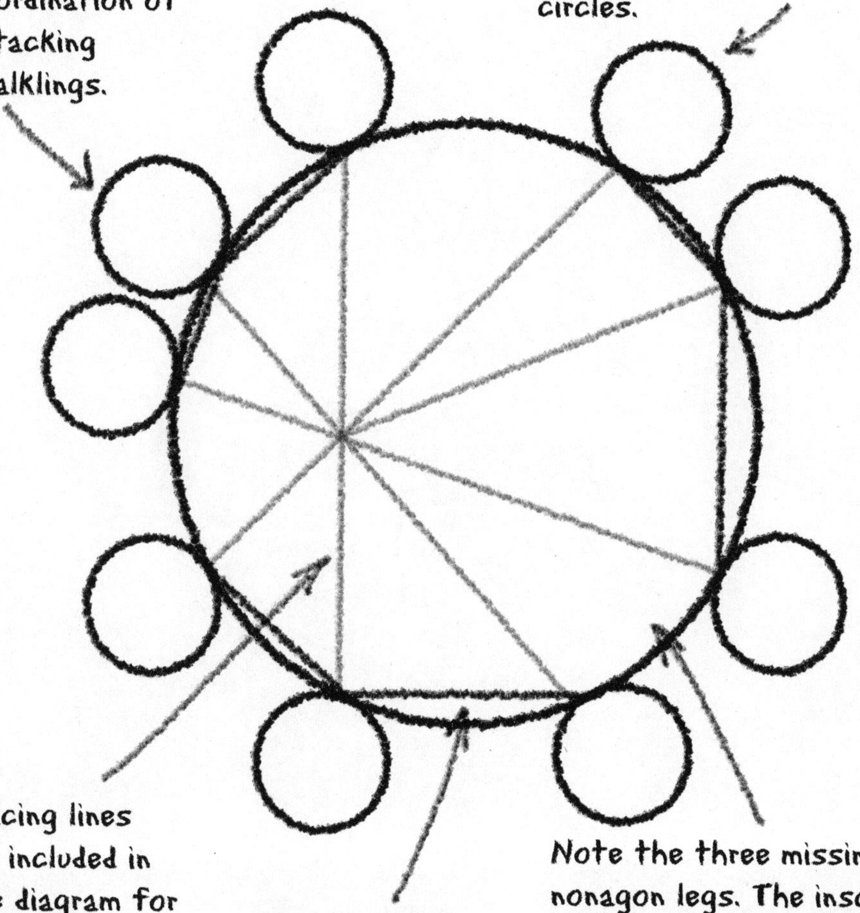

Nine circles on the bind points help with defense and coordination of attacking chalklings.

Variations of the Easton include binding defensive chalklings to these external circles.

Tracing lines are included in the diagram for instruction purposes, but would not be drawn on the actual defense.

The irregular nonagon inside gives this defense a great deal of stability.

Note the three missing nonagon legs. The inscribed polygon adds stability and protection in case of breach, but restricts movement.

Lilly's lamp blew out as she bolted down the hallway. She threw the lamp aside, splashing oil across the painted wall and fine rug. The liquid glistened in the moonlight.

The house was empty. Silent, save for her panicked breathing. She'd given up on screaming. Nobody seemed to hear.

It was as if the entire city had gone dead.

She burst into the living room, then stopped, uncertain what to do. A grandfather clock ticked in the corner, illuminated by moonlight through the broad picture windows. The city skyline spread beyond, buildings rising ten stories or more, springrail lines crisscrossing between them. Jamestown, her home for all sixteen years of her life.

I am going to die, she thought.

Desperation pushed through her terror. She shoved aside the rocking chair in the middle of the room, then hurriedly rolled up the rug so that she could get to the wooden floor. She reached into the pouch tied to a loop on her skirt and pulled out a single bone-white length of chalk.

Kneeling on the wood planks, staring at the ground, she tried to clear her mind. *Focus.*

She set the tip of the chalk against the ground and began to draw a circle around herself. Her hand shook so much that the line was uneven. Professor Fitch would have been quite displeased to see such a sloppy Line of Warding. She laughed to herself—a desperate sound, more of a cry.

Sweat dripped from her brow, making dark spots on the wood. Her hand quivered as she drew several straight lines inside the circle—Lines of Forbiddance to stabilize her defensive ring. The Matson Defense . . . how did it go? Two smaller circles, with bind points to place Lines of Making—

Scratching.

Lilly snapped her head up, looking down the hallway at the door leading to the street. A shadow moved beyond the door's clouded window plate.

The door rattled.

"Oh, Master," she found herself whispering. "Please . . . please . . ."

The door stopped rattling. All was still for just a moment; then the door burst open.

Lilly tried to scream, but found her voice caught in her throat. A figure stood framed in moonlight, a bowler hat on his head, a short cape covering his shoulders. He stood with his hand on a cane to his side.

She could not see his face, backlit as he was, but there was something horribly sinister about that slightly tipped head and those shadowed features. A hint of a nose and chin, reflecting moonlight. Eyes that watched her from within the inky blackness.

The *things* flooded into the room around him. Angry, squirming over floor, walls, ceiling. Their bone-white forms almost seemed to glow in the moonlight.

Each was as flat as a piece of paper.

Each was made of chalk.

They were each unique, tiny picturelike monsters with fangs, claws. They made no noise at all as they flooded into the hallway, hundreds of them, shaking and vibrating silently as they came for her.

Lilly finally found her voice and screamed.

PART
ONE

THE FOUR RITHMATIC LINES

Line of WARDING

Line of FORBIDDANCE

Line of MAKING
(chalkling)

Line of VIGOR

Boring?" Joel demanded, stopping in place. "You think the 1888 Crew-Choi duel was *boring*?"

Michael shrugged, stopping and looking back at Joel. "I don't know. I stopped reading after a page or so."

"You're just not imagining it right," Joel said, walking up and resting one hand on his friend's shoulder. He held his other hand in front of him, panning it as if to wipe away their surroundings— the green lawns of Armedius Academy—and replace them with the dueling arena.

"Imagine," Joel said, "it's the end of the Melee, the biggest Rithmatic event in the country. Paul Crew and Adelle Choi are the only two duelists left. Adelle survived, against all odds, after her entire team was picked off in the first few minutes."

A few other students stopped on the sidewalk to listen nearby as they passed between classes.

"So?" Michael said, yawning.

"So? Michael, it was the finals! Imagine everyone watching, in silence, as the last two Rithmatists begin their duel. Imagine how nervous Adelle would have been! Her team had never won a Melee before, and now she faced down one of the most skilled Rithmatists of her generation. Paul's team had shielded him at their center so that the lesser players fell first. They knew that would get him to the end practically fresh, his defensive circle almost completely untouched. It was the champion against the underdog."

"Boring," Michael said. "They just sit there and draw."

"You're hopeless," Joel replied. "You are going to the very school where Rithmatists are trained. Aren't you even a little interested in them?"

"They have enough people interested in them," Michael said with a scowl. "They keep to themselves, Joel. I'm fine with that. I'd rather they weren't even here." A breeze ruffled his blond hair. Around them spread the green hills and stately brick buildings of Armedius Academy. Nearby, a clockwork crab continued its quiet duty, chopping at the grass to keep it level.

"You wouldn't think that way if you understood," Joel said, getting out some chalk. "Here, take this. And stand here." He positioned his friend, then knelt and drew a circle on the sidewalk around him. "You're Paul. See, defensive circle. If that gets breached, you lose the match."

Joel paced back a ways on the concrete quad, then knelt and drew his own circle. "Now, Adelle's circle was nearly breached in four places. She quickly began to shift from the Matson Defense to . . . Okay, you know what, that's too technical. Just know that her circle was weak, and Paul had a strong, dominant position."

"If you say so," Michael said. He smiled at Eva Winters as she walked past, holding books in front of her.

"Now," Joel said. "Paul started pounding her circle with Lines of Vigor, and she knew she wouldn't be able to shift defenses quickly enough to recover."

"Pounding . . . Lines of what?" Michael asked.

"Lines of Vigor," Joel said. "Duelists shoot them at each other. That's the point; it's how you breach the circle."

"I thought they made little chalk . . . things. Creatures."

"That too," Joel said. "They're called chalklings. But that's not why everyone remembers the 1888 Melee, even some twenty years later. It was the lines she shot. Conventional wisdom would have been for her to last as long as she could, draw out the match, make a good showing of it."

He set his chalk out in front of his circle. "She didn't do that," he whispered. "She saw something. Paul had a small weakened section on the back of his circle. Of course, the only way to attack it would be to *bounce* a shot off *three* different lines left by other duelists. It was an impossible shot. She took it anyway. She drew one Line of Vigor as Paul's chalklings ate at her defenses. She fired it and . . ."

Caught up in the moment, Joel finished drawing the Line of Vigor in front of him, raising his hand with a flourish. With surprise, he realized that some thirty students had gathered to listen to him, and he could feel them holding breaths, expecting his drawing to come to life.

It didn't. Joel wasn't a Rithmatist. His drawings were just ordinary chalk. Everyone knew that, Joel most of all, but the moment somehow broke the spell of his story. The gathered students continued on their way, leaving him kneeling on the ground in the middle of his circle.

"And let me guess," Michael said, yawning again. "Her shot got through?"

"Yeah," Joel said, suddenly feeling foolish. He stood up, putting away his chalk. "The shot worked. She won the Melee, though her team had been lowest favored in the odds. That shot. It was *beautiful*. At least, so the accounts say."

"And I'm sure you'd love to have been there," Michael said, stepping out of the circle Joel had drawn. "By the Master, Joel. I'll bet if you could travel through time, you'd waste it going to Rithmatic duels!"

"Sure, I guess. What else would I do?"

"Oh," Michael said, "maybe prevent some assassinations, get rich, find out what's really happening in Nebrask. . . ."

"Yeah, I suppose," Joel said, pocketing his chalk, then jumping out of the way as a soccer ball shot past, followed by Jephs Daring. Jephs gave Michael and Joel a wave before chasing down his ball.

Joel joined Michael, continuing across campus. The beautiful, low green hills were topped by flowering trees, and green vines wound their way up the sides of buildings. Students darted this way and that between classes, in a variety of dresses and trousers. Many of the boys wore their sleeves rolled up in the late spring warmth.

Only the Rithmatists were required to wear uniforms. That made them stick out; a group of three of them walked between buildings, and the other students casually made way, most not looking at them.

"Look, Joel," Michael said. "Have you ever wondered if maybe . . . you know, you think about this stuff too much? Rithmatics and all that?"

"It's interesting to me," Joel said.

"Yes, but . . . I mean, it's a little odd, considering . . ."

Michael didn't say it, but Joel understood. He wasn't a Rithmatist, and could never be one. He'd missed his chance. But why couldn't he be interested in what they did?

Michael narrowed his eyes as that group of three Rithmatists passed in their grey-and-white uniforms. "It's kind of like," he said softly, "it's kind of like it's us and them, you know? Leave them alone to do . . . whatever it is they do, Joel."

"You just don't like that they can do things you can't," Joel said.

That earned Joel a glare. Perhaps those words hit too close to home. Michael was the son of a knight-senator, a son of privilege. He wasn't accustomed to being excluded.

"Anyway," Michael said, looking away and continuing to hike down the busy sidewalk, "you can't be one of them, so why keep spending all of your time talking about them? It's useless, Joel. Stop thinking about them."

I can't ever be one of you either, Michael, Joel thought. Technically, he wasn't supposed to be at this school. Armedius was horribly expensive, and you either had to be important, rich, or a Rithmatist to attend. Joel was about as far from any of those three things as a boy could get.

They stopped at the next intersection of sidewalks. "Look, I've got to get to history class," Michael said.

"Yeah," Joel said. "I've got open period."

"Running messages again?" Michael asked. "In the hope that you'll get to peek into a Rithmatic classroom?"

Joel blushed, but it was true. "Summer's coming up," he said. "You going home again?"

Michael brightened. "Yeah. Father said I could bring some friends. Fishing, swimming, girls in sundresses on the beach. Mmmm . . ."

"Sounds great," Joel said, trying to keep the hopeful tone out of his voice. "I'd love to see something like that." Michael took a group each year. Joel had never been invited.

This year, though . . . well, he'd been hanging out with Michael after school. Michael needed help with math, and Joel could explain things to him. They had been getting along really well.

Michael shuffled his feet. "Look, Joel," he said. "I mean . . . it's fun to hang out with you here, you know? At school? But back home, it's a different world. I'll be busy with the family. Father has such expectations. . . ."

"Oh, yeah, of course," Joel said.

Michael smiled, banishing all discomfort from his expression in an instant. Son of a politician for sure. "That's the spirit," he said, patting Joel on the arm. "See ya."

Joel watched him jog off. Michael ran into Mary Isenhorn along the way, and he immediately started flirting. Mary's father owned a massive springworks. As Joel stood on that sidewalk intersection, he could pick out dozens of members of the country's elite. Adam Li was directly related to the emperor of JoSeun. Geoff Hamilton had three presidents in his family line. Wenda Smith's parents owned half of the cattle ranches in Georgiabama.

And Joel . . . he was the son of a chalkmaker and a cleaning lady. *Well*, he thought, *it looks like it will be just me and Davis here all summer again.* He sighed, then made his way to the campus office.

Twenty minutes later, Joel hurried back down the sidewalk, delivering messages around campus during his free period.

Those sidewalks were now mostly empty of students, with everyone else in class.

Joel's moment of depression had vanished the instant he'd looked through the stack. There had been only three messages to deliver today, and he'd done those quickly. That meant . . .

He clutched a fourth message in his pocket, one that he himself had added without telling anyone. Now, with some time to spare because of his speed earlier, he jogged up to Warding Hall, one of the Rithmatic lecture halls.

Professor Fitch was teaching in there this period. Joel fingered the letter he carried in his pocket, penned—after some nervousness—to the Rithmatic professor.

This might be my only chance, Joel thought, shoving down any nervousness. Fitch was a relaxed, pleasant man. There was no reason to be worried.

Joel scurried up the long flight of steps outside the vine-covered, grey brick building, then slipped in the oak door. That brought him into the lecture hall at the very top. It was shaped like a small amphitheater, with tiered seats. Schematics depicting Rithmatic defenses hung on the whitewashed walls, and the plush seats were bolted in rows along the tiers, facing toward the lecture floor below.

A few of the students glanced at Joel as he entered, but Professor Fitch did not. The professor rarely noticed when he got deliveries from the office, and would ramble on for the entire lecture before realizing that a member of his audience wasn't actually a member of the class. Joel didn't mind that one bit. He sat down on the steps eagerly. Today's lecture, it appeared, was on the Easton Defense.

". . . is why this defense is one of the very best to use against an aggressive assault from multiple sides," Fitch was saying down below. He pointed with a long red baton toward the floor where he'd drawn a large circle. The hall was arranged so that the students could look down at his Rithmatic drawings on the ground.

With his pointer, Fitch gestured toward the Lines of Forbiddance he'd affixed to the bind points on the circle. "Now, the Easton Defense is most famous for the large number of smaller circles drawn at the bind points. Drawing nine other circles like this can be time-consuming, but they will prove well worth the time in defensive capabilities.

"You can see that the inner lines form an irregular nonagon, and the number of arms you leave off will determine how much room you have to draw, but also how stable your figure is. Of course, if you want a more aggressive defense, you can also use the bind points for chalklings."

What about Lines of Vigor? Joel thought. *How do you defend against those?*

Joel didn't ask; he dared not draw attention to himself. That might make Fitch ask for his message, and that would leave Joel with no reason to keep listening. So, Joel just listened. The office wouldn't expect him back for some time.

He leaned forward, willing one of the other students to ask about the Lines of Vigor. They didn't. The young Rithmatists lounged in their seats, boys in white slacks, girls in white skirts, both in grey sweaters—colors to disguise the ever-present chalk dust.

Professor Fitch himself wore a deep red coat. Thick, with straight, starched cuffs, the coat reached all the way down to Fitch's feet. The coat buttoned up to a tall collar, mostly obscuring the white suit Fitch wore beneath. It had a militaristic feel to it, with all of those stiff lines and straps at the shoulders almost like rank insignia. The red coat was the symbol of a full Rithmatic professor.

"And that is why a Keblin Defense is inferior to the Easton in most situations." Professor Fitch smiled, turning to regard the class. He was an older man, greying at the temples, with a spindly figure. The coat gave him an air of dignity.

Do you understand what you have? Joel thought, looking over the unengaged students. This was a class of fifteen- and sixteen-year-old students, making them Joel's age. Despite their noble calling, they acted like . . . well, teenagers.

Fitch was known to run a loose classroom, and many of the students took advantage, ignoring the lecture, whispering with friends or lounging and staring at the ceiling. Several near Joel actually appeared to be sleeping. He didn't know their names—he didn't know the names of most of the Rithmatic students. They generally rebuffed his attempts to chat with them.

When nobody spoke, Fitch knelt and pressed his chalk against the drawing he'd done. He closed his eyes. Seconds later, the drawing puffed away, willed by its creator to vanish.

"Well, then," he said, raising his chalk. "If there are no questions, perhaps we can discuss how to *beat* an Easton Defense. The more astute of you will have noticed that I made no mention of Lines of Vigor. That is because those are better talked about from an offensive viewpoint. If we were to—"

The door to the lecture hall banged open. Fitch rose, chalk held between two fingers, eyebrows raised as he turned.

A tall figure strode into the room, causing some of the lounging students to perk up. The newcomer wore a grey coat after the style of a Rithmatic professor of low rank. The man was young, with stark blond hair and a firm step. His coat fit him well, buttoned up to the chin, loose through the legs. Joel didn't know him.

"Yes?" Professor Fitch asked.

The newcomer walked all the way to the floor of the lecture hall, passing Professor Fitch and pulling out a piece of red chalk. The newcomer turned, knelt, and placed his chalk against the ground. Some of the students began to whisper.

"What is this?" Fitch asked. "I say, did I pass my lecture time again? I heard no sound for the clock. I'm terribly sorry if I've intruded into your time!"

The newcomer looked up. His face seemed smug to Joel. "No, Professor," the man said, "this is a challenge."

Fitch looked stunned. "I . . . Oh my. It . . ." Fitch licked his lips nervously, then wrung his hands. "I'm not sure how to, I mean, what I need to do. I . . ."

"Ready yourself to draw, Professor," the newcomer said.

Fitch blinked. Then, hands obviously shaking, he got down on his knees to place his chalk against the ground.

"That's Professor Andrew Nalizar," whispered a girl seated a short distance from Joel. "He gained his coat just three years ago from Maineford Academy. They say he spent the last two years fighting in Nebrask!"

"He's handsome," the girl's companion said, twirling a bit of chalk between her fingers.

Down below, the two men began to draw. Joel leaned forward, excited. He'd never seen a real duel between two full professors before. This might be as good as being at the Melee!

Both began by drawing circles around themselves to block attacks from the opponent. Once either circle was breached, the duel would end. Perhaps because he'd been talking about it, Professor Fitch went to draw the Easton Defense, surrounding himself with nine smaller circles touching the larger one at the bind points.

It wasn't a very good stance for a duel. Even Joel could see that; he felt a moment of disappointment. Maybe this wouldn't be that good a fight after all. Fitch's defense was beautifully drawn, but was *too* strong; the Easton was best against multiple opponents who surrounded you.

Nalizar drew a modified Ballintain Defense—a quick defense with only basic reinforcement. While Professor Fitch was still placing his internal lines, Nalizar went straight into an aggressive attack, drawing chalklings.

Chalklings. Drawn from Lines of Making, they were the core offense of many Rithmatic fights. Nalizar drew quickly and efficiently, creating chalklings that looked like small dragons, with wings and sinuous necks. As soon as he finished the first, it shook to life, then began to fly across the ground toward Fitch.

It didn't rise into the air. Chalklings were two-dimensional, like all Rithmatic lines. The battle played out on the floor, lines attacking other lines. Fitch's hands were still shaking, and he kept looking up and down, as if nervous and unfocused. Joel

cringed as the middle-aged professor drew one of his outer circles lopsided—a major mistake.

The instructional diagram he'd drawn earlier had been far, far more precise. Lopsided curves were easy to breach. Fitch paused, looking at the poorly drawn curve, and seemed to doubt himself.

Come on! Joel clenched his fists. *You're better than this, Professor!*

As a second dragon began to move across the ground, Fitch recovered his wits and snapped his chalk back against the floor. The gathered students were silent, and those who had been dozing sat up.

Fitch threw up a long wiggly line. A Line of Vigor. It was shaped like a waveform, and when it was finished, it shot across the board to hit one of the dragons. The blast threw up a puff of dust and destroyed half of the creature. The dragon began to wriggle about, moving in the wrong direction.

The only sounds in the room were those of chalk against floor accompanied by Fitch's quick, almost panicked breathing. Joel bit his lip as the duel became heated. Fitch had a better defense, but he'd rushed it, leaving sections that were weak. Nalizar's sparse defense allowed him to go aggressive, and Fitch had to struggle to keep up. Fitch continued throwing up Lines of Vigor, destroying the chalk creatures that flew across the board at him, but there were always more to replace them.

Nalizar was good, among the best Joel had ever seen. Despite the tension, Nalizar remained fluid, drawing chalkling after chalkling, unfazed by those that Fitch destroyed. Joel couldn't help but be impressed.

He's been fighting the wild chalklings at Nebrask recently, Joel thought, remembering what the girl had said. *He's used to drawing under pressure.*

Nalizar calmly sent some spider chalklings to crawl along the perimeter of the floor, forcing Fitch to watch his flanks. Next, Nalizar began sending across Lines of Vigor. The snaky lines shot across the board in a vibrating waveform, vanishing once they hit something.

Fitch finally managed to get out a chalkling of his own—a knight, beautifully detailed— which he bound to one of his smaller circles. *How does he draw them so well, yet so fast?* Joel wondered. Fitch's knight was a work of beauty, with detailed armor and a large greatsword. It easily defeated Nalizar's more plentiful, yet far more simply drawn dragons.

With the knight set up, Fitch could try some more offensive shots. Nalizar was forced to draw a few defensive chalklings— blob creatures that threw themselves in front of Lines of Vigor.

Armies of creatures, lines, and waveforms flew across the board—a tempest of white against red, chalklings puffing away, lines hitting the circles and blasting out chunks of the protective line. Both men scribbled furiously.

Joel stood, then took an almost involuntary step down toward the front of the room, transfixed. Doing so, however, let him catch a glimpse of Professor Fitch's face. Fitch looked frantic. Terrified.

Joel froze.

The professors kept drawing, but that worry in Fitch's expression pulled Joel away from the conflict. Such desperate motions, such concern, his face streaked with sweat.

The weight of what was happening crashed down on Joel. This wasn't a duel for fun or practice. This was a challenge to Fitch's authority—a dispute over his right to hold his tenure. If he lost . . .

One of Nalizar's red Lines of Vigor hit Fitch's circle straight on, almost breaching it. Immediately, all of Nalizar's chalklings moved that direction, a frenzied, chaotic mess of red motion toward the weakened line.

For just a moment, Fitch froze, looking overwhelmed. He shook himself back into motion, but it was too late. He couldn't stop them all. One of the dragons got past his knight. It began to claw furiously at the weakened part of Fitch's circle, distorting it further.

Fitch hurriedly began to draw another knight. But the dragon ripped through his border.

"No!" Joel cried, taking another step down.

Nalizar smiled, removing his chalk from the floor and standing. He dusted off his hands. Fitch was still drawing.

"Professor," Nalizar said. "Professor!"

Fitch stopped, and only then did he notice the dragon, which continued to work on the hole, trying to dig it out enough that it could get into the center of the circle. In a real battle, it would have moved in to attack the Rithmatist himself. This, however, was just a duel—and a breach in the ring meant victory for Nalizar.

"Oh," Fitch said, lowering his hand. "Oh, yes, well, I see. . . ." He turned, seeming dazed, regarding the room full of students. "Ah, yes. I . . . will just go, then."

He began to gather up his books and notes. Joel sank down onto the stone steps. In his hand, he held the letter he had written to give to Fitch.

"Professor," Nalizar said. "Your coat?"

Fitch looked down. "Ah, yes. Of course." He undid the buttons on the long red coat, then pulled it off, leaving him in his white vest, shirt, and trousers. He looked diminished. Fitch held the coat for a moment, then laid it on the lecture desk. He gathered up his books and fled the chamber. The door to the ground-floor entrance clicked shut softly behind him.

Joel sat, stunned. A few of the members of the classroom clapped timidly, though most just watched, wide-eyed, obviously uncertain how to react.

"Now then," Nalizar said, voice curt. "I will take over instruction of this class for the last few days of the term, and I will be teaching the summer elective course that Fitch had planned. I have heard reports of rather disgraceful performance among students at Armedius, your cohort in particular. *I* will allow no sloppiness in my class. You there, boy sitting on the steps."

Joel looked up.

"What are you doing there?" Nalizar demanded. "Why aren't you wearing your uniform?"

"I'm not a Rithmatist, sir," Joel said, standing. "I'm from the general school."

"*What?* Why in the name of the heavens are you sitting in my classroom?"

Your classroom? This was Fitch's classroom. Or . . . it should be.

"Well?" Nalizar asked.

"I came with a note, sir," Joel said. "For Professor Fitch."

"Hand it over, then," Nalizar said.

"It is for Professor Fitch personally," Joel said, stuffing the letter into his pocket. "It wasn't about the class."

"Well, be off with you then," Nalizar said, dismissing Joel with a wave of his hand. The red chalk dust scattered on the floor looked like blood. He began dispelling his creations one at a time.

Joel backed away, then rushed up the steps and opened the door. People crossed the lawn outside, many dressed in the white and grey of Rithmatists. One figure stood out. Joel dashed down the stairs across the springy lawn, catching up to Professor Fitch. The man trudged with slumped shoulders, the large bundle of books and notes collected in his arms.

"Professor?" Joel said. Joel was tall for his age, a few inches taller, even, than Fitch.

The older man turned with a start. "Uh? What?"

"Are you all right?"

"Oh, um, why it's the chalkmaker's son! How are you, lad? Shouldn't you be in class?"

"It's my free period," Joel said, reaching and sliding two of the books off the stack to help carry them. "Professor, are you all right? About what just happened?"

"You saw that, did you?" Professor Fitch's face fell.

"Isn't there anything you can do?" Joel asked. "You can't let him take your classes away! Perhaps if you spoke to Principal York?"

"No, no," Fitch said. "That would be unseemly. The right of challenge is a very honorable tradition—an important part of Rithmatic culture, I must say."

Joel sighed. He glanced down, remembering the note in his pocket. A request from him to Fitch. He wanted to study with the man over the summer, to learn as much about Rithmatics as he could.

But Fitch wasn't a full professor any longer. Would that matter? Joel wasn't even certain the man would take a non-Rithmatic student. If Fitch wasn't a full professor, might he have more time for tutoring students? Thinking that immediately made Joel feel guilty.

He almost pulled the letter out and gave it to the man. The defeat in Fitch's face stopped him. Perhaps this wasn't the best time.

"I should have seen this coming," Fitch said. "That Nalizar. Too ambitious for his own good, I thought when we hired him last week. There hasn't been a challenge at Armedius for decades. . . ."

"What will you do?" Joel asked.

"Well," Fitch said as they walked along the path, passing under the shade of a wide-limbed red oak. "Yes, well, tradition states that I take Nalizar's place. He was hired on as a tutoring professor to help remedial students who failed classes this year. I guess that is my job now. I should think I'll be happy to be away from the classroom to have some peace of mind!"

He hesitated, turning to look back toward the Rithmatic lecture hall. The structure was block-shaped, yet somehow still artistic, with its diamond patterns of grey bricks forming the vine-covered wall.

"Yes," Fitch said. "I will probably never have to teach in that classroom again." He choked off that last part. "Excuse me." He ducked his head and rushed away.

Joel raised a hand, but let him go, still holding two of the professor's books. Finally, Joel sighed, turning his own course across the lawn toward the campus office building.

"Well," he said softly, thinking again of the crumpled paper in his trouser pocket, "*that* was a disaster."

TWO-POINT
and
FOUR-POINT CIRCLES

When a Line of Warding is drawn into a complete circle, it gains the ability to be affixed with "bind points."

Each circle can have 2, 4, 6, or 9 bind points, depending on where they are drawn.

Obviously, the two-point circle is the easiest to draw. Here, the dots show locations of bind points, while the lines show the relationship between them. In an actual Rithmatic drawing, neither dots nor lines would be drawn. Instead the Rithmatist would place the other lines at these points, locking them into place by virtue of the circle's nature.

The office sat in a small valley between the Rithmatic campus and the general campus. Like most everything at Armedius Academy, the building was of brick, though this building was red. It was only one story tall and had quite a few more windows than the classrooms did. Joel had always wondered why the office workers got a view outside, but students didn't. It was almost like everyone was afraid to give the students a glimpse of freedom.

". . . heard he was going to make a *challenge* of all things," a voice was saying as Joel walked into the office.

The speaker was Florence, one of the office clerks. She sat on top of her oak desk—rather than in her chair—speaking with Exton, the other clerk. Exton wore his usual vest and trousers, with a bow tie and suspenders—quite fashionable, even if he was a bit portly. His bowler hung on a peg beside his desk. Florence, on the other hand, wore a yellow spring sundress.

"A challenge?" Exton asked, scribbling with a quill, not looking up as he spoke. Joel had never met anyone besides Exton who could write and carry on a conversation at the same time. "It's been a while."

"I know!" Florence said. She was young, in her twenties, and not married. Some of the more traditional professors on campus had found it scandalous when Principal York hired a woman as a clerk. But those sorts of things were happening more and more.

Everyone said it was the twentieth century now, and old attitudes would have to change. York had said that if women Rithmatists could fight at Nebrask and the Monarch could use a woman as a speechwriter, he could hire a female clerk.

"Challenges used to be much more common, back closer to the start of the war in Nebrask," Exton said, still scribbling at his parchment. "Every upstart professor with a new coat would want to jump right to the top. There were some chaotic times."

"Hum . . ." Florence said. "He's handsome, you know."

"Who?"

"Professor Nalizar," she said. "I was there when he approached Principal York about the challenge this morning. Swept right in, said, 'Principal, I believe it right to inform you that I shall soon achieve tenure at this academy.'"

Exton snorted. "And what did York have to say?"

"He wasn't happy, I'll say that. Tried to talk Nalizar out of the plan, but he would have none of it."

"I can imagine," Exton said.

"Aren't you going to ask me *who* he intended to challenge?" Florence asked. She noticed Joel at the side of the room and winked at him.

"I seriously doubt you are going to let me continue my work in peace without hearing about it," Exton said.

"Professor Fitch," she said.

Exton stopped. Finally, he looked up. *"Fitch?"*

She nodded.

"Good luck, then," Exton said, chuckling. "Fitch is the best at the academy. He'll take that upstart to pieces so fast that the chalk dust won't have time to settle before the duel is over."

"No," Joel said. "Fitch lost."

The two fell silent.

"What?" Florence asked. "How do you know?"

"I was there," Joel said, walking up to the counter in front of the clerks. The principal's office was behind a closed door at the back.

Exton wagged his quill at Joel. "Young man," he said, "I expressly remember sending you on an errand to the *humanities* building."

"I ran that errand," Joel said quickly. "And the others you gave me. Fitch's classroom was on the way back."

"On the way back? It's on the complete *opposite* side of campus!"

"Oh, Exton, hush," Florence said. "So the boy's curious about the Rithmatists. The same goes for most of the people on campus." She smiled at Joel, though half the time he was convinced she took his side just because she knew it annoyed Exton.

Exton grumbled and turned back to his ledger. "I suppose I can't fault a person for sneaking into *extra* classes. Have enough trouble with students trying to skip them. Still, fascination with those blasted Rithmatists . . . it's not good for a boy."

"Don't be such a bore," Florence said. "Joel, you said that Fitch actually *lost*?"

Joel nodded.

"So . . . what does that mean?"

"He will switch places in seniority with Nalizar," Exton said, "and lose his tenure. He can challenge Nalizar back in one year's time, and both of them are immune to other challenges until then."

"That poor man!" Florence said. "Why, that's not very fair. I just thought the duel would be for bragging rights."

Exton continued his work.

"Well," Florence said. "Handsome or not, I'm growing less impressed with Mr. Nalizar. Fitch is such a dear, and he *so* loves his teaching."

"He will survive," Exton said. "It's not as if he's out on his ear. Joel, I assume you dallied there in the classroom long enough to watch the entire duel?"

Joel shrugged.

"How was the duel, then?" Exton asked. "Did Fitch acquit himself well?"

"He was quite good," Joel said. "His forms were beautiful. He just . . . well, he seemed out of practice with real dueling."

"Such a brutal way to handle things!" Florence said. "Why, they're academics, not gladiators!"

Exton paused, then looked directly at Florence, eyeing her over the top rim of his spectacles. "My dear," he said, "I don't wonder if there should be quite a few *more* challenges like this. Perhaps today will remind those stuck-up Rithmatists why they exist. Should Nebrask ever fall . . ."

"Oh, don't tell me ghost stories, Exton," she said. "Those stories are simply tools for politicians to keep us all worried."

"Bah," Exton said. "Don't you have any work to be doing?"

"I'm on break, dear," she said.

"I can't help but notice that you always take your breaks whenever *I* have something important to finish."

"Bad timing on your part, I guess," she said, reaching to a wooden box on her desk, then getting out the kimchi-and-ham sandwich packed inside.

Joel glanced at the grandfather clock in the corner. He had fifteen minutes until his next class—too short a time to send him away on another errand.

"I'm worried about Professor Fitch," Joel said, still watching the clock, with its intricate gears. A springwork owl sat on the top of the clock, blinking occasionally, then nibbling at its talons as it waited for the hour to chime so that it could hoot.

"Oh, it won't be so bad," Exton said. "I suspect that Principal York will only assign him a few students. Fitch is due for some time off. He might enjoy this."

Enjoy this? Joel thought. *The poor man was crushed.* "He's a genius," Joel said. "Nobody on campus teaches defenses as complex as he does."

"A true scholar, that one," Exton said. "Maybe too much of a scholar. Nalizar may be better in the classroom. Some of Fitch's lectures could be . . . a little over the students' heads, from what I hear."

"No," Joel said. "He's a great teacher. He explains things and doesn't treat the students like fools, like Howards or Silversmith do."

Exton chuckled. "I've been letting you have too much time

off, haven't I? Do you want me to get into trouble with the Rithmatists again?"

Joel didn't respond. The other Rithmatic professors had made it clear that they didn't want him disrupting their lectures. Without Fitch and his lax attitude, Joel would not be sneaking into any more lectures anytime soon. He felt a twist inside of him.

There might still be a chance. If Fitch was going to teach a few students, why couldn't one be Joel?

"Joel, dear," Florence said, halfway through her sandwich, "I spoke with your mother this morning. She wanted me to see if I could give you a nudge on your summer elective paperwork."

Joel grimaced. There were advantages to living on the campus as the son of academy employees. His free tuition was the biggest of those perks, though he'd only been given that because of his father's death.

There were also disadvantages. Many of the other staff members—like Exton and Florence—earned room and board as part of their employment contract. Joel had grown up with them and saw them every day—and that meant that they were good friends with his mother as well.

"I'm working on it," he said, thinking of his letter to Fitch.

"The last day of the term is coming, dear," Florence said. "You need to get into an elective. You finally get to pick one of your own, rather than sitting in a remedial tutelage. Isn't that exciting?"

"Sure."

Most students went home during the summer. The ones who did not leave only had to attend for half days, and could choose a single elective. Unless they did poorly during the year and needed a remedial tutelage as their elective. Rithmatists were lucky—they had to stay in school all year, but at least their summer elective was a Rithmatics elective.

"Have you given it any thought?" Florence asked.

"Some."

"They're filling up fast, dear," she said. "There are still a few slots left in physical merit class. You want in?"

Three months of standing on a field while everyone ran around him kicking balls at each other, playing a game that they all tried to pretend was half as interesting as Rithmatic duels? "No thanks."

"What, then?"

Math might be fun. Literature wouldn't be too painful. But none would be as interesting as studying with Fitch.

"I'll have one picked by tonight," he promised, eyeing the clock. Time to get to his next class. He picked up his books from the corner—placing Fitch's two books on top—and left the building before Florence could push him further.

BIND POINTS and CIRCLES,
ADVANCED NOTES

Many mistakenly assume that a circle must be oriented with one of the bind points northward, or toward one's opponent. That is, however, false.

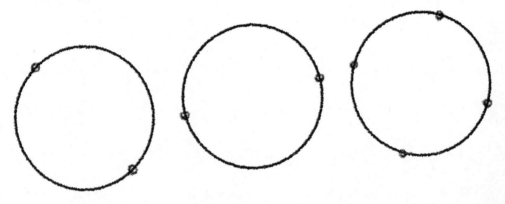

Once again, a Rithmatist MUST be careful not to draw actual dots on their completed figure. These here are used only for illustration purposes.

It is important to touch lines only at bind points, otherwise the circle's integrity will be weakened, forming a point where an opponent can attack, and much more easily breach, the Line of Warding.

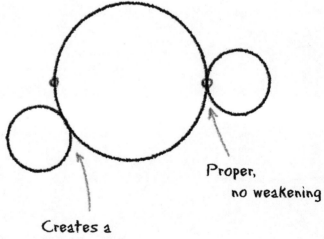

Proper, no weakening

Creates a weak junction

istory class passed quickly that day; they were review-
ing for the next day's final exam. Once it was over, Joel
went to math, his last period. This semester focused
on geometry.

Joel had mixed feelings about math class. Geometry was the
foundation for Rithmatics, so that was interesting. The history
of geometry had always fascinated him—from Euclid and the
ancient Greeks all the way forward to Monarch Gregory and the
discovery of Rithmatics.

There was just so much busywork. Endless problems that
held no interest for him.

"Today, we're going to review formulas for figuring area," said
Professor Layton from the front of the class.

Formulas for figuring area. Joel had memorized those practically before he could walk. He closed his eyes, groaning. How
many times would they have to go over the same things?

Professor Layton, however, didn't let his students lounge
about, even though most of their coursework—including the
final exam—was already done. He insisted on spending the last
week of class covering an exhaustive review of everything they'd
learned.

Honestly. Who reviewed *after* the final exam?

"We get to start today with conic sections!" Layton said. He
was a large-framed man, a tad overweight. Joel always thought

Layton should have been a coach, not a professor of mathematics. He certainly had the motivational speaking part down.

"Remember the great thing about cones?" Layton asked, gesturing at a cone he'd drawn on the board. "You can make so many things just slicing a cone at given points. Look! Slice it in the middle, and you have a circle. Cut it at an angle, and you've got an ellipse. Isn't that incredible!"

The students regarded him blankly.

"I said, isn't that incredible?"

He got some halfhearted responses of "Yes, Professor Layton." The thing was, Professor Layton thought that *every* aspect of mathematics was "incredible." He had boundless enthusiasm. Couldn't he have applied it to something useful, like Rithmatic duels?

The students slumped at their desks. Interspersed through them were several youths in white skirts and pants, with grey sweaters. Rithmatists. Joel leaned back, covertly studying them as Layton went on about different ways to dissect a cone.

The Rithmatic campus had its own specialized classes for the Rithmatists—or Dusters, as some called them. Those courses took up the first hour of each period. During the second hour of each period, then, the Rithmatists attended general education courses with the ordinary students.

Joel always felt it must be hard for them, studying all of the ordinary subjects as well as their Rithmatic learning. But it did make sense that the Rithmatists were held to higher standards than everyone else. After all, the Master himself had chosen them.

They really shouldn't be in here, Joel thought. Since they were in his class, he knew their names, but he knew basically nothing else about them—except that they were in an ordinary math class. And that was important.

Rithmatics was founded on the concepts of geometry and trigonometry, and the Rithmatic classes contained a huge portion of advanced arithmetic studies. The only reason Dusters would end up taking Professor Layton's class would be because they needed basic, remedial help in formulas and shapes.

The two boys, John and Luc, generally sat together in the back corner of the room, looking like they'd rather be *anywhere* than stuck in a math class with a bunch of non-Rithmatists. Then there was the girl. Melody. She had red curls and a face Joel rarely saw, since she spent most of each period leaned over, drawing doodles in her notebook.

Could I maybe figure out a way to get one of them to tutor me? Joel thought. *Talk to me about Rithmatics?* Maybe he could help them with their math in exchange.

"Now," Professor Layton said, "let's review the formulas for a triangle! You learned so much this year. Your lives will never be the same again!"

If only they'd let Joel into a higher-level class. But the higher-level classes were all on the Rithmatic campus. Off-limits to general students.

Hence the letter to Fitch, which Joel still carried in his pocket. He glanced at it as Professor Layton wrote some more formulas on the chalkboard. None of those formulas came to life, moved about, or did anything else unusual. Layton was no Rithmatist. To him, and to Joel—and to most everyone alive—the board was just a board, and chalk just another writing utensil.

"Wow," Layton said, surveying his list of formulas. "Did I mention how incredible those are?"

Someone in the class groaned. Layton turned, smiling to himself. "Well, I suppose you're all waiting for summer electives. Can't say that I blame you. Still, you're mine for today, so everyone get out your notebooks so I can check off last night's assignment."

Joel blinked, then felt a stab of alarm. *Last night's assignment.* His mother had even asked him if he'd had one. He had promised he'd do it. Yet he'd put it off, telling himself that he'd work on it later . . . during his free period.

Instead he'd gone to watch Fitch.

Oh no . . .

Layton moved through the class, glancing at each student's notebook. Joel slowly pulled out his own notebook and opened it to the right page. Ten unworked problems lay there. Undone, ignored. Layton stepped up to Joel's desk.

"Again, Joel?" Layton asked, sighing.

Joel glanced down.

"See me after class," Layton said, moving on.

Joel sank down in his seat. Only two more days. He just had to survive two more days and *pass* his class. He'd meant to get to the assignment; he really had. He just . . . well, hadn't.

It shouldn't matter. Layton put a lot of emphasis on tests, and Joel had achieved a perfect score on every single one. One more missed assignment wouldn't mean much for his grade.

Layton moved up to the front of the room. "All right, well, we've got ten minutes left. What to do . . . Let's work some practice problems!"

This time he got more than a few groans.

"Or," Layton said, "I suppose I could let you go early, since this is the last period of the day, and summer is right around the corner."

Students who had spent the entire period staring at the walls suddenly became alert.

"Very well, go," Layton said, waving.

They were gone in a matter of seconds. Joel remained seated, going through excuses in his head. Through the cramped window, he could see other students moving on the green outside. Most classes were finished with end-of-term tests, and things were winding down. Joel himself only had the one test left, in history. It wouldn't prove much of a problem—he'd actually studied for it.

Joel stood and walked to Professor Layton's desk, carrying his notebook.

"Joel, Joel," Layton said, expression grim. "What am I to do with you?"

"Pass me?" Joel asked.

Layton was silent.

"Professor," Joel said. "I know I haven't been the best with my assignments—"

"By my count, Joel," Professor Layton interrupted, "you've done nine of them. Nine out of *forty.*"

Nine? Joel thought. *I have to have done more than that. . . .*

He thought back, considering the term's work. Math had always been his easiest subject. He'd given very little concern for it.

"Well," Joel said. "I guess, maybe, I was a little too lazy. . . ."

"You think?" Layton said.

"But, my test scores," Joel said quickly. "I've gotten perfect marks."

"Well, first off," Layton said. "School isn't *just* about tests. Graduation from Armedius is an important, prestigious achievement. It says that a student knows how to study and follow instructions. I'm not just teaching you math, I'm teaching you life skills. How can I pass someone who never does their work?"

It was one of Layton's favorite lectures. Actually, Joel's experience was that most professors tended to think their subject was vitally important to a person's future. They were all wrong— except for the Rithmatists, of course.

"I'm sorry," Joel said. "I . . . well, you're right. I was lazy. But you can't really go back on what you said at the beginning of the term, right? My test scores are good enough to let me pass."

Layton laced his fingers in front of him. "Joel, do you know how it looks to an instructor when a student never does their practice assignments, yet somehow manages to get perfect marks on their tests?"

"Like they're lazy?" Joel asked, confused.

"That's one interpretation," Layton said, shuffling a few sheets of paper out of a stack on his desk.

Joel recognized one of them. "My final exam."

"Yes," Layton said, placing Joel's exam on the desk beside one done by another student. The other student had gotten good marks, but not perfect. "Can you see the difference between these two tests, Joel?"

Joel shrugged. His was neat and orderly, with an answer written at the bottom of each problem. The other test was messy, with jotted notes, equations, and scribbles filling the allotted space.

"I'm always suspicious when a student doesn't show their work, Joel," Layton continued, voice hard. "I've been watching you for weeks now, and I haven't been able to figure out how you're doing it. That leaves me unable to make an official accusation."

Joel felt his jaw slip down in shock. "You think I'm *cheating?*"

Layton began to write on his paper. "I didn't say that. I can't prove anything—and at Armedius, we don't make accusations we can't prove. However, it *is* within my power to recommend you for a remedial geometry tutelage."

Joel felt his hopes of a free elective begin to crack—replaced with a horrifying image of spending each and every summer day studying basic geometry. Area of a cone. Area of a triangle. Radius of a circle.

"No!" Joel said. "You can't!"

"I can indeed. I don't know where you got the answers or who was helping you, but we're going to be spending a lot of time together, you and I. You'll come out of your summer elective class knowing geometry one way or another."

"I *do* know it," Joel said, frantic. "Look, what if I do my homework right now? There's still a few minutes left of class. Then I'll have another assignment done. Will that let me pass?" He snatched a pen from its place on Layton's desk, then opened the notebook.

"Joel," Layton said sufferingly.

First problem, Joel thought. *Find the area of the three highlighted sections of the cone.* The figure was of a cone with two segments removed, with lengths and measurements of the various sides given at the bottom. Joel glanced at the numbers, did the calculations, and wrote a number.

Layton put a hand on his shoulder. "Joel, that's not going to help. . . ."

He trailed off as Joel glanced at the second question. The computation was easy. Joel wrote down the answer. The next figure was of a cube with a cylinder cut out, and the problem asked for the surface area of the object. Joel scribbled down an answer for that one.

"Joel," Layton said. "Where did you get those answers? Who gave them to you?"

Joel finished the next two problems.

"If you'd already gotten the answers from someone," Layton

said, "why didn't you just write them down earlier? You went to all the trouble of cheating, then *forgot* to actually do the assignment?"

"I *don't cheat*," Joel said, scribbling the next answer. "Why would I need to do something like that?"

"Joel," Layton said, folding his arms. "Those problems are supposed to take *at least* five minutes each. You expect me to believe you're doing them in your head?"

Joel shrugged. "They're basic stuff."

Layton snorted. He walked to the board, drawing a quick cone, then writing some numbers on the board. Joel took the opportunity to finish the next three problems of his assignment. Then he glanced at the board.

"Two hundred one point one centimeters," Joel said before Layton even finished writing. Joel looked back down at his paper, figuring the last problem. "You need to practice your sketches, Professor. The proportions on that cylinder are way off."

"Excuse me?" Layton said.

Joel joined Layton at the board. "The slant length is supposed to be twelve centimeters, right?"

Layton nodded.

"Then proportionately," Joel said, reaching up and redrawing the cone, "the radius of the bottom circle needs to be *this* long, if you want it to accurately reflect a proportionate measurement of four centimeters."

Layton stood for a moment, looking at the corrected diagram. Then he pulled out a ruler and made the measurements. He paled slightly. "You could tell *by eye* that my drawing was off by a couple centimeters?"

Joel shrugged.

"Draw me a line one third the length of the slant length," Layton ordered.

Joel drew a line. Layton measured it. "Accurate," he said, "to the millimeter! Can you do a circle with that radius?"

Joel did so, drawing a wide circle on the board. Layton measured the circle by getting out a string. He whistled. "Joel, these proportions are *perfect*! The arc on your circle is almost as exact as if it were drawn by a compass! You should have been a Rithmatist!"

Joel glanced away, shoving his hands in his pockets. "About eight years too late for that," he muttered.

Layton hesitated, then glanced at him. "Yes," he said. "I guess it is. But, well, you mean to tell me you sat there in class all this time knowing how to do *this*?"

Joel shrugged.

"You must have been bored out of your mind!"

Joel shrugged again.

"I can't believe it," Layton said. "Look, how about we do your summer elective as a trigonometry study?"

"I know trig already," Joel said.

"Oh," Layton said. "Algebra?"

"Know it," Joel said.

Layton rubbed his chin.

"Look," Joel said. "Can I *please* just pass geometry? I have plans for summer elective. If I can't make them work . . . well, I'll do calculus or something with you."

"Well," Layton said, still regarding the board. "Really is a shame you're not a Rithmatist. . . ."

You're telling me.

"Did you learn this from your father?" Layton asked. "I understand he was something of an armchair mathematician himself."

"Kind of," Joel said. Layton was new to the campus, having arrived at the academy just a few months back. He hadn't known Joel's father.

"All right," Layton said, throwing up his hands. "You can pass. I can't imagine spending three months trying to train you in something you already know so well."

Joel let out a deep sigh of relief.

"Joel, just *try* to do your assignments, all right?"

Joel nodded eagerly, rushing back to get his books from his desk. On top of them were the two books that belonged to Professor Fitch.

Maybe the day wasn't a loss quite yet.

THE BALLINTAIN DEFENSE

A star pattern is often used in Rithmatic sketches to indicate a bind point for a defensive chalkling.

Two outer Lines of Warding help defend the Rithmatist's flanks, while also herding enemy chalklings out away from the main circle.

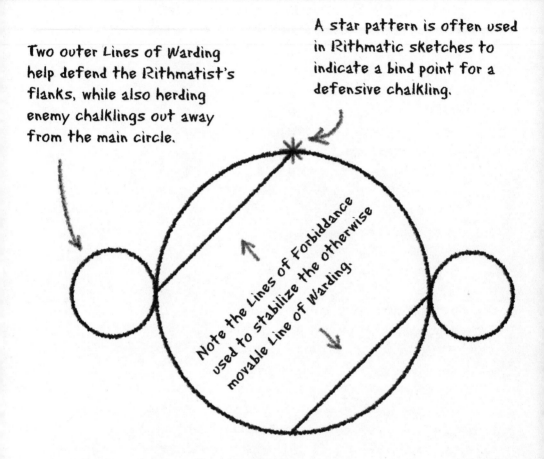

Note the Lines of Forbiddance used to stabilize the otherwise movable Line of Warding.

Straightforward and quick, the Ballintain Defense is one of the more popular defenses built off the four-point circle. It features basic stability lines, along with defensive features in only the most vital locations.

It is favored by aggressive duelists.

Joel left Professor Layton's lecture hall, stepping out onto the grass. A girl in a white skirt and a grey sweater sat outside, back to the brick wall of the building, sketching idly in her notebook. She looked up, curly red hair bouncing as she inspected Joel. It was Melody, one of the Rithmatists in the class.

"Oh, is he done with you?" she asked.

Joel nodded.

"Well, you're still in one piece," Melody said. "I guess that's a good sign. No bite marks, no broken bones . . ."

"You were waiting for me?" Joel asked, frowning.

"No, silly," she said. "Professor *Boring* asked me to stay and talk to him once he was finished with you. Probably means I'm failing. Again."

Joel glanced at her notebook. He'd watched her all semester, imagining the complex Rithmatic defensive circles she was drawing. On the pages, however, he didn't see Lines of Warding, Forbiddance, or even any circles. Instead, he saw a picture of unicorns and a castle.

"Unicorns?" he asked.

"What?" she said defensively, snapping the notebook closed. "The unicorn is a noble and majestic animal!"

"They aren't real."

"So?" she asked, standing with a huff.

"You're a Rithmatist," Joel said. "Why waste your time drawing things like that? You should be practicing your Rithmatic lines."

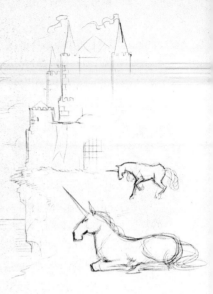

"Rithmatic this, Rithmatic that!" she said, tossing her head. "Protect the kingdom, keep the wild chalklings at bay. Why does everything have to do with *Rithmatics*? Can't a girl spend some time thinking about something else once in a while?"

Joel stepped back, surprised at the outburst. He wasn't certain how to reply. Rithmatists rarely spoke to ordinary students. Joel had tried to talk to some of them during his first few years of classes, but they'd always ignored him.

Now, one was talking to him. He hadn't expected her to be quite so . . . annoying.

"Honestly," Melody said. "Why do *I* have to be the one to deal with all of this?"

"Because the Master chose you," Joel said. "You're lucky. He only picks fewer than one in a thousand."

"He obviously needs better quality control," she said. Then, with a melodramatic sniff, she turned and pushed her way into Professor Layton's classroom.

Joel stared after her, then shook his head and crossed campus. He passed groups of students running toward the spring-rail station. Classes done, it was time to go home for the day. But for Joel, campus *was* home.

A group of students he knew stood on the quad, chatting. Joel strolled up to them, half lost in thought.

"I think it's unfair," Charlington said, folding his arms, as if his opinion were the only one that mattered. "Professor Harris was furious when she didn't show up for her final, but the principal brushed it off."

"But she's a Rithmatist," Rose replied. "Why would she want to get out of the test anyway?"

Charlington shrugged. "Maybe she wanted to get a head start on summer."

Joel had been paying only vague attention to the conversation, but he perked up when they mentioned Rithmatists. He moved over to Davis, who—as usual—stood with his arm around Rose's shoulders.

"What's this?" Joel asked.

"One of the Rithmatist students, a girl named Lilly Whiting," Davis said. "She skipped her history final today. Chuck's missing a gear about it—apparently, he wanted to take the final early so he could join his family in Europe, but he was refused."

"They shouldn't get special treatment," Charlington said.

"She'll probably still have to take the test," Joel said. "It's not like their lives are easy. No free periods, starting early each day, staying in school through the summer . . ."

Charlington frowned at him.

"Trust me, Charlie," Joel said. "If something took her away unexpectedly, she's not off lying on a beach having fun. She might be in Nebrask."

"I suppose," Charlie said. "Yeah, you might be right . . ." He paused, fishing for something.

"Joel."

"Yeah, Joel. I knew that. Well, you might be right. I don't know. Professor Harris was sure upset. I just think it's strange, is all."

A few other students reached the quad, and Charlington joined them, moving off toward the springrail station. Joel could vaguely hear him begin telling the same story to them.

"I don't believe it," Joel said softly.

"What?" Davis asked. "About that student?"

"About Charlington," Joel said. "We've been in classes together for three years, and he still forgets my name every time we talk."

"Oh," Davis said.

"Don't worry about him," Rose said. "Charlington doesn't pay attention to anyone who doesn't have a chest worth staring at."

Joel turned away from the retreating students. "Have you picked summer elective yet?" he asked Davis.

"Well, not exactly." Davis was the son of a professor, and—as such—lived on campus, like Joel. In fact, he was the only other child of an employee who was around Joel's age.

Most of the children of the staff went to the public school nearby. Only the children of professors attended Armedius itself. Well, them and Joel. His father and the principal had been close, before his father's accident eight years ago.

"I have a kind of crazy idea," Joel said. "About my elective. You see . . ."

He trailed off; Davis wasn't paying attention. Joel turned to see a group of students gathering at the front of the campus office building. "What's that?" Joel asked.

Davis shrugged. "You see Peterton there? Shouldn't he be on the 3:15 back to Georgiabama?" The tall senior was trying to peek through the windows.

"Yeah," Joel said.

The door to the office opened, and a figure stepped out. Joel was shocked to recognize the man's sharply militaristic trousers and coat, both navy, with gold buttons. It was the uniform of a federal inspector. The man placed a domed police hat on his head, then bustled away.

"A *federal inspector*?" Joel asked. "That's strange."

"I see police on campus now and then," Rose said.

"Not an inspector," Joel said. "That man has jurisdiction in all sixty isles. He wouldn't come for nothing." Joel noticed Principal York standing in the doorway to the office, Exton and Florence visible behind him. He seemed . . . troubled.

"Well, anyway," Davis said. "About summer elective."

"Yeah," Joel said. "About that . . ."

"I, um." Davis shuffled. "Joel, I'm not going to be spending the summer with you this year. It, uh, turns out I'm not free."

"Not free? What does *that* mean?"

Davis took a deep breath. "Rose and I are going to be with the group Michael is taking this summer. To his summer home, up north."

"You?" Joel said. "But . . . you're not one of them. I mean, you're just . . ." *Like me.*

"Michael is going to be an important man someday," Davis said. "He knows my father has been preparing me for law school, and Michael is planning to go himself. He'll want help, in the years to come. Someday, he'll need good attorneys he can trust. He'll be a knight-senator, you know. . . ."

"That's . . . that's great for you," Joel said.

"It's a wonderful opportunity," Davis said, looking discomforted. "I'm sorry, Joel. I know this means you'll spend the summer alone, but I have to go. This is a *chance* for me, a real chance to move up."

"Yeah, of course."

"You could ask him if you could come. . . ."

"I kind of already did."

Davis winced. "Oh."

Joel shrugged, trying to convey a nonchalance he didn't feel. "He let me down easily."

"He's a classy guy," Davis said. "I mean, you have to admit, everyone treats you pretty well here. You've got a good life, Joel. Nobody picks on you."

That was true. He'd never suffered from bullying. The students at Armedius were too important to waste time bullying. If they didn't like someone, they ostracized them. There were a dozen little proto-political factions on campus. Joel had never been a part of any of them, even the out-of-favor ones.

They probably felt they were doing him a favor. They treated him with civility, laughed with him. But they didn't include him.

He'd have traded that for some good, old-fashioned bullying. At least that would mean someone considered him worth noticing or remembering.

"I've got to go," Davis said. "Sorry."

Joel nodded, and Davis and Rose jogged off to join a group gathering around Michael near the station.

With Davis gone, Joel really *was* going to be spending the summer alone. His grade was practically empty.

Joel hefted Professor Fitch's books. He hadn't meant to take them in the first place, but he had them, so he might as well put them to some use, as the library wouldn't lend Rithmatic texts to ordinary students.

He went looking for a good place to read. And to think.

Several hours later, Joel was still reading beneath the shaded boughs of an out-of-the-way oak tree. He lowered his book and looked upward, peering through the branches of the tree toward the tiny shards of blue he could make out of the sky.

Unfortunately, the first of Fitch's books had proven to be a dud—it was just a basic explanation of the four Rithmatic lines. Joel had seen Fitch loan it out to students who seemed to be struggling.

Fortunately, the second book was far more meaty. It was a recent publication; the most interesting chapter detailed the controversy surrounding a defensive circle Joel had never heard of before. Though a lot of the Rithmatic equations in the book were beyond Joel, he was able to understand the text's arguments. It was engrossing enough that it had consumed him for a good while.

The further he read, the more he'd found himself thinking about his father. He remembered the strong man working late into the night, perfecting a new chalk formula. He remembered times his father had spent, an excited tremble to his voice, describing to the young Joel the most exciting Rithmatic duels in history.

It had been eight years. The pain of loss was still there. It never went away. It just got buried in time, like a rock slowly being covered over by dirt.

The sky was getting dark, nearly too dark for him to read, and the campus was growing still. Lights glowed in some of the lecture halls; many of them had upper stories to provide offices for professors and housing for their families. As Joel stood, he saw old Joseph—the groundskeeper—moving across the campus, winding each of the lanterns on the green in turn. The springworks within them began to whir, the lanterns flaring to life.

Joel picked up his books, deep in thought about the Miyabi Defense's convoluted history and the Blad Defense's nontraditional application of Lines of Warding. His stomach growled in complaint at being ignored.

Hopefully he hadn't missed supper. Everyone ate together—professors, staff, children, even Rithmatists. The only ordinary students who lived on campus were the children of faculty or staff, like Joel. Many of the Rithmatic students lived in the dorms. They either had family who lived too far away to visit, or they needed to accommodate extra study time. All in all, about half of the Rithmatists in Armedius lived in the dorms. The rest still commuted.

The wide-open dining hall was a hubbub of activity and chaos. Professors and spouses sat on the far left side of the room, laughing and talking together, their children seated at separate tables. Staff were on the right side of the chamber, settled at several large wooden tables. The Rithmatic students had their own long table at the back of the room, almost tucked away behind a brick outcropping.

Two long tables in the center of the room were set with the day's offering. While servers dished plates and carried them over to the professors, the family and staff were expected to serve themselves. Most people were already seated on their benches, eating, their chatting causing a low buzz in the room. Dishes clanked, the kitchen staff bustled about, and an amalgamation of scents battled with one another.

Joel made his way to his place across the long table from his mother. She was there already, which relieved him. Sometimes she worked through dinner. She still wore her brown working dress, hair up in a bun, and she picked at her food as she talked to Mrs. Cornelius, one of the other cleaning ladies.

Joel set down his books, then hurried away before his mother could pester him with questions. He piled his plate with some rice and stir-fried sausages. Germanian food. The cooks were getting exotic again. At least they'd moved away from JoSeun dishes, which Joel found far too spicy. After grabbing a flagon of spiced apple juice, he made his way back to his place.

His mother was waiting. "Florence told me that you promised to have a summer elective chosen by tonight," she said.

"I'm working on it," he said.

"Joel," she said. "You *are* going to have a summer elective, aren't you? You're not going to need to go to a tutelage again?"

"No, no," he said. "I promise. Professor Layton just told me today that I'm passing math for sure."

His mother stabbed a sausage chunk with her fork. "Other children try to do more than just *pass* their classes."

Joel shrugged.

"If I had more time to help you with your homework . . ." She sighed. After the meal, she would spend most of the night cleaning. She didn't start work each day until the afternoon, since most of the classrooms she cleaned were occupied during the day.

Like always, she had dark circles under her eyes. She worked far too hard.

"What about alchemics?" she asked. "Will you pass that?"

"Science is easy," Joel said. "Professor Langor already gave us our performance reports—the last days will just be lab, and won't be graded. I'm passing for sure."

"Literature?"

"Handed in my report today," Joel said. He'd gotten that assignment done on time—only because Professor ZoBell had given them writing time in class for two weeks while she poked through a series of novels. Professors tended to get a little bit lazy during the end of term, just like students.

"And history?" his mother asked.

"Term evaluation exam tomorrow."

She raised an eyebrow.

"It's on the history of Rithmatics, Mother," he said, rolling his eyes. "I'll do fine."

That seemed to satisfy her. Joel began to wolf down his food.

"You heard about Professor Fitch and that awful challenge?" his mother asked.

Joel nodded, mouth full.

"Poor man," she said. "You know that he spent twenty years working himself up to full professor? He lost it in a few moments, back down to tutor."

"Mother," Joel said between bites, "have you heard anything about a federal inspector on campus?"

She nodded absently. "They think one of the Rithmatic students ran away last night. She was visiting her family for the evening, and never came back to the school."

"Was it Lilly Whiting?" Joel guessed.

"I think that was her name."

"Charlington said her parents just took her on vacation!"

"That was the story at first," his mother said. "It's hard to keep something like a runaway Rithmatist secret, though. Makes me wonder why they try to flee so often. They have such easy lives. Barely required to work, ungrateful lot . . ."

"They'll find her soon enough," Joel said, jumping in before his mother could go off on *that* particular tangent.

"Look, Joel, you *need* to get into a summer elective. Do you want to end up in labor instruction?"

Many students who couldn't choose—or who chose too late—ended up helping with the landscaping of the school grounds. The official reason for the program, given by Principal York, was to "teach the generally affluent student population respect for those of other economic statuses." That concept had earned him some measure of ire from parents.

"Labor instruction," Joel said. "That wouldn't be so bad, would it? Father was a laborer. Maybe I'll need to do a job like that someday."

"Joel . . ." she said.

"What?" he replied. "What's wrong with being a laborer? You're one."

"You're getting one of the finest educations available. Doesn't that mean *anything* to you?"

He shrugged.

"You rarely do your assignments," his mother said, rubbing her forehead. "Your teachers all say you're bright, but that you don't pay attention. Can't you understand how much other people would do for an opportunity like yours?"

"I do understand," Joel said. "Really. Mother, I'm going to get a summer elective. Professor Layton said I could do math with him if I don't find anything else."

"Remedial?" she asked suspiciously.

"No," he said quickly. "Advanced."

If they'd just let me study the things I want *to,* he thought, shoving his fork into his food, *then we'd all be happy.*

That turned his mind back to the sheet of paper still crumpled in his pocket. Professor Fitch had known his father; they had been friends, to an extent. Now that Joel knew Davis wasn't going to be around for the summer, it made him even more determined to go through with his plan to study with Fitch. He pushed his food around for a few moments, then stood.

"Where are you going?" his mother asked.

He grabbed the two books that belonged to Professor Fitch. "I need to return these. Be back in a few minutes."

THE SIX-POINT CIRCLE

For advanced Rithmatic students, the
six-point circle offers more versatility,
and more defensive capability, than the
two- or four-point versions.

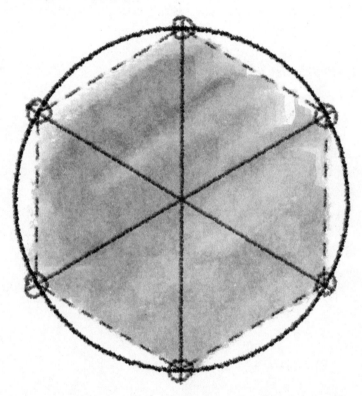

To begin, of course, one simply draws a circle. From there,
however, the Rithmatist must intuit the six bind points
based on where the tips of an inscribed hexagon would
touch the rim of the circle. Determining the location of
these points without actually seeing the hexagon or
drawing the cross-lines is difficult, but is a skill which
should be mastered by any Rithmatic scholar.

The professors sat along their table according to rank, spouses at their sides. Principal York—tall, distinguished, with a drooping brown mustache—sat at the head of the table. He was a large man, wide at the shoulders and tall enough that he seemed to tower over everyone else.

The tenured lecturers came next, Rithmatists and ordinary men interspersed, treated as equals when dining. Joel suspected that the equality had to do with the fact that the principal himself wasn't a Rithmatist. Moving along the table toward the foot, the next group of professors were what were known as "regular" professors—not yet tenured, but well established and respected. There were about six of them. The Rithmatists in their ranks wore blue coats.

The assistant professors in green came next. Finally, there were the three tutoring professors in grey. Professor Fitch, twenty or thirty years older than the people around him, sat in the last chair at the table. Nalizar sat in red near the head of the table. Even as Joel approached, he could hear Nalizar's loud voice.

". . . certainly hope it *does* cause some people to sit up and pay attention," Nalizar was saying. "We are *warriors*. It's been years since most of you held the circle in Nebrask, but *I* was there just a few months ago, on the battlefront itself! Too many academics forget that *we* are the ones who train the next generation of defenders. We can't have sloppy teaching threatening the safety of the sixty isles!"

"Surely your point is made, Nalizar," said Professor Haberstock, another of the Rithmatists. "I mean, no need to unsettle things further!"

Nalizar glanced at him, and in Joel's perception, it looked as if the young professor was barely holding back a sneer. "We cannot afford dead weight at Armedius. We must train *fighters*, not academics."

Fitch turned away, focusing on his food. He didn't seem to have eaten much. Joel stood uncertainly, trying to decide how to approach the man.

"Theory is important," Fitch said quietly.

"What was that?" Nalizar asked, looking down the table. "Did you say something?"

"Nalizar," Principal York said. "You are testing the limits of propriety. You have made your point with your actions; you need not make it with insults as well."

The young professor flushed, and Joel caught a flash of anger in his eyes.

"Principal," Fitch said, looking up, "it's all right. I would have him speak his mind."

"You are a better professor than he, Fitch," the principal said, causing Nalizar to turn even redder. "And a better instructor. I'm not fond of these rules and traditions you Rithmatists have."

"They are ours to follow," Fitch said.

"With all due respect, Principal," Nalizar cut in, "I take exception to your previous statement. Professor Fitch may be a kindly man and a fine academic, but as an instructor? When is the last time one of his students was victorious in the Rithmatic Melee?"

The comment hung in the air. As far as Joel knew, Fitch had never had a student win the Melee.

"I teach defense, Nalizar," Fitch said. "Or, um, well, I used to. Anyway, a good defense is vital in Nebrask, even if it isn't always the best way to win duels."

"You teach wasteful things," Nalizar said. "Theories to jumble their heads, extra lines they don't need."

Fitch gripped his silverware—not in anger, Joel thought, but out of nervousness. He obviously didn't like confrontation; he wouldn't meet Nalizar's eyes as he spoke. "I . . . well, I taught my students to do more than just draw lines," Fitch said. "I taught them to *understand* what they were drawing. I wanted them to be prepared for the day when they might have to fight for their lives, not just for the accolades of a meaningless competition."

"Meaningless?" Nalizar asked. "The Melee is meaningless? You hide behind excuses. *I* will teach these students to win."

"I . . . well . . ." Fitch said. "I . . ."

"Bah," Nalizar said, waving his hand. "I doubt you can ever understand, old man. How long did *you* serve on the front lines at Nebrask?"

"Only a few weeks," Fitch admitted. "I spent most of my time serving on the defensive planning committee in Denver City."

"And," Nalizar asked, "what was your focus during your university studies? Was it offensive theory? Was it, perhaps, advanced Vigor studies? Was it even—as you claim is so important for your students—defense?"

Fitch was quiet for a while. "No," he finally said. "I studied the origins of Rithmatic powers and their treatment in early American society."

"A historian," Nalizar said, turning to the other professors. "You had a *historian* teaching defensive Rithmatics. And you wonder why performance evaluations for Armedius are down?"

The table was silent. Even the principal stopped to consider this one. As they turned back to their food, Nalizar glanced toward Joel.

Joel felt an immediate jolt of panic; he'd already provoked this man once today by intruding in his classroom. Would he remember . . . ?

But his eyes just passed over Joel, as if not even seeing him. Once in a while, it was good to not be memorable.

"Is that the chalkmaker's son standing over there?" Professor Haberstock asked, squinting at Joel.

"Who?" Nalizar asked, glancing at Joel again.

"You'll get used to him, Nalizar," Haberstock said. "We keep having to throw the child out of our classes. He finds ways to sneak in and listen."

"Well, *that* won't do," Nalizar said, shaking his head. "It's sloppy teaching, letting non-Rithmatists distract our trainees."

"Well, *I* don't let him into *my* class, Nalizar," Haberstock said. "Some others do."

"Away with you," Nalizar said, waving at Joel. "If I find you bothering us again, I shall—"

"Actually, Nalizar," Fitch cut in, "I asked the boy to come speak with me."

Nalizar glared at Fitch, but he had little right to contradict instruction given to a student by another professor. He pointedly turned to a conversation about the current state of affairs in Nebrask, of which he was apparently an expert.

Joel stepped up to Fitch. "He shouldn't speak to you like that, Professor," Joel said quietly, hunkering down beside the professor.

"Well, maybe so, but maybe he has a right. I did lose to him."

"It wasn't a fair battle," Joel said. "You weren't ready."

"I was out of practice," Fitch said. Then he sighed. "Truth is, lad, I've never been good at fighting. I can draw a perfect Line of Warding in front of a classroom, but put me in a duel, and I can barely get out a curve! Yes indeed. You should have seen how I shook today during the challenge."

"I did see," Joel said. "I was there."

"You were?" Fitch said. "Ah yes. You were!"

"I thought your sketch of the Easton Defense was quite masterful."

"No, no," Fitch said. "I chose a poor defense for a one-on-one contest. Nalizar *is* the better warrior. He was a hero at Nebrask. He spent years fighting the Tower. . . . I, well, to be honest I rarely did any fighting even when I was there. I tended to get too nervous, couldn't hold my chalk straight."

Joel fell silent.

"Yes, yes indeed," Fitch said. "Perhaps this is for the best. I wouldn't want to leave any students poorly trained. I could never live with myself if one of my students died because I failed to train them right. I . . . I don't rightly think I've ever considered that."

What could Joel say to that? He didn't know how to respond. "Professor," he said instead, "I brought your books back. You walked off without them."

Fitch started. "So, you actually *did* have a reason to speak with me! How amusing. I was simply trying to aggravate Nalizar. Thank you."

Fitch accepted the books, laying them on the table. Then he started to poke at his food again.

Joel gathered his courage. "Professor," he said, reaching into his pocket. "There's something else I wanted to ask you."

"Hum? What?"

Joel pulled out the sheet and flattened it against the table. He slid it over to Fitch, who regarded it with a confused expression. "A request for summer elective?"

Joel nodded. "I wanted to sit in on your advanced Rithmatic defenses elective!"

"But . . . you're not a Rithmatist, son," Fitch said. "What would be the point?"

"I think it would be fun," Joel said. "I want to be a scholar, of Rithmatics I mean."

"A lofty goal for one who cannot himself ever make a line come to life."

"There are critics of music who can't play an instrument," Joel said. "And historians don't have to be the types who make history. Why must only Rithmatists study Rithmatics?"

Fitch stared at the sheet for a while, then finally smiled. "A valid argument, to an extent. Unfortunately, I no longer have a lecture for you to attend."

"Yes, but you'll still be tutoring. I could listen in on that, couldn't I?"

Fitch shook his head. "That's not how it works, I'm afraid.

Those of us at the bottom don't get to choose what or who we teach. I have to take the students the principal assigns to me, and he has already chosen. I'm sorry."

Joel looked down. "Well . . . do you think, maybe, one of the other professors might take over your advanced defenses class?"

"Lad," Fitch said, putting a kindly hand on Joel's shoulder. "I know the life of a Rithmatist *seems* full of excitement and danger, but even Professor Nalizar's talk of Nebrask is much more dramatic than the reality. Most Rithmatic study consists of lines, angles, and numbers. The war against the Tower is fought by a bunch of cold, wet men and women scribbling lines on the ground—interspersed with empty weeks sitting in the rain."

"I know," Joel said quickly. "Professor, it's the theory that excites me."

"They all say that," Fitch said.

"They?"

"You think you are the first young man who wanted to join the Rithmatic classes?" Fitch asked with a smile. "We get requests like this all the time."

"You do?" Joel asked, heart sinking.

Fitch nodded. "Half of them are convinced that something mysterious and exciting must be going on in those lecture halls. The other half assume that if they just study hard enough, they can become Rithmatists themselves."

"There . . . might be a way, right?" Joel asked. "I mean, Dusters like you are just regular people before their inception. So, other normal people can be Rithmatists."

"It doesn't work that way, lad," Fitch said. "The Master chooses his Rithmatists carefully. Once the age of inception has passed, the choices have all been made. In the last two hundred years, not one person has been chosen later than their inception ceremony."

Joel looked down.

"Don't feel so sad," Fitch said. "Thank you for bringing my books back to me. I'm sure I would have searched my entire study three times over for them!"

Joel nodded, turning to go. "He's wrong, by the way."

"Who?"

"Yallard, the author of that book," Joel said, waving toward the second of the two books. "He determines that the Blad Defense should be banned from official duels and tournaments, but he's shortsighted. Four ellipsoid segments combined may not make a 'traditional' defensive Line of Warding, but it's very effective. If they ban it from duels because it's too powerful, then nobody will learn it, and they won't be able to use it in a battle if they need to."

Fitch raised an eyebrow. "So you *were* paying attention in my lectures."

Joel nodded.

"Perhaps it's in the blood," Fitch said. "Your father had some interest in these things." He hesitated, then leaned down to Joel. "What you desire is forbidden by tradition, but there are *always* those who break with tradition. Newer universities, young and eager, are beginning to teach about Rithmatics to anyone who cares to learn. Go to one of those when you're older. That won't make you a Rithmatist, but you *will* be able to learn what you wish."

Joel hesitated. That actually sounded good. It was a plan, at least. Joel would never be a Rithmatist—he accepted that—but to go to one of these universities . . . "I would love that," Joel said. "But will they let me in if I haven't studied under a Rithmatic professor already?"

"Perhaps." Fitch tapped his knife softly against his plate, looking thoughtful. "Perhaps not. If you were to study with me . . ."

Fitch looked toward the head of the table, toward Nalizar and the others. Then he looked down at his food. "No. No, son, I can't agree to this. Too unconventional. I have already caused enough trouble. I'm sorry, son."

It was a dismissal. Joel turned and walked away, shoving his hands in his pockets.

THE MATSON DEFENSE

The Matson Defense is an excellent example of a Rithmatic construction that uses to its advantage all of the bind points of a six-point circle.

In addition, this defense has a large number of bind points for chalklings, allowing the Rithmatist to capitalize on his or her skills in this area.

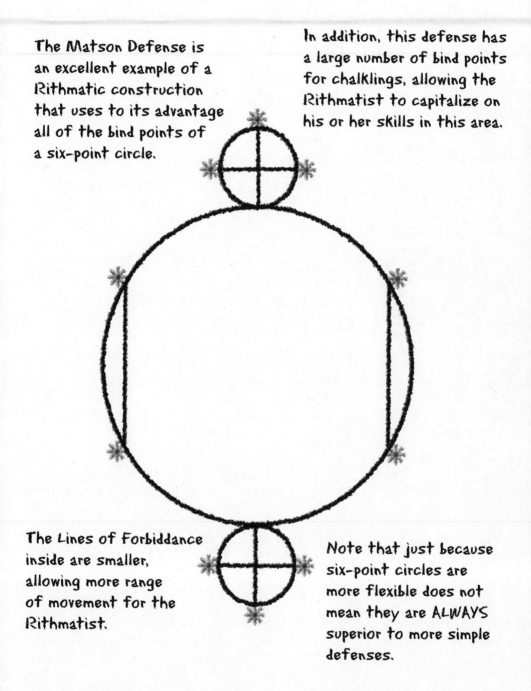

The Lines of Forbiddance inside are smaller, allowing more range of movement for the Rithmatist.

Note that just because six-point circles are more flexible does not mean they are ALWAYS superior to more simple defenses.

J oel hated nights.

Night meant bed, and bed meant lying in the dark, feeling exhausted, yet completely unable to sleep.

He and his mother shared a single room in the family dormitory. They had a closet that doubled as a changing room, and shared a communal bathroom at the end of the hallway outside. The room was tiny: brick walls, a single slit of a window, one bed. When his mother had a holiday from work, Joel slept on the floor. Other days, he made the bed and left it for her to sleep in during the daylight hours when she was off shift.

They'd once lived in larger quarters attached to his father's workshop in the basement of the dormitory. After the accident, Joel's mother had requested that the principal allow them to move into another room. Joel hadn't complained. The chalk workshop held too many memories.

Joel stared at the ceiling. Some nights, Joel went out onto the lawn and read books by lanternlight, but that tended to get him into trouble. His mother was half convinced that his poor showing in school had to do with his nocturnal habits.

Above him, sketched onto the ceiling, he could make out lines, illuminated by the faint light of the grounds' lanterns outside. The Easton Defense, one of the most complicated of the traditional Rithmatic defensive circles. He traced the lines with his eyes, following the inner circle, then the inscribed nonagon with its missing sides, the outer circles.

It was a clumsy sketch, though Joel had been proud of it when he'd drawn it two years back. The nine bind points were off, and a couple of the circles were uneven. If this defense had been used by a Rithmatist in a duel, the circle would have been breached in a matter of heartbeats. Even now, Joel often couldn't do a nine-point circle without a sketch for reference. If he got even one bind point off, it could destroy the integrity of the entire drawing.

The integrity of the drawing. It *had* no integrity. It was just chalk on plaster; it had no power. He blinked, gritting his teeth. Sometimes he hated Rithmatics. It was all about fighting and conflict. Why couldn't it do anything *useful*?

He turned onto his side. Was Michael right? Was Joel too infatuated with Rithmatics? Everyone, from Fitch to his mother, told him that at one point or another.

And yet . . . it was the one thing he cared about, the one thing that he seemed to be skilled at. Without it, what was he? He had been shown, pointedly, that a good education wouldn't elevate him to the status of the other students.

So what did he do now? Follow the course everyone expected of him? Do well enough in school to get a job as a clerk, one step up from a laborer?

Or did he keep chasing a dream? Study Rithmatics at a university. Become a scholar of it, an expert. Fitch had offered him a nibble of something grand, but had snatched away the plate right afterward. Joel felt a flare of anger at that.

He shoved it down. *Fitch did want to teach me,* he thought. *He was so shaken by what happened today that he didn't dare ask.*

Fitch would spend his summer tutoring students assigned to him by Principal York. A plan started brewing in Joel's mind. A desperate, foolish plan.

Joel smiled. He needed to fail history class.

I must remind you, again, how important this exam is," said Professor Kim. He was one of the few foreigners on the faculty.

Even though he spoke without an accent—his family had moved to the United Isles when he was just a baby—his heritage was plainly visible in his Asian skin color and eye shape.

Kim's appointment to the general school had caused a ruckus. Parents had worried about him teaching history to their students—they'd feared that he'd present the JoSeun version of historical events. Joel wasn't sure how the perspective could really get skewed beyond the truth. After all, the JoSeun people had conquered Europe. Could anyone really dispute that as fact?

"The exam is fifty percent of your final grade," Professor Kim said, handing out tests to the students as he moved between their desks. "You have two hours to complete it—take your time."

Professor Kim wore a suit and bow tie—even though other professors, those who had done their university studies in France or Espania, routinely wore JoSeun formal clothing instead of suits or skirts. Kim probably understood that he needed to be even *more* American than the others.

Joel filled in his name at the top of the test and began looking over the three essay questions to be answered.

Discuss the events, and possible causes, that led up to the discovery of Rithmatics.

Discuss the ramifications of the Monarch's exile from Britannia.

Detail the early struggle against the wild chalklings and their eventual isolation in the Tower of Nebrask.

Joel knew the answers. He knew, in depth, about how King Gregory III had been forced out of Britannia during the JoSeun advance. He had been taken in by America, despite the historical tension between the two nations. Gregory, lacking political power, had become primarily a religious leader.

And then the wild chalklings had appeared in the west, a threat to all life in the Isles. King Gregory had discovered Rithmatics, had been the first Rithmatist. He was an old man when it happened.

Was it too much to hope that Joel, despite having passed the age of inception, could also become a Rithmatist? It *had* happened before.

He scrawled answers to the questions. Not the right answers. Terrible ones. This test was fifty percent of his grade. If he failed history, he'd have to spend his summer reviewing with a tutor.

Mother is going to kill me, he thought as he finished, answering the last question with a wisecrack about kimchi, and how the wild chalklings had probably fled to the Tower to escape its stench.

Joel stood just a few minutes after he had begun, then walked up to the front and proffered the exam to Professor Kim.

The man took it hesitantly. He frowned, looking over the three simple answers. "I think you might want to look this over again."

"No," Joel said. "I'm satisfied."

"Joel, what are you doing? Didn't you hear me talk about how *important* this test is?"

"I'm well aware."

Kim stared at the test. "I think you need to have a talk with the principal," he finally said, scribbling a note to the office.

Perfect, Joel thought, taking the note.

He reached the office and pushed open the door. Florence was actually hard at work this time, and the room was quiet save for the scratchings of quills against paper.

Exton looked up as Joel entered. The clerk wore a blue bow tie this day, matched by his suspenders. "Joel," he said. "Is it fifth period already?" He glanced at the clock in the corner, then adjusted his spectacles. "No . . ."

"I have been sent to see the principal," Joel said, holding out the note.

"Oh, Joel," Florence said. "What have you done this time?"

Joel sat at one of the chairs at the side of the office, his view of Exton blocked by the large wooden counter.

"Joel." Florence folded her arms. "Answer me."

"I wasn't prepared for the test," Joel said.

"Your mother said you were quite confident."

Joel didn't respond. His heart thumped nervously in his chest.

Part of him couldn't believe what he'd done. He'd forgotten assignments before, or failed to prepare. However, he'd never *deliberately* sabotaged his grade. This meant he'd failed at least one class each of his four years at Armedius. Students got expelled for things like that.

"Well, whatever it is," Florence said, looking at the note, "you'll have to wait a few minutes. The principal is—"

The door to the office banged open. Nalizar, wearing his red, ankle-length Rithmatic coat, stood in the doorway.

"Professor Nalizar?" Exton asked, standing. "Is there something you need?"

Nalizar swept into the room, blond hair stylishly waved. It didn't seem Nalizar was wearing Fitch's coat—this one looked too new, too well tailored to Nalizar's body. Joel let out a soft hiss of displeasure. That would mean that Nalizar had forced Fitch to give up his coat in front of an entire class when Nalizar already had his own coat ready and waiting.

"It has come to my attention," Nalizar said, "that you have common students delivering messages and interrupting valuable Rithmatic training time."

Though Florence paled, Exton didn't seem the least bit intimidated. "We have messages that must be delivered to the classrooms, Professor. You suggest we force the Rithmatic professors to come to the office between each period to check for notes?"

"Don't be ridiculous," Nalizar said with a wave of the hand. His fingers were dusted red with chalk. "Interruptions are unavoidable. However, I am concerned about the integrity of the Rithmatic campus. It is unseemly to have students who do not belong there loitering about."

"And what do you propose be done about it?" Exton said flatly. "Send Rithmatic students on errands? I asked for one, once, but was told their time was 'too valuable.'"

"Miss Muns, come in, please," Nalizar snapped. A girl in a white skirt trailed into the room, curly red hair standing out sharply against her grey sweater. It was Melody, the girl from Joel's mathematics class.

"Miss Muns has shown unusual ineptitude for basic Rithmatics," Nalizar said. "This lack of dedication could present great danger to both her and those who fight beside her. It has been determined that she should undergo some form of punishment, and so she will come to the office each day after her summer elective to run errands for you to the Rithmatic campus."

Melody sighed softly.

"This will be acceptable, I presume?" Nalizar asked.

Exton hesitated, then nodded.

Joel, however, felt himself beginning to fume. "You did this because of me."

Nalizar finally looked at Joel, then frowned. "And you are . . . ?"

"This is a lot to go through, just to keep one boy out of your classrooms," Joel snapped.

Nalizar looked him up and down, then cocked his head.

Dusts, Joel thought. *He actually doesn't recognize me. Does he pay so little attention?*

"Arrogant child," Nalizar said indifferently. "I must take this action to make certain that Rithmatic students are not bothered now or in the future." He stalked from the room.

Melody sat down in one of the chairs by the door, opened her notebook, and began to sketch.

"I can't believe he did that," Joel said, sitting back down.

"I don't think he cared about you, specifically," Melody said, still sketching. "He's very keen on control. This is just another way for him to get it."

"He's a bully," Joel growled.

"He thinks like a soldier, I guess," Melody replied. "And he wants to keep separation between Rithmatists and others. He said that we needed to be careful how we acted around common people. Said that if we didn't hold ourselves aloof, we'd gain sycophants who would interfere with our work. It—"

"Melody, dear," Florence said. "You're rambling."

Melody blinked, looking up. "Oh."

"Wait," Joel said. "Shouldn't you be going back to class with Nalizar?"

She grimaced. "No. I . . . well, he kind of kicked me out."

"Kicked you out?" Joel said. "Of *class*? What did you do?"

"My circles weren't good enough," she said with a dramatic flip of her fingers. "What is it with circles, anyway? Everyone is so *crazy* over circles."

"The arc of a Line of Warding is vital to the structural integrity of the defensive perimeter," Joel said. "If your circle has an inconsistent arc, you'll be beaten the moment a single chalkling gets to your wall. Drawing an even circle is the first and most important Rithmatic skill!"

"Dusts!" Melody said. "You sound just like a *professor*. No wonder all the students think you're so odd!"

Joel blushed. Even the *Rithmatists* thought he focused too much on Rithmatics, it appeared.

The back door of the office opened. "Florence?" the principal asked. "Who's next?"

Joel stood up and met the principal's eyes. The large man frowned, mustache drooping. "Joel?"

Florence crossed the room and handed him Professor Kim's note. The principal read it, then groaned—a loud, booming sound that seemed to echo. "Come in, then."

Joel rounded the counter. Florence gave him a sympathetic shake of the head as he passed her and entered the principal's office. The wood trim of the chamber was of fine walnut, the carpet a forest green. Various degrees, accolades, and commendations hung on the walls. Principal York had a towering desk to fit his large frame, and he sat, waving Joel toward the chair in front.

Joel sat down, feeling dwarfed by the fine desk and its intimidating occupant. He'd only been in this room three other times, at the end of each year when he'd failed a class. Footsteps fell on the carpet behind, and Florence arrived with a file. She handed it to York, then retreated, pulling the door closed. There were no windows in the room, though two lanterns spun quietly on each wall.

York perused the file, letting Joel sit in silence, sweating. Papers ruffled. Ticking from the lanterns and the clock. As the silence stretched, pulled tight like taffy, Joel began to question his plan.

"Joel," the principal finally said, voice strangely soft, "do you realize the opportunity you are throwing away?"

"Yes, sir."

"We don't allow the children of other staff into Armedius," York continued. "I allowed you in as a personal favor to your father."

"I realize that, sir."

"Any other student," York said, "I would have expelled by now. I have kicked out the sons of knight-senators before, you know. I expelled the Monarch's own grandnephew. With you, I hesitated. Do you know why?"

"Because my teachers say I'm bright?"

"Hardly. Your intelligence is a reason *to* expel you. A child with poor capacity, yet who works hard, is far more desirable to me than one who has a lot of potential, but throws it away."

"Principal, I try. Really, I—"

York held up a hand, stilling him. "I believe we had a conversation similar to this last year."

"Yes, sir."

York sat for a few moments, then pulled out a sheet of paper. It had lots of official-looking seals on it—not a request for a tutor. An expulsion form.

Joel felt a stab of panic.

"The reason I gave you an extra chance, Joel, was because of your parents." The principal took a pen from a holder on his desk.

"Principal," Joel said. "I understand now that I'm—"

The principal cut him off again with an uplifted hand. Joel held in his annoyance. If York wouldn't let him speak, what could he do? In the dark last night, the wild plan had seemed clever and bold. Now, Joel worried it would explode right in front of him.

The principal began to write.

"I failed that test on purpose," Joel said.

York looked up.

"I wrote in answers I knew were wrong," Joel said.

"Why in all of the heavens would you do such a thing?"

"I wanted to fail so that I could get a summer tutelage studying history."

"Joel," York said, "you could simply have asked Professor Kim if you could join his course this summer."

"His elective will study European culture during the JoSeun occupation," Joel said. "I needed to fail *Rithmatic history* so that I could end up studying that."

"You could have approached one of the professors and asked them to tutor you," York said sternly. "Sabotaging your own grades is *hardly* appropriate."

"I tried," Joel said. "Professor Fitch said that ordinary students weren't allowed to study with Rithmatic professors."

"Well, I'm certain that Professor Kim could have come up with an independent study course covering . . . You approached *Fitch*?"

"Yes."

"He's a Rithmatist!"

"That was kind of the point, sir." How could he explain? "I don't really want to study history. I want to study Rithmatic lines. I figure that if I get Professor Fitch alone and start him talking about Rithmatics, I'll be able to learn about the defenses and offenses, even if the tutelage is supposed to be about history."

He gulped, waiting for the scorn he'd received from others.

"Oh, well," York said. "That makes sense then, I suppose—assuming you think like a teenage boy. Son, why didn't you just come *ask* me?"

Joel blinked. "Well, I mean, everyone seems to think that studying Rithmatics would be arrogant of me, that I shouldn't be bothering the professors."

"Professor Fitch likes to be bothered," York said, "particularly by students. He's one of the few true *teachers* we have at this school."

"Yes, but he said he couldn't train me."

"There are traditions," York said, putting aside the form and taking out another one. York regarded it, looking uncertain.

"Sir?" Joel asked, hope beginning to recover within him.

York set the form aside. "No, Joel," he said. "Fitch is right. There are rules against assigning ordinary students to take courses in Rithmatics."

Joel closed his eyes.

"Of course," York said, "I *did* just put Fitch on a very important project. It would be very useful to him to have help. There's nothing forbidding me from assigning him a research assistant from the general school."

Joel opened his eyes.

Principal York pulled out another sheet of paper. "This is assuming, of course, that said assistant wouldn't be a distraction to Professor Fitch. I've already given him a student to tutor. I don't want to overload him."

"I promise not to be a bother," Joel said eagerly.

"I suspect that, with all of his attempts to divide the Rithmatists from the common folk, this will quite upset Professor Nalizar. A tragedy."

York smiled. Joel's heart leaped.

"Of course," York said, glancing at the clock, "I can't give you this assignment unless you have an open summer elective. By my count, you still have forty-five minutes left of Kim's history class. Do you think you could get a passing grade if you were to return and use the rest of your time?"

"Of course I could," Joel said.

"Well then," York said, tapping the sheet with his hand. "This form will be here, ready and waiting, assuming you can get back to me by the end of the day with a passing grade in history."

Joel was out the office door a few heartbeats later, running across the lawn toward history class. He burst into the lecture hall, puffing, startling the students who still sat taking their tests.

His own exam still sat on Kim's desk. "The principal convinced me to try again," Joel said. "Can I . . . have a new test?"

Kim tapped his fingers together. "Did you just go look up the answers while you were out?"

"I promise I didn't, sir!" Joel said. "The office can confirm that I was sitting there the whole time, books closed."

"Very well," Kim said, glancing at the clock. "But you'll still have to finish in the allotted time." He pulled out a fresh test and handed it to Joel.

Joel snatched it, then took a jar of ink and a quill and rushed back to his seat. He scribbled furiously until the clock rang, signaling the end of class. Joel stared at the last question, which he hadn't answered in true depth, lacking time.

Taking a deep breath, he joined the other students at the front of the room turning in their papers. He waited until all of them were gone before handing in his own.

Kim took it, raising an eyebrow as he noticed the thorough answers. "Perhaps I should have sent you to the principal's office months ago, if this was the result."

"Could you, maybe, grade it?" Joel asked. "Let me know if I passed?"

Kim glanced at the clock. He took out a quill, dipped it in ink, then began to read. Joel waited, heart beating, as the professor deducted points here and there.

Finally, Kim totaled up the score at the bottom.

"Do I pass?" Joel asked.

"Yes," Kim said. "Tell me, why did you hand in that other test? We both know you're quite accomplished in this subject."

"I just needed the right motivation, sir," Joel said. "Please, would you write a note to the principal explaining that I passed?"

"I suppose. Would you, by chance, be interested in studying in my advanced history elective this summer?"

"Maybe next year," Joel said, spirits soaring. "Thank you."

When Joel reached the office a short time later, he found the form waiting for him. It was filled out, and it ordered Joel to become Professor Fitch's research assistant for the summer. Beside it was a note from the principal.

Next time, try talking to me. I've been thinking lately that the Rithmatists are too concerned with keeping themselves separate from the rest of the campus.

I'm very curious to see how Professor Fitch handles his current project. Inspector Harding insisted that I put my best

Rithmatist to work on the problem; I found it convenient, if unfortunate, that my best scholar suddenly had plenty of free time.

Keep an eye on things in regards to this project for me, if you don't mind. I may be asking you for the occasional up-date.

—Principal York

PART
TWO

LINES of FORBIDDANCE

It is very important that a Rithmatist pay atten-tion to where they draw each Line of Forbiddance, as one cannot be crossed even by the Rithmatist who drew it.

Here, a Rithmatist has drawn a Line of Forbiddance below their defense for extra protection.

Also, a Rithmatist must realize that if they draw a Line of Forbiddance, it will stop people from being able to pass that way. This can be useful, but can also be dangerous.

They must realize, however, that they now cannot reach past this line to draw chalklings, nor can they launch Lines of Vigor through the line. This can trap the Rithmatist, as it takes four seconds to dismiss a Line of Forbiddance.

Invisible plane of force created above the line

Line of Forbiddance

J oel left the dormitory building early the next morning, crossing over to the Rithmatic campus. He breathed in deeply, enjoying the scent of the flowering trees and the recently cut lawn. The Rithmatic campus consisted of four main buildings of stately brick, named after each of the four Rithmatic lines. The professors made their offices on the upper floors of each building.

Joel opened a door on the outside of Warding Hall, then entered a cramped stairwell. He climbed to the third story, where he found a thick wooden door. It was gnarled and knotted, which gave it the aged feel that prevailed across the Rithmatic campus.

Joel hesitated. He'd never visited any of the Rithmatic professors in their offices. Professor Fitch was a kindly man, but how would he respond to finding out that Joel had gone over his head, approaching Principal York directly?

There was only one way to find out. He knocked on the door. A short time passed with no answer. He reached up to knock again, but at that moment, the door was flung open. Fitch stood inside, his grey Rithmatist's coat unbuttoned, showing the white vest and trousers he wore underneath.

"Yes? Hum?" Fitch asked. "Oh, the chalkmaker's son. What brings you here, lad?"

Joel hesitantly raised the form that Principal York had given him.

"Hum? What is this?" Fitch took the form, looking it over. "Research assistant? You?"

Joel nodded.

"Ha!" Fitch exclaimed. "What a wonderful idea! Why didn't I think of this? Yes, yes, come in."

Joel let out a relieved breath, allowing Fitch to usher him through the door. The chamber beyond felt more like a hallway than a room. It was much longer than it was wide, and was cramped with piles of books. A few slot windows in the right wall illuminated an amalgamation of furniture and knickknacks piled against both walls. Two small springwork lanterns hung from the ceiling, their gears clicking as they shone.

"Indeed," Fitch said, picking his way through the stacks of books, "I should have known York would make everything work out. He's a brilliant administrator. Heaven only knows how he manages to balance all of the egos bumping around this campus. Sons of knight-senators mixing with Rithmatists and men who see themselves as heroes from Nebrask. My, my."

Joel followed the professor. The room ran along the outside of the building; at the corner, it turned at a ninety-degree angle, then continued northward along that wall as well. The room eventually ended at a brick wall, against which sat a small, neatly made bed. The tucked-in sheets and quilted covering seemed quite a contrast to the clutter in the rest of Fitch's dark, brick-walled office.

Joel stood at the corner, watching Fitch rifle through his books, stacking some aside, uncovering a plush stool and matching easy chair. There was a musty scent to the place: the smell of old books and parchment mixed with that of dank brick walls. The air was slightly chilly, despite the approaching summer weather outside.

Joel found himself smiling. The office was much as he had imagined. The left wall was hung with sheets of paper bearing aged Rithmatic sketches. Some were protected in frames, and all were covered with annotations. There were so many books that the piles themselves seemed to pile on top of one another. Exotic knickknacks lay half buried—a flute that looked Asian in origin, a ceramic bowl with a colorful glaze, several Egyptian paintings.

And the Rithmatic Lines . . . they were everywhere. Not just on the wall hangings. They were
printed on the covers of the books, scratched into the
floorboards, woven into the rug, and even sketched
onto the ceiling.

"I asked York for an assistant," Fitch was saying
as he puttered about, "but I would never have dared
ask for a non-Rithmatist. Too untraditional. But there must not
be a rule about it, and . . . Lad?"

Joel looked at the middle-aged Rithmatist. "Yes?"

"You seem distracted," Fitch said. "I'm sorry the place
is such a mess. I keep meaning to clean it, but since
nobody ever comes in here but me—and, well,
I guess now you—there didn't ever seem to be a
point."

"No," Joel said. "No, it's perfect. I . . ." How
could he explain? "Coming in here feels like coming *home*."

Fitch smiled. He straightened his long coat, then settled into
the chair. "Well then," he said, "I suppose I should put
you to work! Let me see—"

He cut off as a quiet knock echoed through
the room. Fitch cocked his head, then stood.
"Now, who . . . Oh yes. The other student."

"Other student?" Joel asked, trailing Fitch as he
rounded the corner and walked down the cluttered
hallway.

"Yes, hum," Fitch said. "York assigned her to me for a remedial tutelage. She gave a very poor showing in my—well, Professor Nalizar's—Rithmatics class."

Joel hesitated. "It's not . . ."

He trailed off as Fitch pulled open the door. Sure enough, the
red-curled Melody stood outside, wearing her white skirt. She'd
traded her grey sweater for a short-sleeved, buttoned blouse. She
was actually kind of pretty—she had nice eyes, at least.

"I'm here," she announced with a loud voice. "Let the flogging commence!"

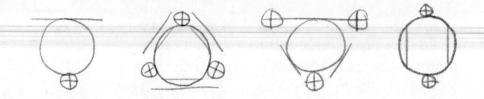

Too bad she was crazy.

"Flogging?" Fitch said. "My dear, are you well?"

Melody stepped into the room. "I'm merely resigned to my fate, Professor."

"Ah, good, very well." Fitch turned around and walked back past Joel, waving for Melody to follow. She stopped beside Joel as Fitch began digging through some piles.

"Tell me honestly," Melody said, whispering to Joel, "are you following me?"

Joel started. "What?"

"Well, you did take the same math class that I did."

"We get assigned our classes by the campus office!" Joel said.

"After that," she continued, speaking as if she hadn't heard his protest, "you got a job at the campus office—the same place that I, unfortunately, have to do service."

"I've had that job since the beginning of the term!"

"And finally," she said, "you followed me to Fitch's office. Pretty suspicious."

"I didn't follow you. I was here *before you*!"

"Yes," Melody said, "a convenient excuse. Just don't show up outside my window at night, or I shall have to scream and throw something at you."

"Ah!" Fitch exclaimed, pulling out a large artist's sketch pad. Then he regarded the wall, rubbing his chin in thought. He eventually pointed at one of the hangings—it depicted a simplified Matson Defense.

Fitch took the hanging off the wall, then shoved aside some books with his foot, making room on the floor. "You, young lady," he said to Melody, "may think that you are a lost cause. I hardly believe that to be the case. You just need some practice in the fundamentals." He set the diagram of the Matson Defense on the

ground, then ripped a sheet out of the large sketch pad and laid it over the top.

Melody sighed. "Tracing?"

"Yes indeed."

"It's something we did back in seventh grade!"

"That, my dear," Fitch said, "is why this is called a *remedial* tutelage. I should think that you'll be able to complete ten copies or so by the time the day is through. Make certain you trace the crosslines in the center and mark the bind points!"

Melody sighed again—she did that a lot, apparently—and shot Joel a glance, as if she blamed him for witnessing her humiliation. He shrugged. Drawing Rithmatic patterns seemed like a fun way to spend the afternoon.

"Get to work, Melody," Fitch said, rising. "Now, Joel, I have something for you to do as well." Fitch began to walk down the hallway, and Joel hurried after, smiling in anticipation. Principal York had said the project Fitch was working on was at the request of the federal inspector, so it must be very important. Joel had spent much of the night lying in bed, thinking about what kind of work Fitch was doing. Something involving Rithmatics, lines, and . . .

"Census records," Fitch said, hefting a pile of hardbound ledgers and handing them to Joel.

"Excuse me?" Joel asked.

"Your job," Fitch said, "is to look through the death notices in these ledgers and search out all of the Rithmatists who have died during the last twenty years. Then I want you to cross-reference those with the lists of Armedius graduates I have over here. Every Rithmatist who has passed away, cross off the list."

Joel frowned. "That sounds like a lot of work."

"That is precisely," Fitch said, "the reason I requested a student assistant!"

Joel glanced through the books Fitch had handed him. They were obituary reports from all across the sixty isles.

"It will be easier than you think, lad," Fitch said. "In those reports, a Rithmatist is always noted by an asterisk, and their obituary will state which of the eight schools they went to. Just scan each page looking for deceased Rithmatists who went to Armedius. When you find one, locate them on this other list and cross them off. In addition, when you find a former Armedius student who died, I want you to read the obituary and note anything . . . odd in it."

"Odd?" Joel asked.

"Yes, yes," Fitch said. "If they died in an unusual way, or were murdered, or something of that nature. Armedius has about twenty Rithmatic graduates a year. Figure an eighty-year period; that means we have over fifteen hundred Rithmatists to look through! I want to know who among them is dead, and I want to know how they passed." The professor rubbed his chin. "It occurred to me that the school should have this information, but a check with Exton at the office informed me that they don't keep strict track of alumni deaths. It is an oversight for which we— well, you—will now have to pay the penalty."

Joel sank down on the stool, looking at the seemingly endless stacks of census reports. To the side, Melody glanced at him, then smiled to herself before turning back to her sketching.

What have I gotten myself into? Joel wondered.

M y life," Melody declared, "is a tragedy."

Joel looked up from his stack of books, names, and dead people. Melody sat on the floor a short distance away; she'd spent hours drawing copies of the Matson Defense. Her tracings were terrible.

Professor Fitch worked at a desk in the corner. He ignored Melody's outburst.

"Why," she continued, "out of all people on the Isles, did *I* have to get chosen to be a Rithmatist? I can't even draw a perfect circle when I'm *tracing*!"

"Actually," Joel said, closing his book, "it's impossible for the unaided human hand to draw a perfect circle. That's one of the things that makes Rithmatic duels so interesting."

She glared at him. "Technicality."

"Here," Joel said, getting down and taking out one of the sheets of paper. He picked up an ink and quill and drew a free-hand circle.

She leaned over, getting a closer look. "That's not bad," she said grudgingly.

He shrugged, glancing about. A piece of string hung from a dusty tome. Joel pulled it free, then used it to measure the circle he'd drawn—sticking one point at the center, then tracing the rest around the perimeter. "See," he said, "I'm off by about half a millimeter."

"So?" she said. "You were still freakishly accurate."

"Yes," Joel said, "but if we were dueling, and you could determine just *where* the arc of my circle was off, you'd be able to attack me there. It's my weak point. Anyway, drawing a Circle of Warding isn't about getting it perfect—it's just about getting as close as you can."

"They should let us use a tool, like that string."

"You can't always count on having a compass," Joel said. "And drawing with a tool takes much longer. My circle here might not be perfect, but it's close enough that finding the weak spots will be tough, particularly when my opponent is sitting inside their own circle five or ten feet away."

He sat back on his stool. "It's just better to learn how to draw a good freehand circle. That will help you more in the long run than pretty much anything else in Rithmatics."

The girl eyed him. "You know a lot about this."

"It interests me."

She leaned in. "Hey, you want to do my tracing for me?"

"*What?*"

"You know, finish this work for me. We'll trade. I can look through those books for you."

"Professor Fitch is sitting *right there*," Joel said, pointing. "He can probably hear everything you're saying."

"Sure can," Fitch said, scribbling at a notebook.

"Oh," Melody said, wincing.

"You're a strange girl," Joel said.

Melody leaned back, crossing her legs beneath her skirt and sighing melodramatically. "Maybe *you'd* be strange too if you'd been forced into a life of abject, *unrelenting* slavery."

"Slavery?" Joel asked. "You should be proud to have been chosen."

"Proud?" she said. "Of being forced into a career since my eighth birthday? Of having to spend my days being told that if I don't learn to draw a stupid circle, it could cost me my life—or even the safety of the entire United Isles? I should be *proud* having no freedom or will of my own? Proud that I'll eventually get shipped off to Nebrask to fight? I figure I have at least a little bit of a right to complain."

"Or maybe you're just spoiled."

Melody's eyes opened wide, and she huffed as she stood and snatched her oversized sketch pad. She marched away, rounding the corner to sit in the other hallway, accidentally knocking over a stack of books as she went.

"More work, please, Joel," Fitch said without looking up from his work. "Less antagonizing of the other student."

"Sorry," Joel said, picking up a ledger.

Fitch was right—the work moved more quickly than Joel had first anticipated. Still, it was boring. What was the point? Was his "important project" nothing more than an excuse to update the school's records? Maybe the principal wanted to search out old graduates and get them to donate money or something to the school.

After all he'd gone through to get into a tutelage with Fitch, he wanted to be involved in something interesting. It didn't have to be spectacular. But bookkeeping?

As he worked, he found his mind drifting toward thoughts of Nebrask. Fitch's work had something to do with why the inspector had visited. Was Lilly Whiting really involved?

Maybe she'd run off to Nebrask. Melody might not want to go, but Joel thought the place sounded terribly exciting. The dark island in the middle of the others, an island where terrible, dangerous chalklings sought to escape and flood the other islands.

The Rithmatists maintained an enormous chalk circle there, the size of a city. Outside the circle, camps and patrols worked to keep the chalklings in. And on the inside, the chalklings attacked the lines, trying to breach, work their way out. On occasion, they'd break through, and the Rithmatists would need to fight.

Wild chalklings . . . chalklings that could kill. Nobody knew who had created them. Joel could imagine that circle though, drawn on concrete poured into the ground. Storms were said to be the worst. Though canopies kept most of the rain off, water would seep in, particularly from the side of the wild chalklings, washing away the chalk, creating breaches. . . .

The grandfather clock in the corner slowly ticked toward noon, the hour when summer elective classes ended. Joel worked on the ledgers, trying to focus, though thoughts of the chalklings, and Rithmatic circles, invaded his mind.

Eventually, Joel closed his latest census book and rubbed his eyes. The clock said fifteen till noon. Joel stood to stretch his legs and walked over to Professor Fitch.

The professor quickly closed his notebook as Joel approached. Joel caught a brief glimpse of some sort of drawing on the page. Rithmatic? A circle that had been breached?

"Yes, Joel?" Fitch asked.

"It's almost time to go," Joel said.

"Ah, is it? Hum, why, yes indeed. So it is. How went the research?"

Research? Joel thought. *I'm not sure that's the right word for it. . . .* "I managed to cross off thirty or so names."

"You did? Excellent! You can continue tomorrow, then."

"Professor? I don't mean to be rude, but . . . well, it would help if I knew the point of this. Why am I looking through census records?"

"Ah . . . hum . . . well, I don't know that I can tell you that," Fitch said.

Joel cocked his head. "This has to do with the inspector who visited the school, right?"

"I can't really say. . . ."

"The principal already told me that much."

"He did?" Fitch scratched his head. "Well, then, I guess you can know that. But really, I shouldn't say more. Tell me, during your research, did you . . . find anything *suspicious*?"

Joel shrugged. "It's a little bit creepy, to be honest—looking through lists and lists of dead people. In a way, they could *all* be suspicious, since there aren't a lot of details. Most of them seem to have died from sickness or old age."

"Any accidents?" Fitch asked.

"A couple. I marked them, like you said."

"Ah, very good. I'll look through those this evening. Excellent work!"

Joel gritted his teeth. *But why? What are you looking for? Does it have to do with the girl who ran away? Or am I just hoping that it does?*

"Well, you should run along then," Fitch said. "You too, Melody. You can go early."

Melody was out the door in a few seconds. Joel stood for a few moments, trying to decide if he should push Fitch further. His stomach growled, however, demanding lunch.

He left to get some food, determined to think of a way to get Fitch to show him the notebook.

The SUMSION DEFENSE

A "Mark's Cross" structure at the top bind point offers further defense while also serving to anchor the entire piece.

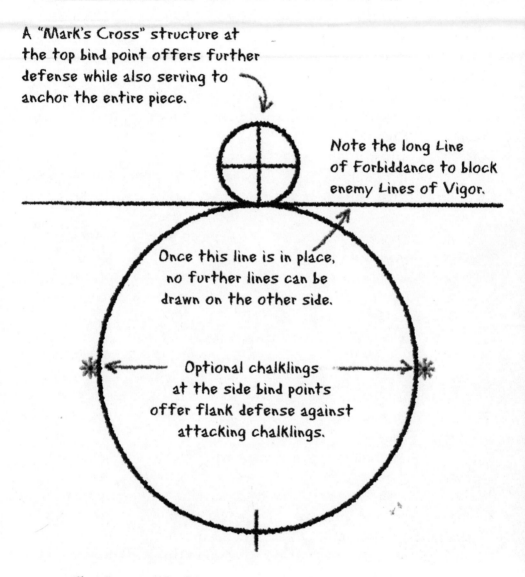

Note the long Line of Forbiddance to block enemy Lines of Vigor.

Once this line is in place, no further lines can be drawn on the other side.

Optional chalklings at the side bind points offer flank defense against attacking chalklings.

The Sumsion Defense is a quick, four-point defense with a long defensive Line of Forbiddance at the top. It is preferred by those who wish to attack from the sides.

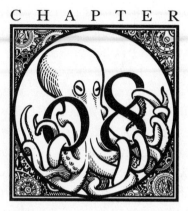

Joel crossed the lawn toward the dining hall. The campus wasn't very full; over half of the students would be gone for the summer. Many of the staff took the summers off too, and even some of the professors were gone—off in France or JoSeun Britannia, doing research and attending symposiums.

Still, lunch was likely to be a little crowded, so he rounded the building and ducked through a back door into the kitchens. They were normally off-limits to students, but Joel wasn't just a student.

Hextilda herself was supervising the lunch duties that day. The large woman nodded to him. "Joel, lad," she said in her thick Scottish accent, "you enjoying your first day of summer?"

"Spent it trapped in a professor's dungeon," Joel said. "He had me reading census records."

"Ha!" she said. "Well, you should know that *I* have news!"

Joel raised an eyebrow.

"M'son has gotten our whole family a traveler's permit to visit the homeland! I'll be leaving in a month's time!"

"That's fantastic, Hextilda!"

"First time any McTavish will have set foot on our own soil since my great-grandfather was driven out. Those dirty Sunnys. Forcing us to have a permit to visit our own land."

The Scots had lasted a long time in their highlands, fighting the JoSeun invasion before being driven out. Trying to convince a Scot that the land was no longer theirs was next to impossible.

"So," Joel said, "want to celebrate by giving me a sandwich so I don't have to wait in line?"

Hextilda gave him a flat look. But less than five minutes later she delivered one of her signature, well-stacked sandwiches. Joel took a bite, savoring the salty flavor of the wood-smoked haddock as he left the kitchens and started across campus.

Something was going on—the way Principal York had acted, the way Fitch had closed the notebook when Joel approached . . . it was suspicious. So how could he get more involved?

Fitch did warn me that the life of a Rithmatist wasn't glamorous, he reminded himself. *But there has to be a way.*

Perhaps he could figure out on his own what Fitch was researching. Joel thought for a moment. Then he looked down at the last few bites of sandwich in his hand, an idea forming in his head. He rushed back to the dining hall.

A few minutes later, he left the kitchen with two more sandwiches, each in a small paper sack. He ran across the campus green to the office.

Florence and Exton looked up when Joel entered. "Joel?" Florence said. "Didn't expect to see you today. It's summer!"

"I'm not here to work; I'm just here to say hello. What, you think that because it's summer I'm never going to drop by?"

Florence smiled. Today she wore a green summer dress, her curly blonde hair tamed in a bun. "How thoughtful. I'm sure Exton will be pleased for the diversion!"

Exton continued to write at one of his ledgers. "Oh yes. I'm excited to have yet another item striving to distract me from the two hundred end-of-term grade reports I must fill out and file before the week is over. Delightful."

"Ignore him, dear," Florence said. "That's his way of saying he's happy to see you."

Joel set the two packages on the countertop. "Well, I have to admit that it's not *just* a social visit. I was in the kitchens, and the cook thought you two might want something for lunch."

"*That's* sweet," Florence said, walking over. Even Exton

grunted in agreement. Florence handed him a bag, and they immediately began to work on the sandwiches. Joel got out the remnant of his own meal, holding it and taking small bites so that he wouldn't look out of place.

"So," he said, leaning against the counter, "anything exciting happen during the four hours since summer started?"

"Nothing much," Florence said. "As Exton already pointed out, there is a lot of busywork this time of year."

"Dull, eh?" Joel asked.

Exton grunted into his sandwich.

"Well," Joel said, "we can't have federal inspectors visiting *every* day, I suppose."

"That's the truth," Florence said. "And I'm glad for it. Quite the ruckus that one caused."

"Did you ever figure out what it was about?" Joel asked, taking a bite of his sandwich.

"Maybe," Florence said, lowering her voice. "I couldn't hear what was going on inside the principal's office, of course. . . ."

"Florence," Exton said warningly.

"Oh, hush you," she said. "Go back to your sandwich. Anyway, Joel, did you hear about that Rithmatic girl who vanished a few days back? Lilly Whiting?"

Joel nodded.

"Poor dear," Florence said. "She was a very good student, by the look of her grades."

"You read her *records*?" Exton asked.

"Of course I did," Florence said. "Anyway, from what *I've* heard, she didn't run away like they're saying in the papers. She had good grades, was well liked, and got along with her parents."

"What happened to her, then?" Joel asked.

"Murder," Florence said softly.

Joel fell silent. Murder. That made sense—after all, a federal inspector was involved. Yet it felt different to have it spoken out loud. It made him remember that they were talking about a real person, not just a logical puzzle.

"Murder," he repeated.

"By a Rithmatist," Florence said.

Joel stiffened.

"Now, that's just useless speculation," Exton said, wagging a finger at her.

"I heard enough before York closed the door," Florence replied. "That inspector thinks a Rithmatist was involved in the killing, and he wanted expert help. It—"

She cut off as the front door to the office behind Joel opened and closed.

"I delivered the message to Haberstock," a female voice said. "But I—"

Joel groaned.

"You!" Melody snapped, pointing at Joel. "See, you *are* following me!"

"I just came to—"

"I don't want to hear your excuses this time," Melody said. "I have *evidence* now."

"Melody," Florence said sharply, "you're acting like a child. Joel is a friend. He can visit the office if he wants."

The redheaded Rithmatist huffed at that, but Joel didn't want another argument. He figured he'd gotten as much out of Florence as he was going to be able to, so he nodded farewell to the clerks and made his exit.

Killed by a Rithmatist? Joel thought once outside. *How would they know?*

Had Lilly died in a duel gone wrong? Students didn't know the glyphs that would make a chalkling dangerous. Usually a chalkling drawn with a Line of Making would be unable to harm anything aside from other chalk drawings. It took a special glyph to make them truly dangerous.

That glyph—the Glyph of Rending—was only taught at Nebrask during the last year of a student's training, when they went to maintain the enormous Circle of Warding in place around the Tower. Still, it was not outside of reason that a student could have discovered it. And if a Rithmatist *had* been involved, it would explain why Fitch had been brought in.

Something is *happening*, Joel thought. *Something important.* He was going to find out, but he needed a plan.

What if he got through those census records as quickly as possible? He could show Fitch how hard he was willing to work, that he was trustworthy. Professor Fitch would have to assign him another project—something more involved, something that gave him a better idea of what was going on.

Plan in place, he headed back toward Fitch's to ask for a few of the census ledgers to take home with him tonight. He'd been planning to read a novel—he'd found an interesting one set during the Koreo Dynasty in JoSeun, during the first days when the JoSeun people had turned the Mongols to their side. It would wait.

He had work to do.

The OSBORN DEFENSE

Note that the side circles are NOT touching the main defense. Ellipses have only two bind points—one at the top and one at the bottom. Better to not let the circles touch, then. These side structures are optional, depending on time and the amount of defense desired.

With only one chalkling bind point, those who use this defense should place a quite detailed Line of Making here for extra defense.

A single line at the back is all that anchors this defense against being moved by a Line of Vigor.

Many see this as the defense's prime drawback.

The Osborn is naturally strong in front, and is good for those who prefer a quick offense.

The Osborn is the only basic defense based on an ellipse. It makes use of the fact that ellipsoid structures have a stronger defense at top and bottom, but are weaker on the sides.

By the end of the week, Joel had discovered something important about himself. Something deep, primal, and completely inarguable.

The Master had *not* meant for him to be a clerk.

He was tired of dates. He was fed up with ledgers. He was nauseated by notes, cross-references, and little asterisks beside people's names.

Despite that, he continued to sit on Fitch's floor, studying page after page. He felt as if his brain had been sucked out, his lips stapled shut, and his fingers given a life of their own. There was something about the rote work that was mesmerizing. He couldn't stop until he was done.

And he nearly was. After one week of hard work, he was well over halfway through the lists. He had started taking records home with him each day, then worked on them until it grew dark. He'd often spent extra hours after that, when he couldn't sleep, working by the light of lanterns.

But soon, very soon, he would be done. *Assuming I don't go mad first,* Joel thought, noting another death by accident on one of his lists.

A paper rustled on the other side of Fitch's office. Each day, Fitch gave Melody a different defensive circle to trace. She was getting better, but still had a long way to go.

Each night at dinner, Melody sat apart from the other Rithmatists. She ate in silence while the others chatted. So he wasn't the only one to find her annoying.

Fitch had spent the last week poking through old, musty Rithmatic texts. Joel had sneaked a look at a couple of them— they were high-level, theoretical volumes that were well beyond Joel's understanding.

Joel turned his attention back to his work and ticked off another name, then moved on to the next book. It was . . .

Something bothered him about that last list—another list of graduates from Armedius, organized by year, for checking off those who had died. One of the names he hadn't checked off caught his attention. *Exton L. Pratt.* Exton the clerk.

Exton had never given any indication that he was an alumnus. He'd been senior clerk in the office for as long as Joel could remember. He was something of a fixture at Armedius, with his dapper suits and bow ties, sharp clothing ordered out of the Californian Archipelago.

"All right, that's it!" Melody suddenly declared. "I, Melody Muns, have had enough!"

Joel sighed. Her outbursts were surprisingly regular. It seemed that she could only stand about an hour or so of silence before she simply *had* to fill it with a dramatic eruption.

"Hum?" Professor Fitch asked, looking up from his book. "What is that?"

"I have had enough," Melody said, folding her arms. "I don't think I can trace another line. My fingers won't do it. They will sooner pull themselves free of my hands!"

Joel rose, stretching.

"I'm just *no good* at this," she continued. "How bad does a girl have to be at Rithmatics before everyone will simply give up and let her move on?"

"Far worse than you are, dear," Fitch said, setting aside his book. "In all my years here, I've only seen it happen twice—and only because those students were considered dangerous."

"I'm dangerous," Melody said. "You heard what Professor Nalizar said about me."

"Professor Nalizar is not the expert in everything he claims," Fitch said. "Perhaps he knows how to duel, but he does not understand students. You, my dear, are far from hopeless. Why, look at how much your tracings have improved in just one week's time!"

"Yeah," she said. "Next time you need to impress a group of four-year-olds, you can send for me."

"You really *are* getting better," Joel said. She still wasn't great, but she'd improved. It seemed that Professor Fitch really did know what he was doing.

"See, dear?" Fitch said, picking up his book again. "You should get back to it."

"I thought you were supposed to be *tutoring* me," she said. "Yet all you do is sit there and read. I think you're trying to shirk your duties."

Fitch blinked. "Tracing Rithmatic defenses is a time-tested and traditionally sound method of training a student to focus on basic techniques."

"Well," she said, "I'm tired of it. Isn't there something else I could do?"

"Yes, well, I suppose seven days spent only on tracing could be a little frustrating. Hum. Yes. Maybe we could all use a break. Joel, would you help me move these books here . . . ?"

Joel walked over, helping Fitch move aside several stacks of books and clear away about a six-foot-long space on the ground.

"Now," Fitch said, settling down on the floor, "there is a lot more to being a successful Rithmatist than lines. The ability to draw is very important—indeed, quite foundational. The ability to *think* is even more important. The Rithmatist who can think faster than his or her opponent can be just as successful as the one who can draw quickly. After all, drawing quickly does you no good if you draw the wrong lines."

Melody shrugged. "I guess that makes sense."

"Excellent," Fitch said, getting a bit of chalk out of his coat pocket. "Now, do you remember the five defenses I had you work on this week?"

"How could I forget?" she said. "Matson, Osborn, Ballintain, Sumsion, and Eskridge."

"Each are basic forms," Fitch said, "each with built-in strengths and weaknesses. With them in hand, we can discuss what Rithmatists often call 'keening.'"

"Keening?" Joel asked. Then he cursed himself. What if Fitch noticed that he was watching, and decided to order him back to his census records?

Fitch didn't even look up. "Yes, indeed. Some younger Rithmatists like to call it 'anticipating,' but that has always felt mundane to me. Let us imagine a duel between two Rithmatists."

He began to draw on the floor. Not a wide, full-sized circle, but a smaller instructional one instead. It was only about a handspan wide, drawn with the very tip of Fitch's chalk so that the lines were rather thin.

"Pretend you are at this duel," he said. "Now, in any given duel, you have three options on how to start. You can pick your defense based on your own strategy—a powerful defense if you want to push for a longer fight, or a weaker defense if you want to get done quickly and attack aggressively.

"However, you could also *wait* to draw your defense until you're certain what your opponent is doing. We call this keening your opponent—you let them take the lead, then gain an advantage by building your defense to counter what they are doing. Let us assume that your opponent is drawing the Matson Defense. What would be your response?"

Fitch filled out the small circle in front of him, drawing smaller circles on the top and bottom bind points, then adding small chalklings at the other bind points. When he finished the first one—a snake—it wiggled to life, then began prowling back and forth in front of the circle. The snake was attached to the front bind point by a small tether around its neck.

"Well?" Fitch asked. "Which of the defenses would be best to use against me?"

"I don't know," Melody said.

"Ballintain," Joel guessed.

"Ah," Fitch said, "and why is that?"

"Because the Matson commits my opponent to drawing a

large number of defensive chalklings. If I can get up a basic defense that is quick to draw, but leaves plenty of space at the top for me to draw Lines of Vigor, I can start shooting before my opponent finishes his defense."

"Excellent," Fitch said. "This is, um, unfortunately the strategy that Nalizar used against me. I doubt that he keened me—he started drawing too fast. Undoubtedly a quick defense is often his style, and he likely knew that I favor complex defenses. He could have predicted that his strategy would be a good one."

Fitch hesitated, laying his chalk against his small circle defense. A few seconds later, it puffed away into dust. Any Rithmatist could dismiss their own lines this way, though one could not dismiss those drawn by someone else. You just had to touch chalk to lines you'd drawn and intentionally will them away.

"But," Fitch said, "don't assume that just because you are aggressive, you will beat a good defense. True, a strong defense is generally more viable against multiple opponents—however, a skilled duelist can build their defense even against a determined offense."

"So," Melody said, "what you're saying is it doesn't *matter* which defense I use."

"That's not what I'm saying at all!" Fitch said. "Or, well, I guess I am. It *doesn't* matter which defense you use, for *strategy* is most important. You have to understand the defenses to know what advantages you gain by picking a certain one. You have to understand your opponent's defense so you can know their weaknesses. Here, what about this?"

He drew an ellipse on the ground, then began to sketch it out with Lines of Forbiddance and a chalkling at the top.

"That's the Osborn Defense," Joel said.

"Very good," Fitch said. "Of course, that shouldn't be too hard to determine, since there's only one basic defense based on an ellipse. Now, which defense would be strong against the Osborn?"

Joel thought for a moment. Osborn was an elliptical defense—which meant that the front and back of the defense were much stronger than the front and back of a circle. At the sides, however, it would be weak.

"I'd use another Osborn," Joel said. "That way, I'd be matched with him in strength, and it would turn into a test of skill."

"Ah," Fitch said. "I see. And you, Melody? Would you do the same thing?"

She opened her mouth, probably to say that she didn't care. Then she hesitated. "No," she said, cocking her red-curled head. "If I'm watching my opponent to see what they are doing, then I *can't* just go with the same defense they do—because I'd have hesitated and let them get ahead! I'd have to play catch-up the entire match."

"Aha!" Fitch said. "Correct."

Joel blushed. He'd spoken too quickly.

"So," Fitch said to Melody, "if you're not going to use another Osborn, which would you use instead?

"Um . . . the Sumsion Defense?"

Joel nodded. Sumsion was a quick defense that was open on the sides. It was often used by people who preferred offensive chalklings—which would be the main way to defeat someone with Osborn. You'd send your chalklings to attack the exposed flanks.

Melody gave Joel a triumphant smirk as Fitch used his chalk to erase his drawing.

Oh, that's it! Joel thought. "Do another, Professor."

"Hum. Shouldn't you be working on those ledgers?"

"Just give me one more chance to beat her," Joel said.

"Very well then. Both of you, get out your chalk."

Joel hesitated. He didn't have any chalk on him at the moment. "Can I . . . borrow a piece?" he whispered sheepishly to Melody.

She rolled her eyes, but handed him one. They both knelt on the ground next to one another. Fitch began drawing. Joel watched, trying to guess which defense he was going to go for. A circle, so it wasn't Osborn. Fitch then placed a smaller circle at the very top, crossed with Lines of Forbiddance.

Sumsion, Joel thought. *It's the Sumsion Defense again.*

Sumsion had a Line of Forbiddance at the front, which—once in place—would block Fitch from drawing further on that side. The Sumsion Defense, then, *started* with a very strong front side, but that front couldn't be protected. The Rithmatist would spend their time drawing chalklings at the sides and sending them out to attack.

I need to strike hard at that front, Joel thought. *Break through in the place where he thinks he's strong, but can't protect himself.*

That probably meant Ballintain was the best. Joel, however, didn't draw that one. He wanted something more dramatic. He scribbled furiously on the rough wood floor, constructing a nine-point circle with a large number of bound chalklings around it, giving himself a very strong defense. He didn't bother with Lines of Forbiddance to anchor himself. He went straight into drawing Lines of Vigor to launch at the very front of Fitch's circle.

"All right," Fitch said, standing. "Let us see here. Hum . . ."

Joel glanced to the side. Melody had drawn the Ballintain Defense, and done a fairly good job of it, for her. The lines were wobbly, and the circle lopsided, but she'd gotten each part in the right place.

"Yes indeed," Fitch said. "That's actually quite good, my dear. You may not have an eye for circles, but you can *think* like a Rithmatist." Fitch hesitated, then leaned down to inspect her work more closely. "And, my! Will you look at that chalkling! Indeed!"

Joel leaned over. Most Rithmatists used simplistic chalklings. Snakes, spiders, occasionally a dragon. Fitch himself favored more intricate drawings—they were stronger, apparently, than ones with fewer lines. Joel hadn't been able to study a lot of chalkling theory.

Melody's single chalkling—there was only room for one on Ballintain—was incredibly detailed and complex, despite the small scale. The tiny bear was shaded with shadows, had little lines for fur, and had perfect proportions. It walked back and forth across the wood in front of her circle, connected to the bind point by a tiny chalk chain, each link drawn individually.

"Wow," Joel said despite himself.

"Yes indeed," Fitch said. "And Ballintain was the correct choice in this instance, I believe—though something with a very strong defense against chalklings would have been good as well."

Fitch glanced at Joel's circle. "Ah, a nine-pointer? Showing off a little, are we?"

Joel shrugged.

"Hum," Fitch continued. "Not bad, Joel, I must say. The third point is a few degrees off, but the others are within reasonable limits. Is that a Hill Defense?"

"A modified one."

"No Lines of Forbiddance?"

"You drew Sumsion," Joel said. "So you probably weren't going to use many Lines of Vigor—not unless you're an expert at reflecting them, but you didn't set yourself up to do that. So you couldn't have pushed me about. That means I didn't need the stabilization."

"Excellent point," Fitch said. "Unless, of course, I were to notice what you'd done. Remember, I could always dismiss the Line of Forbiddance and attack you from the front by surprise!"

"That would take you a few seconds," Joel said. "I'd notice and stabilize my defense."

"Assuming you were watching carefully," Fitch said.

"I would be," Joel said. "Trust me."

"Yes . . . I believe that you would be. Well, that's certainly impressive. I think that both of you might very well have defeated me!"

Doubtful, Joel thought. He'd seen Fitch draw, and the man was good. Uncertain of himself in a duel, true, but quite good. Still, Joel suspected that the professor wasn't trying to be patronizing, just encouraging.

Judging from Melody's response, it was working. She actually seemed excited to be drawing. "What's next?" she asked.

"Well, I suppose we can do a few more," Professor Fitch said, making his lines disappear. Melody did the same.

Joel just stared down at his. "Um . . ." he said. "Do you have an eraser?"

Fitch looked up, surprised. "Oh! Well, hum, let me see. . . ."

After about five minutes of searching through the room's scholarly debris, Fitch managed to produce an eraser. Joel used it, but it didn't work all that well. The lines just smudged on the floor, which hadn't been designed for chalk drawing.

Joel felt his face redden as he brushed harder.

"Perhaps we should have you draw on a board from now on, Joel . . ." Fitch said, digging out a small chalkboard.

Joel looked down at the poorly erased chalk drawing in front of him. It seemed like a sharp and distinct reminder of what he was. No matter how hard he tried or studied, he'd never be a Rithmatist, able to make his chalk lines come alive or vanish with a thought.

"Maybe I should get back to my research," Joel said, standing.

"Oh, do a few more with us," Fitch said, wagging the board as he proffered it. "You've worked too hard on those census reports, and it will be good for Miss Muns to have some competition."

Joel's breath caught in his throat. It was the first time that a Rithmatist had actually *offered* to let Joel participate. He smiled, then reached out to take the board.

"Excellent!" Fitch said. He seemed to find the prospect of teaching them far more exciting than research.

Over the next few hours, they went over a dozen more examples of defenses and counters. Fitch drew more complicated circles, challenging Joel and Melody to discuss two or three ways to attack each one. There were no actual duels. Professor Fitch seemed to shy away from such things.

Instead, he would draw, explain, and coach. They talked about which defenses were best against multiple opponents. They discussed why it was important to think about being surrounded—since on the Nebrask battlefield, a Rithmatist might have to fight

in several directions at the same time. They also discussed timing, drawing to their strengths, and some general theory. All of
this was interspersed with more drawings.

Joel threw himself into it with excitement. Though this wasn't
the deep Rithmatic lecture he'd been hoping for, it was actual
drawing with actual Rithmatists. It was wonderful.

And it was *far* better than looking at census records.

Eventually, Fitch glanced at the clock. "Well, we should move
on for the day."

"What?" Melody demanded, looking up from their latest set
of drawings. "You can't! He's winning!"

Joel smiled smugly. By his count—and he suspected Melody
had kept a similar count in her head—Fitch had approved of Joel's
counter-defenses seven times, while Melody had only done the
right defense three times.

"Winning?" Fitch said. "Why, this isn't a competition."

"Yes, Melody," Joel said. "It's not a competition—at least, it's
not a competition when *you* are involved. None at all."

She flinched, looking like she'd been slapped. Joel hesitated,
realizing how harsh those words had been.

Instead of snapping back a retort, Melody grabbed her sketch-
book. "I'll just . . . keep practicing some more sketches, Professor."

"Yes, dear," Fitch said, shooting a glance at Joel. "That is a
good idea. Joel, I need to run some of these books back to the
library. Would you help me carry them?"

Joel shrugged, then picked up the indicated stack of books and
followed the professor out into the stairwell. Melody remained
behind, sniffling.

They stepped out of the stairwell onto the campus green,
and Joel blinked against the sunlight—it was easy to lose track
of the hours in Fitch's office.

"You're quite accomplished at Rithmatic drawings, Joel," Fitch
said. "I honestly don't know that I've ever seen a student as
skilled as you. You draw like a man with thirty years of practice."

"I usually get the nine-point wrong," Joel said.

"Few Rithmatists even come close with nine-point drawings,"

Fitch said. "Your ability, particularly as a non-Rithmatist, is nothing short of astounding. You are, however, also an insensitive bully."

"A bully!" Joel exclaimed.

Fitch raised a finger. "The most dangerous kind of man is not the one who spent his youth shoving others around. That kind of man gets lazy, and is often too content with his life to be truly dangerous. The man who spent his youth *being* shoved around, however . . . When that man gets a little power and authority, he often uses it to become a tyrant on par with the worst warlords in history. I worry this could become you."

Joel looked down. "I wasn't trying to make her look bad, Professor. I was just trying to draw my best!"

"There is nothing wrong with doing your best, son," Fitch said sternly. "Never be ashamed of aptitude. However, the comment you made in there . . . That was not the sign of a boy who was proud of his aptitude. It was a boy who was proud of being better than another. You disappointed me greatly."

"I . . ." What could he say? "I'm sorry."

"I don't believe I'm the one to whom you should apologize. You are young, Joel. Young enough that you still have time to decide the type of man you would like to become. Do not let jealousy, bitterness, or anger be what guides that path. But, here now, I have probably been too hard on you in turn. Just promise me you will think about what I have said."

"I will."

The two of them continued across campus, Joel feeling shamed to the bones as he carried the books. "Professor, do you really think you can train her to be a great Rithmatist?"

"Melody?" he replied. "Her uncertainty is her only true hindrance. I've looked into the girl's records. It's remarkable that she's kept going, all things considered. I think that, with proper training in the basics—"

"Why, Professor Fitch!" a voice called.

Fitch turned, surprised. Joel hadn't noticed it before, but a small crowd was gathered near the campus quad, where the grass was broken by a hilltop plateau of concrete. A man in a red Rithmatic coat stood there, arms folded as he looked down at Joel and Fitch.

"Professor Nalizar," Fitch said. "Shouldn't you be in class right now?"

"We are having class out here today," Nalizar said, nodding toward the top of the hill, where a large group of Rithmatic students knelt on the concrete, drawing. "The only way to learn is to *do*, and the only way to win is to fight. These students have had enough time of dusty classrooms and lectures."

It also lets him show off, Joel thought, noting the attention Nalizar's display had drawn from the students and professors who had been playing soccer nearby.

"Hum," Fitch said. "Yes. Interesting. Well, have a nice day."

"Are you certain you wouldn't like to come up here, Professor?" Nalizar called. "Have a little match, you and I? Give the children another glimpse of how it is *really* done? I let them each duel me in turn, of course, but they hardly give me a fair contest."

Fitch paled. "Um, I don't think—"

"Come now," Nalizar asked. "Considering the rather *unimpressive* display you gave last time, I should think you'd be eager for a chance to redeem yourself!"

"Go on, Professor," Joel whispered. "You can beat him. I've seen you draw. You're way better than he is."

"No thank you, Professor," Fitch called, laying a hand on Joel's shoulder and turning him away. That hand, Joel noticed, was shaking noticeably.

Joel reluctantly allowed Fitch to pull him away. He could hear as Nalizar barked something to his class. It was followed by laughter.

"Why?" Joel asked as they walked. "Why not duel him?"

"It would be meaningless, Joel," Fitch said. "I couldn't earn my tenure back for another year. If I fought and lost, I'd be humiliated again. If I won, all I would do is make an ever *bigger* enemy of Nalizar."

"He's a hypocrite," Joel said. "All that talk about keeping non-

Rithmatists out of his classroom, and then he comes out here in the open and displays his students for everyone to see?"

"They will be on display at the Melee as well," Fitch said. "I suspect Nalizar wishes to acclimatize them to drawing in front of a crowd. But, yes, I see what you mean. Regardless, I will not put myself in a position where I must fight him again. It wouldn't be gentlemanly in this situation."

"Nalizar doesn't deserve to be treated like a gentleman," Joel snapped. He clenched his fists. If anyone was a bully, it was Nalizar. "You really should have dueled him again. Pride or no pride. You don't have anything to lose—everyone already assumes that Nalizar is better. However, if you *did* win, you'd be making a statement."

Fitch fell silent for a time. "I don't know, Joel. I'm just . . . well, I'm just not good at dueling. He defeated me, and deserved to. No. No, I should not like to duel him again, and that is that. We shall have no more of it."

Joel couldn't help but notice that the professor was still trembling slightly as they continued on their way.

Three strong internal Lines of
Forbiddance make this defense
very firm and immobile.

However, these same
lines block some of the
Rithmatist's ability
to draw.

The Lines of Forbiddance
inscribed in the smaller
circles should be oriented
toward opponents.

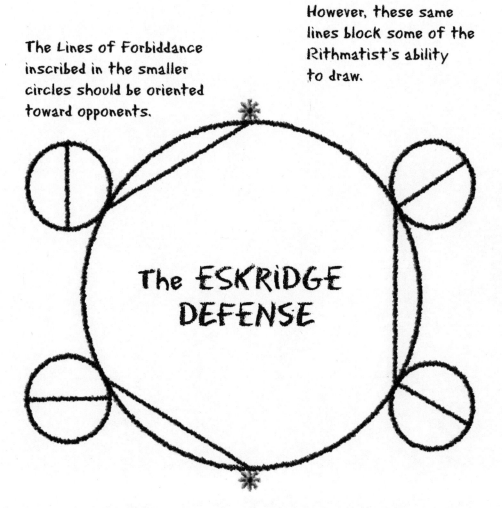

The ESKRIDGE
DEFENSE

The Eskridge Defense is one of the more
complex circles taught to students. It is a
strong defense, designed to stand against
multiple opponents while still offering a good
amount of flexibility.

There! Joel thought with satisfaction, snapping the book closed. After two weeks, he'd finished all of the census records.

He flipped through the stack of papers. The oldest page listed the graduates eighty years back, and he'd been able to cross off every name on that list. The same for the next seven or eight years. The lists went all the way up to the graduates from one year ago. Only one of those had died—during an accident at Nebrask.

Along with the other reports, Joel had also included a special list of Rithmatists who had vanished, their whereabouts unknown. There weren't any of those that had happened recently—save for Lilly Whiting—but he figured that Fitch might be interested.

He reached over to twist the key in the lantern beside his library desk, letting the clockwork wind down and the light spin out. He was surprised at the sense of accomplishment he felt.

He tucked the pile of sheets under his arm, grabbed the books he'd been working on, and walked through the library. It was late—he had probably missed dinner. He'd been so close, he hadn't been able to stop.

The library was a maze of bookshelves, though most of them were only about five feet tall. Other people worked in some of the alcoves, their lamps giving each one a flickering light. The building would close soon, expelling its hermitlike occupants.

Joel passed Ms. Torrent, the librarian, then pushed his way out onto the green. He crossed the grounds in the near darkness, trying to decide if he'd be able to beg some food off the kitchen staff. However, he'd just finished something big—he didn't want to go eat; he wanted to share it with someone.

It isn't even ten yet, Joel thought, glancing toward the Rithmatic campus. *Professor Fitch will still be up.* He'd want to know that Joel was finished, wouldn't he?

Decision made, Joel took off across the grounds, passing between pockets of light shining from clockwork lanterns, with their spinning gears and shining coils. He passed a familiar figure sitting on the green outside the Rithmatist dormitory.

"Hey, Melody," he said.

She didn't look up from her sketch pad as she drew by the light of the lantern.

Joel sighed. Melody, apparently, knew how to hold a grudge. He had apologized for his wisecrack three times, but still she wouldn't speak to him. *Fine,* he thought. *Why should I care?*

He moved past her quickly and arrived at Warding Hall with a spring in his step. He climbed the stairs to Fitch's door and knocked eagerly.

The professor opened the door a few moments later. Joel was right—the man hadn't even gotten ready for bed. He still wore his white vest and long Rithmatist's coat. He looked frazzled— hair disheveled, eyes unfocused. But, then, that wasn't odd for Fitch.

"What? Hum?" Fitch said. "Oh, Joel. What is it, lad?"

"I finished!" Joel said, holding up the stack of papers and books. "I'm *done,* Professor. I got through every single ledger!"

"Oh. Is that so?" Fitch's voice was almost monotone. "Wonderful, lad, that's wonderful. You worked so hard." With that, Fitch walked away, almost as if he were in a daze, leaving Joel at the door.

Joel lowered the stack of papers. *That's it?* he thought. *I spent two weeks on this! I worked evenings! I stayed up late when I should have been sleeping!*

Fitch wandered back to his desk at the corner of the L-shaped office. Joel entered and pushed the door closed. "It's just what you wanted, Professor. All the names indexed. Look, I even kept a list of disappearances!"

"Yes, thank you, Joel," Fitch said, sitting. "You can leave the papers on that stack over there."

Joel felt a sharp disappointment. He set the papers down, and a sudden horror struck him. Had it all been busywork? Had Fitch and the principal devised this entire research assistant plan to keep Joel out of trouble? Would his lists be forgotten and gather dust like the hundreds of tomes crammed into the hallways?

Joel looked up, trying to dismiss those thoughts. Professor Fitch sat huddled over his desk, leaning with his left elbow on the top, left hand on the side of his face. His other hand tapped a pen against a piece of paper.

"Professor?" Joel asked. "Are you all right?"

"Yes, fine," Fitch said in a tired voice. "Well, I just . . . I feel I should have figured things out by now!"

"Figured what out?" Joel asked, picking his way through the room.

Fitch didn't answer—he seemed too distracted by the papers on his desk. Joel tried another tactic.

"Professor?"

"Hum?"

"What would you like me to do now? I've finished the first project. I assume you have something else to fill my time?" *Something having to do with what you're working on?*

"Ah, well, yes," Fitch said. "You did so well at that research; worked far more quickly than I expected. You must enjoy that sort of thing."

"I wouldn't say that . . ." Joel said.

Fitch continued. "It would be very useful if you tracked down the locations of all the Rithmatists living here on the island who have retired from their service in Nebrask. Why don't you get started on that?"

"Track down . . ." Joel said. "Professor, how would I even start something like that?"

"Hum? Well, you could look through the last year's census, then compare the names on it to the names on the lists of graduates from the various academies."

"You're kidding me," Joel said. He knew just enough to realize that the project Fitch was talking about could take months to get through.

"Yes, yes," Fitch said. He was obviously barely paying attention. "Very important . . ."

"Professor?" Joel asked. "Is something wrong? Did something happen?"

Fitch looked up, focusing, as if seeing Joel there for the first time. "Something happen . . . ?" Fitch asked. "Didn't you hear, lad?"

"Hear what?"

"Another student vanished last night," Fitch said. "The police released information about it this afternoon."

"I've been in the library all afternoon," Joel said, stepping up to the desk. "Was it another Rithmatist?"

"Yes," Fitch said. "Herman Libel. A pupil from my old class."

"I'm sorry," Joel said, noting the distressed look in Fitch's eyes. "Do they still think a Rithmatist is behind the disappearances?"

Fitch looked up. "How do you know that?"

"I . . . Well, you have me searching out the locations of Rithmatists, and the principal told me you were working on an important project for the federal inspectors. It seemed obvious."

"Oh," Fitch said. He glanced down at the papers. "So, you know this is my fault, then."

"*Your* fault?"

"Yes," Fitch said. "I was the one in charge of deciphering this puzzle. But so far I have nothing! I feel useless. If I'd been able to figure this out earlier, then perhaps poor Herman wouldn't have . . . well, who knows what happened to him?"

"You can't blame yourself, Professor," Joel said. "It's not your fault."

"It is," Fitch said. "I'm responsible. If I hadn't proven unable to do this task . . ." Fitch sighed. "Perhaps York should have given this problem to Professor Nalizar."

"Professor!" Joel said. "Nalizar might have beaten you in a duel, but he's not even twenty-five years old. You've spent a *lifetime* studying Rithmatics. You're a far better scholar than he is."

"I don't know . . ." Fitch said. On the desk, Joel could see several sheets with detailed notes and drawings, all in ink.

"What's this?" Joel asked, pointing at a sketch. It appeared to be a simplified Matson Defense. Or, rather, what was *left* of one. The detailed sketch showed numerous chunks missing—as if pieces of the defense been clawed free by chalklings. Even where the lines weren't breached, they were scored and uneven.

Fitch covered the sheet with his arms. "It's nothing."

"Maybe I can help."

"Lad, you just told me that Professor Nalizar seemed too inexperienced at age twenty-four. You're sixteen!"

Joel froze. Then he nodded, wincing. "Yes, of course. I'm not even a Rithmatist. I understand."

"Don't be like that, lad," Fitch said. "I don't mean to disparage you, but . . . well, Principal York told me to be very quiet about this. We don't want to create a panic. To be honest, we don't even know if foul play is involved—perhaps it's just coincidence, and those two young people both decided to run away."

"You don't believe that," Joel said, reading Professor Fitch's expression.

"No," he admitted. "There was blood found at both scenes. Not a lot of it, mind you, but some. No bodies though. The children were hurt, then taken somewhere."

Joel felt a chill. He knelt down beside the desk. "Look, Professor, the principal gave me to you as a research assistant, right? Wouldn't that imply that he *expected* me to be involved in this project? I know how to keep a secret."

"It's more than that, lad," Fitch said. "I don't want to involve you in anything dangerous."

"Whatever is going on," Joel said, "it only seems to target Rithmatists, right? So, maybe *that*'s why Principal York sent me. I know a lot about Rithmatics, but I can't make the lines. I should be safe."

Fitch sat for a moment in thought. Then he moved his arms to show the notes on his desk. "Well, the principal *did* give you this assignment. And to be honest, it would be nice to have someone I could talk to about it. I've looked these sketches over hundreds of times!"

Joel leaned in eagerly, looking over the drawings.

"They were made by police at the scene of Lilly Whiting's disappearance," Fitch said. "I can't help but wonder if the officers who did the sketches might have missed recording something. The intricacies of Rithmatic sketches should not be left to laymen!"

"It's the remnants of a Matson Defense," Joel said.

"Yes," Fitch said. "Lilly and her parents attended a dinner party the evening of the disappearance. She left the party early, sometime around ten. When her parents got home a few hours later, they found the front door broken in and this chalk drawing in the middle of the living room floor. Lilly was nowhere to be found, either at the house or at the academy."

Joel studied the sketch. "Her lines were attacked by chalklings. Lots of them."

"Poor child," Fitch said softly. "They found blood inside the circle. Whoever did this knew the Glyph of Rending. That implies they were at Nebrask."

"But she could still be alive, right?"

"We can hope."

"What are *you* supposed to do?" Joel asked.

"Discover who is doing this," Fitch said. "Or at least provide the inspector with as much information as I can about the perpetrator."

"All from one drawing?" Joel asked.

"Well, there are these," Fitch said, pulling over two more papers. They were sketches, realistically rendered, much like one might see an art student do of a bowl of fruit. The first was what appeared to be a sketch of a wooden floor, the second a section of a brick wall. Both had fragments of lines crossing them.

"What are those lines?" Joel asked.

"I'm not sure. They were drawn with chalk, the first on the entryway right inside the house, the second on the wall outside the house."

"Those aren't Rithmatic lines," Joel said. The first was sharp and jagged, like spiked peaks. The second was a looping line that spun around upon itself, like a child's swirl. Something about that one seemed oddly familiar to Joel.

"Yes," Fitch said. "Why would someone draw these lines? Are they to throw us off and confuse us? Or is there more?"

Joel pointed back at the first sketch, the one that was a reproduction of a Matson Defense. "We assume Lilly drew this?"

"A cast-off piece of chalk was discovered near the circle," Fitch said. "It was of Armedius composition. In addition, this Matson pattern is one of my own. Each professor teaches the defenses in a slightly different way, and I recognize my students' work. This was Lilly's circle for certain. She was one of my best, you know. Very bright."

Joel studied the circle. "That . . . was attacked by a *lot* of chalklings, Professor," he said. "Maybe too many. They would have gotten in the way of each other. Whoever did this didn't have a very good strategy."

"Yes," Fitch said. "Either that, or his strategy was simply to overwhelm."

"Yes," Joel said, "but last week—when you had Melody and me draw for you—you told us that the Matson Defense was *strong* against Lines of Making. You said that the best thing to use against it was Lines of Vigor. There aren't any Vigor blast marks on this circle—just chews and claw marks from chalklings."

"Very good, Joel," Fitch said. "You *do* have a good eye for Rithmatics. I noticed that too, but what does it tell us?"

"He couldn't have drawn that many chalklings quickly," Joel said. "To get through a Matson, he'd have to have very detailed, strong chalklings. The defender always has an advantage, since the bind point gives their chalklings strength. Considering that, it's doubtful that the attacker could have completed enough strong chalklings to do *this* kind of damage in the same amount of time it took the defender to draw a Matson."

"Which means . . ."

"The chalklings were already drawn," Joel realized. "That explains why there was no circle discovered for the attacker! He didn't need one to defend himself, since Lilly wouldn't have had time to mount any kind of offense. The attacker must have had his chalklings waiting somewhere, blocked off by Lines of Forbiddance until Lilly was close. Then he let them loose."

"Yes!" Fitch said. "Precisely what I think!"

"But that would be nearly impossible," Joel said. Chalklings were very difficult to control—one had to give them precise, simple instructions. Things like: walk forward, then turn right when you hit the wall. Or: walk forward, then attack when you find chalk. "How could someone possibly have managed to break through the door, then guide an army of chalklings at Lilly?"

"I don't know," Fitch said. "Though I wonder if it has to do with these other two lines. I've spent the last two weeks searching for clues in my texts. Perhaps this jagged line was to be a Line of Vigor, but was drawn poorly? Some lines, if not executed well, will have no Rithmatic properties—they'll just be chalk on the ground. This other one could be a Line of Warding, perhaps. The chalk does strange things sometimes, and we don't know why."

Joel pulled the stool over, sitting down. "This doesn't make sense, Professor. If chalklings were easy enough to control to do something like *this*, then we wouldn't need Circles of Warding. We could just have little boxes of chalklings ready to attack."

"That is true," Fitch said. "Unless someone has discovered something we don't understand. New instructions for chalklings? This almost feels like . . ."

"What?"

Fitch was silent for a time. "Wild chalklings."

Joel grew cold. "They're trapped," he said. "On Nebrask. That's hundreds of miles away."

"Yes, of course. That's silly. Besides, wild chalklings wouldn't run off with a body like this. They'd chew it to bits, leaving a mangled corpse. Whoever did this *took* Lilly away with him. I—"

He cut off as a knock came at the door. "Now, who . . . ?" Fitch said, walking to the door and opening it. A tall man stood in the entryway. He carried a blue police officer's helmet underneath his arm and had a long, thin rifle slung over his shoulder.

"Inspector Harding!" Fitch said.

"Professor," Harding said. "I have just returned from the second crime scene. May I come in?"

"Certainly," Fitch said. "Certainly. Oh, hum, I apologize for the mess."

"Yes," Harding said. "No offense, my good man, but sloppy quarters like this would *never* pass battlefield inspection!"

"Well, good thing we're not on the battlefield, then, I should say," Fitch said, closing the door after the inspector.

"I have vital information for you, Fitch," the inspector said. He had a deep, resounding voice; he seemed like a man who was accustomed to speaking loud and being obeyed. "I'm expecting great things from you on this case, soldier. There are lives at stake!"

"Well, I will do my best," Fitch said. "I don't know how much help I can be. I've been trying hard, you know, but I may not be the best man to help you. . . ."

"Don't be so humble!" Harding said, stomping into the room. "York speaks extremely highly of you, and there's no better recommendation for a man than the one which comes from his commander! Now, I think we need to—"

He cut off when he saw Joel. "I say, who is this young man?"

"My research assistant," Fitch said. "He's been helping me with this problem."

"What's his security clearance?" Harding asked.

"He's a good lad, Inspector," Fitch said. "Very trustworthy."

Harding eyed Joel.

"I can't do this work alone, Inspector," Fitch said. "I was hoping that we could maybe include the boy in this project? Officially, I mean?"

"What's your name, son?"

"Joel."

"Not a Rithmatist, I see."

"No, sir," Joel said. "I'm sorry."

"Never be sorry for what you are, son," Harding said. "I'm not a Rithmatist either, and I'm proud of that. Saved my life a few times on the battlefront! The creatures out there, they go for the Dusters first. They often ignore us ordinary men, forgetting that a bucket of good acid will wipe them off the ground as quickly as any Rithmatist's lines will."

Joel smiled at that. "Sir," he said. "Forgive me for asking . . . but are you a police officer or a soldier?"

Harding looked down at his gold-buttoned blue policeman's uniform. "I served for fifteen years on the Nebrask eastern front, son," he said. "Military police. Recently transferred out here to the civilian division. I . . . well, I've had a little bit of trouble adjusting." With that, the inspector turned back to Fitch. "The lad seems solid. If you vouch for him, then that's good enough for me. Now, we need to talk. What have you discovered?"

"Nothing more than I told you two days ago, unfortunately," Fitch said, walking to his desk. "I'm most certain we're dealing with a Rithmatist—and a very powerful and clever one. I'm going to have Joel look through census records and gather names of all the Rithmatists living in the area."

"Good," Harding said. "But I've already had that done down at the police station. I'll send you over a list."

Joel let out a sigh of relief.

"I also had him look through the old census records," Fitch said. "Searching for Rithmatists who died or disappeared in strange ways. Maybe there's a clue from the past that can help."

"Excellent idea," Harding said. "But what of the drawings themselves? My people can do research about numbers, Fitch. It's the Rithmatics, this blasted *Rithmatics*, that stops us."

"We're working on that," Fitch said.

"I have confidence in you, Fitch!" Harding said, slapping the professor on the shoulder. He took a scroll out of his belt and set it on the desk. "Here are crime scene drawings from the second disappearance. Let me know what you discover."

"Yes, of course."

Harding leaned down. "I think these children are still alive, Fitch. Every moment is of the most essential importance. The slime who's doing this . . . he's taunting us. I can *feel* it."

"What do you mean?"

"The first girl," Harding said, settling his rifle on his shoulder. "Her home was just three houses down from a federal police station. After she vanished, I doubled our street patrols. This second student was taken from a building on the very *block* where we were patrolling last night. This isn't just about kidnapping. The ones behind this, they want us to *know* that they're doing it, and that they don't care how close we are."

"I see," Fitch said, looking disturbed.

"I'm going to get him," Harding said. "Whoever is doing this, I'm going to *find* him. You don't attack children during my watch. I'm counting on you to help me know where to look, Fitch."

"I will do my best."

"Excellent. Have a good night, men, and work hard. I'll check with you soon." He nodded with a crisp motion to Joel, then let himself out.

Joel watched as the door closed, then turned eagerly to Fitch. "Let's see what those new sheets contain. There might be more to the puzzle!"

"Joel, lad," Fitch said. "Remember, this is a young man's life we are talking about, not just a puzzle."

Joel nodded solemnly.

"I'm still not convinced that involving you was a good idea," Fitch said. "I should have talked to your mother first." Fitch reluctantly undid the tie on the roll of paper. The top sheet was a police report.

VICTIM: Presumed to be Herman Libel, son of Margaret and Leland Libel. Age sixteen. Student at Armedius Academy. Rithmatist.
INCIDENT: Libel was accosted and kidnapped in his bedroom at the family estate, which he had visited for the weekend according to school protocol. The parents slept just three rooms

down and reportedly heard nothing. The family servants also reported no sounds.

SCENE: Blood on the floor. Curious chalk drawings (Rithmatic?) discovered on the floor of the bedroom and outside the window.

PERPETRATOR: Unknown. No witnesses. Likely a Rithmatist.

MOTIVE: Unknown.

Professor Fitch flipped to the next page. It was labeled "Chalk drawings discovered at the scene of Herman Libel's disappearance. Blood spots marked with X's."

The picture was of several large squares, each inside one another, with a circle at the middle. The squares had been breached at the corners, and their lengths were scored in the same way as the circle at Lilly Whiting's house. There were other bits of lines scattered about, the remnants of destroyed chalklings, Joel guessed—but it was hard to tell.

"Hum," Professor Fitch said. "He boxed himself in."

Joel nodded. "He saw the chalklings coming, and he surrounded himself with Lines of Forbiddance."

It was a terrible dueling tactic—a Line of Forbiddance not only blocked chalklings, but physical objects as well. The Rithmatist himself couldn't reach past one to draw lines and defend himself. By boxing himself in, Herman had sealed his fate.

"He shouldn't have done that," Joel said.

"Perhaps," Fitch said. "But, if he feared being overwhelmed, this could have been the only way. Lines of Forbiddance are stronger than a Circle of Warding."

"Except at the corners," Joel said.

Lines of Forbiddance had to be straight—and straight lines had no bind points. The chalklings had gotten in at the corners. But perhaps Fitch was right. Chalklings were fast, and running might have been a bad idea.

The only option would be to bunker in, drawing lots of lines, locking yourself in place and yelling for help. Then you'd wait, hoping someone would hear you and be able to do something.

You'd sit, watching while a squirming mass of chalk drawings chewed and clawed their way closer, getting past the lines one at a time. . . .

Joel shivered. "Did you notice these specks?"

Fitch looked more closely. "Hum. Yes."

"They look like they might be remnants of chalklings," Joel said. "After they get torn apart."

"Maybe," Fitch said, squinting. "They weren't re-created very well. Blast! The police sketch artists don't know what is important and what isn't!"

"We need to see the scene itself," Joel said.

"Yes," Fitch said. "However, it is probably too late now. The police will have moved about, scuffing the chalk, throwing acid on the Lines of Forbiddance to remove them so that they can search the room. And that means . . ."

He trailed off.

We won't be able to look at a crime scene unless there's another incident, Joel thought, *and the police know not to touch anything until we get there.*

That meant waiting for another person to disappear, which seemed like a bad idea. Better to work on what they had at the moment.

"Here," Fitch said, looking at the third—and final—sheet. It contained a pattern of looping lines, like the one that had been discovered at Lilly's house. The sketch was labeled "Strange pattern of chalk discovered on the wall outside the victim's room."

"How odd," Fitch said. "The same one as before. But that's not a Rithmatic pattern."

"Professor," Joel said, taking the sheet and raising it to the light. "I've *seen* that pattern somewhere before. I know I have!"

"It's a fairly simple design," Fitch said. "Perhaps you've just seen it on a rug or some stonework. It has an almost Celtic feel, wouldn't you say? Perhaps it's the symbol of the killer . . . or, um, kidnapper."

Joel shook his head. "I feel like I've seen it somewhere having to do with Rithmatics. Maybe one of the texts I read?"

"If that is the case," Fitch said, "it's no text I've seen. That's *not* a Rithmatic pattern."

"Couldn't there be lines we don't know about yet?" Joel said. "I mean, we didn't even discover Rithmatics was *possible* until a few centuries back."

"I suppose," Fitch said. "Some scholars talk about such things."

"Why don't you draw that pattern? Maybe it will do something."

"I guess I could try. What harm could it do?" He got a piece of chalk out of his coat pocket, then cleared off the table.

He hesitated.

A thought struck Joel. *What harm could it do? Potentially a lot, if the design really does have something to do with the kidnappings.*

In his head, Joel imagined Fitch's sketch inadvertently calling forth an army of chalklings or drawing the attention of the person who controlled them. One of the professor's lamps began to wind down, the light fading, and Joel quickly rushed over to rewind it.

"I guess we'll have to try it sometime," Fitch said. "Perhaps you should wait outside."

Joel shook his head. "So far, only Rithmatists have disappeared. I think I should stay, to watch and help in case something happens to you."

Fitch sat for a moment, then finally he sighed and reached out to sketch a copy of the looping swirl on the desk.

Nothing happened.

Joel held his breath. Minutes ticked by. Still nothing. He walked nervously over to the desk. "Did you draw it right?"

"Hum. Well, I think so," Fitch said, holding up the sketch. "Assuming the officers at Herman's house copied it right in the first place." He reached out and touched his chalk against the looping pattern, obviously trying to dismiss it. Nothing.

"It has no Rithmatic properties," the professor said. "Otherwise, I'd be able to make it puff away." He paused, then cocked his head. "I . . . appear to have made quite a mess on the top of my desk. Hum. I didn't consider that."

"We need to do more tests," Joel said. "Try different variations."

"Yes," Fitch said. "Perhaps that is what I shall do. You, however, should go home and return to bed. Your mother will be worried!"

"Mother is working," Joel said.

"Well, you are probably tired," Fitch said.

"I'm an insomniac."

"Then you should go and *try* to sleep," Fitch said. "I am not going to have a student in my office until the early hours of the morning. It's *already* too late. Be off with you."

Joel sighed. "You'll share anything you discover, right?"

"Yes, yes," Fitch said, waving.

Joel sighed again, louder this time.

"You're beginning to sound like Melody," Fitch said. "Go!"

Melody? Joel thought, walking away. *I am not!*

"And . . . Joel?" Professor Fitch said.

"Yes?"

"Keep to the . . . well-lit parts of campus on your way to the dormitories, lad. All right?"

Joel nodded, then shut the door.

Chalk Drawings found at the scene of Lilly Whiting's disappearance.

Figure #2

Unknown figure. Appears to be a cross between a Line of Vigor and a Line of Forbiddance.

Figure #1

Note the broken lines and many scratches. Indicative of a large number of chalklings surrounding and attacking the perimeter.

Figure #3

strange looping pattern found on outside wall of building.

The next morning, Joel rose early and left for Fitch's office. As he crossed the dew-wetted green, he heard a clamor coming from the direction of the campus office. He rounded the hill to find a small crowd outside the building.

A crowd of adults, not students.

Frowning, Joel walked to the edge of the crowd. Exton stood to the side, wearing a red vest with dark trousers and a matching bowler. The rest of the people were dressed similarly—nice clothing, with bright, single-piece dresses for the women, and vests and trousers for the men. None wore coats in the summer heat, but most wore hats.

The adults muttered among themselves, a few shaking fists toward Principal York, who stood in the doorway of the office.

"What's going on?" Joel whispered to Exton.

The clerk tapped his cane against the ground. "Parents," he said. "The bane of *every* school's existence."

"I assure you that your children are safe at Armedius!" the principal said. "This academy has *always* been a haven for those chosen to be Rithmatists."

"Safe like Lilly and Herman?" one of the parents yelled. Others rumbled in assent.

"Please!" Principal York said. "We don't know what is happening yet! Don't jump to conclusions."

"Principal York," said a woman with a narrow face and a

nose pointy enough it could poke out someone's eye if she turned in haste. "Are you denying that there is some threat to the students here?"

"I'm not denying that," York said. "I simply said that they are safe on *campus*. No student has come to harm while on school grounds. It was only during visits outside the walls that incidents occurred."

"I am taking my son away!" one of the men said. "To another island. You can't stop me."

"The ordinary students can leave for the summer," said another. "Why not ours?"

"The Rithmatic students need training!" York said. "You know that! If we act rashly now, we could undermine their ability to defend themselves at Nebrask!"

This quieted them somewhat. However, Joel heard one father muttering to another. "He doesn't care," the man said. "York isn't a Rithmatist—if they die here or die in Nebrask, what is it to him?"

Joel noticed a few sharply dressed men standing quietly to the side, making no complaints. They wore vests of muted colors and triangular felt hats. He couldn't make out any signs of emotion on their features.

York finally managed to break up and dismiss the group of parents. As the people trailed away, the men walked up to Principal York.

"Who are they?" Joel asked.

"Private security," Exton whispered back. "The ones on the left are employed by Didrich Calloway, knight-senator of East Carolina. His son is a Rithmatist here. I don't know the other ones, but I suspect they're employed by some very influential people who also have Rithmatist children here at Armedius."

The principal looked troubled.

"He's going to have to let them go, isn't he?" Joel asked. "The children of the very important."

"Likely," Exton said. "Principal York has a lot of influence, but if he butts heads with a knight-senator, there's little doubt who will win."

A small group of Rithmatic students watched from a hillside a short distance away. Joel couldn't tell if their miserable expressions came from the fact that they were worried about the kidnappings, or if they were embarrassed at having their parents show up at school. Probably both.

"Very well," Joel faintly heard Principal York say from the office doorway, "I see that I have no choice. Know that you do this against my wishes."

Joel turned to Exton. "Has anyone sent for Inspector Harding?"

"I don't believe so," Exton said. "I couldn't even get into the office! They were here before I was, crowding the way in."

"Send Harding a messenger," Joel suggested. "He might want to hear about the parents' reactions."

"Yes," Exton said, watching the security men with obvious hostility. "Yes, that's a good idea. This isn't going to do much to ease tensions on campus, I'd say. If those students weren't afraid before, they will be now."

Joel moved away toward Fitch's office, passing James Hovell being walked by his parents to class. He walked with shoulders slumped, eyes toward the ground in embarrassment. Perhaps there were advantages to having a mother who worked all the time.

Fitch took a long time to answer Joel's knock. When he did pull open the door, he looked bleary-eyed, still wearing a blue dressing gown.

"Oh!" Fitch said. "Joel. What hour is it?"

Joel winced, realizing that Fitch had probably been up late studying those strange patterns. "I'm sorry for waking you," Joel said. "I was eager to find out if you discovered anything. About the patterns, I mean."

Fitch yawned. "No, unfortunately. But it wasn't for lack of trying, I must say! I dug out the other version of that pattern—the one copied from Lilly's house—and tried to determine if there were any variations. I drew a hundred different modifications on the theme. I'm sorry, lad. I just don't think it's a Rithmatic line."

"I've seen it *somewhere* before," Joel said. "I know I have,

Professor. Maybe I should go to the library, look through some of the books I've read recently."

"Yes, yes," Fitch said, yawning again. "Sounds like . . . a capital idea."

Joel nodded, heading toward the library and letting the professor go back to sleep. As he crossed the green toward the central quad, he noticed one of the parents from before—the woman with the sharp nose and pinched face—standing on the green, hands on hips, looking lost.

"You," she called to him. "I don't know the campus very well. Could you tell me where might I find a Professor Fitch?"

Joel pointed toward the building behind him. "Office three. Up the stairwell on the side. What do you want him for?"

"My son mentioned him," she said. "I just wanted to chat with him for a short time, ask him about things here. Thank you!"

Joel arrived at the library and pushed open the door, passing out of the crisp morning air into a place that somehow managed to be cool and musty even during the warmest summer days. The library didn't have many windows—sunlight wasn't good for books—and so depended on clockwork lanterns.

Joel walked through the stacks, making his way to the familiar section dedicated to general-interest books on Rithmatics, both fiction and nonfiction. He'd read a lot of these—pretty much everything in the library that he was allowed access to. If he really had seen that pattern somewhere, it could have been in any of these.

He opened one book he remembered checking out a few weeks ago. He only vaguely recalled it at first, but as he flipped through, he shivered. It was an adventure novel about Rithmatists in Nebrask.

He stopped on a page, reading—almost against his will—paragraphs on a man being gruesomely eaten by wild chalklings. They crawled up his skin under his clothing—they only had two dimensions, after all—and chewed his flesh from his bones.

The account was fictionalized and overly dramatic. Still, it made Joel feel sick. He'd wanted very badly to be involved in

Professor Fitch's work. And yet, if Joel were to face an army of chalklings, he wouldn't be able to build himself a defense. The creatures would crawl right over his lines and get at him. He'd be no better off than the man in the book.

He shook himself free from imaginings of chalklings scrambling up and down his body. He had wanted this. If he was really going to become a scholar of Rithmatics—if that was his goal—he'd have to live with the idea that it could be dangerous, and he would not be able to defend himself.

He put the novel away—it had no illustrations—and moved to the nonfiction section. Here, he grabbed a stack of books that looked familiar and walked to a study desk at the side of the room.

An hour of searching left Joel feeling even more frustrated than when he'd started. He groaned, sitting back, stretching. Perhaps he was just chasing shadows, looking for a connection to his own life so that he could prove useful to Fitch.

It seemed to him that his memory of the pattern was older than this. Familiar, but from a long, long time ago. He had a good memory, particularly when it came to Rithmatics. He gathered his current stack of books and walked back toward the shelves to return them. As he did so, a man in a bright red Rithmatic coat walked into the library.

Professor Nalizar, Joel thought. *I sure hope that someday, some upstart young Rithmatist challenges* him *to a duel and takes away his tenure. He . . .*

The first student hadn't disappeared until Nalizar arrived at the school. Joel hesitated, considering that fact.

It's just a coincidence, Joel thought. *Don't jump to conclusions.*

And yet . . . hadn't Nalizar talked about how dangerous the battlefield in Nebrask was? He thought the students and professors at Armedius were weak. Would he go so far as to do something to make everyone more worried? Something to put them all on edge and make them study and practice more?

But kidnapping? Joel thought. *That's a stretch.*

Still, it would be interesting to know what books Nalizar was looking at. Joel caught sight of a swish of red coat entering the Rithmatic wing of the library. He hurried after Nalizar.

As soon as Joel reached the doorway to the Rithmatic wing, a voice called out to him.

"Joel!" said Ms. Torrent, sitting at her desk. "You know you're not supposed to go in there."

Joel stopped, cringing. He'd hoped she wouldn't be paying attention. Librarians seemed to have a sixth sense for noticing when students were doing things they weren't supposed to.

"I just saw Professor Nalizar," Joel said. "I wanted to go mention something to him."

"You can't enter the Rithmatic section of the library without an escort, Joel," Torrent said, stamping pages in a book, not looking up at him. "No exceptions."

He ground his teeth in frustration.

Escort, he thought suddenly. *Would Fitch help?*

Joel rushed out of the library, but realized that Fitch might still not be dressed or might have returned to bed. By the time Joel got the man back to the library, Nalizar would probably be gone. Beyond that, he suspected that Fitch would disapprove of spying on Nalizar—he might even be afraid to do so.

Joel needed someone who was more willing to take a risk. . . .

It was still breakfast time, and the dining hall was just a short distance away.

I can't believe I'm doing this, he thought, but took off at a dash for the dining hall.

Melody was sitting at her usual place. As always, none of the other Rithmatists had chosen to sit next to her.

"Hey," Joel said, stepping up to the table and taking one of the empty seats.

Melody looked up from her plate of fruit. "Oh. It's you."

"I need your help."

"To do what?"

"I want you to escort me into the Rithmatic section of the library," he said quietly, "so I can spy on Professor Nalizar."

She stabbed a piece of orange. "Well, all right."

Joel blinked. "That's it? Why are you agreeing so easily? We could get in trouble, you know."

She shrugged, dropping her fork back to the plate. "Somehow, *I* appear to be able to get into trouble just by sitting around. How much worse could this be?"

Joel couldn't refute that logic. He smiled, standing. She joined him, and they rushed from the room back across the lawn.

"So, is there any particular reason why we're spying on Nalizar?" she asked. "Other than the fact that he's cute."

Joel grimaced. "Cute?"

"In an arrogant, mean sort of way." She shrugged. "I assume you have a better reason?"

What could he tell her? Harding was worried about security, and . . . well, Melody didn't seem the safest person to tell a secret.

"Nalizar got to Armedius right about the same time those students started disappearing," Joel said, sharing only what he'd figured out on his own.

"And?" Melody replied. "They often hire new professors before summer elective starts."

"He's suspicious," Joel said. "If he was such a great hero back at the battlefront, then why did he come here? Why take a low-level tutor position? Something's going on with that man."

"Joel," she said. "You're not *honestly* implying that Nalizar is behind the disappearances?"

"I don't know," Joel said as they reached the library. "I just want to know what books he's looking at. I'm hoping Ms. Torrent lets me use a student for an escort."

"Well, all right," Melody said. "But I'm only doing this because I get to take a peek at Nalizar."

"Melody," Joel said. "He's *not* a good person."

"I never said anything about his morality, Joel," she said, opening the door. "Only his face." She swished into the room, and he followed. Ms. Torrent looked up as they passed her desk.

"He," Melody said, pointing dramatically at Joel, "is mine. I need someone to carry books for me."

Ms. Torrent looked like she wanted to protest, but—thankfully—she decided not to do so. Joel hurried after Melody, but stopped in the doorway to the Rithmatic wing.

He'd spent years trying to find a way to get into this room. He'd asked Rithmatic students before to bring him in, but nobody had been willing. Nalizar wasn't the only one who was stingy with Rithmatic secrets. There was an air of exclusion to the entire order. They had their own table at dinner. They expressed hostility toward non-Rithmatic scholars. They had their own wing of the library, containing all the best texts on Rithmatics.

Joel took a deep breath, following Melody—who had turned toward him and was tapping her foot with an annoyed expression. Joel ignored her, reveling. The room even *felt* different from the ordinary library wing. The shelves were taller, the books older. The walls contained numerous charts and diagrams.

Joel stopped beside one that detailed the Taylor Defense—one of the most complicated, and controversial, Rithmatic defenses. He'd only ever seen small, vague sketches of it. Here, however, its various pieces were dissected and explained in great detail, along with several variations drawn smaller to the sides.

"*Joel*," Melody snapped. "I didn't abandon half my breakfast so you could stare at pictures. Honestly."

He reluctantly turned his attention to their task. The bookshelves here were high enough that Nalizar wouldn't be able to see Joel or Melody enter the room—which was good. Joel hated to contemplate the ruckus Nalizar would cause if he caught a non-Rithmatist poking around these texts.

Joel waved to Melody, quickly moving down the rows. They seemed placed more haphazardly than back in the main wing, though the library wasn't really *that* big. He should be able to find—

Joel froze midstep as he walked past an aisle between shelves. There was Nalizar, not five feet from where Joel stood.

Melody pulled Joel aside, out of Nalizar's line of sight. He stifled a grunt and joined her in the next row. They could peek through a crack between bookshelves and catch a glimpse of Nalizar, though the poor view didn't let Joel read the title of the book the professor had.

Nalizar glanced up toward where Joel had been. Then he turned—never noticing Joel and Melody peering through the small slit at him—and walked away.

"What books are shelved there?" Joel whispered to Melody.

She rounded the other side—it wouldn't matter if Nalizar saw her—and took one off the shelf. She wrinkled her nose and held the book up toward the crack for Joel. *Theoretical Postulations on Developmental Rithmatics, Revised Edition, with a Foreword by Attin Balazmed.*

"Dry stuff," she said.

Theoretical Rithmatics, Joel thought. "I need to know the exact books Nalizar is carrying!"

Melody rolled her eyes. "Wait here," she said, then walked off.

Joel waited nervously. Other Rithmatic students poked about. Those who saw him gave him odd looks, but nobody challenged him.

Melody returned a few minutes later and handed him a slip of paper. On it was written the titles of three books. "Nalizar gave these to the librarians," she said, "then left for class, instructing the staff to check the books out to him and deliver them to his office."

"How'd you get this?" Joel asked with excitement, taking the paper.

"I walked up to him and mentioned how much I hated my punishment running errands."

Joel blinked.

"It made him give me a lecture," Melody said. "Professors *love* giving lectures. Anyway, while he was chastising me, I was able to read the titles on the spines of the books in his arms."

Joel glanced again at the titles. *Postulations on the Possibility of New and Undiscovered Rithmatic Lines,* the first one read. By Gerald Taffington. The other two had more vague titles having to do with theoretics, but that first one seemed an absolute gem.

Nalizar was researching new Rithmatic lines.

"Thank you," Joel said. "Really. Thank you."

Melody shrugged. "We should get going. I just got a lecture from Nalizar—I don't want to get one from Fitch for being late."

"Yeah, sure," he said. "Just a second." He glanced at the shelves full of books. He'd tried for so long to get in. "I have to get a few of these," he said. "Will you check them out for me?"

"You can take *one*. I'm determinedly impatient today."

He decided not to argue, and instead looked over the nearby stack where Nalizar had been idling.

"Come on," she said.

Joel grabbed a volume that looked promising. *Man and Rithmatics: Origins of Power.* He handed her the book and they left. Ms. Torrent gave them another dissatisfied glance, but reluctantly checked the book out to Melody. Joel let out a deep breath as they walked out onto the green.

Melody handed him the book, and he tucked it under his arm. At the moment, however, it seemed far less important than the little slip of paper. Joel had proof that Nalizar was interested in new Rithmatic lines.

Of course, Fitch was convinced that the looping swirl was not Rithmatic. This was really just another suspicious connection—it wouldn't prove that Nalizar was involved. *I need to get that book,* Joel thought. *If it contains anything like this looping pattern, I'll have evidence.*

That sounded extremely dangerous. Perhaps it would be best for Joel to simply go to Harding and express his concerns. Undecided, he folded the paper and stuffed it in his pocket. Melody walked beside him in her white skirt, binder held against her chest. She had a distant expression on her face.

"Thank you again," he said. "Really. I think this is going to be a big help."

"Good to be useful for something, I suppose."

"Look, about what I said the other day. I didn't mean it."

"Yes you did," she said, voice uncharacteristically soft. "You were only being honest. I *know* I'm no good at Rithmatics. My reaction only makes me doubly a fool for trying to deny the truth, right?"

"You're not being fair to yourself, Melody. You're *really* good with chalklings."

"For all the good it does me."

"It's a great skill," Joel said. "You're way better at that than I am."

She rolled her eyes. "Okay, you're laying it on thick. There's no need to be so melodramatic—I know you're just trying to make yourself feel better. I forgive you, all right?"

Joel blushed. "You're an annoying person. You know that?"

"Okay," she said, holding up a finger. "Now, see, you've gone too far the other direction. If you try *really* hard, you should be able to find a happy medium between patronizing me and insulting me."

"Sorry," Joel said.

"Regardless," she said, "the fact of the matter is that no matter *how* good I am with Lines of Making, I still can't build myself a decent defense. One good shot with a Line of Vigor will take me out of a duel."

"Not necessarily," Joel said. "You know, for all Professor Fitch's talk about keening, maybe that strategy isn't right for you."

"What do you mean?" she asked, eyeing him suspiciously, apparently expecting another insult.

"Have you ever tried the Jordan Defense?"

"Never heard of it."

"It's advanced," Joel said. "One of the most advanced I've ever read about. But it could work. You have to draw a Forbiddance net, then . . ." He hesitated. "Here, I'll just show you. You have chalk?"

She rolled her eyes. "Of course I have chalk. During your first year at Rithmatic school, if any professor catches you without chalk, they're allowed to make you scrub floors for two hours."

"Really?"

She nodded, handing him a piece. The quad was nearby, and it didn't look like anyone was using it. Joel rushed up the hill,

Melody following. "Hey," she said. "Aren't we going to get into trouble for being late to Fitch's office?"

"I doubt it," Joel said, reaching the concrete-covered top of the hill. "Fitch was up late last night, and he got interrupted a couple of times this morning. I'll bet he's still dozing. Okay, here, watch this."

Joel set his book aside and knelt, doing a rough sketch of the Jordan Defense. It was an ellipsoid defense, with a line at each bind point to stabilize it. The main feature of the defense wasn't the primary ellipse, however, but the large cage made from Lines of Forbiddance around the outside. It reminded Joel a little bit of what Herman Libel had tried.

"That boxes you in," Melody said, squatting down beside him. "You can't do anything if you surround yourself with Lines of Forbiddance. That's basic Rithmatics—even *I* know that."

"That's a basic rule of thumb, true," Joel said, still drawing. "A lot of advanced Rithmatic designs break with early wisdom. The really good duelists, they know *when* to take a risk. Look here." He pointed with his chalk to a section of the design. "I've made a large box on either side. The theory with the Jordan is to fill these boxes full of offensive chalklings. If you're good with chalklings, you should be able to instruct them to wait and not attack your own line from behind.

"So, while your opponent is wasting time blasting away at your front, you are building a single overpowering attack. When you're ready, you let out the burst of chalklings, then quickly re-draw that Line of Forbiddance. You use Lines of Vigor to destroy any enemy chalklings that got inside while your defenses were down, then you build another wave of chalklings.

"While you might be slower than your opponent, it doesn't matter because your attacks come in huge rushes that leave him confused and unable to respond. Matthew Jordan, the one who designed the defense, won a couple of very high-profile duels with this and caused an uproar among academics because of how unconventional it was."

Melody cocked her head. "Dramatic," she said.

"Want to give it a try?" Joel said. "You can use my little sketch as a pattern."

"Probably shouldn't," she said. "I mean, Professor Fitch . . ."

"Come on," Joel said. "Just once. Look, I got you into the library so you could ogle Nalizar, didn't I?"

"*And* get yelled at by him."

"That was your idea," Joel said. "Are you going to draw or not?"

Melody set down her notebook and knelt on the concrete. She took out her chalk, eyed Joel's miniature drawing, then began to draw an ellipse around herself.

Joel began to draw as well. "I'm going with the Ballintain," he said, drawing a circle all the way around himself. "But with your Jordan Defense, you don't need to pay much attention to what I'm doing. Just draw as fast as you can."

She got into it, doing a defensive rectangle around the Circle of Warding, then quickly beginning her chalklings.

Joel drew, hoping his instincts were right. The big weakness in the Jordan Defense was the chalklings. Controlling them in this way was difficult; it was only possible because it was a formal duel, and she could orient them right at her target.

For some reason, chalklings were difficult to control if you wanted them to just wait around. That was why most Rithmatists either sent them out to attack or stuck them on a bind point.

I really need to study more chalkling theory, Joel thought as he finished his defense. *Maybe I can get Melody to check out a few books on it.*

"Okay," he said, reaching out to draw a few Lines of Vigor. "This is going to take some imagination, since I can't make my lines do anything. Pretend that I'm good at drawing Vigor Lines— which I am, by the way—and that each of these is hitting your defense at the same point, weakening it. A well-drawn Line of Warding can take about six hits from a Vigor; a Line of Forbiddance can take ten. When you see where I'm shooting, draw another Forbiddance line behind your first to slow me down."

She did so, drawing a line.

"Now I have to get through *two* lines of Forbiddance and one Line of Warding. That means that with this defense, you have about twenty-six Vigors to get your chalklings done. That's not much time, with how—"

He fell silent as she whipped her hand forward and laid her chalk against the inside of her Line of Forbiddance to release her chalklings.

So fast! he thought. *I only got through six of my Lines of Vigor!* True, he hadn't been going as quickly as he could, but even still . . .

Melody's line puffed away—it took four seconds to dismiss a line—and a wave of eight complete chalklings rushed across the ground toward him.

"Wow," he said.

Melody looked up, brushing a bit of curly red hair from her eyes. She blinked in surprise, as if shocked that she'd actually done it. Joel scrambled to draw a few more Lines of Vigor and defend himself against the creatures.

But, of course, that did nothing. In the heat of battle, Joel almost forgot that he wasn't a Rithmatist.

The chalklings reached his defenses and hesitated. For a moment, he felt a stab of fear—similar to what he assumed Herman Libel must have felt while sitting defenseless against an attacking group of chalk monsters.

Joel doubted that Herman had been forced to face down unicorns though.

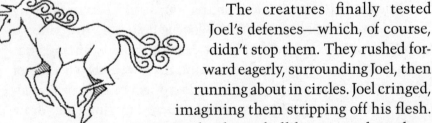

The creatures finally tested Joel's defenses—which, of course, didn't stop them. They rushed forward eagerly, surrounding Joel, then running about in circles. Joel cringed, imagining them stripping off his flesh. Fortunately, these chalklings were harmless.

"Unicorns?" he asked sufferingly.

"The unicorn is a very noble and majestic animal!"

"It's just an . . . undignified way to be defeated, particularly with them prancing about like that."

"Well," she said, rising, "at least I don't have any pink chalk. They won't let us use colors until we're juniors."

Joel smiled. "You did really well. I can't believe you drew those so quickly!"

She walked over and placed her chalk against one of the unicorns. It stopped prancing immediately, freezing in place as if it had become simply a drawing again. Four seconds later, it was gone. She repeated the process with the others. "That wasn't hard," she said. "I just had to get my chalklings to wait before attacking."

From what little Joel had read, it hadn't sounded that easy. If you didn't give the chalklings precisely correct instructions, they'd attack your own Line of Forbiddance. Then, when you dismissed it, they'd be confused and mill about instead of rushing your opponent.

"I *told* you Jordan would work for you," Joel said, standing.

"You went easy on me," she said. "Plus, my lines weren't that great. I'll bet you could have broken through my Forbiddance wall with half as many shots as it would otherwise have taken."

"Maybe," Joel said. "I didn't expect you to work so quickly. Your ellipse was a disaster—but that didn't matter. You did a great job, Melody. You *can* do this. You just need to find patterns and defenses that work for your skills."

She smiled hesitantly at that. "Thanks."

"It's true."

"No," she said. "Not for the compliment. For showing me this. I doubt it's going to revolutionize my style—I'm never going to be a good Rithmatist unless I can learn circles. But, well, it's nice to know I can do *something* right."

Joel smiled back. "All right. Well, maybe *now* we should get to class. Professor Fitch . . ."

He trailed off, noticing a figure in the distance—a figure in a policeman's uniform and hat, sitting astride a large horse.

Remembering that he'd asked Exton to send for the inspector, Joel waved.

"Joel?" Melody asked.

"Just a moment," he said. "You can go on ahead. I need to talk to that policeman."

She turned. "Dusts! Is that an Equilix Stallion?"

As she spoke, Joel noticed that she was right. Harding trotted his mount forward, but that mount was not a horse. It was *shaped* like one, true, but it was made of metal, with glass sides that showed the twisting gears and clicking springs.

"Joel, son," Harding said as he walked his mount up, its metal hooves leaving deep prints in the soil. "How goes the academic front?"

"It goes well, Inspector," Joel said.

Joel had seen springwork horses before, of course. They were expensive, but by no means uncommon. An Equilix, however, wasn't just *any* springwork. Built from the newest of springwork technologies out of Egyptia, they were said to be amazingly intelligent. They had a woman there, a genius scientist, who had figured out new ways of winding springs to pull energy through the harmonic winds.

Joel looked into the machine's clear glass eyes, and could see the tiny springs and rotors moving inside, miniature arms popping up and down like the keys of a typewriter, driving the functions of its complicated clockwork brain.

"Now, who is this pretty young lady?" Harding asked. His tone was civil, but Joel could sense the hesitation.

Pretty? She annoyed him so often, he forgot how cute she could be when she smiled. Like she was doing right now. "She's a student of Professor Fitch's," Joel said.

"Miss . . . ?"

"Muns," she said.

Wait, Joel thought. *Muns. I've heard that name somewhere recently. For someone other than Melody. . . .*

"Miss Muns," Harding said, tipping his blue helmet. Then he turned to Joel. "Thank you for the tip about the parents, Joel. We need to secure this campus; I've ordered that from this point forward, no students are to be allowed out for the evenings or weekends. I've asked for reinforcements, making this our base of operations and front line of defense!"

Joel nodded. "I thought it would be a bad idea for the parents to start running off with their children. Anywhere they go, the . . . person could follow."

"Agreed," Harding said.

Melody glanced at Joel, her eyes narrowing.

"By the way, soldier," Harding said to Joel, "have you seen a blonde woman, five foot seven, hair in a bun, about thirty-five years old, wearing a blue dress? She has sharp features and a narrow face."

"I saw her," Joel said. "She's a parent of one of the Rithmatist students."

Harding snorted. "Hardly. That's Elizabeth Warner—reporter."

"A woman reporter?" Joel asked.

"What's wrong with that?" Melody said with a huff.

"Nothing," Joel said quickly. "Just . . . never heard of it before."

"Times are changing," Harding said. "Women Rithmatists fight on the battlefield, and I'll bet there comes a day when even ordinary women join the ranks of soldiers. Regardless, women or not, press are the *enemy*. If they have their way, this entire island will go into a panic! Where did you see her, son?"

"She was heading toward Professor Fitch's office."

"Blast it all," Harding said, turning his mount. Joel could hear clicks and springworks moving inside. "Watch my retreat!" Harding called.

He took off in a gallop toward the Rithmatic campus.

"And *what* exactly was that all about?" Melody asked.

"Uh . . . nothing."

She rolled her eyes with an exaggerated expression. "I'm sure."

"I can't tell you," he said.

"You're going to relegate me to continued ignorance!"

"Uh, no," Joel said, shuffling. "Look, I really don't know anything."

"Is that a lie?"

Joel hesitated. "Yeah."

She sniffed in annoyance. "And I thought we were starting to get along so well." She grabbed her notebook and stalked away. "My life," she snapped, holding her hand aloft, "is a *tragedy*! Even my friends lie to me!"

Joel sighed. He picked up the book she'd checked out for him, then rushed after her toward Fitch's office.

Chalk Drawings
discovered at the scene
of Herman Libel's
disappearance.

Corners, where lines meet, particularly weak.

The drawing is quite good for a freehand circle.

X

Blood spots, marked with 'X's.

X   X

X   X

Debris from dead chalklings?

Note that the initial breach occurred where the circle was off.

Again, numerous broken lines indicate many chalklings.

Well, yes, I did talk to that woman," Professor Fitch said, looking confused. "She was uncertain about letting her son stay at Armedius. She wanted to know that we were making honest efforts to protect the children."

"And so you told her," Inspector Harding said.

"Of course. She was on the edge of tears. Um, my, I can *never* handle women on the edge of hysterics, Inspector. I didn't say much. Just that we were sure a Rithmatist was behind it, but that we hoped the children might still be alive, and that we were working on some strange chalk drawings left at the crime scenes."

"Professor," Harding said, rubbing his forehead, "this is a *terrible* breach of security. If you were a soldier under my command, I'm afraid I'd have to discipline you for this."

"Oh dear," Fitch said. "Well, I guess there's a reason I'm a professor, rather than a soldier."

Joel raised an eyebrow, trying not to feel *too* smug about the fact that both Harding and Fitch had insisted Melody wait outside, but hadn't forbidden Joel.

"Unfortunately," Harding said, pacing up the hallway of Fitch's office, hands clasped behind his back, "it can't be helped now. Our fortifications have been breached, and a spy escaped with our battle plan. We must bear it and hope for the best. I strongly suggest, Professor, that you avoid speaking of these matters with *anyone* else."

"I understand, Inspector," Fitch said.

"Good," Harding replied. "Now, I think you should be aware that I've asked the knight-senator of New Britannia for permission to set up a perimeter here at Armedius. He's agreed to grant me a full legion from the Jamestown militia to use in defending this location."

"You're going to . . . occupy the school?" Fitch asked.

"Nothing so drastic, Professor," Harding said as he paced, spinning on one heel then coming back the other direction. "Rithmatists are one of the Union's greatest resources; we need to make certain they are protected. I will have men patrolling the grounds. Perhaps we can use sheer intimidation to keep this phantom kidnapper from striking again.

"Principal York has assigned me a room on campus to use as a base of operations. My men will not interfere with the day-to-day workings of the school. However, we want to be seen—and to let the students know that they are being protected. Perhaps this will also be of aid in placating the parents, who seem determined to fracture morale and isolate their children for easy defeat."

"What's this?" Fitch asked. "The parents are doing what?"

"Some of the parents of Rithmatist children are pulling their students out of the school," Harding said. "Young Joel was quickwitted enough to warn me of this. Unfortunately, I wasn't able to secure the grounds quickly enough. A good dozen children—mostly Rithmatists—were pulled out this morning."

"That doesn't sound good," Fitch said. "All of the attacks happened *off* campus. Why would they want to take their children away from Armedius?"

"Parents are unpredictable when their children are involved," Harding said. "I'd much rather fight a squadron of Forgotten than deal with an affluent mother who thinks her son is in danger."

Fitch glanced at Joel, though Joel wasn't certain what to make of the look.

"You are now briefed on the situation, men," Harding said. "I must get back to my rounds, assuming there's nothing else we need to discuss."

I should tell them, Joel thought. *I can't just sneak about and try to fight Nalizar on my own.*

"Actually," Joel said, "I . . . um . . . Well, there's something I should probably mention."

They both turned toward him, and suddenly he felt self-conscious. How exactly did one accuse a professor of being a kidnapper?

"It's probably nothing," Joel said. "But, well, I saw Professor Nalizar acting suspiciously earlier today. These kidnappings didn't start happening until he got hired by the principal, you know."

"Joel!" Professor Fitch said. "I realize that you're upset with the man for dueling me, but this is uncalled-for!"

"It's not that, Professor," Joel said. "It's just . . . well . . ."

"No," Harding said. "It's good, Joel. You should mention things like this. However, I don't think we have anything to worry about from Andrew Nalizar."

Joel looked over. "You know him?"

"Of course I do," Harding said. "Nalizar's a legend back in Nebrask. I know a good two dozen men who owe their lives to him—and I count myself among them."

"You mean he really *is* a hero, like he keeps telling everyone?"

"Of course he is," Harding said. "Not a humble one, I'll admit, but I can forgive something like that if it's earned. Why, there was a time when the chalklings had penetrated along the river to the eastern front! If they'd passed us by, they could have flanked our force—maybe taken the entire eastern front. From there, it would only be a matter of sailing on fallen logs to invade the nearby islands and wreak havoc.

"Anyway, my squad was in serious trouble. Then Nalizar arrived and built us a fortification all on his own. He stood against hundreds of chalklings. Dusts be cast aside if he didn't save all of our lives. I could share more than one story like that. I've rarely seen a Rithmatist as skilled and level-headed as Andrew Nalizar. It was a shame that . . ."

He trailed off.

"What?" Joel asked.

"Sorry, son," Harding said. "I just realized you don't have clearance for that. Regardless, Nalizar is no threat. In fact, I'm happy he's here on campus. It feels good to have that man at my back."

Harding nodded to them—he appeared to almost give them a salute, before halting himself—and made his way out of the room and down the stairs.

"I didn't expect that," Joel said. "About Nalizar, I mean."

"To be honest, Joel," Fitch said, "neither did I."

"Nalizar *can't* be a hero," Joel said. "He's a pompous windbag!"

"I will agree with the adjective," Fitch said, "but the noun . . . Well, he *did* defeat me quite handily. Regardless, it is unseemly for a student to be referring to a professor of the school in such a manner. You must show respect, Joel."

A knock came at the door. It flew open a second later, revealing Melody, who had obviously decided not to wait for someone to answer her knock.

"I *assume*," she said with a huff, "that all the *secret, valuable, interesting* discussion is finished with, and we *ordinary* people can come in now?"

"Melody, dear," Fitch said. "It's not that we wanted to exclude you, it's just—"

She held up a hand. "I assume I'm going to have to do more tracing today?"

"Well, um, yes," Fitch said. "It's very good for you to practice that, Melody. You will thank me someday."

"Right," she said. She gathered up a sketch pad and a pen, then turned to leave.

"Melody?" Professor Fitch asked. "Where are you going?"

"I'm going to sketch out here," she said, "on the mundane, unimportant doorstep. That way, I won't be able to interfere with *significant* conversations you two might need to have."

With that, she pulled the door shut behind her.

Fitch sighed, shaking his head and walking back to his desk.

"I'm sure she'll get over it," he said, sitting and shuffling through his papers.

"Yeah," Joel said, still looking after her. Would this make her bitter against him again, after he'd just gotten on her good side? He was having a devil of a time figuring that girl out. "What do you want me to do, Professor?"

"Oh, hum? Ah. Well, I honestly don't know. I planned for you to be working on those census reports for a few more weeks yet. Hum." Fitch tapped the table with his index finger. "Why don't you take the day off? You worked so hard the last few weeks. It will give me an opportunity to sort through what Harding has given me. I'm certain I'll have something for you to do to-morrow."

Joel opened his mouth to protest—he could certainly help with the professor's research into the strange lines—but then hesitated. He glanced at the book he was still carrying, the one Melody had checked out for him.

"All right," he decided. "I'll see you tomorrow."

Fitch nodded, turning back to his papers. Joel pulled open the door to walk out. He nearly stumbled over Melody, who had indeed set up drawing right in front of the doorway. She grumpily made way for him, and he left via the stairwell, intent on finding a shady spot in which to poke through the tome in peace.

Joel sat beneath a tree, book in his hands. Some students played soccer as their summer elective on a field in the distance, kicking the ball back and forth toward the goal. Joel could hear their shouting, but it didn't bother him.

Police officers patrolled the grounds, but they kept to themselves, as Harding had promised. A bird whistled in the branches above him, and a small springwork crab puttered along on the green, clipping at patches of grass. Long metal feelers dangled in front of it, keeping it from wandering off the green and from clipping things it shouldn't.

Joel leaned back against the trunk of the tree, staring up at the sparkling leaves. When he'd chosen the book, he'd assumed from the title—*Origins of Power*—that it had to do with the way that Rithmatics had been discovered, back in the early days when the United Isles had still been new. He'd expected an in-depth look at King Gregory and the first Rithmatists.

The book, however, was about how people *became* Rithmatists.

It happened during the inception ceremony, an event that occurred every Fourth of July. Every boy or girl who had turned eight since the last inception ceremony was brought to their local Monarchical chapel. The group was blessed by the vicar. Then, one at a time, the children walked into the chamber of inception. They stayed inside for a few minutes, then walked out the other side—a symbol of new birth. They were then given chalk and asked to draw a line. From that point on, some could create sketches with Rithmatic power. The others could not. It was that simple.

And yet, the book made the process sound *anything* but simple. Joel leafed through it again, frowning in confusion as the groundskeeping crab clipped its way closer, then turned around as its feelers brushed his leg. The book assumed that the reader was a Rithmatist. It talked of things like the "chaining" and spoke of something known as a "Shadowblaze."

There was apparently far more to the inception than Joel had originally thought. Something happened in that room— something that physically changed some of the children, giving them Rithmatic power. It wasn't just the invisible touch of the Master.

If what the book said was true, then Rithmatists had some sort of special vision or experience inside the chamber of inception, one they didn't speak of. When they went outside to draw their first line, they already *knew* that they had become Rithmatists.

It flew in the face of everything Joel understood. Or, at least, that was what it *seemed* to say. He considered himself well educated when it came to Rithmatics, but this text was completely over his head.

The chaining of a Shadowblaze, fourth entity removed, is an often undeterminable process, and the bindagent should consider wisely the situation before making any decisions regarding the vessels to be indentured.

What did that even mean? Joel had always assumed that if he could just get into the Rithmatic section of the library, he'd be able to learn so much. It hadn't occurred to him that many of the books would be beyond his understanding.

He snapped the book closed. To the side, the springwork crab was starting to run more slowly. The hour was late, and the groundskeeper would probably pass by soon and either wind the device or pack it up for the evening.

Joel stood, tucking the book under his arm, and began to wander toward the dining hall. He felt odd, having just spent an afternoon studying. The entire campus was coming under an increasingly tight lockdown, and students were disappearing in the night. It felt *wrong* to simply sit about and read a book. He wanted to be helping somehow.

I could get that book Nalizar checked out, he thought. Despite Harding's words, Joel just didn't trust the professor. There *was* something important in that book. But what? And how to get it?

With a shake of the head, he entered the dining hall. His mother was there—which was good—and so Joel went and dished himself up some of the evening's main dish: stir-fried spaghetti and meatballs. He dumped some parmesan cheese on, grabbed a pair of chopsticks, then made his way to the table.

"Hey, Mom," he said, sitting down. "How was your day?"

"Worrying," she said, glancing toward a small group of police officers sitting at a table and eating together. "Maybe you shouldn't be out alone at night."

"This campus is probably the safest place in the city right now," Joel said, digging into his food. Spaghetti mixed with fried peppers, mushrooms, water chestnuts, and a tangy tomato soy sauce. Italian food was one of his favorites.

His mother continued to watch the officers. They were probably there to remind people, as Harding had said, that the campus was being protected. However, the officers seemed to also make people more nervous by reminding them that there was danger.

The room buzzed with the sounds of low conversation. Joel heard mention of both Herman and Lilly several times, though as some of the cooks passed, he also heard them grumbling about "those Rithmatists" bringing danger to the campus.

"How can they be so foolish?" Joel asked. "We need the Rithmatists. Do they want the chalklings to get off of Nebrask?"

"People are frightened, Son," his mother said. She stirred her food, but didn't seem to be eating much of it. "Who knows? Perhaps this whole thing *is* the result of a squabble between Rithmatists. They're so secretive. . . ."

She looked toward the professors. Fitch wasn't there—probably working late on the disappearances. Nalizar wasn't at his seat either. Joel narrowed his eyes. He was involved somehow, wasn't he?

At the table of the student Rithmatists, the teens whispered among themselves, looking worried, anxious. Like a group of mice who had just smelled a cat. As usual, Melody sat at the end of the table with at least two seats open on either side of her. She looked down as she ate, not talking to anyone.

It must be hard for her, he realized, to not have anyone to talk with, particularly at this time of tension. He slurped up some spaghetti, thinking of how much she'd overreacted to being excluded from his meeting with Fitch and Harding. And yet . . . perhaps she had a reason. Was it because she was so commonly excluded by the rest of the Rithmatists?

Joel felt a stab of guilt.

"Joel," his mother said, "maybe it isn't a good idea for you to be studying with Professor Fitch during this time."

Joel turned back to her, guilt overwhelmed by alarm. His mother could end his studies with Fitch. If she went to the principal . . .

A dozen complaints flashed through his mind. But no, he

couldn't protest too much. If he did, his mother might dig in her feet and decide it needed to be done. But what, then? How?

"Is that what Father would want?" Joel found himself asking.

His mother's hand froze, chopsticks in her spaghetti, motionless.

Bringing up his father was always dangerous. His mother didn't cry often about him, not anymore. Not often. It was frightening how a simple springrail accident could suddenly upend everything. Happiness, future plans, Joel's chances of being a Rithmatist.

"No," she said, "he wouldn't want you to ostracize them the way others are. I guess I don't want you to either. Just . . . be careful, Joel. For me."

He nodded, relaxing. Unfortunately, he found his eyes drifting back toward Melody. Sitting alone. Everyone in the room kept glancing at the Rithmatists, whispering about them, as if they were on display.

Joel shoved his chopsticks into the spaghetti, then stood up. His mother glanced at him, but said nothing as he crossed the room to the Rithmatist table.

"What?" Melody asked as he arrived. "Come to flatter me some more so that you can get me to sneak you into another place where you shouldn't be?"

"You looked bored," Joel said. "I thought, maybe, you'd want to come eat over with my mother and me."

"Oh? You sure you're not going to just invite me over, then kick me out as soon as you have to talk about something important?"

"You know what? Never mind," Joel said, turning around and stalking away.

"I'm sorry," she said from behind.

He glanced back. Melody looked miserable, staring down at a bowl filled with brownish red spaghetti, a fork stuck into the mess.

"I'm sorry," she said again. "I'd . . . really like to join you."

"Well, come on then," Joel said, waving.

She hesitated, then picked up her bowl and hurried to catch up with Joel. "You know how this is going to look, don't you? Me running off with a boy twice in one day? Sitting with him at dinner?"

Joel blushed. *Great,* he thought. *Just what I need.* "You won't get into trouble for not sitting with the others, will you?"

"Nah. We're encouraged to sit there, but they don't *make* us. I've just never had anywhere else I could go."

Joel gestured toward his open spot at the servants' table across from his mother, and some people on each side made room for Melody. She sat down, smoothing her skirt, looking somewhat nervous.

"Mom," Joel said, sitting and grabbing his chopsticks, "this is Melody. She's studying with Professor Fitch over the summer too."

"Nice to meet you, dear," his mother said.

"Thank you, Mrs. Saxon," Melody said, picking up her fork and digging into her spaghetti.

"Don't you know how to use chopsticks?" Joel asked.

Melody grimaced. "I've never been one for European food. A fork works just fine."

"It's not that hard," Joel said, showing her how to hold them. "My father taught me when I was really young."

"Will he be joining us?" Melody asked politely.

Joel hesitated.

"Joel's father passed away eight years ago, dear," Joel's mother said.

"Oh!" Melody said. "I'm sorry!"

"It's all right," Joel's mother said. "It's actually good to sit with a Rithmatist again. Reminds me of him."

"Was he a Rithmatist?" Melody asked.

"No, no," Joel's mother said. "He just knew a lot of the professors." She got a far-off look in her eyes. "He made specialty chalks for them, and in turn they chatted with him about their work. I could never make much sense of it, but Trent loved it. I guess that because he was a chalkmaker, they almost considered him to be one of them."

"Chalkmaker?" Melody asked. "Doesn't chalk just come from the ground?"

"Well, normal, mundane chalk does. It's really just a form of limestone. However, the chalk you Rithmatists use doesn't have to be a hundred percent pure. That leaves a lot of room for experimentation. Or so Trent always said.

"The best chalk for Rithmatists, in his opinion, was that which is constructed for the purpose. It can't be too hard, otherwise the lines won't come down thickly. It also can't be too soft, otherwise it will break easily. A glaze on the outside will keep it from getting on the Rithmatist's fingers, and he had some compounds he could mix with it that would make it put out less dust."

Joel sat quietly. It was difficult to get his mother to talk about his father.

"Some Rithmatists demand certain colors," she said, "and Trent would work for hours, getting the shade just right. Most schools don't employ a chalkmaker, though. Principal York never replaced Trent—could never find someone he thought was competent enough for the job. The truth is, a chalkmaker isn't really *necessary*, since ordinary chalk will work.

"But Trent always argued with those who called his work frivolous. Taste is frivolous when eating, he'd say—the body can get the same nutrients from bland food as it can from food that tastes good. Colors for fabric, paintings on walls, beautiful music—none of these things are necessary. However, humans are more than their need to survive. Crafting better, more useful kinds of chalk was a quest for him.

"At one point, he had belts filled with six different kinds of chalk—different hardnesses and curves to their tips—for use in drawing on different surfaces. A lot of the professors wore them." She sighed. "That's past, though. Those who want specialty chalk now just order it in from Maineford."

She trailed off, then glanced at the large ticking clock set into the wall. "Dusts! I have to get back to work. Melody, nice to meet you."

Melody stood up as Joel's mother rushed away. Once she was

gone, Melody sat back down, digging into her meal. "Your father sounds like he was an interesting person."

Joel nodded.

"You remember much of him?" she asked.

"Yeah," Joel said. "I was eight when he died, and we have some daguerreotypes of him hanging in our room. He was a kind man—big, burly. More like a fieldworker than an artisan. He liked to laugh."

"You're lucky," Melody said.

"What?" Joel asked. "Because my father died?"

She blushed. "You're lucky to have had a parent like him, and to be able to live with your mother."

"It's not all that fun. Our room is practically a closet, and Mother works herself near to death. The rest of the students are nice to me, but I can't ever make good friends. They're not sure how to treat the son of a cleaning lady."

"I don't even have that."

"You're an orphan?" Joel asked with surprise.

"Nothing so drastic," she said with a sigh, scooping at her spaghetti with the fork. "My family lives down in the Floridian Atolls. My parents are perfectly healthy, and they are also perfectly uninterested in visiting me. I guess after their fourth Rithmatist child, the novelty kind of wears off."

"There are *four* Rithmatists in your family?"

"Well, six if you count my parents," she said. "They're both Rithmatists too."

Joel sat back, frowning. Rithmatics wasn't hereditary. Numerous studies had proven that if there was a higher likelihood of a Rithmatist having Rithmatist children, it was very slight at best.

"That's impossible," Joel said.

"Not impossible," she said, taking a bite of spaghetti. "Just unlikely."

Joel glanced to the side. The book he'd spent all day reading still sat on the table, dark brown cover aging and scuffed. "So," he said offhandedly. "I've been reading about what happens to Rithmatists when they enter the chamber of inception."

Melody froze, several lines of spaghetti hanging from her mouth and down to her bowl.

"Interesting reading," Joel continued, turning the book about. "Though, there are some questions I had about the process."

She slurped up the spaghetti. "That?" she said. "*That's* what the book is about?"

Joel nodded.

"Oh, dusts," she said, grabbing her head. "Oh, *dusts*. I'm going to be in big trouble, aren't I?"

"I don't see why. I mean, what's the problem? Everyone goes into the chamber of inception, right? So, it's not like everything about the place has to be kept secret."

"It's not secret, really," Melody said. "It's just . . . well, I don't know. *Holy.* There are things you're not supposed to talk about."

"Well, I mean, I've read the book," Joel said. *Or, at least, as much of it as I could make out.* "So, I already know a lot. No harm in telling me more, right?"

She eyed him. "And if I answer your questions, will you tell me about the things you and Fitch talked about with that police officer?"

That brought Joel up short. "Um . . . well," he said. "I gave my word not to, Melody."

"Well, *I* promised I wouldn't talk about the chamber of inception with non-Rithmatists."

Dusts, Joel thought in annoyance.

Melody sighed. "We're not going to argue again, are we?"

"I don't know," Joel said. "I don't really want to."

"Me neither. I have far too little energy for it at this present moment. That comes from eating this slop the Italians call food. Looks far too much like worms. Anyway, what are you up to after dinner?"

"After dinner?" Joel asked. "I . . . well, I was probably just going to read some more, see if I can figure out this book."

"You study too much," she said, wrinkling her nose.

"My professors would generally disagree with you."

"Well, that's because *they're* wrong and *I'm* right. No more reading for you. Let's go get some ice cream."

"I don't know if the kitchen has any," Joel said. "It's hard to get in the summers, and—"

"Not from the kitchen, stupid," Melody said, rolling her eyes. "From the parlor out on Knight Street."

"Oh. I've . . . never been there."

"What! That's a *tragedy*."

"Melody, *everything* is a tragedy to you."

"Not having ice cream," she proclaimed, "is the culmination of all disasters! That's it. No more discussion. We're going. Follow."

With that, she swept out of the dining hall. Joel slurped up a last bite of spaghetti, then followed in a rush.

The front line is drawn in place first, then dismissed once a chalkling force is ready to attack.

This smaller line is usually drawn only after the front is breached, and then only in the place needed.

In this space, the Rithmatist draws chalklings with instructions to wait until the front line vanishes, then attack.

The Jordan is easy to draw, but difficult to use. It depends on keen timing and an ability to control one's chalklings with great finesse.

In this space, the Rithmatist draws chalklings with instructions to wait until the front line vanishes, then attack.

Many traditional Rithmatists still hesitate to teach such an unconventional defense.

The JORDAN DEFENSE

S
o, what's it about Rithmatists that makes you so keen on being one?" Melody asked in the waning summer light. Old Barkley—the groundskeeper—passed them on the path, moving between campus lanterns, twisting the gears to make them begin spinning and giving out light. Melody and Joel would have to be back from this outing soon to obey Harding's curfew, but they had time for a quick trip.

Joel walked beside Melody, his hands in his trouser pockets, as they strolled toward the campus exit. "I don't know," he said. "Why *wouldn't* someone want to be a Rithmatist?"

"Well, I know a lot of people *think* they want to be one," Melody said. "They see the notoriety, the special treatment. Others like the power, I think. That's not you, Joel. You don't want notoriety—you're always hiding about, quiet and such. You seem to like to be alone."

"I guess. Maybe I just want the power. You've seen how I can get when I'm competing with someone."

"No," she said. "When you explain the lines and defenses, you get excited—but you don't talk Rithmatics as a way to get what you want or make others obey you. A lot of people talk about those kinds of things. Even some of the others in my class."

They approached the gates to the school grounds. A couple of police officers stood watching, but they didn't try to bar the exit. Beside the men were buckets. Acid, for fighting off chalklings. It wasn't strong enough to hurt people, at least not much, but it would destroy chalklings in the blink of an eye. Harding wasn't taking any chances.

One of the guards nodded to Joel and Melody. "You two take care," he said. "Be careful. Be back in an hour."

Joel nodded. "You sure this is a good idea?" he asked Melody.

She rolled her eyes dramatically. "Nobody has disappeared from ice cream parlors, Joel."

"No," he said, "but Lilly Whiting disappeared on her way home from a party."

"How do you know that?" Melody said, looking at him suspiciously.

He glanced away.

"Oh, right," she said. "Secret conferences."

He didn't respond, and—fortunately for him—she didn't press the point.

The street looked busy, and the kidnapper had always attacked when students were alone, so Joel probably didn't have to worry. Still, he found himself watching their surroundings carefully. Armedius was a gated park of manicured grass and stately buildings to their right. To their left was the street, and the occasional horse-drawn carriage clopped along.

Those were growing less and less common as people replaced their horses with springwork beasts of varying shapes and designs. One shaped like a wingless dragon crawled by, its gears clicking and twisting, eyes shining lights out to illuminate the street. It had a carriage set atop its back, and Joel could see a mustached man with a bowler hat sitting inside.

Armedius was settled directly in the middle of Jamestown, near several bustling crossroads. Buildings rose some ten stories in the distance, all made from sturdy brick designs. Some bore pillars or other stonework, and the sidewalk itself was of cobbled patterns, many of the individual bricks stamped with the seal of New Britannia. It had been the first of the islands colonized long ago when the Europeans discovered the massive archipelago that now made up the United Isles of America.

It was Friday, and there would be plays and concerts running on Harp Street, which explained some of the traffic. Laborers in trousers and dirty shirts passed, tipping their caps at Melody—who, by virtue of her Rithmatist uniform, drew their respect. Even the well-dressed—men in sharp suits with long coats and canes, women in sparkling gowns—sometimes nodded to Melody.

What would it be like, to be recognized and respected by everyone you passed? It was an aspect of being a Rithmatist that he'd never considered.

"Is that why you don't like it?" he asked Melody as they strolled beneath a streetlamp.

"What?" she asked.

"The notoriety," Joel said. "The way everyone looks at you, treats you differently. Is that why you don't like being a Rithmatist?"

"That's part of the reason. It's like . . . they all expect something from me. So many of them depend on me. Ordinary students can fail, but when you're a Rithmatist, everyone makes sure you know that you *can't* fail. There are a limited number of us—another Rithmatist cannot be chosen until one of us dies. If I'm bad at what I do, I will make a hole in our defenses."

She walked along, hands clasped in front of her. They passed underneath the springrail track, and Joel could see a train being wound up in the Armedius station to his right.

"It's such pressure," she said. "I'm bad at Rithmatics, but the Master *himself* chose me. That implies that I must have the aptitude. So, if I'm not doing well, it must mean that I haven't worked hard enough. That's what everyone keeps telling me."

"Ouch," Joel said. "Harsh."

"Yeah."

He wasn't certain what else to say. No wonder she was so touchy. They walked in silence for a time, and Joel noticed for the first time that a smaller number of those they passed didn't seem so respectful of Melody as the others. These glared at Melody from beneath worker's hats and muttered to their companions. Joel hadn't realized that the complaints about Rithmatists extended beyond the jealousy of the students on campus.

Eventually, they passed the downtown cathedral. The imposing structure had broad metal gates set with clockwork gears twisting and counting off the infinite nature of time. Springwork statues and gargoyles stood on the peaked walls and roof, occasionally turning their heads or shaking wings.

Joel paused to look up at the cathedral framed by the dusk sky.

"You never did answer my question," Melody said. "About why you want to be a Rithmatist so badly."

"Maybe it's just because I feel like I missed my chance."

"You had the same chance as anyone else," Melody said. "You were incepted."

"Yeah," Joel said. "But in December instead of July."

"What?" Melody asked as Joel turned away and started walking again. She rushed up in front of him, then turned to face him, walking backward. "Inception happens in July."

"Unless you miss it," Joel said.

"Why in the world would you miss your inception?"

"There were . . . complications."

"But by December, all the year's Rithmatists would already have been chosen."

"Yeah," Joel said. "I know."

Melody fell into step beside him, looking thoughtful. "What was it like? Your inception, I mean."

"I thought we weren't supposed to talk about these things."

"No. *I'm* not supposed to talk about them."

"There's not much to tell," Joel said. "My mother and I went to the cathedral on a Saturday. Father Stewart sprinkled me with water, marked my head with some oil, and left me to pray in front of the altar for about fifteen minutes. After that, we went home."

"You didn't go into the chamber of inception?"

"Father Stewart said it wasn't necessary."

She frowned, but let the matter drop. They soon approached the small commercial district that thrived outside of Armedius. Awnings hung from the fronts of brick buildings, and wooden signs swung slightly in the wind.

"Wish I would have worn my sweater today," Melody noted, shivering. "It can get cold here, even in summer."

"Cold?" Joel asked. "Oh, right. You're from Floridia, aren't you?"

"It's so cold up here in the north."

Joel smiled. "New Britannia isn't cold. Maineford—*that's* cold."

"It's *all* cold," she said. "I've come to the conclusion that you northerners have never experienced what it is to be *really* warm, so you accept a lesser substitute out of ignorance."

"Aren't you the one who suggested ice cream?" Joel asked, amused.

"It won't be cold in the parlor," she said. "Or . . . well, maybe it will. But *everyone* knows that ice cream is worth the trouble of being cold. Like all things virtuous, you have to suffer to gain the reward."

"Ice cream as a metaphor for religious virtue?" Joel said. "Nice."

She grinned as they strolled along the brick-cobbled sidewalk. Light from whirring lanterns played off her deep red hair and dimpled cheeks.

Yeah, Joel thought, *when she's not acting crazy—or yelling at me—she really is quite pretty.*

"There!" Melody said, pointing to a shop. She dashed across the street; Joel followed more carefully, staying out of the way of vehicles. The parlor was, apparently, a popular one. He'd never been here before—he didn't go to the commercial district much. What would he buy? The academy provided for his family.

Joel recognized some of the students inside from Armedius. Richardson Matthews was outside, and gave Joel a little wave— the tall student was a year ahead of Joel, and had always been nice to him. He eyed Melody, then winked at Joel.

Well, Joel thought. *If there weren't rumors about Melody and me before, there will be now.* He wasn't certain what he thought of that.

He walked toward Richardson, intending to chat with him. Melody went to read the ice cream flavors.

Then Joel saw the prices hanging beside the list of flavors. That stopped him flat.

He cursed himself for a fool. He should have realized, should have stopped to think. He rarely left campus, and he almost *never* spent money on anything.

"Melody," he said, grabbing her arm before she could enter. "I . . . can't afford this."

"What?" she asked.

Joel pointed at the prices hanging on the window outside. "Nine cents for a scoop? That's ridiculous!"

"Well, it *is* June," she said. "Still, it's not that bad. I doubt you'll be able to find a scoop for less than seven cents anywhere on the island, and five is the cheapest I've seen in winter."

Joel blinked. Were things *really* that expensive?

"How much do you have?" she asked.

Joel reached in his pocket and pulled out a single silver penny. It was as wide as his thumb, and thin, stamped with the seal of New Britannia. His mother made him carry it with him, should he need to pay cab fare or buy a ticket on the springrail.

"One penny," Melody said flatly.

Joel nodded.

"That's all the allowance you get a week?"

"A week?" he asked. "Melody, my mother gave me this for my birthday last year."

She stared at it for a moment. "Oh, wow. You really *are* poor."

He flushed, stuffing the penny in his pocket. "You just get what you want. I'll wait out—"

"Oh, don't be silly," she said, grabbing his arm and pulling him into the warm parlor room. She stepped into line behind Richardson and a long-lashed girl that Joel didn't know. "I'll pay for both of us."

"I can't let a girl pay for me!"

"Vain masculine pride," she said, reaching into her pocketbook. She pulled out a shiny gold half-dollar. "Here," she said, handing it to him. "Now you can pay for us."

"That's ridiculous!" he protested.

"You'd better order, because it's our turn."

Joel hesitated, glancing at the soda jerker behind the counter. The man raised an eyebrow at him.

"Uh . . ." Joel said. "Hi."

"Oh, you're hopeless," Melody said, elbowing Joel aside. "I'll take a triple-scoop chocolate sundae with fudge sauce and chocolate sprinkles." She eyed Joel. "He'll have vanilla. Two scoops. Cherries. And a cherry soda for each of us. Got that?"

The soda jerker nodded.

"He'll pay," Melody said, gesturing to Joel.

Joel handed over the half-dollar. He got a couple of pennies in change.

Melody gestured to a table, and Joel followed her. They sat down, and he tried to hand her the change.

Melody waved indifferently. "Keep it. I absolutely *hate* carrying small coins. They rattle about."

"How much money do you *have*?" Joel asked, looking down at the coins.

"I get a dollar a week from my family," Melody said, pulling out a full golden dollar, about two inches in diameter.

Joel gaped. He'd never held a full dollar before. It was complete with a glass face on either side to show the gears inside, marking its authenticity.

Melody turned it over in her fingers, then took out a small key and wound the tiny gears. They began to click softly, spinning around and around inside the glass face.

A dollar a week, Joel thought with amazement.

"Here," she said, rolling it across the table to him. "It's yours."

"I can't take this!" he protested, stopping the dollar before it rolled off the table.

"Why not?"

"It wouldn't be right. I . . ." He'd never held so much money before. He tried to give it back, but Melody snapped her pocketbook closed.

"Nope," she said. "I've got like fifty of those back in my rooms. I never can figure out what to do with it all."

"That's . . . that's amazing!"

She snorted. "Compared to most of the students at this school, that's nothing. There's a kid in one of my classes who gets ten dollars a week from his family."

"Dusts!" Joel said. "I really *am* poor." He hesitated. "I still can't take this, Melody. I don't want handouts."

"It's not a handout," she said. "I'm just tired of carrying it. Why don't you use it to buy your mother something nice?"

That made him pause. Reluctantly, he put it in his pocket.

"Your mother looks like she could use a break," Melody said. "She works a lot, doesn't she?"

Joel nodded. "A *lot*."

"So where does her money go? To pay for your education?"

Joel shook his head. "The principal gave me free tuition when my father died."

"Your mother has to get more compensation than just room and board," Melody said, nodding to the server as he brought their order. Joel felt daunted by the mound of frozen cream topped with sliced cherries and whipped cream. And his was only two-thirds the size of Melody's chocolate behemoth.

She dug right in. "So, where does your mom's money go?"

"I don't know," he said. "I never thought about it before, I guess." He fingered the dollar coin in his pocket again. So much. Did Rithmatists really get that much money from their stipend?

They had to fight for a decade at Nebrask. They could stay longer if they wanted, but so long as they put in their ten years, they could retire from the battlefront, only to be called up if needed. That happened rarely—only once in the last thirty years, when a large breach in the circle had occurred.

For those ten years of service, they were given a stipend for the rest of their lives. Joel didn't know the exact numbers, but if Rithmatists needed more money, they could work for the spring-rail companies. Those had contracts from the government allowing them to use chalklings—drawn with the Glyph of Rending to let them affect the world, and not just chalk—to wind the enormous springs that powered the rail line.

Joel knew very little of this—it was one of those things Rithmatists didn't discuss with others. He wasn't even certain how chalklings could *push*. They did, though, and the work paid Rithmatists very, very well.

"The money seems like a pretty good reason to be a Rithmatist," he said. "Easy income."

"Yeah," Melody said softly. "Easy."

Joel finally took a bite of his ice cream. It was *way* better than the stuff the cooks at Armedius served. He found it difficult to enjoy, noting how Melody had begun stirring hers about disconsolately, eyes downcast.

What did I say? he thought. Had their discussion reminded her of her lack of skill? "Melody," he said, "you really *are* good at Rithmatics. You're a genius with chalklings."

"Thanks," she said, but didn't perk up immediately. That didn't seem to be what was bothering her.

Still, she soon began digging into her sundae again. "Chocolate," she said, "is the greatest invention of *all time*."

"What about springworks?" Joel said.

She waved indifferently. "Da Vinci was a total hack. Everyone knows that. Completely overrated."

Joel smiled, enjoying his sundae. "How did you know what flavor to get for me?"

"Just felt right," she said, taking another bite. "Joel . . . did you mean what you said about chalklings a bit ago? About my skill?"

"Of course," Joel said, and took a sip of his soda. "I've snuck into a lot of lectures, and I've never seen a professor on campus create chalklings anywhere near as detailed as yours."

"Then why can't I get the *other* lines right?"

"So you *do* care?"

"Of course I do. It wouldn't be nearly as much of a tragedy if I didn't."

"Maybe you just need more practice."

"I've practiced a *ton*."

"I don't know, then. How did you keep your chalklings back behind your defenses? It didn't seem tough to you at all, but it's supposed to be very difficult."

"Supposed to be?"

"I don't know for certain," Joel said, shoveling a bite into his mouth. He savored the sweet, creamy flavor, and then licked the spoon. "I haven't studied much about chalkling theory. There isn't a lot of material about them in the ordinary stacks, and Professor Fitch doesn't teach chalkling classes—he's the only one who would let me sneak in and listen on a regular basis."

"That's a shame. What do you want to know about them?"

"You'll tell me?" Joel asked with surprise.

"I don't see why not."

"Because you flipped out when you realized that I was learning about inception ceremonies."

"That's *way* different," she said, rolling her eyes. "Are you going to ask or not?"

"Well," Joel said, "I know that sometimes, chalklings respond better to instructions than other times. Why?"

"I don't know if anyone knows that. They usually do what *I* want them to, though others have more trouble."

"So, you know the instruction glyphs better than others?"

"I wouldn't say that," Melody said. "Chalklings . . . they're not quite like the other lines, Joel. A Line of Forbiddance only does one thing. You draw it, and it sits there. Chalklings, though . . . they're versatile. They have a life of their own. If you don't build them correctly, they won't be able to do what they're supposed to."

Joel frowned. "But, what does 'building them correctly' even mean? I keep looking through the books, and what I *can* find says that detail will make a chalkling stronger. But . . . well, it's just chalk. How can the chalkling tell if you drew it with a lot of detail or not?"

"Because it can," Melody said. "A chalkling knows when it's a good picture."

"Is it the *amount* of chalk that's important? A lot of chalk makes a 'detailed' drawing instead of a nondetailed one?"

Melody shook her head. "Some students my first year tried to simply draw circles and color them in as their chalklings. Those ones always died quickly—some just rolled away, not going where they were supposed to."

Joel frowned. He'd always seen Rithmatics as . . . well, something scientific and measurable. A Line of Warding's strength was proportionate to the degree of its curve. The height of a Line of Forbiddance's blocking power was proportional to its width. The lines all made direct, measurable sense.

"There's got to be some number involved," he said.

"I told you," Melody said. "It has to do with how well they are drawn. If you draw a unicorn that *looks* like a unicorn, it will last longer than one with bad proportions, or one that has one leg too short, or one that can't tell if it's supposed to be a unicorn or a lion."

"But how does it *know*? What determines a 'good' drawing or a 'bad' drawing? Is it related to what the Rithmatist sees in their head? The better a Rithmatist can draw what he or she envisions, the stronger the chalkling becomes?"

"Maybe," she said, shrugging.

"But," Joel said, wagging his spoon, "if that were the case, then the best chalkling artists would be the ones with poor imaginations. I've seen your chalklings work, and they're strong—they're also very detailed. I doubt that the system rewards people who can't imagine complicated images."

"Wow. You really get into this, don't you?"

"Lines of Making are the only ones that don't seem to make sense."

"They make perfect sense to me," she said. "The prettier the drawing is, the stronger it is and the better it's able to do what you tell it to. What's confusing about that?"

"It's confusing because it's vague," Joel said. "I can't understand something until I know *why* it happens the way it does. There *has* to be an objective point of reference that determines what makes a good drawing and what doesn't—even if that objective point of reference is the subjective opinion of the Rithmatist doing the drawing."

She blinked at him, then took another bite of ice cream. "You, Joel, should have been a Rithmatist."

"So I've been told," he said with a sigh.

"I mean seriously," Melody said, "who *talks* like that?"

Joel turned back to his own ice cream. After how much it

had cost, he didn't want it to melt and get wasted. To him, that was secondary to the flavor, good though it was. "Aren't those members of your cohort?" he asked, pointing at a group of Rithmatic students at a table in the corner.

Melody glanced over. "Yeah."

"What are they doing?" Joel asked.

"Looking at a newspaper?" Melody said, squinting. "Hey, is that a sketch of Professor Fitch on the front?"

Joel groaned. *Well, that reporter certainly does work quickly.*

"Come on," he said, downing his soda and shoving the last spoonful of ice cream in his mouth, then standing. "We need to find a copy of that paper."

LINES OF VIGOR
PART ONE: BASIC USAGE

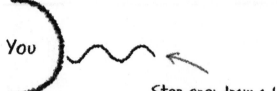

You

Enemy

Step one: draw a Line of Vigor,
starting outward and moving in.

When the chalk is lifted, if the
line completes at least two waveforms, it will
shoot straight out and continue on until
it strikes something.

If aimed correctly, the line will
leave an opponent's defense scarred
or broken. Note: it usually takes several
strikes in the same place to break through
a Line of Warding, depending on the circle's
strength. Most chalklings are easier to destroy.

(It is important to remember that Lines of Vigor CANNOT
affect real creatures or items. Only those made of chalk.)

CHAPTER

P rofessor Fitch,' " Melody read from the paper, " 'is a little
squirrel of a man, huddled before his books like they
were the winter's nuts, piled and packed carelessly in his
den. He's deceptively important, for he is at the center of the
search to find the Armedius Killer.' "

"Killer?" Joel asked.

Melody held up a finger, still reading.

Or, at least, that's what one source speculates. "Yes, we fear
for the lives of the kidnapped students," the unnamed source
said. "Every officer knows that if someone goes missing this
conspicuously, chances are good that they'll never be found.
At least not alive."

Professor Fitch is more optimistic. He not only thinks that
the children are still alive, but that they can be recovered—
and the secret to their whereabouts might have to do with the
discovery of some strange Rithmatic lines at the crime scenes.

"We don't know what they are or what they do," Professor Fitch explained, "but those lines are definitely involved."
He declined to show me these drawings, but he did indicate
that they weren't composed of any of the basic four lines.

Fitch is a humble man. He speaks with a quiet, unas-
suming voice. Few would realize that upon him, our hopes
must rest. For if there really is a Rithmatist madman on the

loose in New Britannia, then it will undoubtedly take a Rithmatist to defeat him.

She looked up from the paper, their empty ice cream dishes and soda glasses sitting dirty on the table. The parlor was growing less busy as many of the students left for Armedius to make curfew.

"Well, I guess now you know the whole of it," Joel said.

"That's it?" she said. "That's all you were talking about with the inspector?"

"That's pretty much it." The article contained some frightening details—such as the exact nature of Lilly's and Herman's disappearances, including the fact that blood was found at each scene. "This is bad, Melody. I can't believe that got printed."

"Why?"

"Up until now, the police and Principal York were still implying that Herman and Lilly might have just run away. Parents of Rithmatists at the academy guessed otherwise, but the people of the city didn't know."

"Well, it's best for them to know the truth, then," Melody proclaimed.

"Even if it causes panic? Even if ordinary people hide in their homes because they're afraid of a killer who may not exist, and who undoubtedly isn't going to hurt them?"

Melody bit her lip.

Joel sighed, standing. "Let's get back," he said, folding up the newspaper. "We have to make curfew, and I want to get this to Inspector Harding, just in case he hasn't seen it yet."

She nodded, joining Joel as he walked out onto the street. It felt darker now, and Joel again wondered at the wisdom of going out when there could be a killer about. Melody seemed to be in a similar mood, and she walked closer to him than she had before. Their steps were quick, their conversation nonexistent, until they finally arrived back at the gates to Armedius.

The same two officers stood at the entryway. As Joel entered, the campus clock beat fifteen minutes to the hour. "Where is Inspector Harding?" Joel asked.

"Out, I'm afraid," one of the men said. "Is there something we can help you with?"

"Give him this when he gets back in," Joel said, handing one of them the paper. The officer scanned it, his face growing troubled.

"Come on," Joel said to Melody, "I'll walk you back to your dorm."

"Well," she said, "aren't you chivalrous all of a sudden?"

They strolled down the path, Joel lost in thought. At least the article hadn't been belittling of Fitch. Perhaps the reporter had felt guilty for lying to him.

They reached the dormitory. "Thank you for the ice cream," Joel said.

"No, thank you."

"*You* paid for it," he said. "Even if you gave me the money first."

"I wasn't thanking you for paying," Melody said airily, pulling open the door to the dormitory.

"For what, then?" he asked.

"For not ignoring me," she said. "But, at the same time, for ignoring the fact that I'm kind of a freak sometimes."

"We're all freaks sometimes, Melody," he replied. "You're just . . . well, better at it than most."

She raised an eyebrow. "Very flattering."

"That didn't come out as I meant it."

"I'll have to forgive you then," she said. "How boring. Good night, Joel."

She vanished into the dormitory, door closing behind her. He slowly crossed the lawn, his thoughts a jumble, and found himself wandering around the Rithmatic campus.

He knew where most of the professors lived, so it was easy for him to determine which previously unused office probably housed Nalizar. Sure enough, he soon found the door bearing Nalizar's nameplate resting on the outside wall of Making Hall.

Joel loitered outside the hall, looking up at the dark second floor. Making Hall was the newest of the four, and had a lot more windows than the older ones. The windows of Nalizar's rooms were dark. Did that mean he wasn't in, or that he'd retired already?

Melody said that Nalizar wanted the books delivered to his office. They're probably sitting on his desk, or maybe waiting at the top of this stairwell. . . .

Joel found himself reaching for the doorknob.

He stopped himself. *What am I doing?* Was he really considering breaking into the professor's office? He needed to think before trying something so drastic. He walked away across the lawn. As he did, he heard something and turned.

The door to Nalizar's stairwell opened, and a figure with a dark cloak and blond hair stepped out. Nalizar himself. Joel felt his heart leap, but he was standing far enough away—and shadowed enough in darkness—that Nalizar didn't notice him.

The professor put on a top hat and strode off down the sidewalk. Joel felt his heart beating in his chest. If he had gone up those stairs, Nalizar would have caught him for sure. He took a few deep breaths, calming himself.

Then he realized that *now* he knew for certain that the professor was gone.

And if he returns quickly? Joel thought. He shook his head. If he *did* decide to sneak into the professor's room, he'd need to have more of a plan.

He kept moving, but didn't feel like going home. He was too awake. Eventually, he decided on a different course of action. There was someone he *knew* would be up late this night, someone he could talk to.

He knew all the normal places to check for his mother, and he tried those first. He didn't find her, but he *did* find Darm, one of the other cleaning ladies. She sent him to the right place.

It turned out that his mother was cleaning the dueling arena. Joel walked up to the door, which was propped open slightly, and peeked in. He heard the sounds of scrubbing echoing inside, so he pulled open the door and slipped in.

The dueling arena was in the middle of Making Hall and took up most of the central space in the building. The room's ceiling was of glass squares with iron supports between. Rithmatic duels, after all, were best watched from above. During the Melee, professors and local dignitaries watched from the best seats up there.

Joel had never seen that room, though he had been lucky enough to get a lower seat for a couple of the Melees. The room was shaped like an ice-skating rink. There was the playing field floor below—black so that chalk would show up well on it—with enough space for dozens of people to draw defensive circles at once. Seats ran around the outside, though there weren't ever enough for all the people who wanted to attend the Melee.

There were dueling competitions throughout the year, of course. The Melee, however, was the most popular. It was the last chance for the juniors to show off their skill before they were shipped to Nebrask for their last year of training. Winners in the Melee were given important posts in Nebrask, and would have a much better chance of becoming squad leaders and captains.

Joel's mother crouched on hands and knees in the middle of the room, scrubbing at the blackrock floor, a single springwork lantern beside her. She wore her hair tied back with a kerchief, her sleeves rolled up, her brown skirt dusty from crawling around.

Joel felt a sudden stab of anger. Other people went to plays, lounged in their rooms, or slept while his mother scrubbed floors. The anger immediately turned to guilt. While his mother scrubbed floors, he had been eating ice cream.

If I were a Rithmatist, he thought, *she wouldn't have to do this.*

Melody had spoken with disdain about the money and power many Rithmatists coveted. She obviously had no concept of what it was like to have to go without.

Joel walked down the steps between the bleachers, his steps echoing. His mother looked up. "Joel?" she said as he stepped onto the blackrock floor. "You should be getting ready for bed, young man."

"I'm not tired," he said, joining her and picking up the extra brush floating in her bucket. "What are we doing? Scrubbing the floor?"

She eyed him for a moment. Finally, she turned back to her work. She was far more lax with his sleep habits in the summer. "Don't ruin your trousers," she said. "The floor has a rough texture. If you aren't careful, you'll scuff your knees and fray the cloth."

Joel nodded, then began to work on a section that she hadn't yet scrubbed. "Why do we need to clean this place? It doesn't get used that often."

"It has to look good for the Melee, Joel," she said, brushing a stray lock of hair away from her face and tucking it behind her ear. "We have to apply a finish each year to keep the color dark. The playing field needs to be clean before we can do that."

Joel nodded, scrubbing. It felt good to be active, rather than just sorting through books.

"That girl seemed nice," his mother said.

"Who? Melody?"

"No, the *other* girl you brought over for dinner."

Joel blushed. "Yeah, I suppose. She's a bit strange."

"Rithmatists often are," his mother said. "I'm glad to see you with a girl, though. I worry about you. You always seem to have people to talk to, but you don't go out in the evenings. You have a lot of acquaintances. Not a lot of friends."

"You've never said anything."

She snorted. "One doesn't have to be a professor to know that teenage boys don't like hearing about their mothers' worries."

Joel smiled. "You have it easy with me. As teenage sons go, I'm not much of a headache."

They continued to work for a time, Joel still feeling annoyed that his mother should have to do such hard work. Yes, Rithmatists were important—they helped protect the Isles from the dangers in Nebrask. Yet, wasn't what his mother did important as well? The Master chose Rithmatists. Didn't he, in a way, choose cleaning ladies as well?

Why was it that people valued what his mother did so much

less than what someone like Professor Fitch did? She worked twice as hard as anyone Joel knew, and yet she gained no notoriety, no wealth or prestige.

Melody had wondered where his mother's money went, and it was a good question. His mother worked long hours. So where did their money go? Was his mother saving it all?

Or was there something else? An expense Joel had never considered. . . .

He sat upright, feeling a chill. "The principal didn't really give me free admittance to Armedius, did he? That's just what you tell me, to keep me from feeling guilty. You're paying for me to go here."

"What?" his mother asked, still scrubbing. "I could never afford that."

"Mother, you work double shifts most days. That money has to be going somewhere."

She snorted. "Even with double shifts, I couldn't afford *this* place. Do you have any idea how much in tuition most of those parents pay?"

Joel thought for a moment, remembering that Melody had spoken of a student who got ten dollars a week in *allowance*. If that much was simple spending money, then how much were they paying for the students to go to Armedius?

Joel didn't want to know.

"So, where *does* it go?" he asked. "Why work all these extra hours?"

She didn't look up. "Your father left more than a family behind when he died, Joel."

"What does that mean?"

"We have debts," she said, continuing to scrub. "It's really nothing for you to worry about."

"Father was a chalkmaker," Joel said. "His workroom was provided by the school, as were his materials. Where did he get debts?"

"From a lot of different things," she said, scrubbing a little bit harder. "He traveled a lot, meeting with Rithmatists and talking about their work. The springrail wasn't as cheap then as it is now.

Plus there were the books, the supplies, the time off to work on his various projects. He got some from Principal York, but he got the greater part from outside sources. The type of men who would lend money to a poor craftsman like your father . . . well, they aren't the kind of men you can ignore when they come asking for payment."

"How much?"

"It doesn't matter to you."

"I want to know."

His mother glanced at him, meeting his eyes. "This is *my* burden, Joel. I'm not going to have it ruining your life. You'll be able to start fresh and clean with a good education, thanks to Principal York. I'll deal with your father's problems."

Obviously, she considered that the end of the conversation. She turned back to her scrubbing.

"What did Father spend all that time working on?" Joel asked, attacking a section of floor. "He must have believed in it a lot, if he was willing to risk so much."

"I didn't understand a lot of his theories," she said. "You know how he would go on, talking about chalk composition percentages. He thought he was going to change the world with his chalk. I believed in him, Master help me."

The room fell silent, save for the sound of brushes against stone.

"It was his goal to send you to Armedius, you know," she said softly. "He wanted to be able to afford to send you here, to study. I think that's why Principal York gave you the scholarship."

"Is that why you always get so mad at me for not doing well in my classes?"

"That's part of it. Oh, Joel. Don't you see? I just want you to have a better life than we did. Your father . . . he sacrificed so much. He might have made it, too, if his blasted research hadn't ended up costing his life."

Joel cocked his head. "He got wounded in a springrail accident."

She paused. "Yes. That's what I meant. If he hadn't been out traveling on one of his projects, he wouldn't have been on the train when it derailed."

Joel eyed her. "Mother," he said. "Father *did* die from a spring-rail accident, didn't he?"

"You saw him in the hospital, Joel. You sat with him while he died."

Joel frowned, but couldn't dispute that fact. He remembered the sterile rooms, the physicians bustling about, the medications they gave his father and the surgeries they did on his crushed legs. Joel also remembered the forced optimism they'd all displayed when telling Joel that his father would get better.

They'd known he would die. Joel could see it now—they'd all known, even his mother. Only the eight-year-old Joel had hoped, thinking—no, *knowing*—that his father would eventually wake up and be just fine.

The accident had happened the third of July. Joel had spent the fourth—the day of inception—at his father's side. His stomach twisted inside. He'd held his father's hand as he died.

Trent hadn't ever woken up, despite the hundred prayers Joel had offered during that day.

Joel didn't realize he was crying until a teardrop splatted to the black stone in front of him. He wiped his eyes quickly. Wasn't time supposed to dull the pain?

He could still remember his father's face: kindly, set with affable jowls and eyes that smiled. It hurt.

Joel stood up, putting his brush back in the bucket. "Maybe I *should* go get some sleep," he said, and turned away, worried that his mother might see his tears.

"That would be for the best," his mother said.

Joel walked for the exit.

"Joel," she called after him.

He paused.

"Don't worry about things too much," she said. "The money, I mean. I have it under control."

You work yourself half to death, he thought, *and spend the*

rest of the time worrying yourself sick. I have to find a way to
help you. Somehow.

"I understand," he said. "I'll just focus on my studies."

She turned back to her scrubbing, and Joel left, crossing the green to their dorm. He climbed into bed without changing, suddenly exhausted.

Hours later, sunlight shining on his face, he blinked awake and realized that—for once—he'd fallen asleep with ease. He yawned, climbed out of the bed, and made it for when his mother got done with work in an hour or so. He changed into some clothing from the small trunk at the end of the bed.

The room was basically empty, otherwise. A dresser, the trunk, the bed. The room was so small that he could almost touch the walls opposite one another at the same time. Yawning, intending to make his way to the restroom at the end of the hall, he opened the door.

He stopped in place as he saw people rushing about in the hallway outside, talking excitedly. He caught the arm of one woman as she hurried past.

"Mrs. Emuishere?" he said. "What's going on?"

The dark-skinned Egyptian woman eyed him. "Joel, lad! Haven't you *heard*?"

"Heard what? I just woke up."

"A third disappearance," she said. "Another Rithmatist. Charles Calloway."

"Calloway?" Joel said. He recognized that name. "You mean . . . ?"

She nodded. "The son of the knight-senator of East Carolina, Joel. The boy was kidnapped right out of his family's private estate late last night. They should have listened to the principal, I say. Poor kid would have been far safer here."

"The son of a knight-senator!" This was bad.

"There's more," she said, leaning in. "There were deaths, Joel. The boy's servants—ordinary men, not Dusters—were found at the scene, their skin ripped off and their eyes chewed out. Like . . ."

"Like they were attacked by wild chalklings," Joel whispered.

She nodded curtly, then bustled off, obviously intent on sharing the news with others.

The son of a knight-senator kidnapped or killed, Joel thought numbly. *Civilians murdered.*

Everything had just changed drastically.

PART

THREE

INSTRUCTING CHALKLINGS

For some reason, chalklings made by humans have rather weak minds. They must be told exactly what to do at all times, or they will wander off. The glyphs used are not standard, and vary between Rithmatists. Meanings of glyphs, however, ARE standard.

1. Most Rithmatists draw the chalkling first.

2. They then add instructions via glyphs written beside the chalkling.

3. Once the instructions are finished, they vanish and the chalkling follows them.

SOME BASIC GLYPHS

↑   X   —   ↱   ↑
GO   ATTACK   WAIT   TURN   8⤶   Go for 8 heartbeats

Example of a glyph sequence:

↑ ↱↑ ↱↑ ↱↑ X
4 45 3 45 1 45

Joel ran across the campus to Professor Fitch's office. He knocked on the door and got no answer. So he tested the doorknob, and found it unlocked.

He pushed it open.

"Just a moment!" Fitch called. The professor stood next to his desk, quickly gathering up a bunch of scrolls, writing utensils, and books. He looked even more disheveled than usual, hair sticking up, tie askew.

"Professor?" Joel asked.

"Ah, Joel," Fitch said, glancing up. "Excellent! Please, come help me with these."

Joel hastened to help carry an armful of scrolls. "What's going on?"

"We've failed again," Fitch said. "There's been another disappearance."

"I know," Joel said, following Professor Fitch toward the door. "But what are *we* doing about it?"

"Don't you remember?" Fitch said, closing the door behind Joel, then hurriedly leading the way down the steps. "You suggested that we needed to see the crime scene before it was contaminated by police officers. As good as they are, they have no realistic understanding of Rithmatics. I explained this to Inspector Harding."

"Will they actually wait until we get there to look things over?"

"They can't start until Harding arrives," Fitch said. "And he's here at Armedius. The disappearance wasn't discovered until just a short time ago. And so, if we—"

"Fitch!" a voice called from ahead. Joel looked up to see Inspector Harding standing with a group of police officers. "Double-time, soldier!"

"Yes, yes," Fitch said, quickening his pace.

Harding gestured, and his police officers scrambled away. "I've told the engineer to hold the springrail," Harding said as Fitch and Joel joined him. "My men are securing the campus— no more Rithmatic students are going to leave this place without police protection until we know what is happening."

"Very wise," Fitch said as Harding and he strode toward the station. Joel hurried along behind, carrying the scrolls. Students had gathered on the green nearby to watch the police, and Joel caught sight of some familiar red curls among them.

"Hey!" Melody said, pushing through the students and rushing up to Joel. "What's going on?"

Joel winced as Professor Fitch turned. "Ah, Melody, dear. I left some defenses for you to trace in my office. You can work on that today while I'm gone."

"Tracing?" Melody demanded. "We're in the middle of a crisis!"

"Now, now," Fitch said. "We don't have all the facts yet. I am going to go see what is going on. However, *you* need to continue your education."

She glanced at Joel, and he shrugged apologetically.

"Come on, soldiers!" Harding said. "We must move quickly while the crime scene is still fresh!"

They left Melody behind. She watched with hands on her hips, and Joel had a feeling that he was going to have to listen to another tirade when he got back.

They arrived at the station, a large brick building that was open on the ends. Joel had rarely ridden one of the trains. Joel's grandparents lived on the same island, and a carriage trip to see them was cheaper. Other than them, there was little reason for him to leave the city, let alone the island.

He smiled in anticipation as he walked up the ramp behind Harding and Fitch. They had to fight traffic as the usual morning crowd of students moved down the ramp around them.

"You haven't shut down the station, Inspector?" Fitch asked, looking at the flood of students.

"I can't afford to," Harding said. "If this campus is going to become a haven for the students, we need to let them *get* here first. Many of the non-Rithmatists live off campus. I want to let as many of them as possible come here for refuge. Now that civilians have died, we don't know for certain if ordinary students are safe."

The three of them stepped into the rectangular brick station. Springrail trains hung beneath their tracks, and so the track was high in the air, about ten feet up; it ran through the building and out the ends. The train cars were long and slender, designed like ornate carriages.

The vehicle's clockwork engines sprouted from the tops of the first two train cars, wrapping around the track above like large iron claws. A group of workers labored above on catwalks, lowering down and attaching an enormous, drum-shaped spring battery onto the first engine. It had been wound in another location; it could take hours to wind a single drum. The powerful springs inside had to be strong enough to move the entire train. That was why chalklings to do the work were preferable.

Harding hurried Fitch and Joel onto the train, and they were followed by a set of policemen. The officers cleared out a few annoyed people from a cabin at the very front of the train, and there made space for Fitch, Harding, and Joel.

Joel sat down eagerly. The situation was gloomy—another student kidnapped, innocent people murdered—yet he couldn't banish the thrill of being able to ride the springrail. And in his own cabin, no less.

The train clanked and shook as the workers attached the spring drum above. Outside, Joel saw annoyed people leaving the train and going to stand out on the platform.

"You're evacuating the train?" Fitch asked.

"No," Harding said. "My men are just informing everyone on the vehicle that it will be canceling all stops until we reach East Carolina. Anyone who doesn't want to go there will have to get off and wait for the next train."

The drum locked into place with a powerful clamping sound. Then the workers moved down to the second car, and similar sounds came as they began to attach a second drum to the gear-work engine there. Joel imagined the massive springs and gears inside of the drums, incredibly taut with power just waiting to be released.

"Inspector," Fitch said, leaning forward. "Was it *really* Sir Calloway's son who was taken?"

"Yes," the officer said, looking troubled.

"What does it mean?" Fitch said. "I mean, for Armedius and the isle?"

The inspector shook his head. "I don't know. I've never understood politicians, Fitch. I'm a fighting man; I belong on the battlefield, not in a conference room." He turned to meet Fitch's eyes. "I *do* know that we'd better figure out what's going on, and quickly."

"Yes," Fitch said.

Joel frowned. "I don't understand."

Fitch eyed him. "Haven't you had classes on government?"

"Of course I have," Joel said. "Government was . . . uh, the class I failed last year."

Fitch sighed. "Such potential wasted."

"It wasn't interesting," Joel protested. "I mean, I want to learn about *Rithmatics,* not politics. Let's be honest, when am I *ever* going to need to know historical government theories?"

"I don't know," Fitch said. "Maybe right *now.*"

Joel winced.

"It's more than that, of course," Fitch said. "Joel, lad, school is about learning *to* learn. If you don't practice studying things you don't like, then you'll have a very hard time in life. How are you going to become a brilliant Rithmatic scholar and attend university if you don't learn to study when you don't feel like it?"

"I never really saw it that way."

"Well, perhaps you should."

Joel sat back. He'd only recently learned that there were liberal universities where non-Rithmatists studied Rithmatics. He doubted those universities would admit a student who had a habit of failing at least one class every term.

He gritted his teeth, frustrated with himself, but there was nothing he could do about years past. Perhaps he could change the future. Assuming, of course, the recent troubles didn't lead to Armedius getting shut down. "So why would New Britannia be in danger because of events at Armedius?"

"The Calloway boy was the son of a knight-senator," Harding said. "The Calloways are from East Carolina, which doesn't have its own Rithmatic school, so people there send their Rithmatists to attend Armedius. Some of the isles, however, complain that they have to pay for a school away from their own shores. They don't like entrusting their Rithmatists to another island's control, even for schooling."

Joel nodded. The United Isles were all independent. There were some things the isles all paid for together, like Rithmatists and the inspectors, but they weren't totally a single country—at least not like the Aztek Federation in South America.

"You're saying the knight-senator could blame New Britannia for his son's disappearance," Joel said.

Harding nodded. "Tensions are high, what with the trade problems between the northeastern coalition and the Texas coalition. Blast it all! I hate politics. I wish I were back on the front lines."

Joel almost asked why he *wasn't* still on the front lines, but hesitated. Something about Harding's expression implied that might not be a good idea.

Fitch shook his head. "I worry that all of this—the disappearing children, the strange drawings at the crime scenes—is all a cover-up to mask what just happened. The kidnapping of an influential knight-senator's son. This could be a political move."

"Or," Harding added, "it could be the move of some rogue organization trying to build its own force of Rithmatists. I've seen a well-drawn Line of Forbiddance stop bullets, even a *cannonball*."

"Hum," Fitch said. "Perhaps you're on to something there, Inspector."

"I hope I'm not," Harding said, pounding the armrest of his seat. "We can't afford to fight each other. Not again. The last time nearly doomed us all."

Wow, Joel thought, feeling cold. It had never occurred to him just how much Armedius might influence the politics of the world. Suddenly, the future of the school seemed a whole lot more weighty than it had just moments earlier.

The second drum locked into place, and the last of the annoyed commuters climbed out of the coaches. The track wound into the sky ahead; the line of steel was filled with crenellations where the teeth of the massive gears above would grip it and pull the train along. A sharp grating sound of steel against steel screeched from above as the engineer released the locking mechanism on the first gear drive, and the train began to move.

It went slowly at first, clicks sounding from the gears, the entire vehicle shaking. The train steadily gained speed, climbing out of the station and up the track into the air. There was something awe-inspiring about being above everything else. As the train gathered speed, it passed straight through the middle of the downtown skyline, rising over the tops of some of the shorter buildings.

People milled about on the streets, looking like dolls or tin soldiers jumbled together after a child forgot to clean them up. The springrail dipped down, moving toward another station— but didn't slow, passing through the center of the building without stopping.

Joel imagined he could see the annoyed expressions on the people waiting on the platforms, though they were just a blur as their train shot by. The train wove through the city, ignoring several more stops; then the track turned sharply south. In seconds they raced out across the water.

Jamestown was on the coast of New Britannia, and the few times Joel had ridden the springrail, it had been to go to the beach. Once with his father, back when times had been better. Once a few years after, with his mother and grandparents.

That trip hadn't been as fun. They'd all spent the time thinking of the one they'd lost.

Regardless, Joel had never actually crossed the waters. *My first time visiting another of the isles.* He wished it could be under more pleasant circumstances.

The track stood elevated by a series of large steel pillars, their bases plunging into the ocean. The water was relatively shallow between islands—perhaps a hundred feet deep—but even still, constructing the springrail tracks had been an enormous undertaking. New tracks were continually being laid, connecting the sixty isles in an intricate web of steel.

Up ahead, he saw a junction where five different tracks met up together. Two headed southwest, toward West Carolina and beyond, and another curved southeastward, probably heading toward the Floridian Atolls. None of them went directly east. There was talk of building a springrail line all the way to Europe, but the depths of the ocean made the project difficult.

Their train hit the loop of track that ran in a circle around the inside of the junction. They rounded this, Joel watching out the window, as the engineer threw a lever that raised a hooked contraption above the train. The hook tripped the proper latch, and a few seconds later they were shooting southward toward East Carolina.

Fitch and Harding settled back for the trip, Fitch looking through a book, Harding scribbling notes to himself on a pad. The earlier sense of urgency now seemed an odd counterpoint to their relaxed attitudes. All they could do was wait. While the isles were relatively close to one another, it still took several hours to cross the larger swaths of ocean.

Joel spent the time sitting and watching the ocean waves some fifty feet below. There was something mesmerizing about the way they crashed and churned. As the minutes passed, the train began to slow, the gears methodically running out of spring power.

Eventually, the train stopped, sitting still on its track above the water. The car shook, and a distant *clink* sounded as the second gear drive was engaged. Motion started again. By the time Joel spotted land, almost exactly two hours had passed from the time they left Armedius.

Joel perked up. What would East Carolina look like? His instincts told him that it wouldn't be all that different from New Britannia, since the two islands were next to one another. In a way, he was right. The green foliage and bushy trees reminded him a lot of his own island.

And yet, there were differences. Instead of concrete cities, he saw forested patches, often dominated by large manor houses that seemed to be hiding within the thick branches and deep greenery. They passed no towns larger than a couple dozen buildings. The train eventually began to slow again, and Joel saw another scattering of homes ahead. Not a town, really—more a set of wooded mansions distant enough from one another to feel secluded.

"Is the entire island filled with mansions?" Joel asked as the train descended.

"Hardly," Fitch said. "This is the eastern side—a favorite spot for country estates. The western side of the island is more urban, though it doesn't contain anything like Jamestown. You have to go almost all the way to Denver to find a city as magnificent."

Joel cocked his head. He'd never considered Jamestown magnificent, really. It simply *was*.

The train clinked into the station and stopped. Not many people got off, and most who did were police. The train's other occupants were apparently heading for the western side of the isle, where the train would soon continue.

Joel, Fitch, and Harding left their coach and walked into a muggy heat as workers began to change the spring drums atop the waiting train.

"Quickly now, men," Harding said, rushing down the steps and out of the station. His urgency seemed to have returned now that they were off the train. Joel followed, once again carrying

Fitch's scrolls and books, though he now had a large shoulder bag, borrowed from one of the police officers.

They crossed a gravel-strewn road, passing beneath the shade of the train above. Joel expected to take a carriage, but apparently the mansion in question was the enormous white one that stood just down the road. Fitch, Harding, and the other officers hurried toward it.

Joel wiped his brow with his free hand. The mansion had a large iron fence, much like the one at Armedius. Trees dotted the lawn, keeping most of the green shaded, and the front of the mansion sported stately white pillars. The lawn smelled freshly cut and was well-groomed.

Police officers scuttled about the front lawn, and a contingent of them stood guarding the gate. Near them gathered a large number of men in expensive suits and top hats. As Harding, Joel, and Fitch walked up the green toward the mansion, a couple of officers rushed over.

"I *really* need to institute the practice of saluting among police officers," Harding muttered as the men approached. "Everybody just seems so dusting informal."

"Inspector," one of the men said, falling into step beside them, "the area is secure. We've kept everyone out, though we cleaned away the bodies of the servants. We haven't entered the boy's room yet."

Harding nodded. "How many dead?"

"Four, sir."

"Dusts! How many witnesses do we have?"

"Sir," the police officer said, "I'm sorry . . . but, well, we're guessing those four men *were* the witnesses."

"Nobody saw anything?"

The police officer shook his head. "Nor heard anything, sir. The knight-senator himself discovered the bodies."

Harding froze in place on the lawn. "He was *here*?"

The police officer nodded. "He spent the night sleeping in his chambers at the end of the hallway—only two rooms down from where the boy was taken."

Harding glanced at Fitch, and Joel saw the same question in both of their expressions. *The perpetrator—whoever he is—could have killed the knight-senator with ease. Why, then, just take the son?*

"Let's go," Harding said. "Professor, I hope you're not disturbed by the sight of a little blood."

Fitch paled. "Well, uh . . ."

The three of them hustled up the marble steps to the front doors, which were made of a fine red wood. Just inside the white entryway, they found a tall man wearing a top hat, hands on a cane that rested tip-down on the floor in front of him. He wore a monocle on one eye and a scowl on his face.

"Inspector Harding," the man said.

"Hello, Eventire," Harding said.

"And who is this?" Fitch asked.

"I am Captain Eventire," the man said. "I represent Sir Calloway's security forces." He fell into step beside Harding. "I should say that we are *most* displeased by these events."

"Well, how do you think *I* feel?" Harding snapped. "Bubbly and happy?"

Eventire sniffed. "Your officers should have dealt with this issue long before now. The knight-senator is *irritated*, you might say, with your New Britannia police force for letting your problems spill over onto his estate and endanger his family."

"First of all," Harding said, raising a finger, "I'm a *federal* inspector, not a member of the New Britannia Police. Secondly, I can't very well bear the blame for this. If you will remember, *Captain*, I was here just last evening, trying to persuade the knight-senator that his son would be safer back at Armedius! That fool has nobody to blame but himself for ignoring my warnings." Harding stopped, pointing directly at Eventire. "Finally, Captain, I should think that your security force should be the first ones to draw your lord's 'irritation.' Where were all of *you* when his son was being kidnapped?"

Eventire flushed. They stared at each other before Eventire finally looked away. Harding began moving again, walking up the steps to the second floor. Joel and Fitch followed, as did Eventire. "These are your Rithmatists, I assume?"

Harding nodded.

"Tell me, Inspector," Eventire said, "why is it that the federal inspectors don't employ a Rithmatist full time? One should think that if your organization were really as important and capable as everyone claims, you would be prepared for events like this."

"We're not prepared," Harding said, "because dusting Rithmatists don't normally kill people. Now, if you'll *excuse* me, my men and I need to do some investigations. Look after your lord, Eventire, and stay out of my business."

Eventire stopped and waited behind, watching them go with obvious displeasure.

"Private security forces," Harding said once they were out of earshot. "No better than mercenaries. Can't trust them on the front lines; their loyalty only goes as far as the coin in their pockets. Ah, here we are."

Here they were indeed. Joel paled as they rounded a corner and found a small hallway marked with several splotches of blood. He was glad the bodies had been removed. The sight of the dried, brownish red stains was disturbing enough.

The hallway was white with white carpeting, which only made the red more stark. It was nicely decorated, with fancy-looking floral paintings on the wall. A small chandelier hung from the ceiling; its clockwork mechanism flickered, clicking softly.

"That fool," Harding said, surveying the bloodied carpet. "If only the knight-senator had *listened*. Maybe this will make the others listen to reason and send their children back to Armedius."

Fitch nodded, but Joel could see that the blood had unsettled him. The professor walked on shaky feet as Harding stepped up to one of the ranking police officers at the scene, a tall man with Aztek heritage. "What do we have, Tzentian?" Harding asked.

"Four bodies discovered in the hallway here, sir," the police officer said, pointing at the bloodstains. "Method of death seems consistent with chalkling attacks. The boy's room is over there." The officer pointed at an open doorway in the middle of the hallway. "We haven't gone in."

"Good," Harding said, walking around the bloodstains and moving to the doorway.

"Sir—" the officer said as Harding tried to step through the doorway.

Harding stopped flat as if he'd hit something solid.

"Sir, there's a Rithmatic line on the floor," Tzentian said. "You didn't want us to breach the scene, so we haven't removed it yet."

Harding waved for Fitch to approach. The professor walked on shaky feet, obviously trying not to look at the blood. Joel joined them, kneeling down beside the doorway. He reached out, pressing his hand against the air.

It stopped. Something pushed back, softly at first, then harder as he pressed. With a lot of effort, he could get a few hairs closer to the invisible wall, but never *quite* felt like he could touch it. It was like trying to press two magnets together with the same poles facing.

The hallway had a carpet, but the boy's room had a wood floor. The Line of Forbiddance was easy to see. It was broken in places, with holes large enough for chalklings to get through. At these points, Joel could reach his hand through and into the room.

"Ah, hum," Fitch said, kneeling beside Joel. "Yes." He pulled out a piece of chalk and drew four chalklings shaped like men with shovels. Watching closely, Joel could see the glyphs the professor wrote below each chalkling as he drew it, giving them instructions to march forward, then attack any chalk they discovered.

One at a time, the chalk drawings began to dig at the Line of Forbiddance. "There," Fitch said, standing. "That will take a few minutes, I'm afraid."

"Inspector," one of the officers said. "If you have a moment, you may want to see this."

Harding followed the officer a short way down the hallway. Joel stood. "You all right, Professor?"

"Yes, yes," Fitch said. "I just . . . well, I'm not good with things like this, you know. Part of why I never did well in Nebrask."

Joel nodded, then set his bag down and walked over to where the inspector knelt beside something on the floor. The bloodstain was shaped like a footprint.

"The prints lead down that direction," the officer was saying, "and out the back door. We lose them after that."

Harding studied the print, which was indistinct because of the carpet. "It'll be hard to tell anything from this."

The officer nodded.

"Are all the prints the same size?" Joel asked.

The officer glanced at Joel, as if noticing him for the first time. He nodded.

"That means there's probably only one person doing this, right?" Joel asked.

"Unless only one of them stepped in the blood," Harding said.

"What about other chalk drawings?" Joel asked. "Were there any besides the ones in the boy's room?"

"Actually, there are a few," the officer said. "One on either side of this hallway." He led them to a wall, set with the same looping pattern of swirls that had been drawn at the other scenes. Joel waved a hand in front of the pattern, but wasn't repelled or affected in any way.

"Professor?" Joel called, drawing Fitch's attention. The professor approached.

"Draw a chalkling on the wall here," Joel said, pointing. "Have it move through this pattern."

"Hum, yes. . . . Yes, very good idea, lad." Fitch began to draw.

"What is the point of this exercise?" Harding asked, standing with hands behind his back.

"If that pattern is really a Rithmatic sketch," Joel said, "then the chalkling will have to attack the chalk to get through it. If this pattern *doesn't* have any Rithmatic powers, then the chalkling will just be able to walk over it as if it weren't there."

Fitch finished his chalkling. The crab crawled across the wall in front of them, then hesitated beside the looping pattern. The chalkling appeared to consider, then took another step forward.

And stopped.

Joel felt a chill. It tried again, but was repelled. Finally, it began to claw at the looping pattern, digging through it quite easily.

"Well I'll be . . ." Fitch said. "It *is* Rithmatic."

"So?" Harding said. "Soldier, I'm at a *distinct* disadvantage in this area. What's going on?"

"There are only four Rithmatic lines," Fitch said. "So we assume." He looked thoughtful, as if considering something deep. "Joel, tell me. Do you think this could be a Line of Warding? After all, we didn't know about ellipses during the early years. Maybe this is just something like that."

"But why draw such a small Line of Warding? And on the wall? It doesn't make sense, Professor. Besides, the chalkling is breaking through *far* too easily for that to be a Line of Warding. If it is one, it isn't working very well at all."

"Yes . . ." Fitch said. "I believe you are right." He reached up, dismissing his chalkling. "Odd indeed."

"Didn't you say there was a second drawing on the wall?" Harding asked the police officer.

The man nodded, leading Harding and Joel to the other end of the hallway. There was another copy of the same swirling line at this end of the hallway.

Joel ran his fingers around the perimeter, then frowned.

"What is it, son?" Harding asked. "You look troubled."

"This one has a break in it," Joel said.

"It was attacked by a chalkling?"

"No," Joel said. "It doesn't look scraped. It just looks unfinished, like it was drawn too quickly." Joel looked down the hallway. "You found this drawing at Lilly Whiting's house. Which wall was it on there?"

"Does it matter?"

"I don't know. Maybe?"

"It was on the front outside wall of the house," Harding said. "Toward the street."

"And at Herman's house?"

"Outside his door," Harding said, "in the hallway."

Joel tapped the wall. "This is the first time that someone *other* than the Rithmatist has been harmed. The four dead men."

Harding nodded. "From the reports, they were probably up playing cards in the servants' kitchen."

"Where's the kitchen?" Joel asked.

Harding pointed down the stairs.

"This side of the hallway," Joel said. "Near the broken symbol. Maybe there's a connection."

"Maybe," Harding said, rubbing his chin. "You've got a good eye for this sort of thing, son. You ever consider becoming a police officer?"

"Me?" Joel said.

Harding nodded.

"Well . . . not really."

"You should think about it, soldier. We can always use more men with a good eye for detail."

An inspector. Joel *hadn't* given it any thought. More and more, he wanted to go study Rithmatics, as Fitch had suggested. But this . . . well, that was another option. He would never be a Rithmatist—he had accepted that years ago—but there were other things he could do. Exciting things.

"Inspector?" Fitch called. "The Line of Forbiddance is down now. We can go in."

Joel glanced at Harding, then together they crossed the hallway and walked into the room.

The SHOAFF DEFENSE

Note the use of
Lines of Forbiddance
only where absolutely
necessary to anchor
the defense.

This Defense is often used by
advanced Rithmatists who
specialize in Lines of Vigor.

The Shoaff Defense is a
nine-point defense which has a
focus on leaving the Rithmatist with
lots of open room to shoot Lines of
Vigor. It eschews the traditional use
of circles at the bind points, instead
using ellipses, which leave more room
open for the drawing of Vigor
Lines. Chalklings with long
tethers should be bound
to each ellipse.

The Shoaff is
versatile, but is
weak against
Lines of Vigor.

It is best
against a
strong
chalkling
offense.

This is interesting, for the defense is
itself good if one prefers to DRAW Lines
of Vigor.

B y the Master," Fitch breathed, standing just inside the doorway. Beyond was a short hallway that turned right, running a short distance into the room itself.

The hallway was *filled* with broken Rithmatic drawings. Circle upon Circle of Warding, dozens of Lines of Forbiddance. Joel looked on, amazed by the sheer amount of chalk on the floor.

"This looks like a battlefield," Harding said from the doorway. "I've seen it before. Not with chalk, of course—with men."

Joel looked at him. "What do you mean?"

"It's easy to see," Harding said, pointing. "The Calloway boy drew an initial circle near the doorway, then blocked off the sides with lines so he couldn't get surrounded. When his front was breached, he abandoned that circle, drawing another one behind it. Like an army slowly retreating on a battlefield."

"He was good," Joel said. "Those defenses are intricate."

"Yes," Fitch said. "I never had Charles in my class, but I heard much of him. He was supposed to be something of a trouble-maker, but his skill was unrivaled."

"The three kidnapped students had that in common," Joel said. "They were the best Rithmatic students in the school." He stepped forward—he could walk over the Lines of Warding that formed the circles, though the Lines of Forbiddance at the sides would block him if he tried to go through them.

"Please try not to step on any of the chalk," Fitch said, getting out rolls of paper and settling down to make sketches of each of the defensive lines. "Don't disturb anything!"

Joel nodded. There were a lot of small lines and dots that, when he looked closely, he could tell were the remnants of chalklings that had been destroyed. Inspector Harding motioned for his officers to remain outside the room, then edged around Fitch and carefully picked his way through the hallway with Joel.

"There," Harding said, pointing to the last circle in the line. "Blood."

Indeed there was. Just a few drops, like at the other scenes. Joel rounded the defense and whistled softly, squatting down.

"What?" Harding asked.

"Shoaff Defense," Joel said. "A nine-pointer. He got it right on, too." He reached over, picking up a slip of paper that lay discarded near the circle. It detailed the Shoaff Defense.

Joel held it up for the inspector. "Cheat sheet. Even with a pattern, it's hard to do a nine-pointer."

"Poor lad," Harding said, taking off his round policeman's hat and tucking it under his arm in respect. He looked back past the line of seven circles leading out of the room. "He put up one *dusting* good fight. Real trooper."

Joel nodded, glancing at those drops of blood. Again, there was no body. Like at the other scenes. Everyone assumed the students were being kidnapped, but . . .

"How did they get him out?" Joel asked.

The others looked at him.

"We had to go through a Line of Forbiddance at the doorway," Joel said. "If they're kidnapping the Rithmatists, how did they get him out of the room?"

"They must have redrawn the line," Harding said, scratching at his chin. "But it had holes in it, as if attacked. So they redrew it, then attacked it again? But why would they do that? To cover up taking the boy? Why bother? We're obviously going to know he was kidnapped."

None of them had an answer to that. Joel studied the defenses for a moment, then frowned, leaning closer to the broken, ripped Shoaff Defense. "Professor Fitch, you should look at this."

"What is it?"

"A drawing," Joel said. "On the floor—not a Rithmatic pattern. A picture."

It was done in chalk, but it looked like a charcoal drawing someone would do in art class. It was hastily done, more a silhouette than a real drawing. It depicted a man wearing a bowler hat and holding a long, oversized cane to his side, tip down against the ground.

The man's head seemed too big, and there was a large undrawn section on the face, like a gaping open mouth. It was smiling.

Beneath the picture were a few short, hastily written paragraphs.

I can't see his eyes. He draws in scribbles. Nothing he does keeps its shape. The chalklings are distorted, and there seem to be hundreds of them. I destroy them, and they return to life. I block them, and they dig through. I scream for help, but nobody comes.

He just stands there, watching with those dark, unseen eyes of his. The chalklings aren't like any I've seen. They writhe and contort, never keeping a single shape.

I can't fight them.

Tell my father that I'm sorry for being such a bad son. I love him. I really do.

Joel shivered, all three of them silent as they read Charles Calloway's final words. Fitch knelt and drew a chalkling on the ground, then used it to check the sketch, in case it was Rithmatic. The chalkling just walked over the picture, ignoring it. Fitch dismissed the chalkling.

"These paragraphs make little sense," Fitch said. "Chalklings that return to life after they're destroyed? Rithmatic shapes that don't hold their forms?"

"I've seen such things," Harding said. He looked up and met Fitch's eyes. "At Nebrask."

"But this is so far from there!" Fitch said.

"I don't think we can deny it any longer, Professor," Harding said, rising. "Something has escaped the Tower. It got here, somehow."

"But it's a *man* who is doing this," Fitch said, hands shaking as he tapped the drawing Charles had done. "That's no Forgotten shadow, Harding. It's in the shape of a person."

As Joel listened, he realized something: there was a *whole* lot more going on at Nebrask than people knew.

"What is a Forgotten?" Joel asked.

Both turned to him, then grew quiet.

"Never mind that, soldier," Harding said. "You're a great help here, but I'm afraid I don't have clearance to tell you about Nebrask."

Fitch looked uncomfortable, and suddenly Joel knew what Melody felt like, being excluded. He wasn't surprised, though. The details of what happened at Nebrask were kept nearly as quiet as the secrets of complex Rithmatics.

Most people were actually fine with that. The battlefield was a long way away, out in the central isles. People were content to ignore Nebrask. The fighting had been pretty much constant since the days of King Gregory, and it wouldn't ever go away. Occasionally there were deaths—but they were infrequent, and were always either Rithmatists or professional soldiers. Easily ignored by the general public.

Unless something managed to get out. Joel shivered. *Something strange is happening, even by Nebrask standards*, he thought, studying Harding and Fitch. Harding had spent over a decade on the battlefront, and he seemed dumbfounded by what was occurring.

Eventually, Harding returned to inspecting the room and Fitch returned to his drawing. Joel knelt, reading the paragraphs one last time.

He draws in scribbles. . . .

With some persuasion, Joel got Fitch to let him help do sketch replicas of the defenses. Harding went outside to organize his men to search for other information, such as signs of forced entry.

Joel drew quietly, using charcoal on the paper. Charcoal would have no Rithmatic properties, even if drawn by a Rithmatist, but it approximated chalk fairly well. The trouble was, no sketch would exactly re-create the drawings on the floor, with all of their subtle scratch marks and broken lines.

After Joel finished a few sheets, he walked over to Fitch, who was again studying the circle where Charles had made his final stand.

"Notice how he outlined the entire room in chalk to keep the chalklings from crawling around his lines by going on the walls?" Fitch said. "Very clever. Have you noticed, yet, that the format of this attack reinforces our thoughts on the previous ones?"

Joel nodded. "Lots of chalklings, attacking in mass."

"Yes," Fitch said. "And we have some evidence, now, that this attacker . . . this *Scribbler* . . . is probably a male, which lets us narrow our results. Would you mind going out and making copies of those swirling patterns on the walls so that we have several versions done by different hands? I suspect that will help us be more accurate."

Joel nodded, grabbing a roll of paper and some charcoal, then picking his way out. Most of the officers were down below, now. Joel hesitated in the doorway, looking back into the room.

Charles had blocked himself in, just like Herman. He had even drawn Lines of Forbiddance around the window, and those lines showed signs of being attacked from the outside. Perhaps he had intended to climb out, and had found his escape route blocked. He'd been out of options.

Joel shivered, thinking of the hours Charles must have spent during the night, resisting the chalklings with defense after defense, trying desperately to survive until morning.

Joel left the doorway and walked to the first of the two wall marks. This crime scene seemed to give more questions than answers. Joel put his paper up against the wall, then eyed the swirling pattern and began to do a sketch. It was—

Something moved in the hallway.

Joel spun, catching sight of it scuttling along the floor of the room, barely visible against the white carpet. A chalkling.

"Professor!" Joel yelled, charging after the thing. "Inspector Harding!"

The chalkling moved down the steps. Joel could barely see it against the white marble, and lost sight of it once he reached the base of the stairs. He glanced about, shivering, imagining it crawling up his leg and gnawing at his skin.

"Joel?" Fitch asked, appearing at the banister above.

There! Joel thought, catching sight of a flash of white as the chalkling crossed the wooden doorway and moved down the steps outside.

"A chalkling, Professor!" he yelled. "I'm chasing it."

"Joel! Don't be a fool! Joel!"

Joel was out the door, running after the chalkling. Some officers saw him immediately, and they charged over. Joel pointed at the chalkling, which was much easier to see now that it moved across grass, its lines conforming to the shape and contours of the blades much as a shadow would look when it fell on an uneven surface.

The police called for more backup, and Fitch appeared at the doorway of the building, looking frazzled. Joel kept running, barely keeping pace with the chalkling. The things were very fast and completely tireless; it would outdistance him eventually. But for the moment, he and the police kept up.

The chalkling reached the fence and shot underneath; Joel and the officers charged out the gate. The chalkling moved over to a large oak tree with thick branches, then—oddly—moved up the side of the trunk.

It was then that Joel finally got a good look at the shape of the chalkling. He froze.

"A unicorn?" *Oh no . . .*

The police officers piled around the base of the tree, looking up, lifting clockwork rifles. "You!" one called. "Come down *immediately!*"

Joel walked up to them. Melody sat in the tree. He heard her sigh dramatically.

"Bad idea?" she called down to him.

"You could say that," he replied.

Y ou *will* explain yourself," Harding said, standing with hands on hips.

Melody grimaced, sitting in a chair in the mansion's kitchen, her white skirt dirtied from climbing the tree. To the side, one of the police officers meticulously wound the gears in his rifle. The clicking sounds rang in the small kitchen.

"Is that really necessary?" Fitch asked, glancing at the gun.

"Please do not interrupt, Professor," Harding said. "You may understand Rithmatic study, but *I* understand spies."

"I'm not a spy!" Melody said. Then she paused. "Well, okay, yeah. I'm a spy. But only for myself."

"And what interest do you have in this operation?" Harding asked, placing his hands behind his back, walking in a slow circle around Melody. "What did you have to do with the deaths?"

She shot a glance at Joel, and he could see that she finally seemed to be realizing just how much trouble she might be in. "I didn't have *anything* to do with that! I'm just a student."

"You're a Rithmatist," Harding said. "These crimes were committed by a Rithmatist."

"So?" Melody said. "There are a lot of Rithmatists in the area."

"You have shown a persistent, undeniable interest in this investigation," Harding said.

"I'm curious!" Melody said. "Everybody *else* gets to hear what is going on. Why not me?"

"No questions from you," Harding said. "Do you realize that I have the power to imprison you until this investigation is over? Do you realize that you are now our *prime* suspect for having caused the murders?"

She paled.

"Inspector," Joel said. "Could I . . . talk to you? Outside, maybe?"

Harding eyed Joel, then nodded. The two of them left by the

side doors and went a little ways down, where they could speak in private.

"We'll go back in a few minutes," Harding said. "It'll be good for her to sweat a bit."

"Inspector," Joel said, "Melody *isn't* behind the murders or the kidnappings. Trust me."

"Yes," Harding said. "I suspect that you are right, Joel. However, I have to pursue every lead. That young woman puts me on edge. Makes me suspicious."

"She puts a lot of us on edge," Joel said. "But that doesn't mean she's the Scribbler. I mean, it's obvious how she got here. She *saw* us leave Armedius, and everyone knows who it was that got kidnapped. I can vouch for her."

"Are you *absolutely* sure you know her, Joel?" Harding asked. "How can you be sure she's not fooling you? Part of me keeps worrying that the person behind this is hiding right in front of us, moving about Armedius itself. It would be the best place for a Rithmatist to hide without looking suspicious."

Like Nalizar! Joel thought. *He left his rooms last night, going somewhere.*

But, then, how well *did* Joel know Melody? Could her silliness and friendship all be an act? Harding's suspicion got to Joel for just a moment. He realized he knew very little about Melody's past, or why her family didn't seem to care about what happened to her.

She was also genuine. She didn't hide her feelings—she belted them out, trumpeted them. She was straightforward with him. With everyone, it seemed.

And, he realized, he liked that about her.

"No," Joel said. "It's not her, Inspector."

"Well, a vote of faith from you means a lot, in my estimation."

"You'll let her go, then?"

"After just a few more questions," Harding said, walking back toward the kitchen. Joel followed.

"All right," Harding said, entering. "Joel has vouched for you, young lady, and that makes me more likely to listen to what you have to say. But you are *still* in serious trouble. Answer my questions, and perhaps I won't have to bring charges against you."

She glanced at Joel. "What questions?"

"My men reported that you sent a chalkling all the way to the building," Harding said. "How in the name of the *Master* did you manage such a thing?"

She shrugged. "I don't know. I just did."

"Dear," Fitch said, "I know many of the most skilled Rithmatists in the world. The string of glyphs you'd need to use in order to instruct a chalkling to cross that distance, climb the stairs, then go to the room . . . Why, that list would be incredible! I had no idea you had that kind of ability."

"What was the point?" Harding asked. "Why make a chalkling go all that way, then come back? Were you *trying* to get caught?"

"Dusts, no!" Melody said. "I just wanted to know what was going on."

"And you expected a *chalkling* to tell you?"

She hesitated. "No," she finally admitted. "I just . . . well, I lost control of it, all right? I made it to distract some of the officers."

Joel frowned. *She's lying*, he thought, noticing how she looked down when she spoke. As he'd noted earlier, she was genuine, and her lie was easy to see.

She's strangely good with chalklings, he thought. *She wouldn't have lost control of that one.* But . . . did that mean that she *did* expect it to report to her on what it found? Chalklings couldn't talk. They were like springwork creatures—they didn't think beyond what they were told to do.

Yet that unicorn chalkling had fled directly back to Melody.

"Chalklings *do* act very strangely sometimes, Inspector," Fitch said.

"Believe me," Harding said, "I'm aware of this. I heard that excuse from Rithmatists every week on the battlefield. I'm amazed you people can ever make them do *anything*, considering how often they simply go off in the wrong direction for no reason."

Melody smiled wanly.

"You, young lady, are still suspicious," Harding said, pointing.

"Inspector," Fitch said. "Really. We now know from the drawing above that the Scribbler is a man, or at least a woman dressed very convincingly as one. I doubt Melody could have managed that, and I'm certain there are those who can vouch for her location last night."

Melody nodded eagerly. "I have two roommates in my dormitory room."

"Beyond that, Inspector," Fitch said, raising a finger, "the description we discovered in Charles's room indicated that the kidnapper's Rithmatic lines act very oddly. I have seen Miss Muns's lines, and they are quite normal. To be honest, they're often rather poorly drawn."

"Fine," Harding said. "You may go, Miss Muns. But I *will* be keeping an eye on you."

She sighed in relief.

"Excellent," Fitch said, standing from his chair. "I have more sketches to complete. Joel, would you walk Melody to the station? And, uh, make certain she doesn't get into any more trouble along the way?"

"Sure," Joel said.

Harding went back to his work, though he did assign two officers to go with Joel and Melody, making certain she left the building. She went sullenly, Joel trailing along behind, and she gave the officers a world-class scowl once they reached the door.

The police remained inside; Joel strolled along the lawn outside with Melody.

"That," she declared, "was decidedly *less* than enjoyable."

"What did you expect," Joel asked, "spying on a crime scene?"

"They let *you* in."

"What's that supposed to mean?"

She looked up at the sky, then shook her head. "I'm sorry. I just . . . well, it's frustrating. It seems like every time I want to be involved in something, I'm told that's the *one* thing I can't do."

"I know how you feel."

"Anyway," Melody said, "thanks for vouching for me. I think you kept that vulture from ripping me apart."

He shrugged.

"No, really," she said. "I'll make it up to you. I promise."

"I'm . . . not sure if I want to know what that will entail."

"Oh, you'll enjoy it," she said, perking up. "I've got an idea already."

"Which is?"

"You have to wait!" she said. "No spoiling surprises."

"Great." A surprise from Melody. That would be wonderful. They neared the station, but didn't enter, instead sticking to the comfortable shade of the trees as they waited for Fitch. Melody tried to get Joel to talk some more, but he found himself giving uninvolved answers.

He kept thinking of that hurried picture with the frightened words beneath it. Charles Calloway had known he was going to die, yet he'd left notes on as much as he could figure out. It was noble—probably more noble than anything Joel had ever done in *his* life.

Someone needs to stop this, he thought, leaning back against a tree trunk. *Something needs to be done.* It wasn't just the students, not just Armedius, who were in danger. Ordinary people had been killed. And if what Fitch and Harding said was true, these kidnappings were threatening the stability of the United Isles themselves.

It comes back to those strange chalk drawings, Joel thought. *That looping pattern. If only I could remember where I saw it before!*

He shook his head and glanced at Melody. She was sitting on a patch of grass a short distance away. "How *did* you do it?" he asked. "With that chalkling, I mean."

"I just lost control of it."

He gave her a flat stare.

"What?" she said.

"You're obviously lying, Melody."

She groaned, flopping back on the grass, staring up at the trees. He figured she was probably going to ignore the question.

"I don't *know* how I do it, Joel," she said. "Everyone in classrooms always talks about instructing the chalklings, and about how they are completely without will themselves, like clockwork. But . . . well, I'm not really that good at the instructional glyphs."

"Then how do you make them obey so well?"

"They just *do*," she said. "I . . . well, I think they understand me, and what I want of them. I explain what I want, then they go do it."

"You *explain* it?"

"Yeah. Little whispers. They seem to like it."

"And they can bring you information?"

She shrugged, which was an odd gesture, considering that she was lying down. "They can't talk or anything. But the way they move around me, the things they do, well . . . yeah, sometimes I feel like I can understand what they mean." She rolled her head to the side, looking at him. "I'm just imagining things, aren't I? I just *want* to be good with chalklings to make up for the fact that I'm bad with the other lines."

"I don't know. I'm the last person who could tell you about chalklings. As far as I'm concerned, they probably *do* listen to you."

She seemed to find that comforting. She smiled, staring up at the sky until Professor Fitch arrived. Apparently Harding was going to stay at the mansion to investigate more. Joel found himself glad to be returning to Armedius. He hadn't eaten anything all day, and his stomach had begun to rumble.

They walked into the station and climbed up onto the empty platform, waiting for the next train.

"This adds some very disturbing elements to our situation," Fitch said.

Joel nodded.

"Wild chalklings," Fitch continued. "Unknown Rithmatic lines . . . I think that, perhaps, I shall need to have you begin helping me look through some of the more obscure Rithmatic texts. There *has* to be mention of things like this somewhere in the records."

Joel perked up, feeling a surge of excitement. Yet it was dulled by the realities of their situation. He glanced at Melody, who stood behind them, probably too far to hear; she obviously felt sheepish around Fitch since she'd been caught spying.

"Troubled times," Fitch said, shaking his head as the track began to shake, a train approaching. "Troubled times . . ."

A short time later, they were riding back across the waters and toward Armedius.

NINE-POINT CIRCLES

Nine-point circles are the most complicated and difficult of Rithmatic circles to draw. Unlike the two-, four-, and six-point circles, the nine-point circle's points are NOT equidistant from one another. The points are actually relative to an imagined triangle within which the circle is drawn. For every non-obtuse triangle, one can draw a circle inside it that will pass through nine significant points.

The midpoint of each side of the triangle leads us to three of the points.

Rithmatists who use nine-point circles generally practice over and over until they can intuit the locations of the points.

The altitude of each triangle side gives us the other six points.

Many Rithmatists never master drawing the nine-point, for if even one of the points is off, it can weaken the entire defense.

T he first European encounters with wild chalklings are
the subject of some debate, the book read.

Joel sat with his back to the brick wall of Professor
Fitch's office. "The subject of some debate" was a terrible under-
statement. So far—despite a week of studying—he hadn't been
able to find two sources that agreed about when the first wild
chalklings had been sighted.

This is because of the poor recordkeeping practices maintained by many who traveled westward across the oceans
after initial contact was made between Aztek ships and the
Old World.

Though many of these early explorers—such as Jacques
Cartier and the infamous Francisco Vásquez de Coronado—
worked on the behalf of European nations, they truly sought
personal fame or fortune. This was a time of expansionism
and exploration. The American Isles presented an unknown
landscape to conquer, control, and—hopefully—use.

There were already rumblings of war in Asia at this time,
and the JoSeun Empire was beginning to flex its muscles.
Many an enterprising man realized that if he could get a foothold in the New World, he might be able to establish himself
as independent, freed from the oppression—either perceived
or actual—of his European masters.

After being rebuffed by powerful South American empires—which had been galvanized by centuries of warfare and struggles against the chalklings—the explorers turned to the isles. They were never told what dangers would await them. The Aztek nations were very xenophobic and reclusive during this era.

The Tower of Nebrask is, of course, a central feature in early records. Of obviously ancient date, the Tower was one of the wonders of the islands, as it was the only freestanding structure of apparent human design to be discovered there.

Numerous explorers described the Tower. Yet these same explorers would swear that the next time they returned to Nebrask, the Tower would be gone. They claim that it moved about the island, never quite being in the same place as it was before.

Obviously, these reports are to be taken with skepticism. After all, the Tower now appears perfectly stable. Still, there are some legitimate oddities. The total lack of human life on the isles should have been a clue that something was wrong in America. Someone built the Tower of Nebrask; someone once occupied the islands. Had it been the Azteks?

They would not speak of Nebrask, only to call it an abomination. So far, their records provide no insight. They used an acid made from local plants to fight the chalklings that tried to gain a foothold in their lands, and they accepted refugees from the islands, but they themselves did not explore northward. Of those purported refugees—now some five hundred years integrated into Aztek culture—their stories are completely oral, and have deteriorated over time. They tell legends and speak of terrible horrors, of bad luck and omens, and of nations slaughtered. But they give no details, and each story seems to contradict its fellows.

Early North American explorers do say they happened across an occasional native on the isles. Indeed, many of the names of the islands and cities they bear come from such early reports. Once again, questions pile atop one another. Were these natives Azteks, or the remnants of some other culture?

If some peoples had lived on the isles, as Aztek legends claim, what happened to the signs of their cities and towns?

Some of the early settlers reported feeling an almost eerie emptiness to the isles. A haunted, troubling stillness. We can only conclude that there must be some truth to Aztek stories—that the peoples who lived here before us were driven southward. Either that or destroyed by the wild chalklings, as we almost were.

In this author's opinion, the Estevez report seems the most trustworthy and accurately dated of all the early European chalkling sightings, even if it is disturbing in concept.

Joel slid the book closed, leaning his head back against the wall and rubbing his eyes with the fingers of one hand. He knew about the Estevez report—he'd just read of it in another book. It spoke of a group of Spanish explorers searching for gold who had crossed into a strange, narrow canyon on one of the southwestern isles—Bonneville or Zona Arida or something like that.

These explorers—led by Manuel Estevez—had found a group of small, human-shaped pictures on the canyon walls. Primitive figures, like one might find in caves left by long-ago inhabitants.

The explorers had camped there for the night, enjoying the quiet stream and shelter from the winds. However, not long after sunset, they reported that the pictures on the walls began to dance and move.

Estevez himself had described the drawings in great detail. Most importantly, he had insisted that the drawings weren't scratched or carved, but instead drawn in a whitish, chalky substance. He had even done drawings of the figures and put them in his log, which survived to the present day.

"Joel, lad," Fitch said, "you look exhausted."

Joel blinked, looking up. Fitch sat at his desk, and from the dark circles under his eyes, Joel figured the man must feel at least twice as tired as Joel did. "I'm all right," Joel said, battling a yawn.

Fitch didn't look convinced. The two of them had spent the past week searching through tome after tome. Fitch mostly assigned Joel the historical books, as the high-level texts were simply beyond Joel's abilities. Joel intended to learn and to study until he *could* figure out those books. For the moment, it was better for him to focus on other subjects.

Inspector Harding was pursuing the investigation to track down the kidnapper. That wasn't a job for Joel and Fitch; they were scholars. Or, well, Fitch was. Joel still wasn't certain what he himself was. Other than *tired*, of course.

"Anything of note in that book?" Fitch asked hopefully.

Joel shook his head. "It mostly talks about other reports and comments on their validity. It is a fairly easy read. I'll keep going and see if there's anything useful."

Fitch was convinced that if there were other Rithmatic lines, there would be mentions of them in such records. Drawings, like Estevez had done, lost in time but now suddenly relevant.

"Hey," Joel said, noticing what Fitch was reading, "are those my notes about the census reports?"

"Hum? Oh, yes. I never did get a chance to go over these."

"You probably don't need to worry about it now. I doubt those death records will be all that helpful."

"Oh, I don't know," Fitch said, leafing through the pages. "Perhaps this isn't the first time events like the ones here have occurred. What if there were other such disappearances, but they were so isolated that they were never connected? We just . . ."

He trailed off, holding up one of the sheets.

"What?" Joel asked. "Did you find something?"

"Hum? Oh, no, I didn't." Fitch quickly put the sheet back down. "I should get back to work on my other reading. . . ."

Fitch, Joel decided, was a terrible liar. Probably came from the man's inability to stand confrontation of any type. So what had Fitch seen on that sheet that had caught his attention? And why didn't he want to mention it to Joel?

Joel was trying to figure out a way to inconspicuously glance at the stack of sheets on Fitch's desk when the door at the end of the narrow chamber opened and Melody entered. Her class with Fitch had ended a half hour ago. Why had she returned?

"Melody?" Fitch asked. "Did you forget something?"

"Hardly," she said, leaning against the doorway frame. "I'm here on official business."

"Official?" Fitch asked.

"Yeah," she said, holding up a slip of paper. "Nalizar still has me running errands after classes, you know. By the way, I've realized that my sorry state is *completely* your fault, Joel."

"Mine?"

"Sure," she said. "If you hadn't gotten yourself into trouble visiting all those Rithmatic classes, then I wouldn't have had to end up running all over campus every afternoon like a windup toy. Here's your note, Professor—it says the principal wants Joel to come to the office."

"Me?" Joel asked. "Why?"

She shrugged. "Something about your grades. Anyway, I have more menial, tedious, obnoxious busywork to be about. See you at dinner?"

Joel nodded, and she took off. He walked over to take the note, which she'd stuffed between two books. Grades. He knew that he should have felt alarmed, but something as mundane as grades seemed distant to him at the moment.

The note had been sealed shut, of course, but Joel could see where Melody had pried it open on the side to peek in. He walked over to grab his book bag. "I'm going to go, then."

"Hum?" Fitch said, already absorbed in a book. "Ah, yes. Very well. I will see you tomorrow."

Joel walked past the desk—and quickly scanned what Fitch had been reading—on his way out. It was one of the census lists of students who had graduated Armedius in a given year. Joel had marked the ones who had died suspiciously. There were two of these, but Joel didn't recognize either name as being all that important. Why, then . . .

He almost missed it, just like last time. Exton's name was at the top of the list, among the graduates from the general school that year. Was that what Fitch had noticed, or was it just a coincidence?

Outside, Joel crossed the green, heading toward the office.

Armedius had changed during the last seven days. The police were far more plentiful now, and they checked identification at the front gates and the springrail station. Rithmatic students weren't allowed off campus without an escort. He passed several nearby, grumbling that Armedius was starting to feel like a prison.

He also passed a group of regular students playing soccer on the field. Their efforts seemed subdued, and there were far fewer of them than before. Most parents of ordinary students had pulled their children out of the academy for the summer, and they were being allowed to continue to do so. While non-Rithmatists had been killed now, it was clear that the Rithmatists were still the targets. Normal students should be safe off campus.

There hadn't been another disappearance since Charles Calloway. A week had passed, and everyone just seemed to be waiting. When would it come? What would happen next? Who was safe and who wasn't?

Joel hurried along, passing closer to the front gates. Outside them was one of the other big changes at the academy.

Protesters.

They carried signs. GIVE US THE TRUTH. DUSTERS ARE DANGEROUS! SEND THEM TO NEBRASK!

Numerous editorialists around the Isles had decided that the deaths of the four Calloway servants had been the fault of the Rithmatists. These editorialists saw some sort of hidden war—some called it a conspiracy—between sects of Rithmatists. There were even those who thought that all of it—the existence of Rithmatists, the inception ceremony, the fight at Nebrask—was a giant hoax used to keep the Monarchical Church in power.

And so, a small—but very vocal—group of anti-Rithmatist activists had set up a vigil outside the front of Armedius. Joel didn't know what to make of such nonsense. He *did*, however, know that several homes of Rithmatic students—all of whom were now staying full-time at the school—had been vandalized in the night. The policemen at the gates, fortunately, kept most troublemakers away from Armedius. Most of them. Two nights ago, someone had tossed in a series of bricks painted with epithets.

Joel didn't stop to listen to the protestors, but the sounds of their chanting followed him. "We want the truth! Stop Rithmatist privilege! We want the truth!"

Joel hurried up the path to the office. Two rifle-bearing policemen stood at the sides of the doorway, but they knew Joel and let him enter.

"Joel!" Florence said. "We didn't expect you to come so quickly." Despite the grim circumstances on the rest of the campus, the blonde clerk insisted on wearing a bright yellow summer dress, complete with a wide-brimmed sun hat.

"Of course he came quickly," Exton said, not looking up from his work. "*Some* people don't ignore their responsibilities."

"Stop being such a bore."

Joel could see over the counter to a newspaper lying on Florence's desk. CRISIS IN NEW BRITANNIA! the top headline read.

"The principal is seeing someone right now, Joel," Florence said. "I'm sure he'll be done soon."

"How are things holding up here?" Joel asked, glancing out the window toward the police officers.

"Oh, you know," Florence said. "Same as always."

Exton snorted. "You seem perfectly willing to gossip other times. Why the coy face now?"

Florence blushed.

"The truth is, Joel," Exton said, setting down his pen and looking up, "things are *not* good. Even if you ignore those fools at the gates, even if you don't mind tripping over a police officer every other step, things are bad."

"Bad how?" Joel asked.

Florence sighed, folding her arms on her desk. "The islands without Rithmatic schools are talking about starting their own."

Joel shrugged. "Would that be such a disaster?"

"Well, for one thing, the quality of education would plummet. Joel, hon, Armedius isn't just a school. It's one of the few places where people from all across the Isles work together."

"Jamestown is different from most cities," Exton agreed. "In most of the world, you don't see JoSeun people and Egyptians mixing. On many isles, if you're a foreigner—even an American from just a few isles over—you're considered an outsider. Can you imagine what will happen to the war effort in Nebrask if sixty different schools—each training Rithmatists in different ways—begin squabbling over who gets to defend what section of land? It's hard enough with eight schools."

"And then there's the talk of what these schools should be like," Florence said, eyeing her newspaper. It was from Maineford, one of the isles to the north. "The editorials make Rithmatists sound like they aren't even really people. A lot of people are calling for the Rithmatists to be pulled out of ordinary classes and be trained only to fight at Nebrask. Like they're nothing but bullets, to be wound up in a gun and then fired."

Joel frowned, standing quietly beside the counter. From her desk, Florence *tsk*ed to herself and turned back to her work.

"Brought it on themselves, they did," Exton said from his place, speaking almost to himself.

"Who?" Joel asked.

"The Rithmatists," Exton said. "Being so exclusive and secretive. Look how they treated you, Joel. Anyone they don't deem *worthy* enough to be on their level, they simply shove aside."

Joel raised an eyebrow. He sensed some pretty strong bitterness in Exton's voice. Something having to do with his days as a student at Armedius, perhaps?

"Anyway," Exton continued, "the way the Rithmatists treat others makes the common people—who pay for this place—begin to wonder if the Rithmatists really need such a fancy school and pensions for the rest of their lives."

Joel tapped the counter with his index finger. "Exton," he said, "is it true that you went to Armedius?"

Exton stopped writing. "Who told you that?"

"I saw it," Joel said, "in the graduation records when I was working on a project for Professor Fitch."

Exton sat quietly for a moment. "Yes," he finally said. "I was here."

"Exton!" Florence said. "You never told me! Why, how did your family manage to pay for your tuition?"

"I don't want to talk about it," Exton said.

"Oh, come on," Florence said.

Exton stopped writing, then stood up. He took his coat and bowler hat off their hooks on the wall. "I'll take my break now, I think."

With that, he left the building.

"Grouch," Florence called after him.

A short time later, the door to the principal's office opened and Inspector Harding walked out, blue suit pressed and neat as always. He picked up his rifle, which he'd left sitting outside the principal's office, then slung it over his shoulder.

"I will see about those patrols," Harding said to Principal York. "We won't let something like the brick incident occur again, sir, I assure you."

York nodded. Harding seemed to regard the principal with quite a bit of respect—perhaps because the principal looked like a battlefield general, with his large frame and drooping mustache.

"I have the most up-to-date list for you, Inspector," Florence said, standing and handing him a sheet.

Harding scanned it, face going slightly red.

"What is it?" Principal York asked.

Inspector Harding looked up. "An oversight on my part, sir. There are still *fourteen* Rithmatist students whose parents refuse to send them to the academy for protection. That is unacceptable."

"It's not your fault that parents are stubborn, Inspector," York said.

"I make it my responsibility, sir," Harding said. "If you'll excuse me." He walked out of the room, nodding to Joel as he passed.

"Ah, Joel," Principal York said. "Come in, son."

Joel crossed into the principal's office and, once again, sat down in the chair before the overly large desk, feeling like a small animal looking up at a towering human master.

"You wanted to talk to me about my grades, sir?" Joel asked as York sat down.

"Actually, no," York said. "That was an excuse that you will forgive, I hope." He folded his arms before him on the desk. "Things are happening on my campus, son. It's my job to keep an eye on them all as best I can. I need information from you."

"Sir?" Joel said. "With all due respect, I'm just a student. I don't know how much help I can be. I don't really like the idea of spying on Professor Fitch, anyway."

York chuckled. "You're not spying, son. I had Fitch in here yesterday, and I just talked to Harding. I trust both men. What I really want is unbiased opinions. I need to *know* what is happening, and I can't be everywhere. I'd like you to tell me about the things you've seen and done while working with Fitch."

And so, over the next hour, Joel did so. He talked about the census studies, his experience visiting the scene of Charles Calloway's disappearance, and the things he'd read. York listened. As the hour progressed, Joel found his respect for the principal growing.

York *did* care, and he was willing to listen to the opinions and thoughts of a simple, non-Rithmatic student. As Joel neared the end of his explanation, he tried to decide if he should mention his suspicions about Nalizar. He eyed the principal, who had gotten out his pen and had begun scribbling notes as Joel spoke.

"All right," York said, looking up. "Thank you, Joel. This is precisely what I needed."

"You're welcome, sir," Joel said. "But . . . well, there is one other thing."

"Yes?"

"Sir," Joel said. "I think Nalizar might have something to do with all of this."

York leaned in. "What makes you say that?"

"Nothing really substantial," Joel said. "Coincidences, really. Nalizar showing up when he did mixed with some of the things he'd done."

"Such as?"

Joel flushed, realizing how foolish he sounded. He was sitting in the principal's office, accusing one of the men York himself had hired.

"I . . ." Joel said, his eyes dropping. "I'm sorry, sir. I spoke out of turn."

"No you didn't. I'm suspicious of Nalizar too."

Joel looked up with a start.

"I can't decide," York said, "if it's simply my *dislike* of the man that is making me react this way, or if there is more. Nalizar has spent a lot of time in the office trying to find out more about the investigation. I keep asking myself if that's because he wants to know how much *we* know, or if he's just jealous."

"Jealous?"

York nodded. "I don't know if you realize this or not, but Professor Fitch is gaining quite a bit of notoriety. The press got hold of his name, and now he's mentioned in nearly every article having to do with the disappearances. Apparently, he's the federal inspectors' 'secret weapon against the kidnappers.'"

"Wow," Joel said.

"Either way," York continued, "I wish I'd never hired Nalizar. He has tenure, however, and firing him would be very difficult—and I really have no proof he is involved. So I ask again: What specifically makes you suspect him?"

"Well," Joel said, "do you remember what I told you about new Rithmatic lines? I saw Nalizar checking out a book from the library that was *about* new Rithmatic lines and their possible existence."

"Anything else?"

"He left his building the other night," Joel said. "The night Charles Calloway was kidnapped. I was out walking and saw him."

York rubbed his chin. "You're right," he said. "That's hardly compelling evidence."

"Principal," Joel said. "Do you know why Nalizar is even here? I mean, if he's such a great hero at Nebrask, then why is he at a school teaching rather than fighting the wild chalklings?"

York studied Joel for a few seconds.

"Sir?" Joel finally asked.

"I'm trying to decide if I should tell you or not," the principal said. "To be honest, son, this is somewhat sensitive information."

"I can keep a secret."

"I don't doubt that," York said. "It's still my responsibility to decide what I tell and what I don't." He tapped his fingers together. "There was an . . . *incident* at Nebrask."

"What kind of incident?"

"The death of a Rithmatist," York said. "Regardless of what many people here in the east claim, a death at Nebrask is *always* treated with solemnity by the war cabinet. In this case, there were lots of fingers pointed, and it was decided that some men—such as Nalizar—would be better off reassigned to nonactive duty."

"So he killed someone?"

"No," York said, "he was involved in an incident where a young Rithmatist was killed by the wild chalklings. Nalizar was never implicated, and shouldn't have been, from what I read. When I interviewed him for his job here, Nalizar blamed political forces for trying to save their own hides from a blemish on their records. That sort of thing is common enough that I believed him. Still do, actually."

"But . . ."

"But it's suspicious," York agreed. "Tell me, what do these new lines you discovered look like?"

"Can I have a pen?"

York loaned him one, then gave him a sheet of paper. Joel drew the swirling, looping pattern that had been discovered at all three crime scenes. "Nobody knows what it is, but at least we know that it *is* Rithmatic now."

York rubbed his chin, holding up the paper. "Hum . . . yes. You know, it's strange, but this looks oddly *familiar* to me for some reason."

Joel's heart skipped a beat. "It does?"

York nodded. "Probably nothing."

Why would he have seen it? Joel thought. *Principal York hasn't studied Rithmatics. What do the two of us have in common? Just the school.*

The school, and . . .

Joel looked up, eyes widening as he remembered—finally—where he'd seen that pattern before.

LINE STRENGTHS

Lines of Forbiddance have strength based on how straight the line is. Their stability is based on the material they are drawn upon, and the height their force wall extends depends on the width of the line.

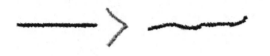

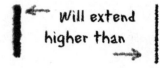

Will extend higher than

Lines of Warding have strength based on how even the line is, and how sharp the curvature is. (So a circle is equally strong all around, but an ellipse has varying strength.)

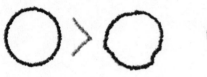

Will be stronger where it curves more than a circle, and be weaker where it curves less than one.

Lines of Vigor have strength based on how large the curve of their wave is.

Is stronger, but harder to draw, than

Lines of Making have strength based on the complexity, creativity, and asthetic beauty of the chalkling that is drawn.

Joel left the office, giving a rushed farewell to York and Florence. He didn't tell anyone what he'd just realized. He needed to confirm it for himself first.

Joel took off down the path toward the dormitory building, moving at a brisk walk. He resisted running—with how tense the campus was, that would probably draw more attention than he wanted.

Unfortunately, he caught sight of Melody walking back down the path toward the office, her deliveries apparently finished. He winced, ducking to the side. But of course she saw him.

"Joel!" she called. "I have decided that I'm *brilliant*!"

"I don't have much time right now . . ." he said as she rushed over to him.

"Blah, blah," she said. "Look, I've got something *exciting* to tell you. Aren't you thrilled!"

"Yeah," Joel said, starting down the pathway again. "I'll talk to you about it later."

"Hey!" Melody said, then pulled up beside him. "Are you trying to ignore me again?"

"Again?" Joel said. "I've never tried to ignore you."

"Yeah, right."

"Look, during those first weeks, weren't you mad at me because you thought I was *stalking* you?"

"Past, gone, dead," she said. "No, listen, this is *really* important. I think I found a way for you to become a Rithmatist."

Joel nearly tripped over his own feet.

"Ha!" Melody said. "I figured that would get your attention."

"Did you say that just to get me to stop?"

"Dusts, no. Joel, I *told* you, I'm brilliant!"

"Tell me about it as we walk," Joel said, moving again. "There's something I need to check on."

"You're strange today, Joel," she said, catching up to him.

"I've just figured something out," he said, reaching the family dormitory building. "Something that's been bugging me for a long time." He climbed the steps up to the second floor, Melody tagging along behind.

"I don't appreciate being treated like this, Joel," she said. "Don't you realize that I've spent days and days working on a way to pay you back for vouching for me in front of Harding? Now, I come to tell you, and you repay me by running about like a crazy man? I'm starting to take it personally."

Joel stopped, then sighed, looking toward her. "We've discovered new kinds of Rithmatic lines at each of the crime scenes where students were kidnapped."

"Really?"

"Yeah. One of them looked familiar to me. I couldn't remember why, but Principal York just said something that reminded me of where I'd seen it. So I'm going to make sure."

"Ah," she said. "And . . . once you're done with that, you'll be able to give proper attention to my *stunning, brilliant, amazing* announcement?"

"Sure," Joel said.

"Fair enough," she said, tagging along as he continued down the hallway to the room he shared with his mother. He pushed inside, then went to the dresser beside the bed.

"Wow," Melody said, peeking into the room. "You sleep here, eh? It's, uh, cozy."

Joel pulled open the top drawer of the dresser, which was filled with knickknacks. He began to rummage in it.

"Where are the rest of your rooms? Across the hallway, here?"

"No, this is it," Joel said.

"Oh. Where does your mother live?"

"Here."

"You *both* live in this room?" Melody asked.

"I use the bed during the nights; she uses it during the days. She's out today, though, visiting her parents. It's her day off." *She takes precious few of those.*

"Incredible. You know, this is way smaller than my dormitory room. And we all complain about how tiny they are."

Joel found what he was looking for, pulling it out of the dresser.

"A key?" Melody asked.

Joel pushed past her, rushing to the stairwell. She trailed behind. "What's the key for?"

"We didn't always live in that room," Joel said, passing the first floor and continuing on to the basement. The door he wanted was at the bottom of the stairwell.

"So?" Melody asked as he unlocked the door.

He looked at her, then pushed the door open. "We used to live here," he said, pointing toward the room beyond.

His father's workshop.

The large chamber was filled with shadowed shapes and a dusty scent. Joel walked in, surprised at how familiar the place felt. He hadn't stepped foot past that door in eight years, yet he knew just where to find the wall lamp. He wound it, then twisted the gear at the bottom, making it begin to hum and shine out light.

Illumination fell on a dusty room filled with old tables, stacks of limestone blocks, and an old kiln used for baking sticks of chalk. Joel walked reverently into the room, feeling his memories tingle and shake, like taste buds encountering something both sour and sweet.

"I slept over there," he said, pointing to the far corner. A small bed stood there, and a couple of sheets hung from the ceiling, arranged so that they could be pulled to give him privacy.

His parents' bed was in the other corner, with similar hanging sheets. Between the two "rooms" was furniture—some chairs, chests of drawers. His father had always talked about building walls to split the shop into rooms. After he'd died, they hadn't been able to fit any of the furniture in the new room, so Joel's mother had just left it.

Joel smiled faintly, remembering his father humming as he smoothed chalk at his table. Most of the chamber had been dedicated to the workshop. The cauldrons, the mixing pots, the kiln, the stacks of books about chalk composition and consistency.

"Wow," Melody said. "It feels . . . peaceful in here."

Joel crossed the room, feet scraping the dusty floor. On one of the tables, he found a line of chalk sticks running the entire spectrum of colors. He slid a blue one off the table and rubbed the length of chalk between his fingers, the coating on the outside keeping his fingers from getting color on them. He walked over to the far side of the room, the one opposite the beds. There, hung on the wall, were chalk formulas detailing different levels of hardness.

The chalk formulas were surrounded by pictures of the different Rithmatic defenses. There were dozens of them, drawn by Joel's father, with notations along the sides explaining who had used them and during which duel. There were newspaper clippings about famous duels, as well as stories on famous duelists.

Trent's voice drifted into Joel's head from memory. His father reading out loud about those duels, explaining to Joel with excitement about brilliant plays. Remembering that enthusiasm brought back a menagerie of other memories. Joel pushed those aside for the moment, focusing on something else. For in the middle of all those formulas, defenses, and newspaper clippings was a particularly large sheet of paper.

Drawn on it was the looping Rithmatic pattern they'd found at each of the crime scenes.

Joel breathed out slowly.

"What?" Melody asked as she stepped up beside him.

"That's it," Joel said. "The new Rithmatic line."

"Wait, your *father* is the kidnapper?"

"No, of course not. But he knew, Melody. He borrowed money; he took time off; he visited with Rithmatists at all eight schools. He was working on something—his passion."

Melody glanced to the side, looking over the clippings and the pictures. "So *that*'s why," she whispered.

"Why what?"

"Why you're so fascinated by Rithmatics," she said. "I asked you once. You never answered. It's because of your father."

Joel stared at the wall, with its patterns and defenses. His father would talk about them at length, telling Joel which defenses were good against which offensive structures. Other boys had played soccer with their fathers. Joel had drawn defenses with his.

"Father always wanted me to attend Armedius," Joel said. "He wanted so badly for me to turn out to be a Rithmatist, though he never said anything. We drew together all the time. I think he became a chalkmaker so that he'd be able to work with Rithmatists."

And he'd done something wonderful. A new Rithmatic line! It hadn't been discovered by men like Fitch or Nalizar, Rithmatists with years of experience. It had been discovered by Joel's father, a simple chalkmaker.

How? What did it mean? What did the line even do? So many questions. His father would have notes, wouldn't he? Joel would have to search them, tracking his father's studies during his last days. Discover how this was related to the disappearances.

For the moment, Joel reveled. *You did it, Father. You accomplished something none of them did.*

"All right," Joel said, turning to Melody, "what is your big news?"

"Oh," she said. "It's kind of hard to declare it properly now. I don't know. I just . . . well, I've been doing some studying."

"Studying?" Joel asked. "You?"

"I study!" she said, hands on hips. "Anyway, you shouldn't complain, because it was about you."

"You studied about me? Now who's the stalker?"

"Not about you personally, idiot. It was about what happened to you. Joel, your inception was handled wrong. You are *supposed* to go into the chamber of inception."

"I told you," Joel said, "Father Stewart said I didn't need to."

"He," Melody said, raising a hand dramatically, "was *dead* wrong. Your eternal soul could be in danger! You weren't incepted. The ceremony was botched! You need to do it again."

"Eight years later?"

"Sure," Melody said. "Why not? Look, the Fourth of July is less than a week away. If we can convince the vicar that you are in peril of losing your soul, he might let you try again. The right way, this time."

Joel considered that for a moment. "You sure I can go through it again?"

"Positive," Melody said. "I can find you the references."

I'm too old. But . . . well, King Gregory became one after he was eight. So, maybe I could too. He smiled. "That might actually be worth a try."

"I *knew* you'd appreciate it," Melody said. "Tell me I'm a genius."

"You're a genius," Joel said, then glanced back at the pattern on the wall. "Let's go get Fitch. I want him to see this. We'll worry about the vicar later."

F rom what I can tell," Fitch said, sitting at a chair beside a table in the middle of the workshop, "your father was *convinced* that there were other Rithmatic lines. Here, look at this."

Fitch pulled a page from the stack of books and old papers. Over the last few hours, Joel and Melody had helped him organize the workshop and sort through Joel's father's papers. The workshop almost seemed to be in use again.

The page fluttered as Fitch handed it over to Joel. It looked like some kind of legal document.

"That," Fitch said, "is a contract of patronage."

"Valendar Academy," Joel said. "That's in the Californian Archipelago, isn't it? One of the other schools that trains Rithmatists?"

Fitch nodded. "There are four of those sheets in here, each from one among the eight schools, including Armedius. They promise your father and his family patronage for a period of one hundred years should he prove the existence of a Rithmatic line beyond the original four."

"Patronage?" Melody asked.

"Money, dear," Fitch said. "A stipend, rather large. With such an income from *four* different schools, Joel's father would have become a very wealthy man. I must say, I'm astounded at the level of your father's understanding of Rithmatics! These writings are *quite* advanced. I should think the other professors would be very surprised to discover these things. I now realize that we never gave him the credit he deserved."

"He convinced someone," Joel said, pointing at the contract of patronage.

"Ah, yes. Indeed, it appears that he did. He must have worked hard, and presented some *very* convincing evidence, to get those contracts. From what I can see here, he researched with the various schools. He even went to Europe and Asia to meet with scholars and professors there."

And in doing so, racked up quite a large number of debts, Joel thought, sitting down on the stool beside the worktable-turned-desk that Fitch was using.

"But he found the line," Melody said, pointing at the drawing on the wall. "So why didn't he get rich?"

"He couldn't make it work," Fitch said, digging out a sheet of paper. "Just as we haven't been able to. I draw that line exactly, and it doesn't do anything. The kidnapper knows something we don't."

"So it's meaningless," Joel said. "My father didn't know anything more than we do. He figured out that other lines existed—he even managed to draw a replica of one—but couldn't make it work."

"Well," Fitch said, sorting through the papers. "There is one important point here, a theory from your father as to why the symbol didn't work. You see, there is a group of scholars who believe that a Rithmatic line functions based on the Rithmatist's *goals* in drawing it. They point to the fact that if we write words in chalk—or even doodle in chalk—nothing comes to life unless we're specifically attempting to do a Rithmatic drawing. None of the straight lines in the alphabet accidentally turn into Lines of Forbiddance, for example.

"Therefore, the Rithmatist's *desires* affect what he draws. Not in a quantifiable way—for instance, a Rithmatist can't simply *wish* his Lines of Forbiddance to be stronger. However, if a Rithmatist doesn't intend to draw a Line of Forbiddance, the line simply won't work."

"So, the reason you couldn't make the swirl pattern do anything . . ." Joel said.

"Was because I don't know what it's *supposed* to do," Fitch said. "Your father believed that unless he could match the proper type of line with the knowledge of what it did, nothing would come of it."

Fitch pulled out another sheet. "Some laughed at him for that, I fear. I, um, vaguely remember some of these incidents. At one point, your father convinced some Rithmatists to draw his lines—I wasn't involved, and didn't pay much attention at the time, or I might have remembered his interest in new Rithmatic lines earlier. But he wasn't able to make those lines do anything, even though he had a large number of possible intentions for them to try out. From his writings here, he saw that as a major defeat."

There was a loud sigh from the floor, where Melody lay, listening and staring up at the ceiling. *She must have to launder her skirts daily,* Joel thought, *considering how much she likes to sit on the floor, and climb trees, and lie on the ground.*

"Bored, dear?" Fitch asked her.

"Only mildly," Melody said. "Keep going." Then, however, she sighed again.

Fitch raised an eyebrow toward Joel, who shrugged. Sometimes, Melody just liked to remind everyone else that she was around.

"Regardless," Fitch said, "this is a wonderful discovery."

"Even if it doesn't tell us what the line does?"

"Yes," Fitch replied. "Your father was meticulous. He gathered stacks of texts—some of them quite rare—and annotated them, listing any that contained hints or theories about new Rithmatic lines. Why, it's almost like your father looked forward in time and saw *just* what we needed for this investigation. His notes will save us months!"

Joel nodded.

"I daresay," Fitch said, almost to himself, "we really *should* have taken Trent far more seriously. Yes indeed. Why, the man was a closet genius. It's like discovering that your doorman is secretly a scholar of advanced springwork theory and has been building a working Equilix in his spare time. Hum . . ."

Joel ran his fingers across one of the volumes, imagining his father working in this very room, crafting his chalk, all the while thinking on Rithmatic wonders. Joel remembered sitting on the floor, looking up at the table and listening to his father hum. He remembered the smell of the kiln burning. His father baked some of his chalks, while he dried others in the air, always searching for the ideal composition, durability, and brightness of lines.

Melody sat up and brushed some curly red hair out of her eyes. "You all right?" she asked, watching him.

"Just thinking about my father."

She sat there for a time, looking at him. "So," she finally said, "tomorrow is Saturday."

"And?"

"The day after that is Sunday."

"All right. . . ."

"You need to talk to the vicar," she explained. "You have to get him to agree that you should be allowed to go through the inception."

"What's this?" Fitch asked, looking up from a book.

"Joel's going to be incepted," Melody said.

"That wasn't done when he was eight?" Fitch asked.

"Oh, it was," Melody said. "They screwed it up. We're going to make them let him do it again."

"I doubt we can *make* them do anything, Melody," Joel said quickly. "I don't even know if this is the right time to worry about that."

"The Fourth of July is *next week*," Melody said. "If you miss it, then you'll have to wait an entire year."

"Yes, well," Joel said. "There are much bigger things to worry about right now."

"I can't believe this!" Melody said, flopping back down. "You spend your entire life mooning over Rithmatics and Rithmatists, and now you have your chance to become one, and you're just going to ignore it?"

"It's not *that* good of a chance," Joel said. "I mean, only one in a thousand get chosen anyway."

Fitch was watching with interest. "Now, wait. Melody, dear, what *exactly* makes you think they'll let Joel try again?"

"He didn't get to go into the chamber of inception," Melody said. "So, he couldn't . . . well, you know."

"Ah," Fitch said. "I see."

"*I* don't," Joel noted.

"It's not fair," Melody said, staring up at the ceiling. "You've seen how good he is at Rithmatics. He never even had a chance. He should get a chance."

"Hum," Fitch said. "Well, I'm no expert on church procedure. I think, however, you will have a difficult time convincing the vicar to let a sixteen-year-old young man take part in an inception ceremony."

"We'll make it work," Melody said stubbornly, as if Joel didn't have a say in the matter at all.

A shadow darkened the doorway. Joel turned to see his mother standing outside, on the landing at the bottom of the stairwell. "Oh," he said, noting her stunned look. "Um . . ."

"Mrs. Saxon," Fitch said, standing. "Your son has made a *wonderful* discovery."

She walked into the room, wearing her blue travel dress, her hair tied back.

Joel watched her with trepidation. What would she think of

them invading the chamber she'd locked up and left behind so long before?

She smiled. "It's been years," she said. "I thought about coming back down, but I always worried that it would hurt too much. I worried it would remind me of him." She met Joel's eyes. "It *does* remind me of him, but it doesn't hurt. I think . . . I think it's time to move back in here."

TYPES of CHALKLINGS

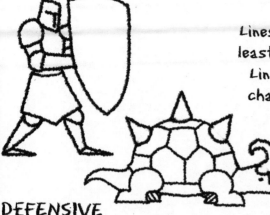

DEFENSIVE CHALKLINGS

Lines of Making continue to be the least quantifiable of the Rithmatic Lines. It appears that the type of chalkling drawn affects its ability to follow instructions. For instance, a chalkling shaped like a Knight is generally stronger when bound to a defensive point than when it is sent to attack. A chalkling with large claws or teeth is good for attacking, but weak at defense. Large, bloated chalklings can take more hits from a Line of Vigor, but are slow to move. Chalklings with lots of legs can move quickly, but often can't chew through enemy lines as quickly.

OFFENSIVE CHALKLINGS

Good for absorbing hits

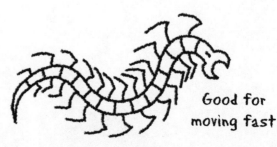

Good for moving fast

Joel sat in the broad cathedral hall, arms resting on the back of the pew in front of him, head resting on his arms, thoughts refusing to rest at all.

"The Master gave life to the lifeless," Father Stewart proclaimed, droning on at his sermon. "We are the lifeless now, needing his atoning grace to restore light and life to us."

Light shone through the stained glass windows, which were each set with a clock that ticked away the time. The main window—a brilliant blue circular one—was inset with the most magnificent clock on the island, the gears and spindles themselves formed of stained glass.

The pews filled the nave of the cathedral, with a single aisle running down the center. Above them, in the reaches of the domed cathedral interior, statues of twelve apostles watched over the crowd of devout. The statues moved occasionally, their internal clockwork mechanisms giving them a semblance of life. Life from the lifeless.

"The bread of life," Father Stewart said, "the water of life, the power of the resurrection."

Joel had heard it all before. Priests, he had long since noted, had a distinct tendency to repeat themselves. This day, Joel was finding it even more difficult than usual to pay attention. It seemed strange to him—even unsettling—that his life should have intersected so keenly with the important developments at

Armedius. Was it fate that had placed Joel where he was? Was it instead the will of the Master, as Father Stewart spoke of so often?

He looked up at the stained glass windows again. What would it mean for the church if public opinion turned against the Rithmatists? Several of the windows depicted King Gregory, the Monarch in Exile. He was always surrounded by Rithmatic drawings.

Cut into the stonework of the walls were interlocking patterns of circles and lines. While the building itself had the shape of a cross, the center where the cathedral arms met was circular, set with pillars marking the points on a nine-point circle.

Apostles watched, and the Master himself was symbolized on the rood. A statue of Saint da Vinci drew circles, gears, and Rithmatic triangles before itself on the ground. He had been canonized and adopted into the Monarchical Church, even though—or perhaps because—he had been a rebel Christian.

Even the most oblivious of men knew of the connection between Rithmatics and the Monarchical Church. No man gained Rithmatic powers without first agreeing to be incepted. They didn't have to stay faithful—in fact, they didn't even have to profess belief. They simply had to agree to be incepted, thereby taking the first step toward salvation.

Muslims called Rithmatics blasphemy. Other Christian churches grudgingly accepted the necessity of the ceremony, but then disputed that it proved the Monarchical Church's authority. The JoSeun people ignored the religious side of the experience, remaining Buddhist despite their inceptions.

However, no man could deny that without the Monarchical Church, there would be no Rithmatics. That simple fact allowed the church—once on the brink of extinction—to eventually become the most powerful in the world. Would the church stand up for the Rithmatists if the public tried to bring them down?

Joel's mother sat next to him, listening devoutly to the sermon. She and Joel had spent the previous day moving back down into the workroom. It hadn't taken very long; they didn't own much. Every time Joel stepped into the workroom, though, he felt as if he were eight years too old and about two feet too tall.

Something poked Joel in the back of the neck. He started, then turned around, surprised to find Melody sitting on the bench behind him. She'd been on the other side of the building when he'd last seen her.

"He's almost done," she hissed. "You going to ask him, or should I?"

Joel shrugged noncommittally.

A few moments later, she slid onto the bench beside him. "What's up with you?" she asked quietly. "I thought this was everything you ever wanted."

"It is," he whispered.

"You don't sound like it. You've been dragging your feet ever since I told you my plan! You act like you don't *want* to be in-cepted."

"I do, I just . . ." How could he explain? "It's stupid, Melody, but I'm worried. For so long, I've defined myself by the fact that I *missed* the opportunity to become a Rithmatist. Don't you see? If this works, but I'm still not chosen, I won't have that to fall back on anymore."

Joel had studied, learning the patterns and defenses, follow-ing in the footsteps of his father. But all the while, he'd been able to feel secure in the knowledge that he wasn't a failure or a reject. He'd simply missed his chance, and for a good reason.

Joel hadn't destroyed his father's hopes for a Rithmatist child. Joel couldn't be blamed if he hadn't had an opportunity, could he?

"You're right, that *is* silly," Melody said.

"I'll go through with it," Joel replied. "I just . . . It makes me feel sick. That's all."

Logically, he saw problems in that reasoning. One couldn't be "blamed" for not being a Rithmatist. Still, logic didn't always change the way a person felt. He'd almost rather be left with the *possibility* that he could have been a Rithmatist than find out for certain.

Melody's insistence that he try again dug up all of the old fears.

Father Stewart finished his preaching. Joel bowed his head for the ritual prayer. He didn't hear much of what Stewart said. By the time the "amen" was spoken, however, he'd made up his mind. If there was a chance for him to become a Rithmatist, he was *not* going to lose it. Not again.

He shoved down his nervousness and stood up.

"Joel?" his mother asked.

"Just a second, Mom," he said. "I want to talk to the vicar." He rushed away, Melody quickly joining him.

"I will do it," Joel said. "You don't need to."

"Excellent," Melody said, for once not wearing her school uniform. Instead, she wore a white dress that was quite fetching. It came down to her knees, showing off quite a bit of leg.

Focus, Joel thought. "I still don't think this will work."

"Don't be so pessimistic," she said, eyes twinkling. "I've got a few tricks planned."

Oh dear, Joel thought.

They arrived at the front of the nave and stopped before Father Stewart. The vicar glanced at them, adjusting his spectacles, the miter on his head waggling. The large headdress was yellow—like his robes—and was marked with a nine-point circle circumscribing a cross.

"Yes, children?" Father Stewart asked, leaning forward. He was growing quite old, Joel realized, and his white beard came almost all the way down to his waist.

"I . . ." Joel faltered momentarily. "Father, do you remember my inception?"

"Hum, let me see," the aged man said. "How old are you, again, Joel?"

"Sixteen," Joel said. "But I wasn't incepted during the usual ceremony. I . . ."

"Ah yes," Stewart said. "Your father. I remember now, son. I performed your inception myself."

"Yes, well . . ." Joel said. It didn't feel right to outright accuse the aged priest of having done it wrong.

To the sides, other people were lining up—there were always those who wanted to speak to Father Stewart after the sermon. Candles burned atop candelabra near the altar, flickering in the wind of opening doors, and footsteps echoed in the great hall of the building. Beyond the altar, at the back of the cathedral, sat the chamber of inception, a small stone room with doors on either end.

Melody nudged him.

"Father," Joel said, "I . . . don't want to be disrespectful, but I'm bothered by my inception. I didn't go into the chamber."

"Ah yes, child," Stewart said. "I can understand your worry, but you needn't fear for your salvation. There are places all over the world where the church isn't prominent enough to warrant a full cathedral, and they have no rooms of inception there. Those people are just as well off as we are."

"But they can't become Rithmatists," Joel said.

"Well, no," Stewart said.

"I didn't have a chance," Joel said. "To become one, then. A Rithmatist."

"You *did* have a chance, son," Stewart said. "You simply were unable to take it. Child, too many people dwell on this issue. The Master accepts both Rithmatists and non-; all are the same to him. To be a Rithmatist is to be chosen for service—it is not meant to make a man powerful or self-centered. To seek after such things is a sin that, I fear, too many of us ignore."

Joel blushed. Stewart seemed to consider the conversation over, and he smiled warmly at Joel, laying a hand on his shoulder and blessing him. The priest then turned toward the next patron.

"Father," Joel said, "I want to take part in the inception this week."

Father Stewart started, turning back. "Son, you're far too old!"

"I—"

"That doesn't matter," Melody said quickly, cutting Joel off. "A man can be incepted at any age. Isn't that true? It mentions so in the Book of Common Prayer."

"Well," Stewart said, "that usually refers to people who convert to our Master's gospel after the age of eight."

"But it *could* refer to Joel," she said.

"He's already been incepted!"

"He didn't get to go through the chamber," Melody said stubbornly. "Don't you know about the case of Roy Stephens? *He* was allowed to be incepted during his ninth year since he was sick the Fourth of July."

"That happened all the way up in Maineford," Stewart said. "A completely different archdiocese! They do some odd things there. There's no reason to incept Joel again."

"Except to give him a chance to be a Rithmatist," Melody said.

Father Stewart sighed, shaking his head. "You seem to have studied the words well, child, but you don't understand the meanings. Trust me; I know what is best."

"Oh?" Melody said, voice rising as he turned away again. "And why don't you tell Joel why it *really* is that you didn't let him into the chamber of inception eight years ago? Perhaps because the north wall was being worked on due to water damage?"

"Melody," Joel said, taking her arm as she grew belligerent.

"What if the Master wanted Joel to be a Rithmatist?" she continued. "Did you consider that when *you* denied him the opportunity? All because you were renovating your cathedral? Is a boy's soul and future worth that?"

Joel grew more and more embarrassed as Melody's voice rang through the normally solemn chamber. He tried to hush her, but she ignored him.

"I, for one," Melody said very loudly, "think this is a *tragedy*! We should be eager to encourage a person who wants to be a Rithmatist! Will the church side with those who are turning against us? Won't its priests *encourage* a boy who seeks to do the will of the Master? What's *really* going on, Vicar?"

"All right, hush, child," Father Stewart said, holding his forehead. "Enough yelling."

"Will you let Joel be incepted?" she asked.

"If it will shut you up," Father Stewart said, "then I will seek permission from the bishop. If he allows it, Joel can be incepted again. Will that satisfy you?"

"For now, I suppose," Melody said, folding her arms.

"Then go with the Master's blessing, child," Father Stewart said. Then, under his breath, he added, "And whatever demon sent you my way will likely be promoted in the Depths for giving me such a headache."

Melody grabbed Joel's arm and towed him away. His mother stood a short distance down the aisle between the pews. "What was *that* about?" she asked.

"Nothing, Mrs. Saxon," Melody said perkily. "Nothing at all."

Once they had passed, Joel glanced at Melody. "So, that was your big plan, eh? To throw a tantrum?"

"Tantrums are a noble and time-tested strategy," she said airily. "Particularly if you have a good set of lungs and are facing down a crotchety old priest. I know Stewart; he always bends if you make enough noise."

They passed out of the cathedral. Harding stood conferring with a few of his police officers on the landing. A couple of spring-work gargoyles prowled across the ledge above the door into the building.

"Father Stewart said he'd ask for permission," Joel said. "I don't think we've won."

"We have," Melody said. "He won't want me to make another scene, particularly considering the tensions between Rithmatists and ordinary people right now. Come on; let's go get something to eat. Being irate sure can build a girl's appetite."

Joel sighed, but let himself be towed across the street and toward the campus.

BINDING CHALKLINGS

Most Rithmatists use a simple "◇" glyph to represent the "defend" instruction to a chalkling. Any chalkling with this glyph in its programming will actively protect its perimeter against other chalklings that are not bound to the same circle.

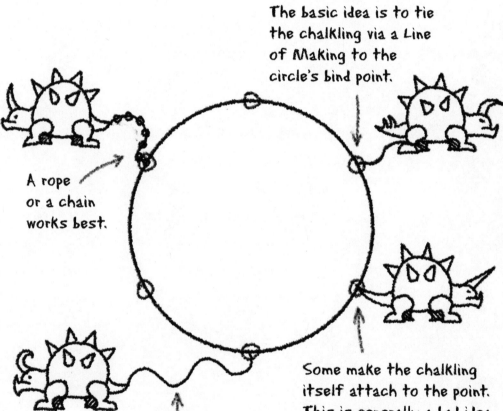

The basic idea is to tie the chalkling via a Line of Making to the circle's bind point.

A rope or a chain works best.

Some make the chalkling itself attach to the point. This is generally a bad idea as the chalkling loses flexibility.

Giving the chalkling a long tether can make its range much larger, but you run the risk of it getting sidetracked and distracted.

T*he circle is divine,* Joel read.

The only truly eternal and perfect shape, it has been a symbol for the Master's works since the ancient Egyptian Ahmes first discovered the divine number itself. Many medieval scholars used the compass—the tool by which a circle is drafted—as a symbol of the Master's power of creation. One can find it scattered throughout illuminated manuscripts.

Before we landed on the American Isles, history entered a dark period for the circle. The Earth was shown to not be a flat circle at all, but a sphere of questionable regularity. The celestial planets were proven to move in ellipses, further weakening belief in the divine circle.

Then we discovered Rithmatics.

In Rithmatics, words are unimportant. Only numbers have meaning, and the circle dominates all. The closer one can come to perfection in its form, the more powerful one is. The circle, then, is proven to be beyond simple human reasoning. It is something inherently divine.

It is odd, then, that something man-made should have played such an important part in the discovery of Rithmatics. If His Majesty hadn't been carrying one of Master Freudland's new-style pocket watches, perhaps none of this would have ever occurred, and man might have fallen to the wild chalklings.

The chapter ended there. Joel sat in the empty workshop, back against the wall. A few thin ribbons of sunlight crept through the windows above, falling through the dusty air to fall in squares on the floor.

Joel flipped through the pages of the old tome. It came from the journal of one Adam Makings, the personal astronomer and scientist of King Gregory III, founder of Rithmatics. Adam Makings was attributed with discovering and outlining the principles surrounding two-, four-, and six-point Rithmatic circles.

The book came from Joel's father's collection, and was apparently quite valuable, since it was a very early copy. Why hadn't Joel's mother sold it—or any of the books—to pay debts? Perhaps she hadn't known the value.

The book contained Makings's theories on the existence of other Rithmatic figures, though he'd never come to any definite conclusions. That last part, however, proved more interesting to Joel than any other.

If His Majesty hadn't been carrying one of Master Freudland's new-style pocket watches, perhaps none of this would have ever occurred, and man might have fallen to the wild chalklings. . . .

Joel frowned, flipping to the next chapter. He was unable to find anything else on the topic of the pocket watch.

Very little was known of how King Gregory discovered Rithmatics. The church's official position was that he had received the knowledge in a vision. Religious depictions often showed Gregory kneeling in prayer, a beacon of light falling around him and forming a circle marked with six points. The inside cover of the book had a similar plate in the front, though this one showed the vision appearing in front of Gregory in the air.

Why would a pocket watch be involved?

"Joel?" A feminine voice rang through the brick hallways of the dormitory basement. A few seconds later, Melody's face appeared in the open doorway to the workshop. She wore a book bag on her shoulder and had on the skirt and blouse of a Rithmatic student.

"You're *still* here?" she demanded.

"There's a lot of studying to—" Joel began.

"You're sitting practically in the dark!" she said, walking over to him. "This place is dreary."

Joel looked around the workshop. "I find it comforting."

"Whatever. You're taking a break. Come on."

"But—"

"No excuses," she said, grabbing his arm and yanking. He let her pull him to his feet. It was Wednesday; tomorrow was the Fourth of July and the inception ceremony. There was still no word from the vicar about whether or not Joel would be able to attend, and the Scribbler had yet to strike again.

Many in the media were claiming Inspector Harding's lock-down to be a success, and the last few holdouts on keeping Rithmatist students away were giving in.

Joel didn't feel their same relief. He felt like an axe was hanging over them, just waiting to fall.

"Come on," Melody said, towing him out of the basement and into the afternoon light. "Honestly, you're going to shrivel up and turn into a professor if you don't watch yourself."

Joel rubbed his neck, stretching. It *did* feel nice to be out.

"Let's go to the office," Melody said, "and see if the vicar has sent you anything yet."

Joel shrugged, and they began walking. The days were growing warm, New Britannia humidity rolling in off the ocean. The heat felt good after a morning spent down in the workshop.

As they passed the humanities building, Joel eyed a group of workers busy scrubbing the building's side where the phrase "Go Back to Nebrask" had been scrawled two nights ago in the darkness. Harding had been furious that someone had managed to penetrate his security.

I wouldn't be surprised if it was done by members of the

student body, Joel thought. There had always been tensions between the rich, non-Rithmatic students and the Rithmatists.

Melody saw it too. "Did you hear about Virginia and Thaddius?"

"Who?"

"Rithmatists," Melody said. "Students from the class ahead of us. They were out yesterday after church services. Ran into a mob of men who *chased* them and threw bottles at them. I've never heard of such a thing happening."

"Are they all right?"

"Well, yes. . . ." Melody said, growing uncomfortable. "They drew chalklings. It made the men scatter in a heartbeat."

Chalklings. "But—"

"No, they don't know the Glyph of Rending," Melody said quickly. "They wouldn't have used it if they'd known it. Using that against people is quite a sin, you know."

"That will still be bad," Joel said. "Stories will spread."

"What would you have them do? Let the mob catch them?"

"Well, no. . . ."

The two walked, uncomfortable, for another few moments. "Oh!" Melody said. "I just remembered. I have to stop by Making Hall."

"What?" Joel said as she spun about.

"It's on the way," she said, adjusting the shoulder strap on the book bag and waving him along.

"It's on the other dusting side of the campus!"

She rolled her eyes exaggeratedly. "What? A little walking is going to kill you? Come on."

Joel grumbled, joining her.

"Guess what?" Melody said.

Joel raised an eyebrow.

"I finally got to move on from tracing," she said. "Professor Fitch is having me work from a pattern now."

"Great!" That was the next step—drawing the Rithmatic forms from a small design to use as a reference. It was something Melody should have mastered years ago, but he didn't say that.

"Yes," she said with a flip of the hand. "Give me another few months, and I'll have this Rithmatics thing down. I'll be able to beat *any* ten-year-old in a duel."

Joel chuckled. "Why do we need to drop by Making Hall, anyway?"

Melody held up a small folded note.

"Oh, right," Joel said. "Office deliveries."

She nodded.

"Wait," Joel said, frowning. "You're doing deliveries? Is *that* why you came down to get me? Because you were bored doing deliveries alone?"

"Of course," Melody said happily. "Didn't you know that you *exist* to entertain me?"

"Great," Joel said. To the side, they passed Warding Hall, where a large number of staff members were moving in and out.

"The Melee," Joel said. "They're getting ready for it." It was coming up on Saturday.

Melody got a sour look on her face. "I can't believe that they're still holding the thing."

"Why wouldn't they?"

"Well, considering recent events . . ."

Joel shrugged. "I suspect Harding will limit attendance to students and faculty. The Scribbler attacks at night anyway. An event like this would be too well attended by Rithmatists to be a good place to try anything."

Melody grumbled something unintelligible as they walked up the hill to Making Hall.

"What was that?" Joel asked.

"I just don't see why they have to have the Melee in the first place," Melody said. "I mean, what's the point?"

"It's fun," Joel said. "It lets the students get some practice in with real duels and prove themselves Rithmatically. What's your problem with it?"

"Every professor has to send at least one student to the thing," Melody said.

"So?"

"So, how many students does Fitch have?"

Joel stopped on the side of the hill. "Wait . . . *you're* going to duel in the Melee?"

"And be thoroughly humiliated. Not that *that's* anything new. Still, I don't see why I have to be put on display."

"Oh, come on. Maybe you'll do well—you're so good at chalklings, after all."

She regarded him flatly. "Nalizar is fielding *twelve* students to fight." It was the maximum. "Who do you bet they'll eliminate first?"

"Then you won't be humiliated. Who would expect you to stand against them? Just enjoy yourself."

"It's going to be painful."

"It's a fun tradition."

"So was witch-burning," Melody said. "Unless you were the witch."

Joel chuckled as they reached Making Hall. They walked along to one of the doors, and Melody reached to pull it open.

Joel froze. It was Nalizar's office. "Here?"

"Yeah," Melody said with a grimace. "The office had a note for him. Oh yeah, I forgot." She reached into her bag, pulling out the book *Origins of Power*, the one that Joel had borrowed a few weeks back. "He requested this, and the library contacted me, since I'd checked it out."

"Nalizar wants *this* book?" Joel asked.

"Uh . . . yeah. That's what I just said. I found it at Fitch's office, where you left it. Sorry."

"Not your fault," Joel said. He'd been hoping that once he'd spent some time studying his father's texts, he'd be able to figure the book out.

"Be back in a sec," Melody said, opening the door and rushing up the stairs.

Joel waited below—he had no desire to see Nalizar. But . . . why did the professor want *that* book?

Nalizar is involved in this somehow, he thought, walking around the building to look up into the office window. *I—*

He stopped short. Nalizar stood there, in the window. The

professor wore his red coat, buttoned up to the neck. He scanned the campus, eyes passing over Joel, as if not noticing him.

Then the professor's head snapped back toward Joel, regarding him, meeting his eyes.

Other times when he'd seen the professor, Joel had found the man haughty. Arrogant in a youthful, almost naive sort of way.

There was none of that in the man's expression now. Nalizar stood in the shadowed room, tall and straight-backed, arms clasped behind him as he stared down at Joel. Contemplative.

Nalizar turned, obviously hearing Melody knock on the door, then walked away from the window. A few minutes later, Melody appeared at the bottom of the stairs, lugging a stack of books, her bag full of others. Joel rushed over to help her.

"Ugh," she said as he took half of the books. "Thanks. Here, you might be interested in this." She slid one book across the top of her stack.

Joel picked it up. *Postulations on the Possibility of New and Undiscovered Rithmatic Lines*, the title read. It was the book he'd wanted to steal from Nalizar, the one the professor had borrowed a few weeks back.

"You *stole* it?" Joel asked with a hushed tone.

"Hardly," Melody said, walking down the slope with her stack of books. "He told me to return these to the library as if I were some glorified errand girl."

"Uh . . . that's what you *are*, Melody. Only without the 'glorified' part."

She snorted, and the two of them continued down the hill. "He sure is checking out a lot of books," Joel noted, looking over the titles in his arms. "And they're all on Rithmatic theory."

"Well, he *is* a professor," Melody said. "Hey, what are you doing?"

"Looking to see when he checked them out," Joel said, balancing the books as he tried to flip to the back cover of each one, looking at the stamp on the card. "Looks like he's had these for less than two weeks."

"So?"

"So, that's a lot of reading," Joel said. "Look, he checked out this one on advanced Vigor reflecting *yesterday*. He's returning it already?"

She shrugged. "It must not have been that interesting."

"Either that, or he's looking for something," Joel said. "Skimming the books for specific information. Perhaps he's trying to develop another new line."

"*Another?*" Melody said. "You still insist on connecting him to the disappearances, don't you?"

"I'm suspicious."

"And if he's behind it," Melody said, "then why did all of the disappearances happen *off* campus? Wouldn't he have taken the students easiest to reach?"

"He wouldn't have wanted to draw suspicion to himself."

"And motive?" Melody said.

"I don't know. Taking the son of a knight-senator changes so much, transforming this from a regional problem to a national crisis. It doesn't make sense. Unless that's what he wanted in the first place."

Melody eyed him.

"Stretch?" Joel asked.

"Yeah. If this were about creating a national crisis, then he could have just taken the knight-senator."

Joel was forced to admit that she was right. What *were* the Scribbler's motives? Was it about Rithmatists, or about driving a wedge between the islands? If it was just about killing or kidnapping students, then where had the new Rithmatic lines come from, and why were the wild chalklings involved? Or were they really? Could ordinary chalklings be instructed to act like wild ones to throw the police off?

Joel and Melody arrived at the library, and they went in, dropping off Nalizar's books. Ms. Torrent gave them one of her trademark looks of displeasure as she checked the books in, then checked the book on potential Rithmatic lines back out to Melody.

They left, and Melody handed the book to Joel.

He tucked it under his arm. "Weren't we going to the office to look for a note from the vicar?"

"I suppose," she said, sighing.

"You're down, all of a sudden."

"I'm like that," she said. "Wild mood swings. It makes me more interesting. Anyway, you have to admit that it hasn't been a pleasant afternoon you've shown me. I got to see Nalizar—dreamy as he is—but I was also forced to think about the Melee."

"You almost sound like it's my fault," Joel said.

"Well," she said, "I wasn't going to say it myself, but since you pointed it out, I find myself persuaded. You really should apologize to me."

"Oh please."

"Don't you feel the least bit sorry for me?" she asked. "Having to go and be laughed at by the entire school populace?"

"Maybe you'll hold your own."

She regarded him flatly. "Have you *seen* one of my circles, Joel?"

"You're getting better."

"The Melee is in three days!"

"Okay," he admitted. "You don't have a chance. But, well, the only way to learn is by trying!"

"You really *are* like a professor."

"Hey!" Joel said as they approached the office building. "I resent that. I've worked *very* hard during my school career to be a delinquent. I'll bet I've failed more classes than you have."

"I doubt that," she said haughtily. "And, even if you did, I doubt you failed them as *spectacularly* or as *embarrassingly* as I did."

He chuckled. "Point conceded. Nobody's as spectacularly embarrassing as you, Melody."

"That's *not* what I said."

They approached the office, and Joel could see Harding's police guarding there. "Well, one good part about all this," Melody said. "If Principal York restricts the Melee to students and faculty, then I won't have to be embarrassed in front of my parents."

"Wait. They'd actually come?"

"They *always* come to the Melee," she said, grimacing. "Particularly when one of their children is in it."

"When you talk about them, it sounds like you think they hate you or something."

"It's not that. It's just . . . well, they're important people. Busy doing stuff. They don't have much time for the daughter who can't seem to get Rithmatics right."

"It can't be *that* bad," Joel said.

She raised an eyebrow at him. "I have two brothers and one sister, all older than me, all Rithmatists. Each one won the Melee at least twice during their careers. William won all four years he was eligible."

"Wow," Joel said.

"And I can't even do a straight circle," Melody said, walking quickly. Joel hurried to catch up to her.

"They're not bad people," she said. "But, well, I think it's easy for them to have me here. Floridia is far enough away that they don't have to see me often. I could probably go home on weekends—I did during the early years. Lately, though, with William's death . . . well, it's not really a very happy place at home."

"Wait," Joel said, "*death?*"

She shrugged. "Nebrask is dangerous."

Death, Joel thought. *At Nebrask. And her last name is . . .*

Muns. Joel stopped short.

Melody turned.

"Your brother," Joel said. "How old was he?"

"Three years older than me," Melody said.

"He died last year?"

She nodded.

"Dusts!" Joel said. "I saw his obituary in the lists Professor Fitch gave me."

"So?"

"So," Joel said, "Professor *Nalizar* was involved in the death of a Rithmatic student last year. That's why he was sent away from the battlefront. Maybe it's connected! Maybe—"

"Joel," Melody snapped, drawing his attention.

He blinked, regarding her, seeing the distress in her eyes, hidden behind anger.

"Don't involve William," she said. "I just . . . Don't. If you have to look for conspiracies around Nalizar, do it. But don't talk about my brother."

"I'm sorry," Joel said. "But . . . if Nalizar was involved, don't you want to know?"

"He *was* involved," Melody said. "Nalizar led a team past the Nebrask Circle up to the base of the Tower itself trying to recover my brother. They never even found the body."

"Then maybe he killed your brother!" Joel said. "Maybe he just *said* he couldn't find him."

"Joel," she said, growing quiet. "I'm only going to discuss this one time, all right? William's death was his own fault. He ran out past the defensive lines. Half the contingent saw him get swarmed by chalklings.

"William tried to prove himself a hero, and he put a lot of people in danger. Nalizar did all he could to rescue him. Nalizar *risked his life* for my brother."

Joel hesitated, remembering how she always described Nalizar.

"I don't like what he did to Fitch," Melody said, "but Nalizar *is* a hero. He left the battlefront because of the failure he felt in not being able to rescue William in time."

Something didn't seem right about that to Joel. However, he didn't say anything about it to Melody. Instead, he simply nodded. "I'm sorry."

She nodded as well, apparently considering the topic closed. They walked the rest of the way to the office in silence.

Nalizar suddenly decided he couldn't take failure? Joel thought. *He left the battlefront because of one death? If it was his conscience that made him leave the battlefront, then why did he complain about politics to Principal York?*

Something is *going on with that man.*

They opened the door to the office, and Joel was pleased to find both Inspector Harding and Professor Fitch there. Harding stood talking to Florence about supplies and housing accommodations for his officers. Fitch sat in one of the waiting chairs.

"Ah, Joel," Fitch said, rising.

"Professor?" Joel said. "You weren't looking for me, were you?"

"Hum? What? Ah, no, I have to give a report to the principal about our work. He has me in every couple of days or so. You haven't discovered anything new, have you?"

Joel shook his head. "I'm just keeping Melody company on her errands." He paused, leaning against the wall as Melody walked over to get another stack of notes to deliver. "Though there *was* one thing."

"Hum?"

"Do you know much about the original discovery of Rithmatics?" Joel asked. "Back when King Gregory was alive?"

"I know more than most," Fitch said. "I am, after all, a historian."

"Was there some involvement of *clocks* in the discovery?"

"Ah," Fitch said. "You're talking about the Adam Makings report, are you?"

"Yes."

"Ha! We'll turn you into a scholar yet, lad. Very nice work, very nice. Yes, there are some strange references to the workings of clocks in the early records, and we haven't been able to figure out why. Early chalklings reacted to them, though they no longer do so. The power of the gears over chalklings is one of the reasons that springworks are used so often in Monarchical churches, you know."

"It's a metaphor," Exton added from the other side of the room. Joel looked up; he wasn't aware the clerk had been paying attention.

"Ask the vicar about it sometime," Exton continued. "The priests see time in an interesting way. Something about how it is divided by man bringing order to chaos."

There was a chuckle from the side of the room, where Florence had turned from her conversation with Inspector Harding. "Exton! I thought you were too busy to chat!"

"I *am*," he muttered. "I have nearly given up on getting anything done in this madhouse. Everyone bustling about and making noise all the time. I'm going to have to find a way to do work when nobody is around."

"Well," Joel said to Professor Fitch, "the clock thing is probably a dead end then, if people have already noticed it and researched it." He sighed. "I'm not certain I'll be able to find anything of use in these books. I keep being shocked by how little I know about Rithmatics."

Fitch nodded. "I feel the same way sometimes."

"I remember sitting and watching your duel with Nalizar," Joel said. "I thought I knew it all, just because I understood the defenses you were using. There's a lot more to all of it than I once thought."

Fitch smiled.

"What?" Joel asked.

"What you just said is the *foundation* of all scholarship." Fitch reached out, putting a hand on Joel's shoulder, which stood a bit taller than Fitch's own. "Joel, son, you've been *invaluable* to this investigation. If York hadn't given you to me as an assistant . . . well, I don't know where we would be."

Joel found himself smiling. Fitch's sincerity was touching.

"Aha!" a voice declared.

Joel spun to find Melody holding a letter. She rushed across the office room, prompting a frown from Exton. She stretched across the counter between the office area and the waiting area, handing the letter to Joel. "It's from the vicar," she said. "Open it, open it!"

Joel accepted it hesitantly. It was marked with the clockwork cross. He broke the seal, then took a breath, opening the letter.

Joel, I have reviewed your case and have spoken with the bishop of New Britannia, as well as the principal of your school. After some deliberation, we have determined that— indeed—your request has merit. If there is a chance that the Master wishes you to be a Rithmatist, we should not deny you the opportunity.

Arrive at the cathedral on Thursday at eight sharp, and you will be fitted for a robe of inception and be allowed an opportunity to enter the chamber before the regular ceremony begins. Bring your mother and any with whom you might wish to share this event.

Vicar Stewart

Joel looked up from the note, stunned.

"What does it *say?*" Melody asked, hardly able to contain herself.

"It means there's still hope," Joel said, lowering the note. "I'm going to get a chance."

ANCHORING DEFENSIVE CIRCLES

Lines of Vigor, if drawn with a large arc, can be used to move other lines about.

(This is very hard against Lines of Forbiddance, but easy against chalklings and Lines of Warding.)

Because of this, it is important to anchor a defensive circle with a few Lines of Forbiddance attached at bind points. The more lines used, the greater the stability. Use too many, however, and you will find yourself unable to move about within your own defense!

The clever Rithmatist watches for defenses that are improperly anchored, and attacks them.

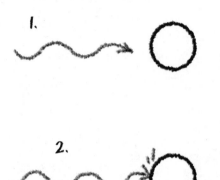

1.

2.

3.

Note: The Line of Vigor will, of course, run out of power quickly. However, moving an opponent's defense even a few inches can often have excellent results.

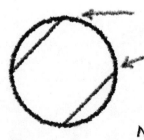

Most Rithmatists choose to connect two bind points via a Line of Forbiddance.

One line is not enough as the circle can be shaken free this way. Use two.
Note: Other strategies for anchoring exist.

L ater that night, Joel lay quietly in bed, trying to sort through his emotions. A clock ticked on the wall of the workshop. He didn't look at it; he didn't want to know the hour.

It was late. And he was awake. The night before his inception.

Less than one in a thousand. That was his chance of becoming a Rithmatist. It seemed ridiculous to hope, and yet his nervousness drove away any possibility of sleep. He was going to get a chance to be a Rithmatist. A real, honest chance.

What would it mean, if he were chosen? He wouldn't be able to draw a stipend until after he'd served in Nebrask, and so his mother would probably have to continue working.

Nebrask. He'd have to go to *Nebrask*. He didn't know much about what happened at the place. There were the wild chalklings, of course. The Rithmatists on the island maintained their enormous chalk Circle of Warding, thousands of feet in diameter, to keep the chalklings and the Tower locked in.

There were the reports of other things on the island as well. Dark, unexplained things. Things Joel would eventually have to face, should he be made a Rithmatist. And he'd only have one year to prepare and learn, while other students had eight or nine.

That's why they don't let older people become Rithmatists, he realized. *They need to be trained and taught when they are young.*

Students went to Nebrask their final year of schooling. Ten years of service came next, then freedom. Some chose to work at the spring-winding stations, but others stayed at Nebrask, Melody said. Not for the money, but for the challenge. For the struggle and the fight. Would this be Joel's future?

This is all moot anyway, Joel thought, rolling over, trying to force himself to sleep. *I'm not going to become a Rithmatist. The Master won't pick me because I won't have enough time to train.*

Yet there was a *chance.* Over the next thirty minutes or so, thinking about that chance kept him from being able to sleep.

Eventually, Joel rose and reached for the lamp beside his bed. He cranked the key on the side, then watched through the glass as the spinners inside began to twirl. Several small filaments grew hot from the friction, giving out illumination, which the reflectors inside concentrated and bounced out the top.

He stooped over, picking through the books beside his bed. He chose one. *The Narrative of the Captivity and the Restoration of Mrs. Mary Rowlandson,* the first page read. A diary, one of the earliest recorded bits of literature from the original settlers of the American Isles. It had happened before the wild chalklings began their main offensive, but after they began to harass people.

The sovereignty and goodness of THE MASTER, together with the faithfulness of his promises displayed, being a narrative of the captivity and restoration of Mrs. Mary Rowlandson. The second Addition Corrected and amended. Written by her own hand for her private use, and now made public at the earnest desire of some friends.

On the tenth of February, sixteenth year of our arrival, came the wild chalklings with great numbers upon Lancaster. Hearing the sounds of splashing, we looked out; several houses were burning, and the smoke ascending to heaven. The monsters were visible upon the ground, dodging between the buckets of water thrown by our men.

Water. It washed away chalk, but not very well. They hadn't yet discovered the composition of acids that would dissolve the chalklings with a single splash.

There were five persons eaten in one house; the father, and the mother and a sucking child, they stripped of skin, then ate out the eyes. The other two they herded out the doorway. There were two others, who being out of their garrison upon some occasion were set upon; one was stripped of all skin, the other escaped.

Another, seeing many of the wild chalklings about his barn, ventured and went out, but was quickly set upon. They ate at his feet until he screamed, falling to the ground, then swarmed above him. There were three others belonging to the same garrison who were killed; the wild chalklings climbing up the sides of the walls, attacking from all sides, knocking over lanterns and beginning fires. Thus these murderous creatures went on, burning and destroying before them.

Joel shivered in the silence of his room. The matter-of-fact narrative was disturbing, but oddly transfixing. How would you react, if you'd never seen a chalkling before? What would your response be to a living picture that climbed up walls and slid beneath doors, attacking without mercy, eating the flesh off bodies? His lantern continued to whir.

At length they came and beset our own house, and quickly it was the dolefulest day that ever mine eyes saw. They slid beneath the door and quickly they ate one man among us, then another, and then a third.

Now is the dreadful hour come, that I have often heard of (in time of war, as it was the case of others), but now mine eyes see it. Some in our house were fighting for their lives, others wallowing in their blood, the house on fire over our heads. Now might we hear mothers and children crying out for themselves, and one another, "Master, what shall we do?"

Then I took my children (and one of my sisters', hers) to go forth and leave the house: but as soon as we came to the door and appeared, the creatures outside swarmed up the hill toward us.

My brother-in-law (being before wounded, in defending the house, his legs bleeding) was set upon from behind, and fell down screaming with a bucket of water in his hands. Whereat the wild chalklings did dance scornfully, silently, around him. Demons of the Depths they most certainly are, many made in the form of man, but created as if from the shape of sticks and lines.

I stood in fright as we were surrounded. Thus was my family butchered by those merciless creatures, standing amazed, with the blood running down to our heels. The children were taken as I ran for the bucket to use in our defense, but it was emptied, and I felt a cold feeling of something on my leg, followed by a sharp pain.

It was at that point that I saw it. Something in the darkness, illuminated just barely by the fire of our burning house. A shape that did seem to absorb the light, created completely of dark, shifting blackness: like charcoal scraped and scratched on the ground, only but standing upright in the shadows beside the house.

It did watch. That deep, terrible blackness. Something from the Depths themselves. The shape wiggling, shaking, like a pitch-black fire sketched in charcoal.

Watching.

Something cracked against the window of Joel's room.

He jumped and saw a shadow moving away from the small pane of glass. The window stood at the very top of the wall, in the small space between where the ground stopped and the ceiling began.

Vandals! Joel thought, remembering the curse that had been painted on the humanities building. He jumped from the bed and rushed for the door, throwing on a coat. He was up the stairs and out the door a few moments later.

He rounded the building to see what the vandals had written. He found the side of the building clean. Had he been wrong?

That was when he saw it. A symbol, written in chalk on the brick wall. A looping swirl. The Rithmatic line they still hadn't been able to identify.

The night was strangely quiet.

Oh no . . . Joel thought, feeling a horrible chill. He backed away from the wall, then opened his mouth to call for help.

His scream came out unnaturally soft. He felt the sound almost get *torn* away from his throat, sucked toward that symbol, dampened.

The kidnappings . . . Joel thought, stunned. *Nobody heard the Rithmatists call for help. Except for a few servants, on the side of the hall where that symbol had been drawn too hastily.*

That's what the line does. It sucks in sound.

He stumbled back. He had to find the police, raise the alarm. The Scribbler had come to the dormitory for . . .

Dormitory. This was the *general* dormitory. There were no Rithmatists in it. Who had the kidnapper come for?

Several shaking white shapes crawled over the top of the building and began to move down the wall.

For Joel.

Joel yelled—the sound dying—and took off at a dash across the green. *This can't be happening,* he thought with terror. *I'm not a Rithmatist! The Scribbler is only supposed to come after them.*

He ran madly, screaming for help. His voice came out as barely a whisper. He glanced back and saw a small wave of whiteness following him across the lawn. There were about a dozen of the creatures—fewer than the attacks indicated had taken the others. But then, Joel wasn't a Rithmatist.

He yelled again, panicking, his heart thumping, his entire body feeling cold. No sound came from his mouth.

Think, Joel, he told himself. *Don't panic. You'll die if you panic.*

That sound-stealing line can't have this long a range. Someone at one of the other crime scenes would have noticed that they couldn't make sound, and that would have given it away.

That means there must be other copies of the symbol nearby. Drawn in a row, because . . .

Because the Scribbler guessed which direction I'd run.

Joel pulled up sharply, looking wildly across the dark green. It was lit only by a few phantom lanterns, but in that light, he saw it. A white line drawn across the concrete walk ahead. A Line of Forbiddance.

He turned, looking behind him. The chalklings continued onward, pushing Joel toward the Line of Forbiddance. Trying to corner him and trap him. There were probably lines to the sides as well—it was hard to draw with chalk on earth, but it was possible. If he got trapped behind Lines of Forbiddance . . .

He would die.

That thought was almost enough to stun him again. The wave of chalklings approached, and he could see what Charles had described in his final note. The things weren't like traditional chalklings. Their forms shook violently, as if to some phantom sound. Arms, legs, bodies melding together. Like the visions of an insane painter who couldn't make up his mind which monstrosity he wanted to create.

Move! something inside of Joel yelled. He sucked in a deep breath, then took off at a dash straight *at* the chalklings. When he drew near, he jumped, soaring over the top of the creatures. He hit the ground and dashed back the way he had come.

Have to think quickly, he told himself. *Can't go to the dormitory. They'll just come under the doors. I have to find the policemen. They have acid.*

Where were Harding's patrols? Joel ran with all his might toward the Rithmatic side of the campus.

His breath began to come in gasps. He couldn't outrun chalklings for long. Ahead, he saw lights. The campus office building. Joel let out a ragged yell.

"Help!"

Blessedly, the sound came in full force. He'd gotten away from the trap. However, though sound was no longer dampened, his voice felt weak. He had been running at full speed for too long.

The door to the office flung open and Exton looked out, wearing his typical vest and bow tie. "Joel?" he called. "What's wrong?"

Joel shook his head, sweating. He dared a glance behind, and saw the chalklings scrambling over the grass just behind him. Inches away.

"Blessed heavens!" Exton shouted.

Joel turned back, but in his haste, he tripped and fell to the ground.

Joel cried out, hitting hard, the breath knocked from him. Dazed, he cringed, waiting for the pain, the coldness, the attacks he had read about.

Nothing happened.

"Help, police, someone!" Exton was screaming.

Joel lifted his head. Why wasn't he dead? The grass was lit only by a lantern shining through the window of the office building. The chalklings quivered nearby, surrounding him, their figures shaking. Small hands, eyes, faces, legs, claws formed periodically around whirling, tempestuous chalk bodies.

They did not advance.

Joel raised himself up on his arms. Then he saw it: the gold dollar Melody had given him. It had fallen from his pocket and lay sparkling on the grass.

The gears inside it ticked quietly, and the chalklings shied away from it. Several of them tested forward, but they were reticent.

There was a sudden splash, and one of the chalklings washed away in a wave of liquid.

"Quickly, Joel," Exton said, holding out his hand from a short distance away, an empty bucket in his other hand. Joel scrambled to his feet, snatching the gold coin and dashing through the hole Exton had made in the ring of chalklings.

Exton rushed back into the office building.

"Exton!" Joel said, following him through the doorway and into the office. "We have to run. We can't stop them here!"

Exton slammed the door shut, ignoring Joel. Then he knelt to the floor and pulled out a piece of chalk. He drew a line in front of the doorway, then up the sides of the wall and around the doorway. He stepped back.

The chalklings stopped outside. Joel could just barely see them begin attacking the line. Exton proceeded to draw another one around Joel and himself, boxing them in.

"Exton," Joel said. "You're a Rithmatist!"

"A failed one," Exton admitted, hands shaking. "Haven't carried chalk in years. But, well, with all the problems here at the school . . ."

Across the room, chalklings moved across the windowpanes, looking for other ways in. A single lantern flickered, giving the office a shadowy illumination.

"What's going on?" Exton asked. "Why were they chasing you?"

"I don't know," Joel said, testing the Line of Forbiddance around them. It wasn't drawn particularly well, and wouldn't hold for long against the chalklings.

"Do you have any more acid?" Joel asked.

Exton nodded toward a second bucket nearby, within their defensive square. Joel grabbed it.

"It's the last one," Exton said, wringing his hands. "Harding left the two here for us."

Joel glanced at the chalklings, visible under the door, attacking at Exton's line. He took out the coin.

It had stopped them. Why?

"Exton," he said, trying to keep the terror from shaking his voice. "We're going to have to make a run for the gates. The policemen will have more acid there."

"Run?" Exton said. "I . . . I can't run! I'm in no shape to keep ahead of chalklings!"

He was right. Portly as he was, Exton wouldn't be able to keep up for long. Joel felt his hands shaking, so he clenched his fists. He knelt down, watching the chalklings beyond the Line of Forbiddance. They were chewing through it at an alarming rate.

Joel took the coin and snapped it to the ground behind the line. The chalklings shied away.

Then, tentatively, they came back and began to work on the Line of Forbiddance again.

Blast, Joel thought. *So it* won't *stop them, not for good.* He and Exton were in trouble. Serious trouble. He turned to Exton, who was wiping his brow with a handkerchief.

"Draw another box around yourself," Joel said.

"What?"

"Draw as many lines as you can," Joel said. "Don't let them touch each other except at corners. Wait here." Joel turned toward the door. "I'm going for help."

"Joel, those *things* are out there." Exton jumped as the window cracked. He glanced toward the glass, where a couple of chalklings were attacking, scraping at the glass with a terrible sound. It cracked further. "They'll be in here soon!"

Joel took a deep breath. "I'm not going to sit here like Herman and Charles did, waiting for my defenses to be breached. I can make it to the gates—it's just a short distance."

"Joel, I—"

"Draw the lines!" Joel yelled.

Exton fumbled, then went down on his knees, boxing himself inside a set of Lines of Forbiddance. Joel turned the coin over in his palm.

Then he picked up the bucket and splashed most of its contents beneath the door, washing away the Line of Forbiddance. The chalklings outside washed away like dirt sprayed off a white wall. Joel threw open the door and, without looking back, took off at a charge toward the gates to the academy.

He knew he'd never be able to run with a bucket of liquid, so he tossed it behind him.

He ran, holding the coin.

What would happen to him if the gates weren't guarded? What if the Scribbler had managed to kill the policemen or make a distraction?

Joel would die. His skin ripped from his flesh, his eyes gouged out. Just like the people in Mary Rowlandson's narrative.

No, he thought with determination. *She survived to write her story.*

I'll survive to write mine!

He yelled, pushing himself in a dash over the dark landscape. Ahead, he saw lights.

People moved near them.

"Halt!" one of the officers said.

"Chalklings!" Joel screamed. "They're following me!"

The officers scattered at his call, grabbing buckets. Joel was thankful for Harding's sense of preparation, as the men didn't even stop to think or question. They formed a defensive bucket line as Joel charged between them and collapsed to his knees, puffing and exhausted, his heart racing.

He twisted about, leaning one hand against the ground. There had been four chalklings following him—more than enough to kill him. They had stopped in the near darkness, barely visible from the gates.

"By the Master," one of the police officers whispered. "What are they waiting for?"

"Steady," said one of the others, holding his bucket.

"Should we charge?" asked another.

"*Steady*," the first said.

The chalklings scrambled away, disappearing into the night.

Joel wheezed in exhaustion, falling backward to the ground and lying on his back. "Another man," he said between breaths, "is trapped inside the office building. You've got to help him."

One of the policemen pointed, motioning for a squad of four to go that direction. He took his gun and fired it upward. It made a *crack* of sound as the springs released and the bullet ripped through the air.

Joel lay, sweating, shaking. The officers held their buckets, nervous, until Harding raced into sight from the east, riding his springwork charger. He had his rifle out.

"Chalklings, sir!" one of the officers yelled. "At the office building!"

Harding cursed. "Send three men to alert the patrols around the Rithmatist barracks!" he yelled, turning his horse and galloping toward the office. He slung his rifle over his shoulder as he went, trading it for what looked to be a wineskin filled with acid.

Joel simply lay, trying to wrap his mind around what had just happened.

Someone tried to kill me.

Two hours later, Joel sat in Professor Fitch's office, holding a cup of warmed cocoa, his mother in tears at his side. She alternated between hugging him and speaking sternly with Inspector Harding for not setting patrols to protect the non-Rithmatists.

Professor Fitch sat bleary-eyed, looking stunned after hearing what had happened. Exton was, apparently, all right—though the police were speaking with him back at the office building.

Harding stood with two policemen a short distance away. All of the people crowded the small, hallwaylike office.

Joel couldn't stop himself from shaking. It felt shameful. He'd almost died. Every time he considered that, he felt unsteady.

"Joel," Fitch said. "Lad, are you sure you're all right?"

Joel nodded, then took a sip of his drink.

"I'm sorry, Son," said his mother. "I'm a bad mother. I shouldn't stay out all night!"

"You act like it's your fault," Joel said quietly.

"Well, it—"

"No, Mother," Joel said. "If you'd been there, you might have been killed. It's better that you were away."

She sat back on her stool, still looking troubled.

Harding dismissed his officers, then approached Joel. "Soldier, we found the patterns you mentioned. There were five—one on the wall outside your room, then four spaced along the ground in the direction you ran. They ended in a box of Lines of Forbiddance. If you hadn't thought as quickly as you did, you would have been trapped."

Joel nodded. His mother began crying again.

"I have the entire campus on alert, soldier," Harding said. "You did well tonight. *Very* well. Quick thinking, bravery, physical adeptness. I'm impressed."

"I nearly wet myself," Joel whispered.

Harding snorted. "I've seen men twice your age freeze in combat when they saw their first chalkling. You did an amazing job. Might well have just solved this case."

Joel looked up with surprise. *"What?"*

"I can't speak now," Harding said, raising a hand. "But if my suspicions prove to be correct, I'll have made an arrest by the morning. You should get some sleep, now." He hesitated. "If this were the battlefield, son, I'd put you in for highest honors."

"I . . ." Joel said. "I don't know that I can go back to the workshop to sleep. . . ."

"The lad and his mother can stay here," Fitch said, rising. "I'll stay in one of the empty rooms."

"Excellent," Harding said. "Ms. Saxon, I will have ten men with acid guarding this doorway all night, two inside the room, if you wish."

"Yes," she said, "please."

"Try not to be too worried," Harding said. "I'm sure the worst of this is through. Plus, as I understand, you have an important day tomorrow, Joel."

The inception ceremony. Joel had almost forgotten about it. He nodded, bidding the inspector farewell. Harding marched out and closed the door.

"Well," Fitch said. "You can see that the bed is already made, and Joel, there are extra blankets underneath for you to sleep on the floor. I hope that's all right?"

"It's fine," Joel said.

"Joel, lad," Fitch said. "You really *did* do well."

"I ran," Joel said quietly. "It's the only thing I *could* do. I should have had acid at the room, and—"

"And what, lad?" Fitch asked. "Thrown one bucket while the other chalklings swarmed you? A single man can't hold the front against chalklings—you learn that quickly in Nebrask. It takes a bucket brigade, dozens of men, to keep a group of the things back."

Joel looked down.

Fitch knelt. "Joel. If it's any help, I can imagine what it feels like. I . . . well, you know I never did very well at Nebrask. The first time I saw a chalkling charge, I could barely keep my lines straight. I can't even *duel* another person and keep my wits. Harding is right—you did very well tonight."

I want to be able to do more, Joel thought. *Fight.*

"Exton is a Rithmatist," he said out loud.

"Yes," Fitch said. "He was expelled from the Rithmatic school his early years at Armedius for certain . . . complications. It happens very rarely."

"I remember you talking about that," Joel said. "To Melody. Professor, I want you to draw that new line we found, the one with swirls."

"Now?" Fitch asked.

"Yes."

"Honey," his mother said, "you need rest."

"Just do this one thing, Professor," Joel said. "Then I'll go to bed."

"Yes, well, all right," Fitch said, getting out his chalk. He knelt to begin drawing on the floor.

"It makes things quiet," Joel said. "You have to know that. It sucks in sound."

"How do you know . . . ?" His voice grew much quieter when he finished the drawing.

Fitch blinked, then looked up at Joel. "Well, that's something," he said, but the voice sounded far diminished, as if he were distant.

Joel took a deep breath, then tried to yell, "I know!" That was dampened even further, so it came out as a whisper. When he whispered, however, that sound came out normally.

Fitch dismissed the line. "Amazing."

Joel nodded. "The ones we found at the crime scenes no longer worked, so the line must run out of power after a time, or something like that."

"Joel," Fitch said, "do you realize what you just did? You solved the problem your father spent his *life* trying to uncover."

"It was easy," Joel said, suddenly feeling very tired. "Someone gave me the answer—they tried to kill me with it."

BOUNCING LINES of VIGOR

Lines of Vigor react against Lines of Forbiddance in an interesting way. Instead of breaking or moving them, the Lines of Vigor reflect OFF them, turning in a new direction.

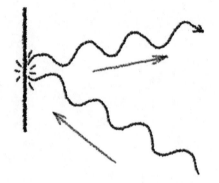

Advanced Rithmatic strategies include learning to draw Lines of Forbiddance specifically for the purpose of reflecting Lines of Vigor. Often, this is one of the only ways to get through a foe's defenses.

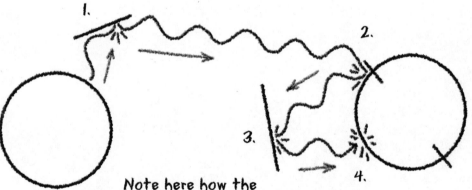

Note here how the Rithmatist bounces her Line of Vigor off her foe's own Lines of Forbiddance to strike at their Circle of Warding.

Harding arrested Exton early the next morning.
Joel heard about it from Fitch as they crossed the
green on their way toward the cathedral for Joel's inception. Joel's mother held to his arm, as if afraid some beast were
going to appear out of nowhere and snatch him away.

"He arrested Exton?" Joel demanded. "It doesn't make sense."

"Well, hum," Fitch said. "Murder rarely makes sense. I can
see why you might be shocked. Exton was a friend of mine too.
And yet, he never *did* like Rithmatists. Ever since he was expelled."

"But he came back to work here!"

"Those who have intense hatred often are fascinated by the
thing they detest," Fitch said. "You saw that drawing at Charles's
house—the man with the bowler and the cane. It looks an awful
lot like Exton."

"It looks like a lot of people," Joel said. "Half the men in the
city wear bowlers and carry canes! It was a small chalk sketch.
They can't use that as proof."

"Exton knew where all of the Rithmatist children lived,"
Fitch said. "He had access to their records."

Joel fell silent. They were fairly good arguments. But *Exton*?
Grumbling yet good-natured Exton?

"Don't worry about it, Son," his mother said. "If he's innocent,
I'm sure the courts will determine that. You need to be ready. If

you're going to be incepted, you should be focused on the Master."

"No," Joel said. "I want to talk to Harding. My inception . . ." It couldn't wait. Not again. But this was *important*. "Where is he?"

They found Harding directing a squad of police officers who were searching through the campus office. Principal York stood a distance off, seeming very dissatisfied, a weeping Florence beside him. She waved to Joel. "Joel!" she called. "Tell them what madness this is! Exton would never hurt anyone! He was such a *dear*."

The police officer at her side quieted her—he was apparently questioning both her and the principal. Inspector Harding stood at the office doorway, leafing through some notes. He looked up as Joel approached. "Ah," he said. "The young hero. Shouldn't you be somewhere, lad? Actually, as I consider it, you should have an escort. I'll send a few soldiers with you to the chapel."

"Is all of that really necessary?" Fitch asked. "I mean, since you have someone in custody . . ."

"I'm afraid it *is* necessary," Harding said. "Every good investigator knows that you don't stop searching just because you make an arrest. We won't be done until we know who Exton was working with, and where he hid the bodies . . . er, where he is keeping the children."

Joel's mother paled at that last comment.

"Inspector," Joel said, "can I talk to you alone for a moment?" Harding nodded, walking with Joel a short distance.

"Are you *sure* you have the right man, Inspector?" Joel asked.

"I don't arrest a man unless I'm sure, son."

"Exton *saved* me last night."

"No, lad," Fitch said. "He saved himself. Do you know why he got expelled from the Rithmatic program thirty years ago?"

Joel shook his head.

"Because he couldn't control his chalklings," Harding said. "He was too much of a danger to send to Nebrask. You saw how wiggly those chalklings were. They didn't have form or shape because they were drawn so poorly. Exton set them against you, but he couldn't really control them, and so when you led them back against him, he had no choice but to lock them out."

"I don't believe it," Joel said. "Harding, this is *wrong*. I know he didn't like Rithmatists, but that's not enough of a reason to arrest a man! Half of the people in the Isles seem to hate them these days."

"Did Exton come to your aid immediately?" Harding asked. "Last night?"

"No," Joel said, remembering his fall and Exton screaming. "He was just scared, and he did help eventually. Inspector, I *know* Exton. He wouldn't do something like this."

"The minds of killers are strange things, Joel," Harding said. "Often, people are shocked or surprised that people they know could turn out to be such monsters. This is confidential information, but we found items belonging to the three missing students in Exton's desk."

"You *did*?" Joel asked.

"Yes," Harding said. "And pages and *pages* of ranting anger about Rithmatists in his room. Hatred, talk of . . . well, unpleasant things. I've seen it before in the obsessed. It's always the ones you don't expect. Fitch tipped me off about the clerk a few days back; something reminded him that Exton had once attended Armedius."

"The census records," Joel said. "I was there when Fitch remembered."

"Ah yes," Harding said. "Well, I now wish I'd been more quick to listen to the professor! I began investigating Exton quietly, but I didn't move quickly enough. I only put the pieces together when you were attacked last night."

"Because of the wiggly lines?" Joel asked.

"No, actually," Harding said. "Because of what happened yesterday afternoon in the office. You were there, talking to Fitch, and he praised how much of a help you'd been to the process of finding the Scribbler. Well, when I heard you'd been attacked, my mind started working. Who would have a motive to kill *you*? Only someone who knew how valuable you were to Fitch's work.

"Exton overhead that, son. He must have been afraid that

you'd connect him to the new Rithmatic line. He probably saw the line when your father was working on it—your father approached the principal for funding to help him discover how the line worked. It wasn't until some of my men searched his quarters and his desk that we found the truly disturbing evidence, though."

Joel shook his head. Exton. Could it actually have been him? The realization that it could have been someone so close, someone he knew and understood, was almost as troubling as the attack.

Things belonging to the three students, in his desk, Joel thought, cold. "The objects . . . maybe he had them for . . . I don't know, reasons relating to the case? Had he gathered them from the students' dorms to send to the families?"

"York says he ordered nothing of the sort," Harding said. "No questions remain except for the locations of the children. I won't lie to you, lad. I think they're probably dead, buried somewhere. We'll have to interrogate Exton to find the answers.

"This is disgraceful business, all of it. I feel terrible that it happened on my watch. I don't know what the ramifications will be, either. The son of a knight-senator dead, a man Principal York hired responsible . . ."

Joel nodded numbly. He didn't buy it, not completely. Something was off. But he needed time to think about it.

"Exton," he said. "When will he be tried?"

"Cases like these take months," Harding said. "It won't be for a while, but we'll need you as a witness."

"You're going to keep the campus on lockdown?"

Harding nodded. "For at least another week, with a careful eye on all of the Rithmatist students. Like I said. An arrest is no reason to get sloppy."

Then I have time, Joel thought. *Exton won't be tried for a while, and the campus is still safe. If it ever was.*

That seemed enough for now. Joel was exhausted, worn thin, and he still had his inception to deal with. He would do that, then maybe have time to think, figure out what was wrong with all of this.

"I have a request of you," Joel said. "My friend, Melody. I want her to attend my inception. Will you let her out of the lockdown for today?"

"Is she that redheaded troublemaker?" Harding asked.

Joel nodded, grimacing slightly.

"Well, for you, all right," Harding said. He spoke to a couple of officers, who rushed off to fetch her.

Joel waited, feeling terrible for Exton sitting in jail. *Potentially becoming a Rithmatist is important,* Joel thought. *I have to go through with this. If I'm one of them, my words will hold more weight.*

The officers eventually returned with Melody, her red hair starkly visible in the distance. When she got close, she ran toward him.

Joel nodded to Harding and walked over to meet her.

"You," she said, pointing, "are in serious trouble."

"What?" Joel asked.

"You went on an adventure, you nearly got killed, you fought chalklings, and you *didn't invite me!"*

He rolled his eyes.

"Honestly," she said. "That was terribly thoughtless of you. What good is having friends if they don't put you in mortal peril every once in a while?"

"You might even call it tragic," Joel said, smiling wanly and joining his mother and Professor Fitch.

"Nah," Melody said. "I'm thinking I need a new word. *Tragic* just doesn't have the effect it once did. What do you think of *appalling?"*

"Might work," Joel said. "Shall we go, then?"

The others nodded, and they again began walking toward the campus gates, accompanied by several of Harding's guards.

"I guess I'm happy you're all right," Melody said. "News of what happened is all over the Rithmatic dorm. Most of the others are red in the face, thinking that the puzzle was solved and they were saved by a *non*-Rithmatist. Of course, half of the red-facedness is probably because none of us can leave yet."

"Yeah," Joel said. "Harding's a careful guy. I think he knows what he's doing."

"You believe him, then?" Melody said. "About Exton, I mean."

Things belonging to each of the students, Joel thought. *And pages of rants about wanting revenge against them. . . .*

They walked the same path Joel had run the night before, terrified in the dark, approaching the police officers. "I don't know," he said.

J oel remembered much of what Father Stewart said from the last time he'd gone through an inception ceremony. He'd been less nervous that time. Perhaps he'd been too young to realize what he was getting himself into.

Joel's knees ached as he knelt in a white robe before Father Stewart, who sprinkled him with water and anointed him with oil. They had to go through the whole ceremony again if Joel wanted to enter the chamber of inception.

Why did everything have to happen at once? He was still fatigued from lack of sleep, and he couldn't stop thinking about Exton. The man had seemed truly frightened. But he would have been, if his own chalklings had come back to attack him.

Joel felt like he had been swept up in something so much larger than he was. There were new Rithmatic lines. He'd solved his father's quest, yet wouldn't get paid for it—all of his father's contracts of patronage had expired when no line had been produced within five years. Still, the world would be shaken by the discovery of a Rithmatic pattern that was so different from the others.

Father Stewart intoned something in Old English, barely recognizable to Joel as from scripture. Above, the apostles turned their springwork heads. To his right, down a hallway, PreSaint Euclid stood inside a mural dedicated to the triangle.

Joel was about to be one of the oldest nonconverts to ever go through the inception ceremony. The world seemed to be becoming a more uncertain place. The disappearances—probably deaths—of Armedius students made the islands bristle, and there was talk of another civil war. The realities of world politics were starting to seem more and more real to Joel. More and more *frightening*.

Life wasn't simple. It never *had* been simple. He just hadn't known.

But how does Nalizar play into all of this? Joel thought. *I still don't trust that man.* Exton had expressed dislike of Nalizar on several occasions, but perhaps it was something to think about. Could he have framed Exton?

Perhaps Joel just *wanted* to find that Nalizar was doing something nefarious.

Father Stewart stopped talking. Joel blinked, realizing he hadn't been paying attention. He looked up, and Father Stewart nodded, his thin white beard shaking. He gestured toward the chamber of inception behind the altar.

Joel stood up. Fitch, his mother, and Melody sat alone on the pews—the regular inception ceremony for the eight-year-olds wouldn't come for another hour yet. The broad, vast cathedral hall sparkled with the light of stained glass windows and delicate murals.

Joel walked quietly around the altar toward the boxy chamber. The door was set with a six-point circle. Joel regarded it, then fished the coin out of his pocket and held it up.

The main gear moving inside had six teeth. The center of each tooth corresponded to the location of one of the six points. The smaller gear to the right had only four teeth. The one to the left, nine teeth, spaced unevenly. The three clicked together in a pattern, one that had to be perfectly attuned to work with the irregular nine-tooth gear.

Huh, Joel thought, tucking the coin in his pocket. Then he pushed open the door.

Inside, he found a white marble room containing a cushion for kneeling and a small altar made from a marble block, topped by a cushion to rest his elbows on. There didn't seem to be anything else in the room—though a springwork lantern shone quite brightly from above, mounted in a crystalline casing so that it cast sparkling light on the walls.

Joel stood, waiting, heart thumping. Nothing happened. Hesitantly, he knelt down, but didn't know what to say.

That was another piece in this whole puzzle. Was there really a Master up in heaven? People like Mary Rowlandson—the colonist he'd read about the night before—believed in God.

The wild chalklings hadn't killed her. They'd kept her prisoner, always stopping her from fleeing. Nobody knew their motives for such an act.

She'd eventually escaped, partially due to the efforts of her husband and some other colonial men. Had her survival been directed by the Master, or had it been simple luck? What did Joel believe?

"I don't know what to say," Joel said. "I figure that if you *are* there, you'll be angry if I claim to believe when I don't. The truth is, I'm not sure I *don't* believe, either. You might be there. I hope you are, I guess.

"Either way, I *do* want to be a Rithmatist. Even with all of the problems it will cause. I . . . I *need* the power to fight them. I don't want to run again.

"I'll be a good Rithmatist. I know the defenses better than almost anyone else on campus. I'll defend the Isles at Nebrask. I will serve. Just let me be a Rithmatist."

Nothing happened. Joel stood. Most people went in and came out quickly, so he figured that there was no point in waiting around. Either he'd be able to draw the lines when he left, or he wouldn't.

He turned to leave.

Something stood in the room behind him.

He jumped, stumbling back, almost falling over the small altar. The thing behind him was a brilliant white. It stood as high as Joel did, and was in the shape of a man—but a very thin one, with spindly arms and only a curved line for a head. It held what appeared to be a crude bow in one hand.

The thing looked as if it had been drawn, but it didn't stick to the walls or floors like a chalkling. Its form was primitive, like the ancient drawings one might find on the side of a cliff.

Suddenly, Joel remembered the story he'd read from before, the tale of the explorer who had found a canyon where the drawings danced.

It didn't move. Joel hesitantly leaned to the side and could see that the thing almost disappeared when looked at from that angle.

Joel leaned back to look at it from the front. What would it do? He took a hesitant step forward, reaching out. He paused, then touched the thing.

It shook violently, then fell to the ground, pasting itself to the floor like a chalk drawing. Joel stumbled back as the thing shot away underneath the altar.

Joel dropped to his knees, noticing a slit at the base of the altar. There was darkness beyond.

"No," Joel whispered, reaching out. "Please. Come back!"

He knelt there for the better part of an hour. A knock finally came at the far door.

He opened it and found Father Stewart standing outside. "Come, child," he said. "The others needing inception will arrive soon. Whatever has happened has happened, and we shall see the result."

He held out a piece of chalk.

Joel left the chamber feeling shocked and confused. He took the chalk numbly, walking over to a stone placed on the ground for the purpose of drawing. He knelt down. Melody, Fitch, and his mother approached.

Joel drew a Line of Forbiddance on the top of the block. Melody reached out with an anxious hand, but Joel knew what would happen.

Her hand passed through the plane above the line. Her face fell.

Father Stewart looked troubled. "Well, son, it appears that the

Master has other plans for you. In his name, I pronounce you a full member of the Church of the Monarch." He hesitated. "Do not see this as a failure. Go, and the Master will lead you to the path he has chosen." It was the same thing that Stewart had told Joel eight years ago.

"No," Melody said. "This isn't right! It was supposed to . . . supposed to be different this time . . ."

"It's all right," Joel said, standing. He felt so tired. With a crushing sense of defeat on top of that, making it difficult for him to breathe.

Mostly, he just wanted to be alone. He turned and walked slowly from the cathedral and back toward campus.

The TAYLOR DEFENSE

This defense is controversial in regular duels because of the two circles. It is allowed, but if the outer circle is breached, that is considered a loss.

It has been argued that this is the most powerful defense in all of Rithmatics.

The Taylor is very good at focusing enemy fire and chalklings into these open corridors.

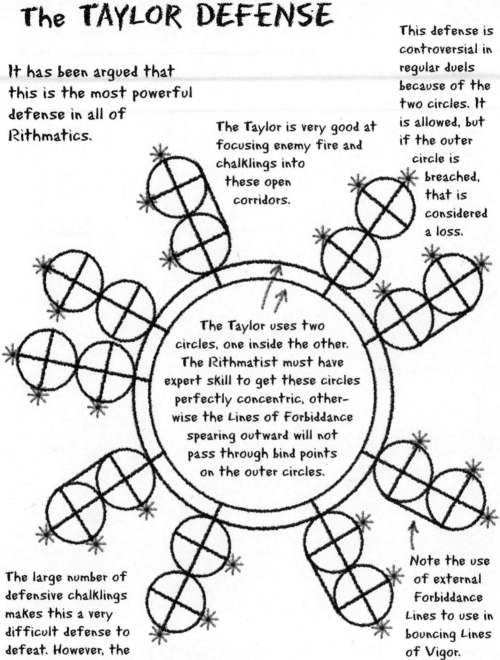

The Taylor uses two circles, one inside the other. The Rithmatist must have expert skill to get these circles perfectly concentric, otherwise the Lines of Forbiddance spearing outward will not pass through bind points on the outer circles.

The large number of defensive chalklings makes this a very difficult defense to defeat. However, the Rithmatist drawing it must be VERY fast.

Note the use of external Forbiddance Lines to use in bouncing Lines of Vigor.

Often called the "Impossible Defense," the Taylor is one of the most difficult known defenses because of its dependence upon not one, but two nine-point circles.

Joel slept through most of the day, but didn't try to go to bed that night. He sat up at his father's table, a springwork lantern whirring on the wall behind him.

He'd cleaned the books off the table, making way for his father's old notes and annotations, which he'd placed alongside a few pieces of the man's best chalk. The notes and diagrams seemed unimportant. The mystery had been solved. The problems were over.

Joel wasn't a Rithmatist. He'd failed his father.

Stop that, he told himself. *Stop feeling sorry for yourself.*

He wanted to throw the table over and scream. He wanted to break the pieces of chalk, then grind them to dust. Why had he dared hope? He'd *known* that very few people got chosen.

So much about life was disappointment. He often wondered how humankind endured so long, and if the few moments when things went right *really* made up for all the rest.

This was how it ended. Joel, back where he had begun, the same as before. He'd done too poorly in his classes to earn himself further education once he was done with Armedius. Now he didn't even have the slight, buried hope that he might find a way to be a Rithmatist.

The three students who had been taken were dead. Gone, left in unmarked graves by Exton. The killer had been stopped, but what did that mean to the families who had lost children? Their pain would continue.

He leaned forward. "Why?" he asked of the papers and notes. "Why does everything turn out like this?"

His father's work would be forgotten in the light of Exton's horrible deeds. The clerk would be remembered as a murderer, but also as the man who had finally solved the mystery of a new Rithmatic line.

How? Joel thought. *How did he solve that mystery? How did Exton, a man who failed his classes, discover things that no Rithmatic scholar has been able to?*

Joel stood up, pacing back and forth. His father's notes continued to confront him, seeming to shine in the light of the lantern.

Joel walked over, digging through them, trying to find the very oldest of the notes. He came up with a yellowed piece of paper, browning on one edge.

> I traveled again to the fronts of Nebrask. And discovered very little. Men speak of strange happenings all the time, but they never seem to occur when I am there.
>
> I remain convinced that there are other lines. I need to know what they do before I can determine anything else.

The page had a drawn symbol at the bottom, the Line of Silencing, with its four loops. "Where?" Joel asked. "*Where* did you get this, Father? How did you discover it? At Nebrask?"

If that had been the case, then others would know about it. Surely the Rithmatists on the battlefront, if they saw lines like these, would intuit their meaning. And who would draw them? Wild chalklings didn't draw lines. Did they?

Joel put the sheet aside, looking through his father's log, trying to date when he'd written that particular passage.

The last date on the log was the day before his father had died. It listed Nebrask as the location of that trip.

Joel sat down, thinking about that. He flipped back to the very first dates of travel. A visit to the island of Zona Arida.

Zona Arida, near Bonneville and Texas. They were all southwestern islands. Joel's father had gone there several times, according to the logs.

Joel frowned, then glanced at the books on the floor. One was the one that Nalizar had checked out, about further Rithmatic lines. Joel picked it up and opened it to the back, looking at the stamped card that listed the book's history. The volume had only been checked out a few times over the years.

Joel's father was one of the first on the list. His father's first visit to Zona Arida had come only a few weeks after he had checked out the book.

Joel flipped open the volume, scanning the chapter lists. One was called "Historical New-Line Theories." He flipped to that one, skimming the contents by the light of a single lantern. It took several hours to find what he wanted.

> Some early explorers reported strange designs upon the cliffs of these islands in the southwest. We cannot know who created them, since much of America was uninhabited at the time of European arrival.
>
> Some have claimed that lines drawn after these patterns have Rithmatic properties. Most scholars dismiss this. Many odd shapes can be drawn and gain chalkling life from a Line of Making. That does not make them a new line.

Joel turned the next page. There, facing him, was a sketch of the very creature he'd seen in the chamber of inception earlier that day.

What is going on here? Joel thought, reading the caption to the picture. It read: *One of the many sketches made by Captain Estevez during his explorations of Zona Arida Island.*

Joel blinked, then looked back at his table.

Something tapped at his window.

He yelped, jumping up out of his chair. He reached for the bucket of acid he'd taken from Inspector Harding, but then saw what was on the other side of the window.

Red hair, wide eyes. Melody grinned at him, waving. Joel checked the clock. It was two in the morning.

He groaned, walking out and then climbing the steps to open the dormitory door, which was locked. Melody stood outside. Her skirt was scuffed, and there were twigs in her hair.

"Melody," he said. "What are you *doing* here?"

"Standing in the cold," she said. "Aren't you going to invite a lady in?"

"I don't know if it would be proper. . . ."

She pushed her way in anyway, walking down to the workroom. Joel sighed, closing the door and following her. Inside, she turned to him, hands on hips. "This," she said, "is *appalling.*"

"What?" he asked.

"It really doesn't work as well as the word 'tragic,' does it?" She flopped down into a chair. "I need a different word."

"Do you know what time it is?"

"I'm annoyed," she said, ignoring his question. "They've had us locked up all day. You're an insomniac. I figured I could come bug you."

"You snuck past the guards?"

"Out the window. Second story. There's a tree close by. Harder to climb down than it looks."

"You're lucky the policemen didn't catch you."

"Nah," she said. "They aren't there."

"What?"

"Oh, there are a couple at the main door," she said. "But only those two. The ones that patrolled below the windows left a short time ago. Guess they changed shift or something. Anyway, that's not important. Joel, the important thing is this *tragedy* I'm trying to tell you about."

"You being locked up?"

"That," she said. "And *Exton* being locked up. He didn't do it, Joel. I know he didn't. The guy gave me half of his sandwich once."

"That's a reason for him not being a murderer?"

"It's more than that," Melody said. "He's a nice man. He

grumbles a lot, but I like him. He has a kind heart. He's also smart."

"The person doing this was smart."

"Exactly. Why would Exton attack the son of a knight-senator? That's a stupid move for him, if he wanted to remain inconspicuous. That's the part of this that doesn't make sense. We should be asking why—why attack Charles? If we knew that, I'll bet the real motive for all of this would come together."

Joel sat thoughtfully.

"Harding has evidence against Exton," Joel said.

"So?"

"So," Joel said. "That's usually what proves that a person is guilty."

"I don't believe it," Melody said. "Look, if Exton got kicked out of here all those years ago, then how in the world was *he* a good enough Rithmatist to create a line nobody else knew of?"

"Yeah. I know." He stood. "Come on," he said, walking out the door.

Melody followed. "Where are we going?"

"Professor Fitch's office," Joel said, crossing the dark campus. They walked in silence for a time before Joel noticed it. "Where are the police patrols?"

"I don't know," Melody said. "See, I told you."

Joel hastened his step. They reached Warding Hall, then rushed up the stairs. Joel pounded on the door for a while, and eventually a very groggy Professor Fitch answered the door. "Hum?"

"Professor," Joel said. "I think something's going on."

Fitch yawned. "What time is it?"

"Early," Joel said. "Look, Professor, you saw the lines that were intended to trap me? The cage of Lines of Forbiddance that Exton supposedly drew?"

"Yes?" Fitch asked.

"How well were the lines drawn?"

"They were good. Expertly straight."

"Professor," Joel said, "I *saw* lines that Exton drew at the door. They weren't shaped right. He did a terrible job."

"So he was trying to fool you, Joel."

"No," Joel said. "He was afraid for his life. I saw it in his eyes. He wouldn't have drawn poor lines in that case! Professor, what if Nalizar—"

"Joel!" Fitch snapped. "I'm tired of your fixation on Professor Nalizar! I . . . well . . . I hate raising my voice, but I'm just fed up! You wake me up at awful hours, talking about Nalizar? He didn't do it, no matter how badly you want him to have."

Joel fell silent.

Fitch rubbed his eyes. "I don't mean to be testy. It's just . . . well, talk to me in the morning."

With that, and a yawn, Fitch closed the door.

"Great," Melody said.

"He's not good with lack of sleep," Joel said. "Never has been."

"So what now?" Melody asked.

"Let's go talk to the policemen at the front of your dormitory," Joel said, rushing down the stairs. "See why the others aren't on their patrol."

They crossed the campus again in the dark, and Joel began to wish he'd brought that bucket of acid with him. But surely Harding's men would—

He pulled up short. The Rithmatic student dormitory was straight ahead, and the door was open. Two forms lay on the grass in front of it.

"Dusts!" Joel said, pelting forward, Melody at his side. The forms proved to be the policemen. Joel checked the pulse of the first one with nervous fingers.

"Alive," Joel said. "But unconscious." He moved over to the other one, finding that he was still alive as well.

"Uh, Joel," Melody said. "You remember what I said this morning, about being angry at you for not inviting me to be attacked with you?"

"Yeah."

"I completely take that back."

Joel looked up at the open doorway. Light reflected distantly inside.

"Go for help," he said.

"Where?"

"The front gates," he said. "The office. I don't know! Just find it. I'm going to see who's inside."

"Joel, you're not a Rithmatist. What can you do?"

"People could be dying in there, Melody."

"I'm the Rithmatist."

"If the Scribbler really is in there," Joel said, "it won't matter which of us goes in. Your lines will be little defense against him. Go!"

Melody stood for a moment, then bolted away at a dash.

Joel looked at the open doorway. *What am I doing?*

He gritted his teeth, slipping inside. At the corner, he found some buckets of acid, and he felt more confident carrying one as he snuck up the stairs. Boys were on the first floor, with girls on the second, some families of professors on the third. There were hall mothers stationed on the second floor to keep watch. If Joel could find one of them, perhaps she could help.

He rounded the top of the stairs on the second floor, slipping into the hallway. It appeared empty.

He heard something on the stairs behind him.

He looked with a panic to see something coming down from the third floor, moving in the darkness there. Barely thinking, Joel hefted his bucket of acid and tossed it.

The something turned out to be a person. The wave of acid completely drenched the surprised Nalizar.

The professor gasped, rubbing his eyes, and Joel yelped, scrambling away down the second-floor hallway. In his panicked mind, he thought to make for Melody's room, where he could use the aforementioned tree to climb away. He heard Nalizar follow, cursing.

Joel smacked straight into something invisible. It threw him backward to the ground, stunned. The hallway was barely lit, and he hadn't seen the Line of Forbiddance on the ground.

"Foolish child," Nalizar said, grabbing him by the shoulder.

Joel yelled and punched as hard as he could at Nalizar's gut.

Nalizar grunted, but didn't let go. Instead, he stuck his foot out, scraping it along the ground. It left a chalk line behind it.

Chalk on the bottom tip of the shoe, Joel thought. *Good idea. Hard to draw straight lines, but good idea.*

Nalizar shoved Joel to the floor, then finished a Box of Forbiddance around him. Joel groaned at the pain in his arm—Nalizar had a powerful grip.

Trapped.

Joel cried out, feeling at the invisible box. It was solid.

"Idiot," Nalizar said, wiping his face with a dry section of his coat. "If you live this night, you're going to owe me a new coat." The professor's skin looked irritated from the acid, and his eyes were bloodshot. The acid used wasn't powerful enough to be truly dangerous to a person, however.

"I—" Nalizar said.

One of the doors in the hallway opened and interrupted him. Nalizar spun as a large figure stepped out into the hallway. Joel could just barely make out the face in the dim light.

Inspector Harding.

Nalizar stood for a moment, dripping acid. He glanced at Joel, then back at Harding.

"So," Nalizar said to Harding, "it *is* you. I've tracked you down at last."

Harding stood still. In the shadowed light, his domed police officer's hat looked an awful lot like a bowler. He lowered his rifle, resting his hand on the butt, the tip against the ground. Like a cane.

His hat was pulled down over his eyes so that Joel couldn't see them. Joel *could* see the inspector's ghastly grin. Harding opened his mouth, tipping his head back.

A swarm of squirming chalklings flooded out of his mouth like a torrent, scurrying down his chest and across his body.

Nalizar cursed, dropping to his knees and drawing a circle around himself. Joel watched as Nalizar completed the Easton Defense with quick, careful strokes.

Harding, Joel thought. *He said there was a federal police station near Lilly Whiting's house. And he said he was on patrol in the very area where Herman Libel was taken—Harding claimed that the Scribbler was taunting him by striking so close.*

And then Charles Calloway. While we were investigating Charles's house, Harding mentioned that he'd been there the very evening before, trying to get the family to send their son back to Armedius.

When Harding charged to the gates after being called on the night I was attacked, he came from the east. From the direction of the general campus, not the Rithmatic one. He'd been over there, controlling the chalklings.

Exton wasn't the only one in the room who heard Professor Fitch say how important I was—Harding was there too.

Dusts!

Joel screamed for help, slamming his fists against the invisible barrier. It all made sense! Why attack the students outside campus? Why take the son of the knight-senator?

To inspire panic. To make the Rithmatic students all congregate at Armedius, rather than staying at their homes. Harding had secured the campus, brought all of the Rithmatists here, including the half who normally lived far away, and had locked them in the dorms.

That way, he had them all together and could take them in one strike.

Joel continued to pound uselessly at the walls of his invisible prison. He yelled, but as soon as his voice reached a certain decibel, the excess vanished. He glanced to the side, and there saw one of the Lines of Silencing, hidden against the white of the painted wall. It was far enough away that it only sucked in his voice when he yelled, not when he spoke normally.

Joel cursed, falling to his knees. Harding dismissed the Line of Forbiddance in the hallway, the one Joel had run into, and the multitude of chalklings swarmed forward and surrounded Professor Nalizar, attacking his defenses. The man worked quickly, reaching out of his circle and drawing Lines of Vigor to shoot off pieces of chalklings. That didn't seem to have much effect. The formless chalklings just grew the pieces back.

Joel pushed at the base of his prison, looking for the place that felt the weakest. He found a section that Nalizar had drawn with his foot that pushed back with less strength. The chalk there wasn't as straight.

Joel licked his finger and began to rub at the base of the line. It was a poor tactic. Lines of Forbiddance were the strongest of the four. He could only rub at the side, carefully wearing away the line bit by bit. It was a process that the books said could take hours.

Nalizar was not faring well. Though he'd drawn a brilliant defense, there were just *so many* chalklings. Inspector Harding stood shadowed in the darkness. He barely seemed to move, just a smiling, dark statue.

His arm moved, the rest of him completely still. He lowered the tip of his rifle, and Joel could see a bit of chalk taped to it. Harding drew a Line of Vigor on the ground.

Only it *wasn't* a Line of Vigor. It was too sharp—instead of curves, it had jagged tips. Like the second new Rithmatic line they had found at Lilly Whiting's house. Joel had almost forgotten about that one.

This new line shot forward like a Line of Vigor, punching through several of Harding's own chalklings before hitting the defenses. Nalizar cursed, reaching forward to draw a curve and repair the piece that had been blown away.

His sleeve dripped acid. That acid fell right on his circle, making a hole in it. Nalizar stared at the hole, and the chalklings shied away from the acid. Then, one threw itself at the drop, getting dissolved. Another followed. That diluted the acid, for the next one that touched the acid didn't vanish. It began attacking the sides of the hole the acid had made.

"You are making a mistake," Nalizar said, looking up at Harding.

Harding drew another jagged line. This one shot through the hole, hitting Nalizar and throwing him backward.

Joel gaped. *It's a Line of Vigor that can affect more than chalk*, he realized. *That's . . . that's amazing!*

The scribbled, shifting chalklings withdrew. Nalizar lay in the middle of his circle, unconscious. Harding smiled, eyes shadowed, then walked to the next door in the hallway, one just to Joel's right. Harding pushed it open, and Joel could see young women slumbering in the beds inside.

Wild chalklings swarmed in behind Harding and flooded the room. Joel screamed, but the Line of Silencing stole his voice. One of the girls stirred, sitting up.

The chalklings crawled over her, swarming her body. Her mouth opened wide, but no sound came out. Another Line of Silencing hung on the wall there, drawn to keep sound from waking the other students.

Joel could only watch, banging against his invisible wall, as the girl shook and writhed, a group of the chalklings climbing into her mouth as she tried to scream. They pinched at her skin, causing pinpricks of blood. More and more of them crawled into her mouth.

She didn't stop shaking. She shook and shook, spasming, falling to the floor and rolling as she seemed to *shrink* and flatten. Her figure began to waver. Joel watched, horrified. Soon the girl was indistinguishable from the other scribbled chalklings.

Harding watched with a broad grin, showing teeth, his eyes lost in shadow.

"Why?" Joel demanded of him. "What is going on?"

Harding made no reply as his chalklings took the other girls in the room. One by one, two other girls were consumed and transformed. The awful sight made Joel look away. The chalklings that had been dissolved in the acid were re-forming, pulling themselves out of the pool and coming back to life.

Harding moved to the next room, passing Joel. He opened the door and stepped inside, and Joel could see a Line of Silencing had already been drawn on the door. Harding had probably done them all first.

The scribbled chalklings flooded the hallway behind Harding, then disappeared into the room. Joel felt sick, thinking of the girls sleeping inside. He dropped to his knees and continued scratching at his line, trying to get through. He wasn't doing much.

A chalkling suddenly moved in front of him and began to attack the line.

Joel jumped back, grabbing his coin and trying to use it to ward the creature away. It ignored both him and the coin.

It was at that moment that Joel realized the chalkling was a unicorn.

He glanced to the side, where a face peeked around the corner ahead of him, farther down the hallway. Melody drew another unicorn, sending it to help the first. Joel stepped back, amazed at how quickly the unicorn made holes in Nalizar's line.

She really is good with those, Joel thought as they broke through a large enough section for him to squeeze past. Sweating, he dashed to her.

"Melody," he whispered. As long as he didn't yell, the Lines of Silencing wouldn't steal his voice. The sound wouldn't carry far enough, he guessed, to hit the lines and activate them.

"Joel," she said. "Something's *very* wrong. There aren't any policemen at the gates *or* at the office. I tried pounding on the doors of the professors, but nobody answered. Is that Professor *Nalizar* on the ground?"

"Yes," Joel said. "Melody, come on, we—"

"You defeated him!" she said with surprise, standing.

"No, I think I was wrong about him," Joel said urgently. "We need to—"

Harding stepped out of the room and looked toward them. He was between them and the way to the stairwell. Melody screamed, but most of it dampened, and Joel cursed, pulling her after him. Together, they scrambled farther down the hallway.

The dormitory hallway was a square, with rooms on the inside and out. If they could go all the way around, they could get to the stairs.

Melody ran beside him, then suddenly yanked him to the side. "My room," she said, pointing. "Out the window."

Joel nodded. She threw open the door, and they were confronted by chalklings crawling in the open window, moving across the walls like a flood of white spiders. Harding had sent them around the outside of the building.

Joel cursed, slamming the door as Melody screamed again.

This scream was dampened less than the others; they were getting away from the Lines of Silencing.

Chalklings crawled under the door. Others scurried down the hallway from Harding's direction. Joel pulled Melody toward the stairs, but froze as he saw another group of chalklings coming from that direction.

They were surrounded.

"Oh dusts, oh dusts, oh dusts," Melody said. She fell to her knees and drew a circle around them, then added a Square of Forbiddance around it. "We're doomed. We're going to die."

Harding rounded the corner. He was a dark silhouette, stepping quietly, not speaking. He stopped as the chalklings began to work on Melody's square, then he reached up and twisted the key on the nearby lantern, bringing light to the hallway.

He seemed even more twisted by the half-light than he had in the dimness.

"Talk to me!" Joel said. "Harding, you're my friend! Why are you doing this? What happened to you out there, in Nebrask?"

Harding began to draw one of his modified Lines of Vigor on the floor. Melody's square had failed, and the chalklings were starting to work on her circle. They squirmed and shook, as if anticipating biting into Joel's and Melody's flesh.

Suddenly, a voice rang in the hallway. Clear, angry.

"You will leave them *alone!*"

Harding turned toward a figure standing in an open Rithmatic coat at the other end of the hallway, holding a piece of chalk in each hand.

Professor Fitch.

Joel's Sketch of the Rithmatic Dorms' second floor that night

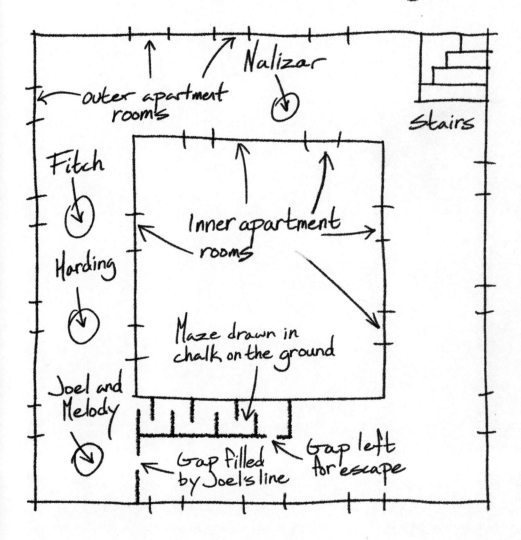

Nalizar

outer apartment rooms

Stairs

Fitch

Harding

Inner apartment rooms

Joel and Melody

Maze drawn in chalk on the ground

Gap filled by Joel's line

Gap left for escape

Professor Fitch was shaking. Joel could see that, even from the distance. The flood of chalklings turned away from Joel and Melody and rushed toward him.

Harding raised his rifle.

Fitch dropped to his knees and drew a Line of Forbiddance on the floor. There was a loud *click* and a rush of air as the rifle fired.

The bullet shot through the hallway, then hit the line's wall and froze a few inches from Fitch's head. The bullet lost its momentum and was pushed back and away. It hit the floor with a *clink*.

Harding let out his first sound then, a roar of anger. It was quieted by the Lines of Silencing. Still, it was loud enough to make Fitch waver, and he looked up, eyes widening in fear. Hesitating.

Then he looked at Joel and Melody, trapped in their failing circle. Fitch's jaw set and his hands stopped shaking. He looked down at the flood of chalklings approaching him, and reached out with both hands to snap his chalk to the ground on either side of him.

Then he drew.

Joel stood up straight, watching with awe as Fitch spun about, using his chalk to draw two Lines of Warding, one inside the other, both as perfect as Joel had ever seen. Fitch added smaller circles on the outside, one after another in rapid succession, one hand drawing each circle even as the other drew a Line of Forbiddance inside each one as an anchor.

The Taylor Defense.

"Professor . . ." Joel whispered. The defense was perfect. Majestic. "I *knew* you could to it."

"Yeah, Joel?" Melody said. "Hello. Pay attention. We need to
get out of here."

She knelt down, using her chalk to dismiss the Line of
Warding around them.

"No," Joel said. He looked down at her. "Melody, those chalklings aren't natural. Fitch can't fight them; they can't be destroyed. We need to help him."

"How?"

Joel looked back. "Dismiss the rest of those lines around us."
As she did so, Joel knelt down, taking a piece of blue chalk
out of his coat pocket.

"Hey, you started carrying some!"
Melody exclaimed.

"My father's chalk," Joel said, sketching out a long rectangular maze pattern
on the floor. "Go draw this in the corridor there. Make it as long as you can,
and leave this little section open on the
side and at the far end."

She nodded, then moved over to begin
drawing. Joel took his chalk and closed
off the hole she left open.

"What good will that do?" she asked,
drawing urgently.

"You'll see," Joel said, spinning back
toward Harding and Fitch. Fitch drew furiously and was faring
far better than Nalizar had. He had managed to enclose a couple
of the Scribbler's chalklings within boxes, trapping them.

Unfortunately, his outer defenses were nearly eaten away.
He wouldn't last long like this.

Joel gave Melody as much time as he dared. Then he yelled,
"Hey, Harding!"

The inspector turned.

"Wednesday night," Joel said, "you tried to kill me. Now is your chance. Because if you *don't*, I'm going to go get help and—" He cut off, yelping. Apparently Harding didn't need any encouragement, for a good third of his chalklings began scrambling back down the hallway toward Joel and Melody, taking some of the pressure off the beleaguered Fitch.

Joel turned and dashed down the hallway. Melody had drawn quickly, and while her lines weren't perfectly straight, they would do. Joel entered the long corridor of chalk she'd made, with Lines of Forbiddance to either side of him, then wove through the short maze of lines.

As he'd expected, the chalklings piled in after him. They could have gotten through to Melody if they'd known that the section of the lines that *Joel* had drawn wasn't Rithmatic—but, just like before, chalklings seemed as fooled by a fake line as a human might be, at least at first.

Joel burst through the hole in the end of the small maze. "Close it!"

Melody did so, blocking the chalklings. The things immediately turned around to escape back out the front of the maze.

"Come on!" Joel said, running, Melody at his side. They raced the chalklings, who had to weave through turns to get to the end. Joel and Melody passed through the gap where he had drawn a non-Rithmatic line, then Melody closed off the entrance to the maze.

She stood, puffing, the chalklings inside shaking angrily. They began to attack the walls.

Joel turned around. "Melody!" he said. Another group of chalklings had broken off from Professor Fitch and were heading toward him and Melody.

She yelped, drawing a line across the corridor, then down the sides of the wall to protect her and Joel.

That trapped them again. Harding left the second batch of chalklings there, chewing on the line blocking Joel and Melody from the combat.

"That's all we can do, Professor!" Joel called, just quiet enough that the Lines of Silencing had no effect. Then, more softly, he added, "Come on. . . ."

Fitch drew with a look of intense concentration on his face. Every time he seemed to waver, he glanced up at Melody and Joel surrounded by chalklings. His face grew more determined, and he continued his work.

Harding—the Scribbler—growled, then began launching his enhanced Lines of Vigor at Fitch. The professor drew expert Lines of Forbiddance to not just block, but deflect the Lines of Vigor.

Joel watched, breathing quickly, following Fitch's moves as Melody shored up their defense, drawing reinforcing lines where the chalklings looked like they might be close to getting through.

"Come on . . ." Joel repeated. "You can do it."

Fitch worked furiously, drawing with both hands. His defense was expert—he coaxed the chalklings toward weak points, then blocked them off inside Lines of Forbiddance.

Then, with a smile, Fitch reached out and drew a jagged Line of Vigor like Harding had been doing.

It shot across the room and hit the surprised inspector, throwing him backward. Harding hit the ground with a grunt. He groaned, then stood back up, drawing a Circle of Warding around himself, followed by a Line of Forbiddance in front of it.

When did Harding become a Rithmatist? Joel thought, realizing the oddity for the first time. *That Line of Warding is almost inhumanly perfect. And he drew it at a distance, with chalk on the end of his rifle!*

Fitch wasn't daunted. He expertly bounced two Lines of Vigor around Harding's front defending wall. Harding was forced to draw Lines of Forbiddance at his sides.

Fitch then bounced a Line of Vigor off the wall Melody had drawn, hitting the back of Harding's defense.

"Wow," Joel said.

Harding bellowed, then drew a line behind himself as well.

"Ha!" Fitch yelled just as the chalklings burst through his circle.

"Professor!" Joel yelled.

Fitch, however, stood up and leaped out of the circle as the chalklings piled into it. They hesitated, and Fitch quickly drew a Line of Forbiddance to block off the circle, trapping them inside his own defense. Then he rushed across the room and drew a Line of Forbiddance across the hallway to trap the chalklings there against Melody's line.

Finally, he turned toward Harding. The man, whatever he was, stood with eyes shadowed. He no longer smiled, but simply waited. The creature knew that soon, the chalklings would break free and attack again.

"Professor," Joel called softly, something occurring to him. It was a long shot, but . . .

Fitch turned toward him.

"A clock," Joel said. "Find a clock."

Fitch frowned, but did as requested. He burst into one of the students' rooms, then came back out with a clock and held it toward Joel. "What do I do with this?"

"Break off the face," Joel said. "Show the creature the gears inside!"

Fitch did so, desperately prying off the front of the clock. He held it up, showing the gears. Harding shied back, dropping his rifle, raising his hands.

Fitch approached, displaying the ticking gears, the winding springs, the spinning circles. Harding cried out, and in the light of the single lantern, Joel could see the creature's shadow begin to shake and twist. The shadow fuzzed, coming to look as if it were drawn in charcoal.

"By the Depths!" Fitch said. "A Forgotten!"

"What the *dusts* is a Forgotten!" Joel said.

"A creature of Nebrask," Fitch said. "They lead the wild chalklings. But . . . how did one get all the way here? And attached to Harding! I wasn't aware that was possible. This is dire, Joel."

"I figured that last part out," Joel said. "How do we kill it?"

"Acid," Fitch said, proffering the clock. "We need acid!"

"Melody, let me out the back."

"But—"

"Do it!" Joel said.

She reached back, dismissing the line. Joel dashed down the

corridor and steps to where the second bucket of acid waited. He grabbed it, then ran back up the stairs. He rounded the hallway in the other direction, passing Nalizar on the ground and coming up behind Professor Fitch.

Joel hesitated beside the professor. Nearby, the chalklings Fitch had trapped inside his defense burst out, swarming across the floor.

Joel took a deep breath, then threw the acid toward Harding's feet. The acid washed away the Line of Forbiddance and the Circle of Warding, splashing across Harding's shadow.

That dissolved, as if it *were* made of charcoal. Or chalk. Blackness melted into the acid.

The inspector screamed, then collapsed to the ground.

The chalklings froze in place.

All fell silent.

Joel waited, muscles tense, watching those chalklings. They continued to remain frozen.

We beat him. We did it!

"My, my," Fitch said. He reached up to wipe his brow. "I actually won a duel. That's the first time I've actually *won*! My hands barely shook."

"You did fantastic, Professor!" Joel said.

"Well, I don't know about that. But, well, after you children left I just couldn't sleep. After how I treated you and all. And, hum. Here you'd been right so many times, and I sent you away without even listening. So I came out to find you. Saw the policemen at the front of the building here, and . . ." He hesitated. "I say," Fitch said, pointing. "What is happening to them?"

Joel glanced at the chalklings. They were beginning to quiver even more furiously than normal. Then they began to expand.

Uh-oh, Joel thought. "Dismiss the lines boxing them in! Quick!"

The other two gave him incredulous stares.

"Trust me!" Joel said as the chalklings began to take shape. Fitch rushed over to his defense and began to release the chalklings he'd captured in small boxes. Melody gave Joel a "you'd better know what you're doing" look, then bent down to release her lines.

The first of the chalklings popped into three dimensions, forming the shape of the young woman Joel had seen taken earlier. Fitch exclaimed in surprise, then reached out with a second piece of chalk, releasing the chalklings more quickly before the people inside of them got squished by their confines.

In minutes, Joel, Melody, and Fitch were surrounded by a group of dazed people. Some of them were students—Joel recognized Herman Libel among the group—but many were older Rithmatists in their twenties, wearing the coats of graduates. Rithmatists from the fight at Nebrask.

"William?" Melody asked, looking at one of the younger Rithmatists—a man with red hair.

"Where the dusts am I?" the young man said. "Mel? What the . . . ?"

Melody's brother trailed off as she grabbed him in an embrace.

At that moment, Joel heard footsteps. A breathless Nalizar appeared around the corner, holding his chalk, still dripping slightly with acid.

"I will save—" he began, then stopped short. "Oh."

"Yeah," Joel said. "Great timing, Professor." He sank down, exhausted, leaning back against a wall.

Melody walked over, hands on hips. "Worn out already?" she asked with a smile, her confused brother trailing along behind her.

"Tragic, eh?" Joel asked.

"Definitely."

ADVANCED EASTON DEFENSE

The Rithmatist has added a large number of defensive chalklings to the outside of the figure. This is an excellent way to monopolize on the Easton's huge number of bind points.

This side of the figure is more defensive, with more circles. A wise Rithmatist will focus on opponents from the southeast first, where the defense is weaker, but more open.

The outer circles have been strengthened with a Mark's Cross inside of each one. This added stability allows the Rithmatist to forgo some of the inner Lines of Forbiddance, giving him or her more room to work.

It is quite informative to compare a basic Easton with one drawn by a more advanced Rithmatist. Note that the Easton is itself a difficult defense to draw, so completing even the basic version under stress is considered an accomplishment.

Joel grinned. "Your gratitude will include a couple of good seats to the Melee, won't it?"

"They're set aside for you, son. Front row."

"Thanks!"

"I believe that *we* are the ones who owe *you* thanks," York said. To the side, Joel noticed some men in very rich-looking suits approaching. One was Knight-Senator Calloway.

"Ah," York said. "If you'll excuse me, there are politicians who need to be entertained."

"Of course, sir," Joel said, and York withdrew.

Joel stood for a long while, watching people enter the broad doors, filling the arena inside. Exton approached with Florence. The two of them seemed to argue a lot less frequently lately.

Harding had been relieved of duty, but claimed he didn't remember anything of what had happened. Joel was inclined to believe the man. He'd seen the change that happened in Harding. The other authorities weren't as quick to understand. Apparently, a Forgotten had never acted in this manner before.

Joel was beginning to suspect that whatever happened to make Rithmatists in the chamber of inception could happen in Nebrask as well. That book he wasn't supposed to have read had said the inception ceremony involved something called a Shadowblaze.

He'd seen one in the chamber of inception. He'd asked several other people who hadn't become Rithmatists, and none had seen one of the things. He already knew that the Rithmatists, Melody included, wouldn't speak of the experience.

Joel wasn't certain why he had seen the Shadowblaze, or why he hadn't become a Rithmatist for it, but his experience hinted that the entire process of inception was far more complex than most people knew.

Harding had no history at all of having Rithmatic abilities, and he could no longer produce lines. Whatever the Forgotten had done to him, it had granted the ability. Was that what a Shadowblaze did for someone during the inception?

That left an uncomfortable knowledge in Joel. There was more

I suppose we owe an apology to Professor Nalizar, don't we?" Principal York asked.

Joel shrugged. "I'd apologize to Exton first, sir."

York chuckled, his mustache quivering. "Already done, lad. Already done."

They stood outside Warding Hall, groups of people piling in for the Melee. York had declared the campus open again after just one day of chaos following the Scribbler's defeat. The principal wanted to make a point that Armedius would continue undaunted; he had been certain to publicize not only the return of the missing students, but the dozens of Rithmatists thought lost at Nebrask. The media was having a frenzy with that.

"And not one, but two new Rithmatic lines discovered," York said, hands behind his back, looking utterly pleased.

"Yeah," Joel said, a little noncommittal.

York eyed him. "I've sent letters to some of my friends who lead the other academies, Joel."

Joel turned.

"I think that, in light of events, several of them can be persuaded to honor some of their contracts with your father. Armedius certainly will. It may not be the riches your father dreamed of, lad, but I'll see your mother's debts paid and *then* some. We owe you and Professor Fitch."

than one way to become a Rithmatist. One of those ways involved something dark and murderous. Could there be other ways?

It opened up hope again. He wasn't sure if that was a good thing or not.

"Joel!" Exton said. The stout man hurried over and grabbed Joel's hand. "Thank you *so* much, lad. Fitch told me how you continued to believe in me, even when they took me into custody."

"Harding almost had me convinced," Joel said. "But some things just didn't make sense. The inspector must have planted the evidence against you when he was investigating the office."

Exton nodded. Both Lilly Whiting and Charles Calloway had identified Harding as the Scribbler.

"Well, son," Exton said. "You are a true friend. I mean it."

Florence smiled. "Does that mean you'll stop grumbling at him?"

"I don't know about that," Exton said. "Depends on if he's interrupting my work or not! And, speaking of work, I have to adjudicate the Melee. Goodness help us if I hadn't been released—nobody else knows the rules to this blasted thing well enough to referee!"

The two of them moved on toward the arena.

Joel continued to wait outside. Traditionally, the Rithmatists didn't come until most of the seats were filled, and this day was no exception. The students began to arrive, making their way through the doors, where Exton had them draw lots to determine where on the arena floor they—or, if they wanted to work in a team, their group—would begin drawing.

"Hey," a voice said behind him.

Joel smiled toward Melody. She wore her standard skirt and blouse, though this particular skirt was divided and came down to her ankles to facilitate kneeling and drawing. She probably wore knee pads underneath.

"Come to see me get trounced?" she asked.

"You did pretty well the other night against the chalklings."

"Those lines barely held them, and you know it."

"Well, whatever happens today," Joel said, "you helped rescue about thirty Rithmatists from the Scribbler. The winners of the competition will have to deal with the fact that while you were saving all sixty isles, they were snoozing a few doors away."

"Good point, that," Melody agreed. Then she grimaced.

"What?" Joel asked.

She pointed toward a small group of people dressed in Rithmatic coats. Joel recognized her brother, William, among them.

"Parents?" he asked.

She nodded.

They didn't look like terrible people. True, the mother had very well-styled hair and immaculate makeup, and the father an almost perfectly square jaw and a majestic stance, but . . .

"I think I see what you mean," Joel said. "Hard to live up to their standards, eh?"

"Yeah," Melody said. "Trust me. It's better to be the son of a chalkmaker."

"I'll keep that in mind."

She sighed with an overly dramatic sound as her parents and brother entered through the doors. "I guess I'd better go get humiliated."

"I'm sure that whatever happens," Joel said, "you'll do it spectacularly."

She moved on. Joel was about to follow when he saw a set of Rithmatists arrive together. Twelve of them, wearing red shirts with their white pants or skirts. Team Nalizar had arrived.

The professor himself was at their head. How was it that simply by association, he could make a group of students seem more haughty, more exclusive? Nalizar stood beside the doorway with arms folded as they entered one at a time.

Joel gritted his teeth and forced himself to enter the building after Nalizar. He spotted the professor walking down a short hallway to the right, heading toward the stairs up to the observation room.

Joel hurried after. This hall was pretty much empty now, though Joel could hear the buzz of people through the arena doors a short distance away.

"Professor," Joel said.

Nalizar turned to him, but gave Joel only a quick glance before continuing on his way.

"Professor," Joel said. "I want to apologize."

Nalizar turned again, and this time he focused on Joel, as if seeing him for the first time. "You want to apologize for telling people that *I* was the kidnapper."

Joel paled.

"Yes," Nalizar said, "I heard about your accusations."

"Well, I was wrong," Joel said. "I'm sorry."

Nalizar raised an eyebrow, but that was his only response. From him, it seemed like something of an acceptance.

"You came here, to Armedius, chasing Harding," Joel said.

"Yes," Nalizar said. "I knew something had gotten loose, but nobody back at Nebrask believed me. Harding seemed like the most likely candidate. I got the authorities to release me on a technicality, then came here. When people started disappearing, I knew I was right. Forgotten can be tricky, however, and I needed proof for an accusation. After all, as you might have figured out, making accusations about innocent people is a terribly unpleasant thing to do."

Joel gritted his teeth. "What was he, then?"

"A Forgotten," Nalizar said. "Read the papers. They'll tell you enough."

"They don't know the details. Nobody will speak of them. I was hoping—"

"I am not inclined to speak with non-Rithmatists about such things," Nalizar snapped.

Joel took a deep breath. "All right."

Nalizar raised his eyebrow again.

"I don't want to fight, Professor. In the end, we were working toward the same goal. If we'd helped one another, then perhaps we could have accomplished more."

"What will accomplish the most," Nalizar said, "would be if you stayed out of my way. Without your ill-planned dump of acid, I would have had the strength to beat that fool Harding. Now, if you'll excuse me, I must get going."

Nalizar began to walk away.

Would have had the strength . . . ? Joel frowned. "Professor?"

Nalizar stopped. "What is it *now*?" he said, not turning around.

"I just wanted to wish you luck—like the luck you had two nights ago."

"What luck two nights ago?"

"The fact that Harding didn't shoot at you," Joel said. "He took a shot at Fitch. Yet against you, he didn't fire his gun, even though you didn't have a Line of Forbiddance up at first to stop a shot."

Nalizar stood quietly.

"And," Joel added, "it's lucky that he didn't attack you with his chalklings once you were unconscious. He ignored you and moved on to the students. If I'd been him, I would have turned the major threat—the trained adult Rithmatist—into a chalkling first."

Joel cocked his head, the conclusions coming to his tongue before he realized what he was doing. *Dusts!* he thought. *I just got done apologizing, and now I'm accusing him again! I really am obsessed with this man.*

He opened his mouth to retract what he'd said, but froze as Nalizar turned back halfway, his face looking shadowed.

"Interesting conclusions," the professor said quietly, the mockery gone from his voice.

Joel stumbled back.

"Any more theories?" Nalizar asked.

"I . . ." He gulped. "Harding. The thing controlling him didn't seem very . . . smart. It boxed itself in with its own Lines of Forbiddance, and it didn't coordinate its chalklings, which let Melody and me escape. It never spoke except to growl or try to shout.

"Yet," Joel continued, "the plot was really intricate. It involved framing Exton, grabbing the perfect students to cause a panic that would end with the majority of the Rithmatists on campus lumped together, where they could be attacked and taken in one swoop. The thing we fought seems to have come out only at night. Harding himself was in control during the day. He didn't make the plans, and the Forgotten didn't seem smart enough to do so either. It makes me wonder . . . was someone else helping it? Maybe something smarter?"

Nalizar turned around all the way. He stood tall, and something about him seemed *different*. Like it had that day when Joel had looked up at the window and Nalizar had looked down at him.

Nalizar's arrogance was gone, replaced by cool calculation. It was like the young upstart was a persona, carefully crafted to make people hate, but ignore, Nalizar as a threat.

The professor strolled forward. Joel began to sweat, and he took a step backward.

"Joel," Nalizar said, "you act as if you are in danger." Behind his eyes, something dark flashed—a fuzzing, charcoal blackness.

"What are you?" Joel whispered.

Nalizar smiled, stopping a few feet in front of Joel. "A hero," he whispered, "vindicated by your own words. The man nobody likes, but one they think has a good heart anyway. The professor who came to the rescue of the students, even if he arrived too late—and was too weak—to defeat the enemy."

"It was a ruse," Joel said. He thought back to Nalizar's surprise at finding Joel in the dorms, and the way he had reacted to Harding. Nalizar hadn't seemed surprised to see Harding, more . . . bothered. As if realizing that he'd just been implicated.

Had Nalizar changed his plans at that moment, fighting Harding to appear like a hero to fool Joel?

"You would have let me live," Joel said. "You would have lain there, presumably unconscious, while your minion turned the students to chalklings. You could have charged over then and saved some of them. You'd have been a hero, but Armedius would still have been decimated."

Joel's voice rang in the empty hallway.

"What would the others think, Joel," Nalizar said, "if they heard you speak such hurtful things? Just a couple of days after publicly admitting that I'm a hero? I daresay it would make you look rather inconsistent."

He's right, Joel thought numbly. *They won't believe me now.*

Not after I vouched for Nalizar myself. Plus, Melody and Fitch reinforced that Nalizar had come to help at the end.

Joel met the professor's eyes, and saw the darkness moving behind them again—a real, tangible thing, clouding the whites with a shifting, scribbly mess of black.

Nalizar nodded to Joel, as if in respect. It seemed such an odd motion from the arrogant professor. "I . . . am sorry for dismissing you. I have trouble telling the difference between those of you who are not Rithmatists, you see. You all look so alike. But you . . . you are special. I wonder why they did not want you."

"I was right," Joel whispered. "All along, I was right about you."

"Oh, but you were *so* wrong. You don't know a fraction of what you *think* you know."

"What are you?" Joel repeated.

"A teacher," he said. "And a student."

"The books in the library," Joel said. "You're not searching for anything specific—you're just trying to discover what we know about Rithmatics. So you can judge where humankind's abilities lie."

Nalizar said nothing.

He came for the students, Joel realized. *The war in Nebrask— the chalklings haven't managed a significant breakout for centuries. Our Rithmatists are too strong. But if a creature like Nalizar can get at the students before they are trained . . .*

A new Rithmatist can only be made once an old one dies. What would happen if instead of dying, all of them were turned into chalkling monsters?

No more Rithmatists. No more line in Nebrask.

The weight of what had just happened pressed down upon Joel. "Nalizar the man is dead, isn't he?" Joel said. "You took him at Nebrask, when he went into the breach to find Melody's brother . . . and Harding was with him, wasn't he? Melody said that Nalizar led an expedition in, and that would include soldiers. You took them both together, then you came out here."

"I see I need to leave you to think," Nalizar said.

Joel reached into his pocket, then whipped out the gold coin, holding it up wardingly at Nalizar.

The creature eyed it, then plucked it from Joel's fingers, holding it up to the light and looking at the clockwork inside.

"Do you know why time is so confusing to some of us, Joel?" Nalizar asked.

Joel said nothing.

"Because man created it. He sectioned it off. There is nothing inherently important about a second or a minute. They're fictional divisions, enacted by mankind, fabricated." He eyed Joel. "Yet in a human's hands, these things have *life*. Minutes, seconds, hours. The arbitrary becomes a law. For an outsider, these laws can be unsettling. Confusing. Frightening."

He flipped the coin back to Joel.

"Others of us," he said, "take more concern to understand—for a person rarely fears that which he understands. Now, if you'll excuse me, I have a competition to win."

Joel watched, helpless, as the creature that was Nalizar disappeared up the steps to meet with the other professors. It had failed, but it didn't seem the type to have only one plan in motion.

What was Nalizar planning for his personal team of students? Why create a group of young Rithmatists who were loyal to him? Those who won the Melee would be given prime positions at Nebrask. Made leaders . . .

Dusts, Joel thought, rushing back toward the dueling arena. He had to do something, but what? Nobody would believe him about Nalizar. Not now.

The students had already been placed on the field, some of them individual, others grouped in teams. He saw Melody, who unfortunately had drawn a very poor location near the very center of the arena. Surrounded by enemies, she'd have to defend on all sides at once.

She knelt out there, head bowed, back slumped in dejection. It twisted Joel's insides in knots.

If Nalizar's students won this Melee, those moving to Nebrask for their final year of training would gain positions of authority over other students. Nalizar wanted them to win—he wanted his people in control, in charge. That couldn't be allowed.

Nalizar's students could not win the Melee.

Joel glanced to the side. Exton was chatting with several of the clerks from the city who would act as his assistant referees. They'd watch to make certain that as soon as a Circle of Warding was breached, the Rithmatist inside was disqualified.

Joel took a breath and walked up to Exton. "Is there any rule against a non-Rithmatist entering the Melee?"

Exton started. "Joel? What is this?"

"Is there a rule against it?" Joel asked.

"Well, no," Exton said. "But you'd have to be a student of one of the Rithmatic professors, which isn't really the case for any non-Rithmatist."

"Except me," Joel said.

Exton blinked. "Well, yes, I suppose being his research assistant over the summer elective counts *technically*. But, Joel, it'd be foolish for a non-Rithmatist to go out there!"

Joel looked across the field. There were some forty students on it this year.

"I'm entering on Professor Fitch's team," Joel said. "I'll take a spot on the field with Melody."

"But . . . I mean . . ."

"Just put me down, Exton," Joel said, running out onto the field.

His entrance caused quite a stir. Students looked up, and the watching crowd began to buzz. Melody didn't see him. She was still kneeling, head down, oblivious to the whispers and occasional calls of laughter that Joel's entrance prompted.

The large clock on the wall rang out, bells marking the hour. It was noon, and once the twelfth chime rang, the students could start drawing. Forty clicks sounded as students placed their chalk against the black stone floor. Melody reached out hesitantly.

Joel knelt and snapped his chalk to the ground beside hers.

She looked up with shock. "Joel? What the dusts are you *doing*?"

"I'm annoyed at you," he said.

"Huh?"

"You came out here to get humiliated, and you didn't even invite me along!"

She hesitated, then smiled. "Idiot," she said. "You're not going to prove anything to me by going down faster than I do."

"I don't intend to go down," Joel said, holding up his blue piece of chalk. The sixth chime rang. "Just draw what I do."

"What do you mean?"

"Trace me. Dusts, Melody, you've practiced tracing all summer! I'll bet you can manage it better than anyone here. Where you see blue, draw over it with white."

She hesitated, and then a broad, mischievous smile split her mouth.

The twelfth bell rang, and Joel began to draw. He made a large circle around both him and Melody, and she followed, tracing his line exactly. He finished, but then stopped.

"What?" Melody said.

"Safe and simple?"

"Dusts, no!" she said. "If we go out, we go out dramatically! Nine-pointer!"

Joel smiled, stilling his hands as he listened to the drawing all around him. He could almost believe himself a Rithmatist.

He set his chalk back down, divided the circle in his head, and began to draw.

Professor Fitch stood quietly on the glass floor, a cup held in his hand, though he didn't drink. He was too nervous. He was afraid his hand would shake and spill tea all over him.

The viewing lounge atop the arena was quite nice, quite nice indeed. Maroon colorings, dim lighting from above as to not distract from what was below, iron girders running between the glass squares so that one didn't get too much of a sense of vertigo by standing directly above the arena floor.

Fitch generally enjoyed the view and the privileges of being a professor. He had watched numerous duels from this room. That, however, didn't make the experience any less nerve-racking.

"Fitch, you look pale," a voice said.

Fitch looked over as Principal York joined him. Fitch tried to chuckle at the principal's comment and dismiss it, but it kind of came out weakly.

"Nervous?" York said.

"Ah, well, yes. Unfortunately. I much prefer the midwinter duel, Thomas. I don't usually have students in that one."

"Ah, Professor," York said, patting him on the shoulder. "Just two days ago you faced down a *Forgotten*, for dusts' sake. Surely you can stand a little bit of dueling stress?"

"Hum, yes, of course." Fitch tried to smile. "I just . . . well, you know how I am with confrontation."

"There is, of course, no contest," another voice said.

Fitch turned, looking through the collection of professors and dignitaries to where Nalizar stood in his red coat. He wore the one that had once belonged to Fitch—the other one had been ruined by acid.

"My students are the best trained," Nalizar continued. "We've been practicing duels all summer. You will soon see the importance of building a strong, quick offense."

A strong, quick offense makes for excellent dueling, Fitch agreed in his head. *But it makes for terrible defensive practice on the battlefield, where you'll likely be surrounded.*

Nalizar couldn't see that, of course. All he saw was the victory. Fitch couldn't really blame the man—he was young. Attacking fast often seemed so important to those who were in their youths.

York frowned. "That one is too arrogant for my tastes," the principal said softly. "I'm . . . sorry, Fitch, for bringing him on campus. If I'd known what he'd do to you . . ."

"Nonsense, Thomas," Fitch said. "Not your fault at all, no, not at all. Nalizar will grow wiser as he ages. And, well, he certainly did shake things up here!"

"A shakeup isn't always for the best, Fitch," York said. "Particularly when you're the man in charge and you *like* how things are running."

Fitch finally took a sip of his tea. Down below, he noticed, the students were already drawing. He'd missed the start. He winced, half afraid to seek out poor Melody. He was taking her reeducation slowly for her own good. She wasn't yet prepared for something like this.

That made Fitch grow nervous again. *Drat it all!* he thought. *Why can't I be confident, like Nalizar?* That man had a gift for self-assuredness.

"Hey," said Professor Campbell. "Is that the *chalkmaker's son?*"

Fitch started, almost spilling his drink as he looked down at the wide, circular arena floor below. In the very center, two figures drew from within the same circle. That wasn't forbidden by the rules, but it was highly unusual—it would mean that a break in the circle would knock them both out of the competition, and that wasn't a risk worth taking.

It slowly dawned on Fitch who those two students were. One didn't wear the uniform of a Rithmatist. He wore the sturdy, yet unremarkable clothing of a servant's son.

"Well, I'll be," York said. "Is that legal?"

"It can't possibly be!" Professor Hatch said.

"I think it actually is," said Professor Kim.

Fitch stared down, mentally calculating the arcs between the points on Joel and Melody's circle. "Oh, lad," he said, smiling. "You got it *right on*. Beautiful."

Nalizar stepped up beside Fitch, looking down. His expression had changed, the haughtiness gone. Instead, there was simply consternation. Fascination, even.

Yes, Fitch thought, *I'm sure he'll turn out to be an all right fellow, if we just give him enough time. . . .*

Joel's blue chalk vibrated between his fingers as he dragged it across the black ground. He drew without looking up. He was surrounded by opponents—that was all he needed to know. Keening would do him no good. He needed defense. A powerfully strong defense before he could move on to any kind of attack.

He scratched out a kind of half-person, half-lizard, then attached it to a bind point before moving on.

"Wait," Melody said. "You call *that* a chalkling?"

"Well, uh . . ."

"Is that a walking carrot?"

"It's a lizard man!" Joel said, drawing on the other side, fixing a circle that had been blown through.

"Yeah, whatever. Look, leave the chalklings to me, all right? Just draw 'X' marks where you want them, and I'll make them to fit the situation."

"You aren't going to draw unicorns, are you?" Joel asked, turning, his back to her as he drew.

"What's wrong with unicorns?" she demanded from behind him, her chalk sounding as it scraped the ground. "They're a noble and—"

"They're a noble and *incredibly girly* animal," Joel said. "I've got my masculine reputation to think of."

"Oh hush, you," she said. "You'll deal with unicorns—maybe some flower people and a pegasus or two—and you'll like it. Otherwise, you can just go draw your own circle, thank you very much."

Joel smiled, growing less nervous. The lines felt natural to draw. He'd practiced so much, first with his father, then alone in his rooms, finally with Professor Fitch. Putting the lines where he did just felt *right*.

The waves of chalklings came first, a surprising number of them. He glanced up to see that Nalizar's students—with their advanced training in dueling—had already eliminated some opponents. Drawing so quickly and offensively had given them an advantage in the first part of the Melee. It would hurt them as time wore on.

Joel and Melody, along with three or four other unlucky students, were in the direct center of the floor. Surrounded by Nalizar's team, who formed a ring. Obviously, their plan would be to eliminate those in the direct center, then fight those at the perimeters.

What's your plan for these students, Nalizar? Joel wondered. *What lies are you teaching them?*

Joel gritted his teeth—the positioning was great for Nalizar's students, but terrible for Joel and Melody. He and she were sur-rounded by a ring of enemies.

Large waves of chalklings swarmed Joel and Melody. By now, however, Melody had up a good dozen of her unicorns. That was one of the great things about an Easton Defense—a large circle with nine bind points, each with a smaller circle bound to it. Each of those smaller circles could theoretically hold up to five bound chalklings.

With Melody on the team, that was a dis-tinct advantage. Her little unicorns frolicked in what Joel thought was a very undigni-fied manner, but they did it even as they ripped apart enemy trolls, dragons, knights, and blobs. The Nalizar chalklings didn't have a chance. As their broken corpses piled up, Melody added a couple more unicorns to her defense.

"Hey," she said, "this is actually kind of fun!"

Joel could see the sweat on her brow, and his knees hurt from the kneeling. But he couldn't help but agree with her.

Lines of Vigor soon began to hit their defenses, blow-ing chunks off Melody's unicorns—which made her quite perturbed—and knock-ing holes in the outer circles.

Nalizar's students had realized that they would have to beat their way through. Fortunately, Joel had built their defense well anchored with Lines of Forbiddance. Too many, maybe. Mel-ody kept running into them and cursing.

He needed to do something. Nalizar's students would even-tually break through.

"You ready to show off?" Joel asked.

"You need to *ask*?"

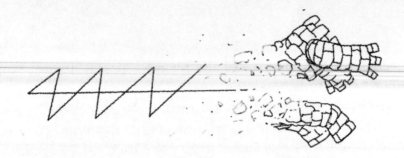

Joel drew the new line—the one that was a cross between a Line of Vigor and a Line of Forbiddance. They were calling it a Line of Revocation, and he'd spent hours practicing it already. It was more powerful than a Line of Vigor, but not really *that* much.

However, it would probably have a big impact on morale. Melody traced his line, and hers shot across the floor—conveniently dusting away Joel's original as it moved. He'd aimed it at a student who hadn't anchored his circle properly, and wasn't disappointed. Joel's Line of Revocation blasted against the unfortunate student's circle, shaking it free and knocking it a few feet out of alignment.

That counted as a disqualification—the student was, after all, now outside of his circle. A referee approached and sent the boy away.

"One down," Joel said, and continued to draw.

The gathered professors and island officials muttered among themselves. Fitch stood directly above Joel and Melody and just watched. Watched the defense repel dozens and dozens of chalklings. Watched it absorb hit after hit but stay strong. Watched Joel's shots—fired infrequently, yet timed so well—slam against enemy circles.

He watched, and felt his nervousness slowly bleed to pride. Beneath him, two students battled overwhelming odds, and somehow managed to start *winning*. Circle after circle of Nalizar's students fell, each breached by a careful shot on Joel's part.

Melody focused on keeping her chalklings up. Joel would lay down a line, then watch, patient, until there was an opening in the enemy waves. Then he'd get Melody's attention, and she'd trace his Line of Revocation without even looking up, trusting in his aim and skill.

Usually, a defense with two people inside of it was a bad trade-off—two circles beside one another would be more useful. However, with a non-Rithmatist on the field, it made perfect sense.

"Amazing," York whispered.

"That's *got* to be illegal," Professor Hatch kept saying. "Inside the same circle?"

Many of the others grew quiet. They didn't care about legality. No, these—like Fitch—watched and understood. Beneath them were two students who didn't just duel. They fought. They understood.

"It's beautiful," Nalizar whispered, surprising Fitch. He would have expected the younger professor to be angry. "I will have to watch those two very carefully. They are amazing."

Fitch looked back down, surprised by just how excited he was. By surviving inside Team Nalizar's ring, Joel and Melody had destroyed the enemy strategy. Nalizar's students had to fight on two fronts. They slowly destroyed the students on the outside of their ring, but by the time they did, Joel and Melody had taken out half of their numbers.

It became six on two. Even that should have been impossible odds.

It wasn't.

Joel heard the bell ring before he understood what it meant. He just kept drawing, working on some outer circles to add a secondary bastion of defense, since their main circles had nearly been breached a dozen times.

"Uh, Joel?" Melody said.

"Yeah?"

"Look up."

Joel stopped, then raised his head. The entire black playing field was empty, the last student in red trailing away toward the doors. The girl walked over broken circles and unfinished lines, moving between the Lines of Forbiddance, scuffing circles with her passing.

Joel blinked. "What happened?"

"We won, idiot," Melody said. "Uh . . . did you expect that?"

Joel shook his head.

"Hum," Melody replied. "Well then, guess it's time for some drama!" She leapt to her feet and let out a squeal of delight, jumping up and down, screaming, "Yes, yes, yes!"

Joel smiled. He looked up, and though the ceiling was tinted, he thought he could see Nalizar's red coat where the man stood, eyes focused on Joel.

I'm watching you, the professor's stance seemed to say.

It was then that the stunned audience erupted into motion and noise, some cheering, others rushing down onto the field.

And I'm watching you back, Nalizar, Joel thought, still looking up. *I've stopped you twice now. I'll do it again.*

As many times as I have to.

TO BE CONTINUED

ACKNOWLEDGMENTS

This book has been a long time in the making.

I first started writing it in the spring of 2007, half a year before I was asked to complete the Wheel of Time. My epic fantasy project at the time, titled *The Liar of Partinel*, just wasn't working for me. It had too many problems, and rather than continue to try to force it, I found my way into a fun, alternate-world "gearpunk" novel that I titled *Scribbler*. It was one of those projects I'm prone to do when I'm supposed to be doing something else—an unexpected book that makes my agent shake his head in bemusement.

The book turned out really well, but like most of my off-the-cuff stories, it had some major flaws that I needed to fix in revision. Unfortunately, with the Wheel of Time on my plate, I couldn't afford the time it would take to revise this story. Beyond that, I didn't think I could release it, as there's an implicit promise of something further in the world, and I knew I wouldn't be able to make good on that promise for many years.

Well, the Wheel of Time is finally done, and I've been able to return to *Scribbler*, which we've renamed *The Rithmatist*. I'm reminded of just how fun this book was. I'm also reminded of the many, many people who gave reads on it over the years. It has now been almost six years since I did the first draft. (Where does all this time go, anyway?) With so much time involved in getting this book ready, I'm worried that I'm going to miss some people. If I do, I'm terribly sorry! Make sure you let me know so I can fix it.

My original writing group on this book included Isaac Stewart, Dan Wells, Sandra Tayler, Janci Patterson, Eric James Stone, and Karla Bennion. They read this in a very early form, and were a huge help in getting it ready. I also want to make note of the early American work *The Narrative of the Captivity and the Restoration of Mrs. Mary Rowlandson*, which makes an (admittedly altered) appearance in this volume.

Other alpha and beta readers include Chris "Miyabi" King, Josh & Mi'chelle Walker, Ben & Ben Olsen, Kalyani Poluri, Austin Hussey, Jillena O'Brien, Kristina Kugler, C. Lee Player, Brian Hill, Adam Hussey, and Ben McSweeney—who was a valuable alpha reader as well as the artist. We toyed with doing a graphic novel along the way; if you can ever corner him, ask to see some of the test pages for that. They're awesome.

Stacy Whitman was also very helpful in getting this book ready. (At one time, as an editor, she wanted to buy it. Thanks, Stacy, for your help!) The copyeditor was Deanna Hoak, and deserves your thanks (and mine) for helping make the manuscript less typo-y. (Though I believe it's beyond the power of any mortal to completely relieve my prose of typos.)

Susan Chang, the book's editor, and Kathleen Doherty at Tor have been wonderful to work with, and have both been big believers in this book for many years. I'm glad we were finally able to release it. As always, I'd like to thank Moshe Feder for his support, Joshua Bilmes for his agent-fu, and Eddie Schneider for his sub-agent-fu.

A special thanks also goes out to Karen Ahlstrom and the intermittent Peter Ahlstrom. For many years, they believed in this book and pushed me to give it the time and love it deserved.

Finally, as always, I want to thank my family and my loving wife, Emily. They don't just put up with me; they encourage me to thrive. Thank you.

—*Brandon Sanderson*

READING AND ACTIVITY GUIDE

The information, activities, and discussion questions that follow are intended to enhance your reading of *The Rithmatist*. Please feel free to adapt these materials to suit your needs and interests.

WRITING AND RESEARCH ACTIVITIES

1. Author Brandon Sanderson is known for writing epic fantasy stories. Go to the library or online to find the literary definition of the term "epic." Write a short essay explaining how *The Rithmatist* fits into the category of epic novels—or how it doesn't. If you have read other epic novels, such as *Redwall* by Brian Jacques, *Dragonriders of Pern* by Anne McCaffrey, or Harry Potter by J. K. Rowling, you may include comparisons to these in your essay.

2. In addition to its epic qualities, *The Rithmatist* has features of a *steampunk* or gearpunk novel. Go to the library or online to learn more about the elements of steampunk and gearpunk literature. Then, using descriptions from the novel, create an illustrated poster depicting steampunk and gearpunk images, concepts, or scenes from the novel.

3. Imagine that you are a non-Rithmatist scholar of things Rithmatic, such as Joel aspires to be. Using information from the novel, create a PowerPoint or other type of illustrated

presentation explaining Rithmatic lines, shapes, and defenses; the relationship between Rithmatists and ordinary people; and the role of the Church in Rithmatist selection. Share your presentation with friends or classmates.

4. In the character of Melody, write a journal entry describing your first morning spent with Professor Fitch and Joel. How do you feel about the prospect of a summer of remedial tracing? Why do believe you don't fit in with the other Rithmatic students? What do you think of Joel?

5. Near the end of the novel, Joel returns to his former home and his father's workshop. In the character of Joel, write a journal entry describing your emotions as you step back through the doorway. Or, write a journal entry comparing your experience reentering your father's space to your experience reentering the inception room as a teen instead of a grade school child.

6. The novel makes reference to a real book from literary history. Mary Rowlandson's seventeenth-century narrative of being held captive by Native Americans has been called America's first bestseller. Go to the library or online to learn more about Rowlandson, her experience, and her publication. Then, write a short essay explaining why you think Brandon Sanderson chose to feature this particular historical work in *The Rithmatist*.

7. Melody invites Joel into town for ice cream and, when he can't afford the cost, she covers it. In the character of Joel or Melody, write an internal monologue exploring your thoughts about seeing the town through the other's eyes, your comfort level and other considerations about giving/receiving money, and whether you feel this trip has changed your relationship in any way.

8. *The Rithmatist* is set in an alternate America with different technology, boundaries, and an ongoing threat posed by the wild chalklings at Nebrask. Do any of these differences call to mind societal or governmental concerns happening in your real world? Bring in two or three current newspaper clippings that reference subject matter that makes you think

of the novel. For each clipping, write a two- to three-sentence description of the connection you see between the novel and the news report.

9. Examining a clockwork-infused coin given to him by Melody, Joel starts to consider the element of time in his understanding of humanity and Rithmatics. With friends or classmates, role-play a conversation between Joel, Professor Fitch, and Father Stewart in which Joel presents his thoughts on time and the two other characters accept, reject, or elaborate upon his thoughts.

10. Melody is stunned when Joel fails to qualify as a Rithmatist for a second time. Were you? Imagine you are a student at Armedius Academy in whom Joel has confided about his second inception room experience. Write a detailed petition statement demanding a third inception ceremony for Joel. If desired, read your statement aloud to friends or classmates and invite them to vote on whether they would be in favor of a third inception ceremony.

11. Use oil pastels or other visual arts media to create a colorful, illustrated postcard invitation—or design a mock Facebook event page—to encourage people to attend the end-of-year student Melee at Armedius Academy.

12. Assume the character of a Rithmatic student in your final year at Armedius before being sent to complete your education at Nebrask. Create your own chalkling, drawn with chalk on a sheet of black construction paper. On a large index card, write a brief description of your chalkling, how you came to draw this particular form, the name of the Rithmatic defense with which it is most effective, and your proudest accomplishment as a fledgling Rithmatist. If desired, create a display of "Rithmatic Artworks" by combining your drawing and description with pictures created by friends or classmates.

QUESTIONS FOR DISCUSSION

1. The prologue of *The Rithmatist* describes something frightening happening to a girl named Lilly. However, it is not until later in the novel that the reader fully realizes what these opening pages have described. How might you interpret the events of the prologue before reading further in *The Rithmatist*? What images and emotions from the prologue resonate through the rest of the novel? After reading the whole novel, how would you reinterpret the prologue? Why, in terms of plot and themes, do you think the author chose to begin his novel with this scene featuring the first Rithmatic student disappearance?

2. From the start of the novel, it is clear that Joel is frustrated by his lack of Rithmatic talent. How does this affect his actions throughout the story? Describe at least two ways in which Joel is an outsider at Armedius Academy. Then, name at least two ways in which Joel is more of a Rithmatist than many of the chosen Rithmatic students.

3. What is Joel's relationship with Professor Fitch? Why is he so upset when Fitch loses the duel to Nalizar? To what important new responsibility does this lead for Joel? Why has Melody found herself under the tutelage of Fitch?

4. Describe Joel's relationships with Exton, Florence, and his mother, all non-Rithmatist characters. What secrets do these characters keep about their connection to Rithmatics? What conclusions might you draw about the relationships between Rithmatists and others in the greater world?

5. Between chapters of the novel, diagrams illustrate the art of Rithmatics. As a reader, how do you connect with these instructional elements? How do they help you to build a clearer sense of the world of Rithmatic fighting? Does this complex scheme, thoroughly taught to only a select few, remind you of any realms of scholarship or leadership in your own world? Explain your answer.

6. At the beginning of Chapter 9, Joel feels certain that

". . . the Master had *not* meant for him to be a clerk." Later, in Chapter 22, Joel muses, "Was there really a Master up in heaven? . . . The truth is, I'm not sure I *don't* believe, either. You might be there. I hope you are, I guess." (p. 322) Have you ever felt uncertainties about your faith or government, such as Joel's, or worries about what path you should choose for your future? What words of support or empathy might you offer to Joel?

7. Geometric shapes versus chalklings. Creativity versus control. Being a Rithmatist versus understanding Rithmatics. The Church versus academia. Could you read *The Rithmatist* as a story about the tensions between art and science, between history and faith? Explain your answer.

8. List all of the characters Joel considers as suspects before the capture of the real kidnapper. What important discovery does Joel make about the mysterious new chalk symbol found at each crime scene that helps him solve the mystery? What might the discovery of this new symbol foretell about the future of Rithmatics?

9. How are the kidnapped children rescued? What is a Forgotten? Do you think the Forgotten has any relationship to the creature Joel sees in the inception room? Why or why not?

10. Why did Harding embark on his kidnapping spree? Do you think any one individual—even Joel—could have stopped him?

11. At the end of the novel, the "Professor Fitch" Melee team of Joel and Melody impress their audience because ". . . they were two students who didn't just duel. They fought. They understood." (p. 369) What is the difference between fighting and dueling? How might Joel and Melody's perceived weaknesses in Rithmatics have led to this impressive victory? Have you ever struggled with a weakness, such as a learning difficulty or family problem, that has ultimately made you stronger?

12. What are your feelings about Nalizar at the end of the novel? Do you think he was trying to harm or save Joel and Melody during their heroic encounter with Inspector Harding?

13. Where is Joel at the end of the novel? How would you describe the danger facing the world now that the kidnapping mystery has been solved? What role do you feel Joel ought to play in this ongoing battle? What might you title the next installment of the Rithmatist series?

MISTBORN

"It's rare for a fiction writer to have much understanding of how leadership works, how communities form, and how love really takes root in the human heart. Sanderson is astonishingly wise."
—Orson Scott Card

"[Sanderson] has created a fascinating world here, one that deserves a sequel."
—*The Washington Post Book World*

THE WELL OF ASCENSION

"This entertaining read will especially please those who always wanted to know what happened after the good guys won."
—*Publishers Weekly*

"Vin's struggles with love and power inject the human element into Sanderson's engaging epic."
—*Booklist*

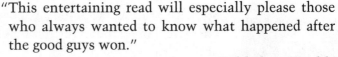

THE HERO OF AGES

"Sanderson is an evil genius. There is simply no other way to describe what he's managed to pull off in this transcendent final volume in his Mistborn trilogy. . . . The characterization is stellar, the world-building solid, and the plot intricate and compelling—if you haven't read the first two books, go and do so immediately, then buy this one. You won't regret it."
—*RT Book Reviews* (gold medal, top pick)

THE ALLOY OF LAW

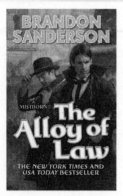

"Sanderson has skillfully woven together an intricate plot with new complex, imperfect heroes. Highly recommended for fantasy fans, especially followers of the original trilogy."

—*Library Journal* (starred review)

WARBREAKER

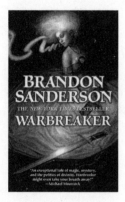

"This very superior stand-alone fantasy proves, among other things, that Sanderson was a good choice to complete the late Robert Jordan's Wheel of Time saga. Sanderson is clearly a master of large-scale stories, splendidly depicting worlds as well as strong female characters."

—*Booklist*

ELANTRIS

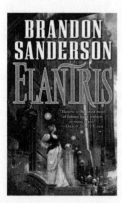

"Sanderson's outstanding fantasy debut, refreshingly complete unto itself and free of the usual genre clichés, offers something for everyone: mystery, magic, romance, political wrangling, religious conflict, fights for equality, sharp writing, and wonderful, robust characters. . . . Sanderson is a writer to watch."

—*Publishers Weekly* (starred review)

ABOUT THE AUTHOR

BRANDON SANDERSON grew up in Lincoln, Nebraska. He lives in Utah and teaches creative writing at Brigham Young University. After Robert Jordan's death, he completed the final three volumes in Jordan's bestselling epic The Wheel of Time® series. Visit him at www.brandonsanderson.com.

BEN McSWEENEY is an illustrator whose work has appeared in *The Way of Kings, The Alloy of Law,* and *The Mistborn Adventure Game.* Find out more at www.inkthinker.net.